HIGHLAND SURRENDER

What really troubled Maldie was that she was making no effort to thwart him in his seductive game. She should be inflicting pain upon the man, breaking free of his hold. Instead she remained still in his arms, thinking with some amusement that he was a handsome rogue.

"So, this is what ye plotted all along," she said, her palms flat against his broad chest in a weak, fraudulent show of resistance.

"Do ye accuse me of base trickery?" he asked, his voice pleasant, almost amused, as he brushed a kiss over her forehead.

"Aye, I do. Do ye deny it?" She shivered with ill-concealed delight as he kissed the hollow behind her ear.

" 'Twas no plot or trickery, bonny Maldie. Merely a thought, something I considered." He grinned when she uttered a short, sharp sound of disgust. "Ye did need to get out of that room."

Just as Maldie opened her mouth to tell him succinctly that he was speaking utter nonsense, he touched his lips to hers. A little voice in her head told her that she was courting danger, but she easily ignored it. The warmth his slow, enticing kiss stirred within her melted away all common sense and resistance. He made her feel good, and, she ruefully admitted, she was too weak to refuse that.

As he deepened the kiss, she curled her arms around his neck and pressed closer to him. The tremor that went through him spread to her own body. It astounded and alarmed her that one simple kiss could so enflame them both.

His unsteady fingers brushed her skin as he unlaced her chemise. She found the strength to murmur a nay, but he kissed away her halfhearted protest. Maldie knew she lacked the strength to shove him away from her, that she was allowing him such freedom, because her skin ached for his touch . . .

Books by Hannah Howell

THE MURRAYS

Highland Destiny
Highland Honor
Highland Promise
Highland Vow
Highland Knight
Highland Bride
Highland Angel
Highland Groom
Highland Warrior
Highland Conqueror
Highland Champion
Highland Lover
Highland Barbarian
Highland Savage
Highland Wolf
Highland Sinner
Highland Protector
Highland Avenger
Highland Master
Highland Guard

THE WHERLOCKES

If He's Wicked
If He's Sinful
If He's Wild
If He's Dangerous
If He's Tempted
If He's Daring

VAMPIRE ROMANCE

Highland Vampire
The Eternal Highlander
My Immortal Highlander
Highland Thirst
Nature of the Beast
Yours for Eternity
Highland Hunger
Born to Bite

STAND-ALONE NOVELS

Only for You
My Valiant Knight
Unconquered
Wild Roses
A Taste of Fire
A Stockingful of Joy
Highland Hearts
Reckless
Conqueror's Kiss
Beauty and the Beast
Highland Wedding

Silver Flame
Highland Fire
Highland Captive
My Lady Captor
Wild Conquest
Kentucky Bride
Compromised Hearts
Stolen Ecstasy
Highland Hero
His Bonnie Bride

Published by Kensington Publishing Corporation

HIGHLAND DESTINY

Hannah Howell

Zebra Books
Kensington Publishing Corp.

http://www.zebrabooks.com

ZEBRA BOOKS are published by

Kensington Publishing Corp.
119 West 40th Street
New York, NY 10018

ISBN-13: 978-1-4201-2235-0
ISBN-10: 1-4201-2235-5

First Printing: July 1998

20   19   18   17   16   15   14   13   12

Printed in the United States of America

Chapter One

Scotland, Spring 1430

"Young Eric is gone."

Balfour Murray, the laird of Donncoill, looked up from the thick venison stew he had been savoring and frowned at his sergeant of arms. The heavily muscled James looked dirty, weary, and pale with concern. It took a great deal to unsettle the placid James, and Balfour felt his insides tighten with unease, effectively killing his appetite.

"What do ye mean—gone?" he asked, rinsing out his mouth with a large swallow of hearty red wine.

James swallowed hard, shifting his feet slightly and making a soft rustle in the fresh rushes scattered over the floor of the great hall. "The lad has been taken," he confessed, eyeing the tall, dark laird of Donncoill with a mixture of shame and wariness. "We were out hunting when we were surrounded by near to a dozen men. Colin and Thomas were cut down, God rest their brave souls, but they accounted for twice their number ere they fell. I told Eric to flee for there was a breach in the enemy's line. He and I rode through it, but the lad's horse faltered. Ere I could aid him, they had captured him. They fled with him. I was no longer of any interest to them, so I hied back here.''

"Who took the boy?" Balfour demanded after ordering a young page to go and find his brother Nigel.

" 'Twas Beaton's men.''

That Sir William Beaton would cause him trouble was no surprise to Balfour. The laird of Dubhlinn had been a thorn in the side of the Murrays for many a year. That the man would take Eric was a shock, however. Eric was the result of a brief liaison between their father and one of Beaton's late wives. The man had callously left the infant exposed on a hillside to die. It had been simple chance that had brought James along that same path as he had returned from a hunt. The tiny Eric had been wrapped in cloth with the Beaton colors, and it had not taken his father long to discover who the child was. That Beaton would leave a helpless bairn to die appalled all of the Murrays. That the man would try to so callously murder a Murray enraged them. The Beatons had always been an irritation. At that moment they became the enemy. Balfour knew his father's hatred for Beaton had run deep, a hatred increased by the sudden and very suspicious death of the woman he had loved. The resulting feud had been fierce and bloody. Upon his father's death, Balfour had hoped for some peace. It was painfully clear that the laird of Dubhlinn cared nothing for peace.

"Why would Beaton want Eric?" Balfour suddenly tensed, gripping his heavy silver goblet so tightly that the ornate carvings on the side cut into his palm. "Do ye think he means to murder the boy? To finish what he tried to do so many years past?"

"Nay," James replied, after frowning in thought for a moment. "If Beaton wanted the laddie dead he would have sent his dogs to kill Eric, nay to just take him as they did. This took planning. It wasnae any chance meeting where a few Beatons and Murrays crossed paths and the Beatons decided 'twas a fine time to cull our numbers. These men were waiting and watching for us, for Eric.''

"Which tells me that we have grown dangerously careless in our guard, but little else. Ah, Nigel," Balfour murmured as his younger brother strode into the great hall. " 'Tis good that ye were found so swiftly."

"The lad ye sent to find me babbled something about Eric being taken?" Nigel sprawled on the bench at Balfour's side and poured himself some wine.

Balfour wondered how Nigel could look so calm. Then he saw that his brother was gripping his goblet in the same way he was, so tightly that his knuckles had whitened. There was also a hard look in Nigel's amber eyes, a look that had darkened them until they were nearly as dark a brown as his own. Balfour doubted that he would ever cease to be amazed at how well and how completely his brother could control strong emotion. He succinctly related what little he knew, then waited impatiently for Nigel to stop sipping at his wine and speak.

"Beaton needs a son," Nigel finally said, the coldness in his deep voice the only hint of the fury he felt.

"He cast Eric aside years ago," Balfour argued, signaling James to come and sit with them.

"Aye, for he had years left in which to breed himself a son. He failed. Scotland is littered with Beaton's daughters, those born of his wives as weel as those born of his mistresses, whores, and even of poor unwilling lasses who had the ill luck to come within his reach."

James nodded slowly and combed his fingers through his graying black hair. "And I have heard that the mon isnae weel."

"The mon is rapping, loudly, on death's door," Nigel drawled. "His kinsmen, his enemies, and his nearest neighbors are all closing in on him. There is no one he has chosen as his heir. He probably fears to choose one, for that mon would surely hasten his death. The wolves are baying at his gates and he is desperately fighting them back."

"When he left Eric on that hillside to die, he told the world and its mother that he didnae believe the bairn was his,'' Balfour said.

"Eric looks more like his mother than a Murray. Beaton could claim him. Aye, few might believe him, but there will be naught they can do for the lad was born of Beaton's lawful wife. A tale of a fit of blind jealousy would be all that was needed to explain away his claims that our father had cuckolded him. The mon is cursed with unthinking rages, and all ken it. They might question that Eric is truly born of his seed, but none would doubt that Beaton could become so enraged he would turn a bairn out to die, even one of his own.''

Balfour cursed and shoved his long fingers through his thick chestnut hair. "So the bastard means to put young Eric betwixt him and his enemies.''

"I have no proof of all of this, but, aye, that is what I think.''

"When I put what I ken of the mon together with all I have heard of late and what ye think, it sounds too much like the truth to argue. Eric is too young to be thrust into that nest of vipers. He may be safe as long as Beaton is alive and fear keeps his men loyal to him, but the moment the mon is too weakened by his ailments to be feared or he dies, I dinnae think Eric will survive for long.''

"Nay, mayhaps not even long enough to see the bastard buried. We cannae leave the lad there. He is a Murray.''

"I wasnae thinking of leaving him with the Beatons, although he has as much claim to what little Beaton leaves behind as any other. I was but wondering how much time we have to pull him free of Beaton's deadly grasp.''

"Mayhap days, mayhap months, mayhap even years.''

"Or mayhap merely hours,'' Balfour said, smiling grimly when Nigel shrugged, revealing that he thought the same.

"We must ride for Dubhlinn as soon as we can,'' James said.

"Aye, it would seem that we must,'' agreed Balfour.

He cursed and took several deep swallows of wine to try and calm himself. There would be another battle. More good men would lose their lives. Women would grieve and children would be left fatherless. Balfour hated it. He had no fear of battle. In defense of his home, the church, or the king, he would be the first to don armor. The constant bloodletting caused by feuds was what troubled him. A lot of Murrays had died because his father had loved and bedded another laird's wife. Now they would die to try and save the child of that adulterous union. Although Balfour loved his brother and felt the boy deserved to be fought for, it was just another part of a long feud that should never have been started.

"We will ride for Dubhlinn in the morning, at first light," Balfour said finally. "Prepare the men, James."

"We will win, Balfour, and we will get wee Eric back," Nigel assured his brother as soon as James had left the great hall.

Balfour studied his brother and wondered if Nigel truly felt the optimism he expressed. In many ways Nigel was just like him, but in just as many ways he was so different as to be a puzzle. Nigel was lighter of spirit, just as he was lighter of coloring. It had never surprised Balfour that Nigel had a greater skill with the ladies, for Nigel had the sweet tongue and charming nature he himself lacked. Nigel also had the gift of fine looks. Balfour had often gazed at himself in the looking glass and wondered how one man could be so brown, from his dark brown hair to his dark brown eyes to his swarthy skin. He sometimes had to fight the sour taste of envy over Nigel's appearance, especially when the ladies sighed over his younger brother's thick reddish brown hair, his amber eyes, and his golden skin. Now, as in so many times in the past, Balfour was drawn to share in Nigel's more hopeful view of the coming battle. His own feeling, however, was that they were all marching to their deaths and could quite easily cause Eric's death as well. Balfour decided he would try to settle his mood at some place in between the two.

"If God is with us, aye, we will win," Balfour finally said.

"Saving a sweet lad like Eric from a bastard like Beaton ought to be a cause God will shed His favor on." Nigel smiled crookedly. "Howbeit, if God truly was paying close heed, He would have struck that adder dead many years ago."

"Mayhap He decided that Beaton was more richly deserving of the slow, painful death he now suffers."

"We shall see that the mon dies alone."

"All ye have said about Beaton's plans makes sense, yet the mon must be completely mad to think that it will work. Aye, he may be able to get others to believe that Eric is his son, or, at best, nay to question it openly. For all his scheming he hasnae considered our wee brother Eric. The laddie might be slight of build and sweet of nature, but he isnae weak or witless. Beaton's plan cannae work unless Eric plays his part as told. The minute the mon eases his guard, the lad will flee that madhouse."

"True, but there are many ways to secure such a slender lad." Nigel sighed and rubbed his chin as he fought yet again to control his emotion. "We also ken that there are many ways to cloud the truth in a person's mind. Grown men, strong, battle-hardened knights, have been forced to confess to crimes they never committed. Confessions were pulled from their lips that then cost them their lives, sent them to deaths that were neither swift nor honorable. Aye, Eric is strong of spirit and quick of wit, but he is still nay more than a slender lad."

"And he is alone," Balfour murmured, fighting the urge to immediately ride for Dubhlinn, sword in hand, screaming loudly for Beaton's head on a pike. "Come the morrow, whether we win or lose, at least the lad will ken that he is not alone, that his clan is fighting for him."

Dawn arrived cloaked in a chill, gray mist. Balfour stood in the crowded bailey of Donncoill and studied his men, struggling to push aside the dark thought that some of them would not return from this battle. Even if Eric was not beloved by all of Donncoill, honor demanded that they free him from their enemy's hold. Balfour just wished that there was a bloodless way to do it.

"Come, brother!" murmured Nigel as he led their horses

over to Balfour. "Ye must look as if ye hunger for Beaton's blood and carry no doubt of victory in your heart."

Balfour idly patted his warhorse's thick muscular neck. "I ken it and ye will ne'er see me waver once we mount. I had but prayed that we would have a time of peace, a time to heal all wounds, gain strength, and work our lands. There is a richness in this land, but we ne'er have the time to fully harvest it. We either neglect it to ride to battle, or our enemies destroy whatever we have built, thus leaving us to begin all over again. I but suffer from a deep weariness."

"I understand, for it has afflicted me from time to time. This time we fight for Eric's life. Aye, mayhap e'en his soul. Think only on that."

"I will. 'Tis more than enough to stir the bloodlust needed to lead men to battle." He mounted, holding his horse steady only long enough for Nigel to get into his saddle, then began to lead his men out of the bailey.

As he rode, Balfour did as Nigel had suggested and thought only of his young, sweet-natured brother. Soon he was more than eager to face Beaton and his men sword to sword. It was also far past time to put an end to the man and his crimes.

Nigel fell from his horse, one arrow protruding from his chest, another from his right leg. Balfour bellowed out a fierce curse, fear and anger strengthening his deep voice. He dismounted and pushed his way through his beleaguered army until he reached Nigel. Even as he crouched by Nigel's side, uncaring of how he was exposing himself to the deadly rain of arrows from the walls of Dubhlinn, he saw that his brother still breathed.

"Praise God," Balfour said and signaled two of his men to pick up Nigel.

"Nay, we must not cease just because I have fallen," Nigel protested as he was carried to the greater safety at the rear of the army. "Ye cannae let the bastard win."

Balfour ordered his men to prepare a litter for Nigel, then

looked down at his brother. "He won this battle ere we had arrayed ourselves upon this cursed field. The mon kenned that we would come after Eric, and he was ready." He grabbed a white-faced page and pulled the boy away from the other youths huddled near the horses. "Have the retreat called, laddie. We will flee this land ere we are all buried in it."

Nigel swore vociferously as the boy hurried away. "May the bastard's eyes rot in his face."

"Defeat is indeed a bitter drink," Balfour said as he knelt by Nigel. "Howbeit, we cannae win this battle. We can only die here. That willnae aid young Eric. Dubhlinn is stronger than I remembered or had planned for. We must flee, lick our wounds, and think of another way to pull our wee brother free of Beaton's grasp. Ye two lads," he called, pointing to the two largest of the terrified pages. "Come and hold Nigel steady as I pull these arrows free of his flesh."

The moment the two boys flanked Nigel and grasped him, Balfour set to work. As he pulled the first arrow out, Nigel screamed and fainted. Balfour knew that would not completely free his brother of the pain, however, and he worked as fast as he dared to remove the second arrow. He tore his own shirt into rags to bind the wounds, wincing over the filth on the cloth. His men were already in full retreat by the time he got Nigel on the litter, and he wasted no time in following them.

Defeat was a hard, bitter knot in his belly, but he forced himself to accept it. The moment he had ridden onto the open land surrounding Dubhlinn he had sensed that he had erred. His men had rushed into the attack before he could stop them. Beaton's defenses had quickly proven to be strong and deadly. Balfour was both saddened and enraged by the deaths and injuries suffered by his men before he was able to pull them free of the slaughter. He could only hope that this folly had not cost him too dearly. As they marched back to Donncoill, a carefully selected group of men watching their backs, Balfour prayed that he could think of a way to free Eric without shedding any more blood, or, at least, not as much blood as had soaked the fields before Dubhlinn on this ill-fated day. Looking down at the slowly rousing Nigel, he also prayed that freeing one brother would not cost him the life of another.

The chilling sounds of battle cruelly destroyed the peace and pleasure of the unusually warm spring morning. Maldie Kirkcaldy cursed and hesitated in her determined march toward Dubhlinn, a march that had begun at her mother's grave three long months ago. As her mother's shrouded body had been lowered into its final resting place, she had sworn to make the laird of Duhblinn pay dearly for the wrongs he had done them. She had carefully prepared for everything—poor weather, lack of shelter, and lack of food. She had never considered the possibility that a battle would impede her advance.

Maldie sat down at the edge of the deeply rutted wagon track and scowled toward Dubhlinn. For a brief moment she considered drawing closer. It might be useful to know which one of the bordering clans was trying to destroy Beaton. She shook that tempting thought aside. It was dangerous to draw too close to a battle, especially when one was not known to either side. Even those who were trailing their clansmen, known to friend and foe alike, risked their lives by lingering too close to the battle. There was, however, always the chance of meeting with Beaton's enemies later, she mused. All she had to do was convince Beaton's enemy that she was his ally, and a good and useful one at that.

Idly drawing a pattern in the dirt with a stick, Maldie shook her head and laughed at her own foolishness. "Aye, and doesnae every fine, belted knight in the land cry out his eagerness to call wee Maldie Kirkcaldy his companion in arms."

After a quick look around to reassure herself that she was still alone, Maldie dragged her hands through her thick, unruly hair and cursed herself. Although slender and small, she had survived three months alone wandering lands she did not know. It would be madness to lose the caution that had kept her alive, especially now when she was so close to fulfilling her vow. She had never spent so long a time so completely alone, her

only companion her own vengeful thoughts, and decided it was
starting to affect her wits. Maldie knew she would have to be
even more careful than she had been thus far. To fail now,
when she was so near to gaining the revenge her mother had
begged for, would be bitter indeed.

The sounds of battle grew less fierce and she tensed, slowly
rising to her feet. Instinct told her the battle was ending. The
road she stood on showed clear signs of a recent passing. That
army would soon return along the road, either heady with
victory or bowed with defeat. Either mood could prove to be
a threat to her. Maldie brushed the dust from her much mended
skirts even as she backed into the thick concealing shrubs and
wind-contorted trees bordering each side of the road. It was
not the most secure shelter, but she felt confident that it would
serve. If the army that would soon pass her way had been
victorious, it would be little concerned about any possible threat.
If it had lost, it would simply be watching its rear flanks. Either
way she should be safe if she remained still and quiet.

After crouching in the bushes and staring down the road for
several moments Maldie began to think that she had guessed
wrong, that no one was coming her way. Then she heard the
faint but distinct jingle of horses' harnesses. She tensed and
frantically tried to decide what to do. Although a prideful part
of her stoutly declared that she was doing very well on her
own, she knew that an ally or two could be very helpful. If
nothing else she might be able to gain a more comfortable place
to wait as she decided the best way to use all the knowledge she
had gained in the last three months.

She had just convinced herself that Beaton's enemies were
her friends, that it could only benefit her to approach them,
when she caught her first sight of the army and her confidence
in her decision faltered. Even from a distance the army marching
away from Dubhlinn looked defeated. If an army of trained
knights, weighted down with armor and weaponry, was not
enough to defeat Beaton, what hope did she have? Maldie
quickly shook aside that sudden doubt in herself. She could
not so easily cast aside or ignore her doubts about the men

stumbling toward her. If Beaton could win against them with all their strength and skill, what use could they be to her? As they drew near enough for her to see the grief, weariness, and pain on their begrimed faces, she knew she had to make her final decision.

A once defeated ally was better than none, she told herself as she slowly rose to her feet. If nothing else they might have knowledge she did not, knowledge that could help her gain what she sought—Beaton's death. That was if they did not kill her first. Praying fiercely that she was not just inviting a quick death, Maldie stepped out onto the road.

Chapter Two

Maldie prayed that the tall, dark knight coming to a cautious halt before her could not hear how swift and hard her heart was beating. He made no threatening move toward her, and she fought to calm her fear. When she had first stepped out of the shelter of the thick brush to stand before the battered, retreating army, the possibility of gaining a few allies had made such a rash move seem worth the risk. Now that she was actually face to face with the men, seeing the cold looks on their faces, the mud and blood of battle smearing their clothes and bodies, she was not so sure. And, worse, she was no longer certain she could adequately explain her presence there, alone, on the road to Dubhlinn, or that she could immediately reveal her dark plans of revenge. These men were warriors, and she was not contemplating a battle, but a righteous murder.

"Might ye explain what a wee lass is doing alone on this road?" Balfour asked, shaking free of the hold of her wide, deep green eyes.

"Mayhap I just wished to get a closer look at how badly old Beaton has defeated you," Maldie replied, wondering a little wildly what it was about the broad-shouldered, dark-eyed man that prompted her to be so dangerously impertinent.

"Aye, that bastard won the battle." Balfour's deep voice was rough and cold with fury. "Are ye one of those carrion who seek to pick o'er the bones of the dead? If ye are, ye had best step aside and keep walking down this road."

She decided to ignore that insult, for it was one she had earned with her own ill-chosen words. "I am Maldie Kirkcaldy, just down from Dundee."

"Ye are a verra long way from home, lass. Why have ye wandered to this cursed place?"

"I seek a few of my kinsmen."

"Who? I may ken the family and can aid ye in the finding of them."

"That is most kind of you, but I dinnae think ye can help me. My kinsmen wouldnae have much call to ken a mon as highborn as yourself." Before he could press for a more informative reply, she turned her attention to the man on the litter. "Your companion looks to be sorely wounded, sir. Mayhap I can help." She stepped closer to the wounded man, ignoring the way the large knight tensed and made a subtle move as if to block her. "I make no false, vain boast when I claim to have a true skill at healing."

The firm confidence weighting her words made Balfour step aside, and then he scowled. It did not please him to be so easily swayed by a woman's words, nor was it wise to so quickly put his trust in a complete stranger. She was unquestionably beautiful, from her wild raven hair to her small booted feet, but he sternly warned himself against letting his wits fall prey to a pretty face. He moved to stand on the opposite side of Nigel's litter and watched the tiny woman carefully as she hiked up her skirts and knelt by his brother.

"I am Sir Balfour Murray, laird of Donncoill, and this mon is my brother Nigel," he said, crouching so that he could watch every move of her pale, delicate hands, and lightly resting his hand on the hilt of his sheathed sword. "He was cut down when our enemy used guile and treachery to lure us into a trap.''

As Maldie studied Nigel's wounds, quickly deciding what needed to be done for the man and silently cursing her lack of the right supplies, she replied, ''I am ever and always amazed o'er how men think every other mon will follow the honorable laws of war. If ye would all tread a wee bit more cautiously, ye might not continue to be cut down in such great numbers.'' She grimaced with distaste as she quickly removed the dirty rags covering the man's wounds.

'' 'Tis nay unreasonable to believe that a mon who has attained the honorable title of a knight will act as befits his position.''

Balfour frowned at the soft, deeply scornful noise she made. It was just a little noise, but it carried within it a wealth of emotion—anger, bitterness, and a complete lack of respect. Although her coarse black gown implied that she was lowly born, she offered no deference to a man of his higher standing, nor to anyone of higher birth if he judged her correctly. Balfour wondered who had wronged her, then wondered why he should even care.

He studied her carefully as she bathed Nigel's wounds and bound them to slow the bleeding. Nigel was already looking more at ease. Balfour decided that her claim of having a healing skill was not an empty one. It was almost as if her mere touch was enough to ease Nigel's pain. As he watched her smooth the hair from Nigel's forehead, Balfour found himself thinking of how her small, long-fingered hands would feel moving against his skin. The way his body tightened startled him. He struggled to shake aside the thought and the ill-timed arousal it had invoked.

There was a lot to be drawn to, he reluctantly conceded as he thoroughly looked her over. She was tiny and her gown was old and worn, fitting her slim, shapely form with an alluring snugness. She had high, full breasts, a tiny waist, and temptingly curved hips. For such a small woman she had very long legs, slim and beautifully shaped, which led to feet nearly as small as a child's. Her wild raven hair was poorly restrained by a blackened strip of leather. Thick, curling tendrils fell forward to caress her pale cheeks. Her rich green eyes were so big they nearly swamped her small, heart-shaped face. Long, thick black lashes framed her lovely eyes and delicately curved dark brows highlighted them perfectly. Her nose was small and straight right to the tip, where it suddenly took a faint turn upward. Beneath full, tempting lips was a pretty, but clearly stubborn, chin. Balfour wondered how she could look so young and delicate yet so sultry at the same time.

I want her, he thought with a mixture of astonishment and some amusement. His amusement was born of wanting such a tiny, impertinent, disheveled woman. His astonishment was born of how quickly and strongly he wanted her, faster and more fiercely than he had ever wanted a woman. The hunger she stirred inside of him was so deep and strong it almost alarmed him. It was the kind of hunger that could make a man act unwisely. He struggled to clear his head and think only of Nigel's health.

"My brother already looks more hale," Balfour said.

"Words courteously spoken, but which tell me that ye ken verra little about healing," Maldie said as she sat back on her heels, wiped her hands on her skirts, and met Balfour's dark gaze. "I have done little more than bathe the blood and filth away and bound the wounds with cleaner rags. I dinnae have what I need to tend his injuries as they need to be tended."

"What do ye need?" His eyes widened as she recited a long list, many of the things unrecognizable to him. "I dinnae carry such things to battle."

"Mayhap ye should. After all, 'tis in battle that ye fools gain such wounds."

" 'Tis nay foolish to try and retrieve one's young brother from the grasp of a mon like Beaton." He made one short slash with his hand when she began to speak, silencing her. "I have lingered here long enough. I cannae be certain Beaton's dogs are back in their kennels. They may weel be baying at our backs. Nigel also needs to be sheltered and cared for."

Maldie stood up and brushed herself off. "Aye, that he does, so ye had best hurry along."

"Ye have done so weel in tending him even without all ye said ye needed. I will be most curious to see what miracles ye can perform when all ye require is right at hand."

"What do ye mean?"

"Ye will journey to Donncoill with us."

"Am I to be your prisoner then?"

"Nay, my guest."

She opened her mouth to give him a firm, rude refusal, then pressed her lips together and swallowed the sharp words. This was not the time to be stubborn or contrary. She struggled to remind herself of the many advantages of joining her fate with that of Sir Balfour. He was at war with Sir Beaton just as she was, and, even though he had lost the battle today, he still had the men and arms to inflict some true and lasting harm to the laird of Dubhlinn. She would also have shelter and food while she plotted her revenge.

There were some disadvantages, too, she mused with an inner grimace. Beaton had clearly done Sir Balfour a great harm. If he discovered the truth of her parentage, she could find herself in danger. There could also be trouble ahead for her if he discovered exactly why she was on the road to Dubhlinn. If she went with him she would have to deceive him, and every instinct she had told her that Sir Balfour Murray would not easily forgive deceit. Her plan to gain an ally was proving itself to be far from simple.

As she studied him, one other possible complication presented itself. She recognized the look in his fine dark eyes. It was one she had seen far too often. He wanted her. What worried her was that she could feel herself responding to that, something she had never done before. This dark knight's lust did not arouse the anger, disgust, and scorn other men's had.

Although that worried her, it also made her curious. He was undeniably handsome, but she had seen other men just as handsome. There was a lean strength to his tall body that any woman with eyes in her head had to appreciate. His face was a delight to look upon with high cheekbones, a long straight nose, and a firm jaw. His deep brown hair was thick and wavy, hanging to his broad shoulders, and faintly gleaming with red wherever the sunlight touched it. It was his eyes that truly drew her interest. They were a soft, rich brown, surrounded by surprisingly thick black lashes and set beneath faintly arced dark brows. A little unsettled by his steady gaze, she glanced at his mouth and quickly decided that was a dangerous place to look. He had a very nice mouth, the bottom lip slightly fuller than the top. She could all too easily imagine how it would feel to kiss him.

She hastily turned away from him and picked up her small sack. " 'Tis most kind of you to offer me shelter, but 'tis late spring and there are but a few short months of fine weather ahead. I cannae pause now. I must find my kinsmen ere I am forced to seek shelter from the ill weather of winter."

"If tending to Nigel takes too long, then ye can shelter at Donncoill." He grabbed her by the arm and tugged her toward his horse. "Nigel is in great need of your skills."

"So, my laird, this isnae an invitation, but a command."

Balfour grabbed her around her tiny waist and set her in the saddle, musing fleetingly that she needed a few good meals, for she was not much heavier than some child. "It would make your stay at Donncoill more pleasant if ye would try to think of this as an invitation."

"Would it? I am nay sure I can tell myself such a large falsehood."

"Try."

He smiled at her and Maldie felt her breath quicken. His smile was alluring in its complete honesty. There was no guile or arrogance behind that crooked grin, just a simple amusement he was silently inviting her to share with him. It was not only his good looks that could prove a danger, she realized, but the man himself. It was beginning to look as if Sir Balfour Murray held a lot of those good qualities she had long ago decided no man could ever have. Maldie knew that could make it very hard to keep her secrets.

She smiled faintly. "As ye wish, m'laird. And, when your brother has healed, I will then be free to leave?"

"Of course," he replied, and wondered why those words had been so hard to say.

"Then we had best ride on, Sir Murray, as the day rapidly wanes and your brother willnae fare weel in the chill that comes with the setting of the sun."

Balfour nodded, signaled his men to begin their march again, and then fell into step by the side of his brother's litter. He noted that little Maldie had no trouble with his horse, despite the litter attached to the animal. In fact, his mount seemed very pleased to have the tiny lady on his strong back, his ears turned back to eagerly catch the words she was murmuring to him.

"The lass has a way with the animals as weel," Balfour said, glancing down at his brother.

"Aye, horses *and* men," Nigel muttered.

"Why are ye so troubled by her? She has eased your pain. I can see the truth of that in your face."

"She has eased my pain. The lass certainly has the touch. She is also a bonny, wee woman with the finest eyes I have e'er seen. Howbeit, ye dinnae ken who she is. The lass has some secrets, Balfour. I am certain of it."

"And why should she tell us everything about herself? She kens who we are no better than we ken her. The lass is just cautious."

"I pray that is all I sense, simply a natural caution with strangers. This is a dangerous time to trust too quickly, or to let one's wits be turned by a sweet face. A misstep now could cost Eric his young life."

Balfour grimaced as he stared at Maldie's back. Nigel was right. This was a poor time to have his thoughts scattered by a bonny lass. He could not bring himself to set her aside and let her walk away, but he swore he would be cautious. His family had already suffered from the consequences of thoughtless lusting. He would not repeat his father's mistakes.

*   *   *

Maldie's first sight of Donncoill came as they cleared a section of thick trees. It sat atop the slowly climbing hill they rode up, looking both secure and threatening. The lands around it looked rich, able to supply the Murrays with a wealth many Scots would envy, but even a cursory glance told her it was not being used to its full potential. Its promise was still locked in wide expanses of untilled soil and ungrazed fields. Maldie suspected that this battle was just one of many, the constant need to fight stealing the time and men it would take to fully harvest the richness of the land. She wondered sadly if men would ever gain the wit to understand what they lost with their constant feuds and battles.

Hastily, she shook aside that dark thought. It did no good to mourn things she could never change. She turned her full attention on the keep they rode toward. Set behind high stone walls, Donncoill had not suffered the neglect the lands had. It had clearly been strengthened and improved from the original square tower house she could still see prominently positioned amongst the additions. On the right of the old, squat tower ran one wing leading to a second narrower tower. Another wing extended to the left of the old structure leading to what was obviously going to be another tower. Her mother had often entertained her with tales of the grand castles of France and England. Maldie began to think Sir Balfour had actually seen such places or heard the same tales, for the castle taking shape behind the thick curtain walls would soon equal any her mother had spoken of with such awe.

"The work proceeds slowly," Balfour said as he walked up beside her and took hold of his horse's reins.

Praying that she did not look as unsettled as she felt, both from his sudden appearance at her side and his nearness, Maldie drawled, "Mayhap ye should put your sword back in its scabbard more often."

"I would be happy to let it rest there, but I fear Beaton doesnae share my hopes for peace."

"Ye speak of peace, yet march to battle. I am fair certain that Beaton didnae invite ye to his walls."

"Oh, aye, he did. If he had sent an herald he couldnae have said it clearer. He stole away my young brother Eric, sent his curs onto my lands whilst the lad was out hunting."

"And so he was expecting you to come clamoring at his gates."

Balfour nodded, embarrassed by what he now saw as his own stupidity. "Aye, he was. I kenned that our attack was a mistake even as we rode onto the clearing before his keep. Then, I called to him to speak with me, to try and settle the matter without bloodshed. He led me to believe that he would do so, and, blind fool that I am, I drew nearer. It was a trap. He but wished me near enough to kill with ease and to make my men less watchful. It almost worked. Howbeit, his arrows fell short of their mark, and my men were wiser than I. They ne'er trusted Beaton's plea for peace."

"Yet ye lingered there so that he could glean your forces."

"Ye dinnae understand, lass." Balfour briefly wondered why he was taking the time to explain himself and the battle to her, then realized that he simply liked speaking to her. He suspected that he was also trying to explain the whole bitter failure to himself. "My men were enraged by this low trickery and wished to extract blood for blood. They are as weary of this constant war as I am, and their fury possessed them. It took but a moment to see that the day was lost, but men caught tight in the grip of battle and bloodlust arenae easy to reason with. When Nigel fell they came to their senses long enough for them to heed my calls for retreat."

"And Beaton still holds fast to your brother." Maldie felt a wave of sympathy for the man, but did not want to. She did not want to become concerned with his trials and tribulations. She had enough of her own.

"Aye, but at least wee Eric now kens that the Murrays will fight for him."

"And why should he think otherwise? He is your brother."

Balfour grimaced and hesitated, then decided there was no need to be secretive. "Eric is but my half brother. My father bedded one of Beaton's wives. Beaton discovered the liaison. When Eric was born he had the bairn set upon a hillside to die. One of our men found the lad. It wasnae hard to discover who he was and why he had been cast aside."

"And thus began the feud."

"Aye, thus began the feud. E'en my father's death didnae end it. Now it takes on a new shape. Beaton tries to claim Eric as the son he could ne'er breed on his own. He means to use the lad as a shield 'twixt him and all those who hunger for what he has. We must rescue Eric ere Beaton's illness makes him too weak to fight off the wolves, or finally takes his life."

"Beaton is dying?"

Maldie bit the inside of her cheek until tears stung her eyes. She did not need the swift narrowing of Balfour's eyes to tell her that she had reacted suspiciously to that news. Her voice had been too sharp, too full of emotion. The thought that Beaton's age and illness might rob her of the chance to gain her revenge infuriated her, even alarmed her. Beaton dying on his own would leave her unable to fulfill her vow to her mother. Maldie knew all of that emotion had been clear to hear in her voice. She prayed she could talk away Sir Murray's blatant curiosity.

"Aye, 'tis what I have been told," Balfour said, watching her closely, confused by the sudden flare of emotion on her lovely face and its equally sudden disappearance.

"I ask your pardon, sir," Maldie said. "For one swift moment all I could think of was that ye had taken up your sword against an ageing, dying mon. Then I recalled your brother's plight."

"Ye dinnae have much faith in the honor of men, do ye, lass?"

"Nay. I have ne'er been given much cause to believe in such a thing." She stared at the huge iron-studded gates of Donncoill as they drew within feet of them. "Surely there is a healing woman within such a fine keep, and thus ye have no real need of my skills.'' She looked at Balfour, but he only spared her a fleeting glance before staring at his keep.

''We had a verra skilled woman, but she died two years past. The woman she tried to train has neither wit nor skill. She favors leeches for all and any ill. I have oft felt that her untender mercies hastened my father's death.''

''Leeches,'' Maldie muttered, then she shook her head. ''They have their uses, aye, but are too often used wrongly. Your brother has already bled freely enough to remove all ill humors and poisons from his body.''

''So I believe.''

''Howbeit, I have no wish to offend the woman.''

''Ye willnae. She doesnae like the chore, does it only because no other can or will, and it does provide her with some prestige. I can easily find her another chore that will give her the same place of honor amongst the other women.''

Maldie just nodded, for all of her attention was on the bailey they were entering. It was crowded with people, few of whom paid her any heed. The sharp sounds of grief began a moment later, and she desperately fought to close her ears to them. Even as a small child she had been able to feel what others felt and the sorrow of those who had lost someone they loved in the battle choked her, their pain knotting her stomach. Yet again she wished that her mother had helped her learn how to shield herself from such emotional assaults, then scolded herself for being such an ungrateful child. There had been a use or two for her odd skill, uses that had gained them some much needed coin from time to time. Taking a few deep breaths, she struggled to calm herself, to clear her mind and heart of the invasive feelings of others.

''Are ye ill?'' Balfour asked as he helped her to dismount, worried about her loss of color and the chill on her skin.

''Nay, just weary,'' she replied and quickly turned her attention to Nigel. ''He must be put abed. The journey on the litter was a rough one and the sun begins to set, taking the day's warmth with it.''

"I think ye need to rest as weel."

She shook her head as she fell into step behind the men carrying Nigel into the keep. "I shall be fine. I think 'twas just riding on a horse. He is a fine steed, needing but a light touch and a soft word to do as he ought, but I am unused to riding. Dinnae fear, Sir Murray, I am hale enough to heal your brother and toss him back into the fray."

Balfour smiled faintly as he watched her follow his brother into the keep. For a moment she had appeared so affected by the grief of the bereaved women in the bailey that she was close to swooning. Then, although still pale and shivering faintly, she had returned to what was clearly her usual state of impertinence. Nigel was right. There was a mystery about the girl. She leapt from sympathy to scorn in a heartbeat. There was also her odd reaction to the news that Beaton was dying. Her explanation for that reaction had not rung true. He still desired little Maldie Kirkcaldy more than he knew was wise, perhaps even more than was sane, but he would be cautious. With Eric's life hanging in the balance, he could not afford to let his passions steal away all wisdom. Maldie Kirkcaldy had a secret or two, and even as he tried to satisfy the desire he felt for her, he would work to find out exactly what those secrets were.

Chapter Three

A soft moan of weariness escaped Maldie as she stood up. She hastily glanced at Nigel, relieved to see that he still slept peacefully, that her groan had not been loud enough to disturb him. For three long days and nights she had nursed the man through a raging fever, allowing herself only brief respites when Balfour took her place by his brother's bedside. The fever had finally broken, but she hesitated to ease her watch.

Maldie moved to a small table set near the arrow slit in the wall that served as the room's window, and poured herself a goblet of spiced cider. It was hard to nurse Nigel all alone, but she had needed only one look at Donncoill's healing woman Grizel to know that she would never let that woman within yards of Nigel Murray. Grizel was filthy and suffered from some skin ailment that left her dotted with ugly sores. Maldie had also sensed a deep, bitter unhappiness in the woman. Grizel not only disliked being the Murrays' healing woman, she disliked everyone and everything. Such a woman would not and could not care if the one she tended to lived or died. The woman would never be a healer no matter how much knowledge she gained, for she had no urge to heal or help anyone, no feeling at all for the afflicted or their pain. Maldie knew that, before she left Donncoill, she would have to try and explain that to Balfour, so that he would not return the woman to the same place of honor and responsibility. It would help if she could find someone with more heart and skill to take Grizel's place, but she needed to get out of Nigel's room to do that.

She grimaced, finished her cider, and refilled her plain silver goblet. Now that she could leave the room, she was reluctant to do so. It would mean that she would have to confront Balfour without Nigel and his wounds as a shield. Maldie knew that she had never once flagged in her duty as a healing woman nor in her determination to keep Nigel alive, but she had also hidden behind the fever-tormented man every time Balfour had drawn near to her.

That cowardice annoyed her even as it alarmed her. Balfour had made no overt attempt to touch her. His deep concern for his brother had been all that had brought him into the room. And, yet, she had felt her blood warm each time he had looked at her. Her every sense had come alive. Despite her exhaustion, it had often been hard to rest when he was in the room, because she had been so intensely aware of him. No matter how often she told herself she was just being vain, she still felt his want, his desire for her. With his every glance, even the briefest, most courteous touch, she had sensed his passion and her whole body had responded to it eagerly. Getting too close to Balfour could be very dangerous. Not only would she have to fight her own desire and attraction to the man, but she would have to try and shield herself from his, as well as the delight it stirred deep within her. Maldie wondered if she should have stayed hidden in those bushes by the side of the road.

"I begin to think that I have taken a grave misstep," she murmured, staring into the goblet.

"Nay, I dinnae think so. My brother looks much improved," came Balfour's deep, rich voice from close behind her.

Maldie squeaked and had to scramble to hold onto her goblet, her surprise at his sudden appearance making her lose her firm grip upon it. "Ye just terrified ten years off my poor wee life."

Balfour bit back a smile. He found her unease around him both encouraging and amusing. At first he had wondered if she was afraid of him, but had quickly shrugged that concern aside. It was not fear he saw in her beautiful eyes, but a reflection of the desire he felt for her. He wished he could know for certain if her unease came from a maidenly aversion to such desire or from the strength of it, from a strong need to give in to it. Such knowledge would make it easier for him to know what step to take next. Then he inwardly laughed at himself. Knowing the truth about how she felt would make little difference to what he planned, except that it might give him leave to act more quickly upon his desire. He wanted Maldie Kirkcaldy and he intended to have her.

"Come, I am nay so frightening," he said softly as he gave in to the urge to gently stroke her thick, unruly hair.

Although his touch was as light and fleeting as a soft spring breeze, Maldie felt its power. Standing so close to him, she could almost smell his desire for her. The heat of it reached deep inside of her, warming her blood, demanding a response. She could feel his seductive thoughts. He did not need to speak them. They were as tangible to her as any caress. She trembled and stepped away from him. As she took a long, deep drink of her cider, she covertly glanced his way and inwardly grimaced. His expression of mild amusement told her that he saw her move for exactly what it was—a cowardly retreat.

"I am nay afeared of you, sir. I but find this situation unsettling." She set her empty goblet down on the table, pleased at how steady her hand was, for her insides were churning like the mud beneath the feet of an advancing army. "Being alone in a bedchamber with a mon I have but recently met was something I was taught ne'er to do."

"Weel, there is a simple answer to that trouble," he said.

"Oh, aye? Ye are leaving?"

"Nay, ye must learn to ken me better." He smiled sweetly at her disgusted glance. " 'Twill nay be so painful, lass. Ye cannae hide away in here for all time."

"True. I shall stay until your brother is weel, and then be on my way."

"It may take months for Nigel to be fully healed yet, already, he doesnae need unceasing care from sunrise to sunrise. Ye need to enjoy the spring."

Maldie watched him closely, her eyes narrowing as her suspicions rose. "I can see the beauty of the spring out of that wee window." The man was flirting with her. She was sure of it.

"Ah, true, but 'tisnae the same as walking in it, as breathing it," he murmured. "Spring must be felt against one's skin." He slid his hand down her slim arm, ignoring the way she jerked free of his touch. "Its sweet breezes must be allowed to tousle one's hair." He lightly dragged his fingers through her hair. She pulled away, faced him squarely, and scowled. "And one must allow the sweet, warm air to soothe away all temper and ill humors."

"I am nay afflicted by any ill humors." She put her hands on her hips and tilted her head to the side, torn between amusement and annoyance. "If ye sense my temper rising 'tis because I dinnae play this game weel, sir."

Balfour hoped his expression of innocence was infallible, but the look she was giving him told him that it probably did not fool her at all. "What game do ye speak of, lass? I play no game."

"Ye are a poor liar, Sir Murray. Ye flirt with me, tease me, play the game of seduction."

"Mayhap ye misjudge me."

"Nay I ken the game verra weel." Simply thinking of the subtle, not so subtle, and even brutal ways men had tried to lure her into their beds angered Maldie. "It has been tried many a time before."

"And failed?" Balfour was not only surprised at how badly he wanted her to be untouched, but alarmed. The state of her innocence should not matter to him at all, but it did. It mattered a lot.

Maldie gaped, unable to believe that he would be so lacking in manners as to ask such a question. At first she was insulted and furious. Many men saw a poor girl as one without morals, and were deeply puzzled when she proved to have some. She had not guessed that Balfour held that insulting attitude.

Then she took a deep breath and let her feelings guide her. It was dangerous to open herself up to the man's emotions. The last thing she wished to discover was that Balfour Murray, like so many men before him, thought that because she was poor, she was a whore. But, for reasons she did not care to examine too closely, she needed to know why he had asked such a rude question.

At first it was difficult to reach beyond his desire for her, and her blind, immediate response to it. She forced herself to look deeper, and felt a calming sense of relief sweep over her. There was no scorn in his heart. She was certain he had not intended to insult her or, worse, thought she was the sort who would not be insulted by the insinuation behind his query. What puzzled her was that the question seemed to have been prompted by anger, fear, and reluctant curiosity. That was what she felt stirring inside of him. It was almost as if he deeply cared about her response, badly wanted it to be *aye*, and she could not understand why he should.

"Of course they failed," she replied, her lingering anger making her voice sharp. "As ye weel ken, I havenae had the wealth or comfort ye have enjoyed for your whole life. I was raised in a rougher world. Aye, men seem to think that, if ye are a poor lass, ye should be happy to do anything for a wee coin or two or just to please those who think they are your betters." She was glad to see him wince slightly, proving that he understood the rebuke. "Howbeit, I chose to learn how to fight rather than to just smile prettily and play the whore."

"I meant no insult," he said.

"Mayhap not, but ye gave one."

He took her hand in his, ignored the way she stiffened, and brushed a kiss over her knuckles. "Then I truly and deeply beg your pardon."

"And, if ye meant that, ye wouldnae still be trying to woo me."

"Oh, aye," he grinned and winked at her. "That I would."

Maldie gasped with a mixture of shock and outrage when he suddenly pulled her into his arms. "Ye have just humbly apologized for insulting me yet, now, clearly, ye intend to insult me again."

"Nay, I but mean to kiss you."

Balfour knew he was stepping over every boundary he had been trained to respect as an honorable man. Maldie might be worldly in knowledge, but she was an innocent in all other ways, had obviously fought hard to remain so. Custom demanded that he treat her with great respect. Instead, he had every intention of stealing a kiss if she did not protest too loudly or struggle too fiercely. It was undoubtedly a mistake, certainly not the way to woo someone as skittish and cleverly elusive as Maldie Kirkcaldy, but he realized that he was too weak to ignore temptation. She was close, she was beautiful, and he ached to kiss her. Had done so since he had first set eyes on her. Balfour just hoped that he would not pay too dearly for his impatient greed.

"Ye go too far, Sir Murray," she said, pushing against his chest.

Maldie inwardly cursed. She had intended to sound outraged and angry, to speak in a firm, sharp, and cold voice. Instead her voice was low, unsteady, and faintly husky. Even to her own ears her rebuke sounded weak, as weak as her attempt to push him away. Instinct told her that any true show of resistance would be respected, but she could not seem to muster up the strength to produce one. She did not really want to push her hands against his broad chest, but smooth them over the snug, soft woolen jerkin he wore, to feel the strength that lay beneath the cloth. She was disgusted with her own weakness, but reluctantly admitted that she wanted him to kiss her. She wanted to kiss him back.

He kept one arm securely wrapped around her, grasped her small chin between his thumb and forefinger, and gently but firmly turned her face up toward his. Maldie held herself taut, but even she was not sure how much of the tension was from resistance, and how much from anticipation. As he lowered his mouth to hers, watching her closely from beneath partly lowered eyelids, Maldie tried one last time to scold herself into acting as she should, and failed miserably. Instead of thinking a firm *nay* and acting upon it forcibly, all she could think of was how warm and dark his eyes were, how long and thick his lashes were, and how temptingly shaped his mouth was.

The moment his lips touched hers Maldie knew she had lost all chance of escape. His lips were soft, warm, and sweet. She knew the heady taste of him could hold her in his arms as firmly as any stout iron chain. He nudged her lips with his tongue and she opened to him, then shuddered. The way he stroked the inside of her mouth left her breathless, but that was not all that made her tremble. It felt as if, by opening her mouth, she had also opened herself up to all that Balfour was feeling, and she realized that her fears had been justified. Not only was she engulfed by the power of her own desires, but by the power of his as well. One fed the other. Even as her passion rose, filling her and stealing all thought, his seemed to flow into her, adding strength to all she felt. It was almost frightening, but her hunger for Balfour conquered that fear, impatiently pushed it aside.

When he pulled his mouth from hers, she clutched at him and muttered a protest. Then he touched a kiss to the side of her neck and she sighed with pleasure. As he covered her throat with kisses she tilted her head back, allowing him unfettered access, and pressed closer to him. His warm lips touched the pulse point in her throat and she gasped as she felt that heat immediately flow throughout her body. He smoothed his big hands over her back, down her sides, and then gently grasped her backside, pressing her closer to him. Maldie heard herself softly groan as she felt his hardness. Instinctively, she rubbed against him, savoring the way it made her feel, and echoing his shudder. They were both breathing hard, as if they had just run for miles, and she knew that that kiss had already driven them beyond clear thought and reason.

''Ye are so sweet,'' Balfour said, his voice thick and husky as he marked the delicate lines of the bones in her face with kisses.

He inwardly cursed the inadequacy of his words. The way Maldie made him feel deserved higher praise, poetry that would make a rock weep. Even if he had such skill, he mused as he began to kiss her again, he doubted he could muster it at the moment. The taste of her, the smell of her, and the feel of her softly trembling body pressed so close to his robbed him of coherent thought. He could only think of one thing. He wanted to bury himself deep inside of her.

"Maldie," he whispered, subtly tugging her toward the bed, "bonny Maldie. Ye feel the heat, too, dinnae ye."

"Aye." Each time he moved away she rushed forward, desperate to keep herself close to his warmth. " 'Tis a spell, I am thinking."

"One we are both caught in."

They bumped against the bed and Nigel groaned. Maldie felt all the warmth leave her body with such speed it made her dizzy. She swayed a little as she pulled free of a shocked Balfour's loosened hold and stared, horrified, at the sleeping Nigel.

Maldie's first clear thought was to briefly thank God that Nigel still slept, that the man had not seen anything. Then anger swept through her, although she was not sure who she was most angry with, Balfour for nearly seducing her into bed, or herself for allowing it. She strode away, neatly eluding Balfour's attempt to grasp her by the arm and hold her at his side. After briskly pacing in front of the massive stone fireplace opposite the end of the bed, she turned to glare at Balfour. He looked wary, but not contrite at all, and that annoyed her.

"Why are ye still here?" she snapped, pushing her tangled hair back over her shoulders with a quick, angry gesture.

Balfour leaned against one of the tall, thick posts at the foot of the bed and studied her. He fought to ignore how full and wet her lips were, his kisses still marking them, as well as the flush upon her cheeks. There would be no returning to her arms, not today. The look on her face told him clearly that the thoughts she now had about him were not kind ones. He had but one chance to stop her anger from turning her cold toward him, and that was to make her realize and accept that, for that brief time she had been in his arms, she had been a very willing, very warm partner. It was true that he had stolen a kiss, had ignored her protest, but it was also true that all that had happened after that had been with her full and passionate willingness.

"But a moment ago I was most welcome," he replied, purposely keeping his voice calm and his tone pleasant.

Despite all of her efforts not to, Maldie blushed. She knew he referred to how greedily she had accepted his kisses, and she could not deny that. However, he was unkind to remind her of her lack of moral strength, she decided. She would never have discovered how weak she was if he had not forced that first kiss upon her. Before his lips had touched hers, she had only suspected that she would be unable to resist the strength of his passion and her own. Now she knew she could not, and she did not appreciate him showing her that hard truth.

"Weel, that welcome has fled." She silently cursed, for, even to her own ears, her voice held a sulky tone. "As ye can see, I have much work to do here."

"Oh? Nigel sleeps. Ye need to watch him do that, do ye? Come, say what ye truly mean. Ye wish me gone for I made ye feel the same passion I do. Ye shared a heat with me, and ye want me far away ere ye start to feel it again."

"Such arrogance. Ye tricked me. I said *nay* to that first kiss and ye ignored me. Like all men, ye decided ye wanted something, so ye reached out and took it."

"Aye, I accept the blame for that first kiss." He straightened up, walked to the door, and looked back at her as he opened it. "But, lass, ye *gave* me the second one, eagerly and with a passion as hot and strong as my own. Aye, ye will probably try hard to deny that once I leave, but I think ye have too much wit to believe such a lie. Ye wanted me, Maldie Kirkcaldy, as greedily as I wanted you. Ye ken it weel, and so do I."

When the door shut behind him, Maldie looked around for something large and heavy to throw at the thick oak panel. By

the time she saw something suitable she knew it would be a
wasted gesture, for he was undoubtedly too far away to hear
anything. She cursed and sat down on the thick lambskin rug
in front of the fireplace. It would have been nice to have slain
him on the spot with cold words, with a sharp wit that would
have shamed him into slinking away like a whipped cur, but
she knew she had failed miserably in doing that. He had said
all he had wished to and left, and she had been unable to mount
a serious defense.

What deeply troubled her and somewhat angered her was
that he was right. She could curse him as ungallant, arrogant,
and vain, but it did not change the fact that he was right. She
had felt the same passion he had, had shared a heat with him.
Their desire was well matched. Their hunger for each other of
an equal strength. Passion had made her as blind and as heedless
as it had made him. It was not really fair to blame him for
what had happened, or what had almost happened.

But she did, she admitted, and inwardly grimaced at her own
confusion. It had always been so easy to scorn passion, to push
away any man who revealed an interest in her. The ease with
which she had cast aside all desire had made her cocky, made
her think she was strong enough not to repeat her mother's
folly. Balfour had slaughtered that confidence, shown her with
one kiss that she could be as foolish and as weak as the most
witless of women. She not only resented him for that uncomfortable revelation, she knew she was now afraid of drawing close
to the man. She had come to Donncoill to join in the destruction
of Beaton, not to become a laird's mistress. By the time Nigel
was well enough to finish recovering without any further nurs-
ing, she was going to have to make the decision as to whether
she would stay and fight Beaton alongside the Murrays, or flee
the temptation of Sir Balfour. There was no doubt in Maldie's
mind that staying could well cost her her hard-fought-for innocence. She briefly suspected that it could also cost her her heart.
Soon she would have to decide just how high a price she wished
to pay for help in killing Beaton.

* * *

Balfour sighed as he stared out at his fields, watching the spring planting with little interest. He was acting like some lovelorn girl and was disgusted with himself. He could not stop thinking about Maldie, about how good she tasted and how perfectly she fit in his arms. It had only been an hour since he had left her and he was aching to see her again, to hold her again. The only thing that stayed him was the certainty that it would be a very big mistake. She was still angry, and she needed time to think about what had happened between them.

"And so do I," he muttered, shaking his head.

The passion she stirred inside of him with her soft, full mouth and her small, lithe body was a delicious, heady thing. It was also unsettling. Something that powerful made it hard to think clearly and, with young Eric's life at stake, Balfour knew that a clear head was vital.

"Has Nigel worsened?" asked James as he walked up to Balfour and leaned against the parapets.

"Nay. He sleeps. The fever shows no sign of returning."

" 'Tis what I heard, yet your expression was so dark I feared the good news had proven false."

" 'Tis not Nigel nor his health I scowl o'er, but his wee nurse."

"A comely lass," James said, watching Balfour closely as the man chuckled.

"Too comely. Too sweet. Too tempting."

"And too ready at hand."

Balfour looked straight at James and slowly nodded. "Aye. We were in sore need of a skilled healer for Nigel and, behold, there she was. A blessing or a trap? Aye, sometimes when one has a great need God miraculously fills it, but I cannae take the chance of believing that now. Too much is at risk."

"Mayhap ye should just send her away."

"I should. She has even said she will leave as soon as Nigel no longer needs her healing skills. My wits said, *'Aye, that was for the best,'* but all else began to plot ways to keep her here.

I fear I learned naught from my father's many follies. I want the lass and 'tis all I can think of.''

"Nay, not all, for ye ken that she has secrets. Ye can see that there are questions that need to be answered.''

"I do." Balfour grimaced. "Howbeit, when I am near her, I dinnae think of getting any answers.''

"Then *I* will.''

Balfour hesitated only a moment before nodding. "My pride pushes me to say that I can do it myself. Fortunately, at this moment, I have more wit than pride. I have a weakness for the lass. I cannae trust myself to do what needs to be done. So, aye, see what ye can discover. She appeared at a time of need, but also at a time of conflict. She could be a bonny angel of mercy, but she could also be an adder slipped into our camp by our enemies. Maldie Kirkcaldy holds fast to many a secret. I must learn what they are. And dinnae take too long in discovering what those secrets are, old friend. I confess, that wee green-eyed lassie makes my blood run hot and my wits scatter. Best ye find out the truth swiftly, ere I am too ensorcelled to believe any ill of her.''

Chapter Four

"Ye take good care of me, lass," Nigel said as Maldie helped him ease his battered body into a seated position, carefully arranging several fat pillows behind his back. "I would have died if ye had not come to my aid."

Maldie inwardly grimaced as she felt Nigel's arm curl around her waist. It had been five days since his fever had broken and, with each day, he had shown an increasing and alarming interest in her. The moment he had regained the strength to move his arm, he had begun to touch her. They were subtle, inoffensive touches, easily excused, except that they were becoming more frequent. There was also far too much warmth in his lovely amber eyes each time he looked at her.

The very last thing she needed, she thought crossly as she neatly eluded his touch and went to collect the tray of food the maid had set on the table near the window, was yet another Murray trying to lure her into his bed. Nigel was being far sweeter and more courteous in his pursuit than Balfour, and it irritated Maldie a little that she had no interest in the younger Murray. Nigel was treating her as a man would treat a fine lady, his skill at flattery far surpassed Balfour's, and he was an extraordinarily handsome man, yet she was completely unmoved by his interest.

"I think I may need your kind aid in eating this stew," Nigel said quietly as she set the tray on his lap.

She glanced at him with some suspicion as she sat down on the edge of the bed and began to feed him the thick venison stew. He idly rested a hand on her knee and she felt no weakness there. The man could probably feed himself, but she decided to allow him to play his game. He did still suffer from weakness, his strength badly depleted by his wounds and the fever. There was always the chance that he feared losing the strength a good long rest had given him and finding himself unable to continue feeding himself partway through his meal or embarrassing himself by making a poor job of it. Since he was still completely harmless, she saw no gain in arguing the matter.

"Why do ye search for your kinsmen here?" Nigel asked as Maldie cut him some bread. "The Kirkcaldy clan roosts many leagues from here."

"Aye, they do. I havenae gotten lost, if that is what ye think," she replied. "I dinnae wish to go to them."

"Why?" He coughed a little when she somewhat roughly stuck a thick slice of bread in his mouth. " 'Tis a reasonable question," he protested, smiling faintly at the look of irritation on her face.

"Mayhap. The Kirkcaldys dinnae want me about. I have made no secret of the sad truth that I am a poor lass and have lived a rough life."

"As have many of the Kirkcaldys, I am certain."

"Aye. Howbeit, what I havenae said is that I am a bastard child." Nigel's eyes widened slightly, but she saw no scorn or distaste there, merely curiosity and the faintest hint of pity. "My mother was the eldest daughter of a Kirkcaldy laird. She allowed herself to be seduced away from her kinsmen. Weel, the mon who stole her away from hearth and home was already wed. When she got with child, he left her. She was too ashamed to go home."

Maldie decided it was safe to tell that much truth about

herself. She would keep well hidden the name of her sire as well as the fact that he had stayed until she was born, until he had seen that his sin had given him a girl child and not the son he craved. Naming her sire could pull her into more trouble than she could deal with, perhaps even put her life at stake. Speaking of the man's craving for a son could easily spawn more questions than she could safely answer.

"Ye could be misjudging the Kirkcaldys." Nigel used both hands to grasp his tankard of wine as he took a drink. "They may not care that ye are a bastard child. Your mother's fear that they would turn her or ye aside could be born of her own sense of guilt and shame. Mayhap ye should return home and speak to her."

"I cannae. She is dead."

"I am sorry for your loss. So, do ye seek out your father's kinsmen?"

That question made Maldie very uneasy and she abruptly stood up. "Nay. That cur has shown no interest in me. I have none in him. Are ye done?"

He nodded and she took the tray away, setting it back on the table near the window. It was now clear that answering a few questions was not enough to satisfy Nigel's curiosity. No matter how carefully she replied, her answer seemed to breed yet another question. The way he was so closely watching her told Maldie that her reaction to the question about her father had only whetted his appetite for more answers. It was not going to be easy to hold fast to her secrets without raising suspicions. If she decided to stay at Donncoill, to take even a small part in the fight against Beaton, she was going to have to think of some story about her past, something detailed and elaborate enough to answer all possible questions. Maldie was not sure she could think of such a complicated lie, nor tell it well.

The sound of the door opening caught her attention and she was surprised at how relieved she was to see Balfour. Since they had kissed she had done her best to stay far away from the man, nearly fleeing the room the moment he cleared the doorway. Even the small, terse courtesies they had exchanged in passing had been enough to make her uneasy. She had often caught a look in his dark eyes that told her he was fully aware of her retreat. Maldie also sensed that he was not going to allow it any longer. Despite that, she tried to slip past him, sighing with resignation when he caught her firmly by the arm.

"I was going to leave ye alone with your brother," she said as she turned to face Balfour, making one faint attempt to pull free of his hand and quickly giving up when he tightened his grip.

"Weel, I have no wish to hurt Nigel's tender feelings," Balfour flashed a quick grin at Nigel before fixing his gaze on Maidie, "but I came here to fetch you."

"Why?"

" 'Tis time ye went outside and had a wee taste of spring."

"I had a verra big taste of it when I walked from Dundee to here."

"The fine weather wasnae here yet. The sky is bluer and the sun warmer now."

"Nigel may need something."

"Aye," agreed Nigel with a sharp haste that caused Balfour to frown. "I dinnae think I should be left alone just yet."

"Ye willnae be alone," Balfour said, watching Nigel closely as he nudged Maldie out of the room. "Old Caitlin is hobbling her way to your room e'en as we speak." He grinned when Nigel groaned a curse. "She cannae wait to spend a few hours with 'her wee, bonny bairn.' "

"What was that all about?" Maldie demanded after Balfour shut the door and started to tug her along the hallway.

"Old Caitlin was Nigel's nursemaid, his milkmother," Balfour replied. "She still sees him as a wee lad, not a mon, and treats him so. And, why have ye suddenly agreed to come with me after fleeing from the sight of me for days?"

Maldie briefly considered telling him the truth, that Nigel was wooing her. She had simply made a choice between the two brothers, both of whom were trying to lure her into bed. There was a chance she could put a stop to Nigel's tentative

seduction before there was any real confrontation. To walk off
with Balfour, who made little secret of what he wanted from
her, might be one way to do that. She brushed aside the thought
of telling Balfour any of that, however. She was courting enough
trouble by simply lingering at Donncoill without setting one
brother against the other or, worse, inspiring them to indulge
in some manly competition where she was the prize.

"I havenae been fleeing from you," she protested, struggling
to sound haughty.

"Aye, ye have. Scurrying off like a wee timid mousie flushed
from the grain."

"Ye think yourself far more important than ye are."

"Racing for the safety of some warren like a wee rabbit
with the hounds after it."

"I was but leaving so that ye and your brother could have
some time to speak privately."

"Bounding off like a deer that has heard the hunter's horn."

"Ye are going to run out of animals soon."

Balfour choked back a laugh. "Slinking off into the shadows
like a whipped cur."

"Wait a moment." Maldie stopped as they left the keep,
yanking on her arm hard enough to halt him and make him
face her. "What happened to bounding, racing, and fleeing?"

"Ye dinnae like the word slinking, eh?"

"I am nay afraid of you, Balfour Murray."

He hooked his arm through hers and started to walk again.
"Nay? Then ye run from me because I am nay as pretty as
Nigel?"

She stumbled slightly and he watched her closely as he
waited for her reply. From the moment Nigel had opened his
eyes after shaking free of the fever's grip, Balfour had sensed
that the man was no longer seeing Maldie as a possible threat.
The gleam he had sometimes caught in his brother's eyes had
not been that of a man seeking to solve a mystery or root out
betrayal. Nigel wanted Maldie, and Balfour began to think his
brother wanted her as badly as he himself did.

The instant he had seen the glint of desire in Nigel's glance,

Balfour had fought the urge to pull Maldie out of his brother's
reach and hide her away, like some greedy child hoarding a
favorite toy. From the time he had been of an age to take an
interest in women, Balfour had seen that most of the ladies
favored Nigel over him. Nigel had been graced with a fair face,
a lighter nature, and an admirable skill with words. The lasses
had always sighed over Nigel's beauty, praised his sweet
tongue, his charm, and his courtly ways. One had even told
Balfour that Nigel's skill in the bedchamber far surpassed his
own. It was an old jealousy, one he had thought he had outgrown
until he had seen Nigel smile so sweetly at Maldie. He had
fought to remain silent, to still his concerns, and just watch the
two together. Balfour had seen no sign that Maldie was swayed
by Nigel in any way, but he wanted to hear her speak of her
indifference aloud.

"I dinnae think there are many men in Scotland who are as
pretty as Nigel," Maldie replied, watching Balfour covertly
and curious about the grimace that so briefly twisted his strong
features. It was as if she had somehow hurt him. "Aye, mayhap
not e'en in the whole world. A verra pretty mon is your
brother."

"The lasses have always sighed o'er him." Balfour inwardly
cursed, for he was sure he had sounded sullen.

Maldie nodded. "I suspect the mon has ne'er had to chase
a lass verra far or verra hard."

"And how hard will he have to work to win you?"

He spoke in a near whisper and Maldie again stopped to
stare at him. The man was jealous. Even scolding herself for
excessive vanity did not alter her opinion. He had seen Nigel's
interest in her and clearly thought that, like so many other
women before her, she would quickly succumb to a bonny face,
a sweet smile, and pretty words. His jealousy was dangerously
flattering, but his unspoken accusation was insulting. Then she
realized that Balfour struggled with an old jealousy, one he
neither wanted nor liked to feel, but one that had undoubtedly
been heartily fed over the years by foolish women. She could
probably push him away, maybe even kill his desire for her,

if she pretended to be swayed by Nigel, to be as easily captivated by beauty and a skillful tongue as other women he had known. But she could not grasp the opportunity presented to her. It was not simply because she could not set one brother against another, either. Sympathy for what he felt stopped her. Maldie understood what he suffered all too well. Because she was poor and a bastard, she had often been ignored or cast aside.

"Verra hard indeed," she replied and started to walk again.

"Aye? I have seen the way he looks at you."

"Ah, that is too bad. I had hoped he would be cured of that ere anyone noticed. The mon but feels a softening toward one who has eased his pain. And, dinnae forget, I am nearly all he has had to look upon for a week and a day."

"A face any mon would take great pleasure in watching."

She felt the heat of a blush on her cheeks and inwardly cursed. Nigel's soft, poetic flatteries had only stirred unease and an occasional smile. Balfour awkwardly telling her that she was pretty caused everything inside of her to soften. Maldie feared she was already past saving, that Balfour had already slinked into her heart. While she had been worrying over the passion they shared and how to fight it, her heart had quietly accepted him as the man it wanted. That meant that she had a lot more than her own errant desires to fight. It also meant that her chances of leaving Donncoill unchanged were a great deal less than she had thought.

Maldie was abruptly pulled from her dark thoughts when Balfour stopped and turned her to face him. She hastily looked around and silently cursed. He had walked her to a deserted, sheltered corner. They were encircled by piles of stone and the irregular walls of the tower he was having built. From the wideness of the grin on his face, she was sure that had been his plan all along. Balfour had not taken her outside to enjoy a warm, spring day, but to lure her to a sheltered place so that he could steal another kiss.

What really troubled Maldie was that she was making no effort to thwart him in his seductive game. She should be inflicting pain upon the man, breaking free of his hold, and

getting back to the safety of Nigel's room as fast as she could
Instead she remained still in his arms, thinking with some
amusement that he was a handsome rogue.

"So, this is what ye plotted all along," she said, her palms
flat against his broad chest in a weak, fraudulent show of
resistance.

"Do ye accuse me of base trickery?" he asked, his voice
pleasant, almost amused, as he brushed a kiss over her forehead

"Aye, I do. Do ye deny it?" She shivered with ill-concealed
delight as he kissed the hollow behind her ear.

" 'Twas no plot or trickery, bonny Maldie. Merely a thought
something I considered." He grinned when she uttered a short.
sharp sound of disgust. "Ye did need to get out of that room.'"

Just as Maldie opened her mouth to tell him succinctly that
he was speaking utter nonsense, he touched his lips to hers. A
little voice in her head told her that she was courting danger,
but she easily ignored it. The warmth his slow, enticing kiss
stirred within her melted away all common sense and resistance.
He made her feel good and, she ruefully admitted, she was too
weak to refuse that.

As he deepened the kiss, she curled her arms around his
neck and pressed closer to him. The tremor that went through
him spread to her own body. It astounded and alarmed her that
one simple kiss could so enflame them both. The thought that
they were behaving no better than animals in rut crossed her
mind and cooled her passion slightly. Before she could grasp
control of herself, however, Balfour slid his hand up her rib
cage and over her breast. He brushed his thumb over her nipple
until it hardened, pressing painfully against the worn linen of
her chemise. The feelings that spread through her left her gasping for air and sanity. The latter proved to be unattainable.

Balfour slowly moved her around until her back was against
one of the partially erected walls of the unfinished tower. She
knew he was unlacing her gown, but could not muster up the
will to push him away, almost aiding him as he tugged her
bodice down until it hung in a lump at her waist. His unsteady
fingers brushed her skin as he unlaced her chemise. She found

he strength to murmur a *nay,* but he kissed away her halfhearted protest. Maldie knew that she lacked the strength to shove him away from her, that she was allowing him such freedom because her skin ached for his touch.

When he opened her chemise the cool afternoon air brushed her skin, chilling her. Then Balfour kissed the soft skin between her breasts and the warmth returned. Maldie sighed her pleasure, threading her fingers through his thick hair, as he gently traced the full shape of her breasts with light kisses. When he enclosed the hardened tip of one breast in his mouth, teased it with his tongue, and then began to suckle, Maldie heard someone groan. It was a moment before she realized that that sound of blind greed had come from her own throat. Then she gave herself over completely to the desire Balfour stirred within her.

It was the sweet sound of children laughing that finally brought Maldie to her senses. She became painfully aware of where she was, that she was half-naked, and that the air was cool on her skin, so quickly she was robbed of breath for a moment. An inarticulate curse escaped her, and she started to push Balfour away only to realize that he had already begun to release her. As she fumbled with the laces on her chemise and gown, she tried not to think on how well he had sensed her change of mood. She forced herself to think not only of how close she had come to losing her innocence outside, against a wall, but steps from a crowded bailey, and how furious that made her, at herself and at Balfour.

Balfour pressed his body against the chill, damp stone of the partially built wall as he watched Maldie fix her gown. It did little to cool the heat in his blood. He had sensed the moment she had shaken free of desire's grip and used all of his willpower to let her go. Knowing that he had done the right thing did not ease the aching want twisting his insides, however. He did not feel noble, just starved for more of the passion they could share. The look of anger settling on her still flushed face told him that it could well be a very long time before he got another chance to taste that passion.

"I am nay better than some witless hedgerow whore," Maldie grumbled as she vainly tried to put some order into her badly tousled hair.

"Nay. A hedgerow whore feels naught," Balfour said as he slouched against the wall, crossing his arms over his chest as he fought the urge to reach for her. "She just lies there, enduring, and waiting for ye to press a coin into her palm."

She bit back the urge to ask him how he knew so much about whores. "At least that serves some practical purpose. 'Tis clear that I am prepared to open my legs for no more than a bonny smile." Maldie was so disgusted with herself, so disappointed by her own weakness, she realized that she had no time or inclination to be embarrassed by what had just happened. "I am no better than my poor mother. I rush to repeat her folly."

"As I seem to rush to repeat my father's. Or so I thought. Howbeit, I have never acted in this way before, have ye?"

"Of course not." Maldie knew she ought to leave before Balfour said anything else. The man had a true skill at speaking simple truths, ones she could not deny.

"Weel, my father bedded any wench who would allow it for miles around and claimed to love half of them. 'Tis a wonder that Donncoill doesnae swarm with his bastards. I have e'er fought hard to keep my blood cool and my head clear. And your mother's folly?"

"She bore me."

"I dinnae see that as a folly," he said softly.

"Oh, but it was. I am the bastard child of a mon who didnae feel bound by his marriage vows." She had to sharply bite the inside of her cheek to keep herself from saying anything else about her father, surprised at how Balfour's soft look made her feel compelled to tell the truth. "The way he left her alone when he got her with child should have made her wary, but it didnae, not for a long time. Aye, she loathed him, yet it didnae seem to stop her from thinking that the next mon would be different. In some ways they were. Most at least gave her some coin or a few gifts. At some time, she ceased to care or feel, simply took the money."

''I cannae believe ye would ever become like that.'' Balfour inwardly cursed, for, although he felt a deep sympathy for the sad life she had had to endure, he also saw how it could give Maldie the strength to fight the passion that flared between them. ''Ye are too strong.''

''My mother was a strong woman.'' Even though she spoke firmly, Maldie realized that she was no longer so certain of that. ''She was brought low by a mon, used and cast aside, twisted by his heartlessness until she grew as heartless as he. No mon will drag me down. I will heed no lies nor be the loser in some mon's game.''

''And I neither lie nor play a game. What flares between us, lass, is heady and sweet. Aye, and methinks it may be stronger than both of us.''

''Nay. 'Tis but a heedless thing, nay more than what possesses the forest beasts in rutting season. I willnae let it win.''

Balfour sighed and watched her walk away. There was nothing he could say to change her mind anyway. He now believed that he and Maldie shared far more than his feckless father had shared with any woman, including his mother. What flared between him and Maldie was fierce and went deeper than lust. He was not sure, however, if it was fate, one of those rare, blinding passions most men dream about but never taste, or the first stirrings of love. Neither did he know exactly what he wanted of Maldie beside bedding her, so he could make her no promises. She would easily sense his uncertainty if he tried to discuss what they felt. It could even make her think he was lying to her just to gain what he wanted. It was hard to put the ring of truth behind one's words when one did not know what the truth was.

They were at an impasse, he decided as he slowly made his way back to the keep, a cold, sleep-robbing impasse. Both of them feared repeating the mistakes of their elders. Maldie would lose her chastity if she succumbed to the passion they shared and, quite often, that was all the dowry a poor girl had. He could not, at least not yet, offer her any more than an equal passion. With Eric's life at risk and a battle looming, it was not the time for him to make any promises to any women, especially to a poor fatherless girl who held close to too many secrets. Balfour sighed again. It began to look as if Maldie was the only one who could solve their dilemma. She was the one who would be risking all for passion. Balfour just wished that he would be given a few more chances to show her what she would deny herself if she turned him away. But, after today, he would be very surprised if Maldie let him within shouting distance.

Chapter Five

"What are you doing, ye great fool?"

Maldie could not believe the sight that greeted her as she stepped into Nigel's room. She had been gone barely an hour, and it appeared that relaxing her guard for even that short a time had been a mistake. In the week since Balfour had nearly succeeded in seducing her, she had gratefully found herself diverted by the battle to keep Nigel from trying to do too much too soon. Looking at him standing there, a young maid unsteadily supporting him as he tried to walk, Maldie did not feel so grateful anymore. Although there was little chance of him opening his wounds, the man could easily and permanently cripple himself.

"Jennie, is it?" Maldie asked as she moved to take over the pale girl's place supporting the trembling, sweating Nigel.

"Aye, mistress." Jennie grimaced and absently rubbed her lower back.

"I ken that this fool can be sweet and cajoling," she ignored Nigel's muttered complaints over her insults as she urged him back to his bed, "howbeit, ye are to ignore his pleas or commands to help him to walk."

"But, mistress," Jennie hesitated at the door, watching a softly cursing Nigel with wide eyes.

"If ye fear disobeying the laird's own brother, dinnae worry o'er it. I can speak to Sir Balfour and he will readily repeat my command. This fool isnae supposed to be up on these wee, spindly legs unless I say so."

"Spindly?" Nigel muttered, as Jennie fled the room and Maldie got him comfortably arranged on his bed.

"Ye wish to be crippled, do ye?" Maldie asked, putting her hands on her hips as she stared down at the man.

"Nay, of course I dinnae wish for that. I will be, howbeit, if I dinnae get my strength back."

"Ye were badly wounded, lost a great deal of blood, and suffered a long, fierce fever less than a fortnight ago. Ye cannae expect to be up and dancing so soon. 'Tis necessary to let your whole body recoup the strength it lost, to renew the blood that poured out of you and make it hearty again. That requires rest and food."

"I at least feel hale enough to *try* and walk again."

"Aye, that is clear enough to see. What can also be seen is that when ye stand up ye sweat and tremble like a man with the ague. 'Tis your body telling you that ye arenae ready at all. Heed it or it will make ye pay dearly for disobeying it." She moved to pour him some wine.

"Ye make it sound as if my body has its own life and rules, seperate from what my mind says."

"It does." She handed him the goblet of wine, frowning when she saw how he had to hold it with both hands because of the faint tremor in his arms. "I think ye have wit enough to ken that your body is now telling you that ye have been verra foolish indeed."

Nigel groaned and tried to thrust the goblet at her, but lacked the strength for such a forcible gesture. He was barely able to hold it out to her with only one unsteady hand without dropping it. "If I must lie abed for verra much longer I may weel be strong enough to walk again, but I will also be drooling mad."

Maldie had to smile as she put the goblet away and gathered

a bowl of water and rag to wash him. "I ken weel how maddening it can be to do naught but lie abed, your mind alert but your body too weak to act upon your wishes. 'Tis why I say ye must heed your body. I cannae say it strong enough or often enough." She began to lightly wash the sweat from his body. "I ken that people think I speak nonsense when I say your body tells you things, but it does. When ye stood up didnae your head swim, didnae ye sweat from head to toe, and didnae ye tremble? That, my fine knight, was your body saying, in the strongest way it could, to get back into bed and get some more rest."

" 'Twould be nice if it had my mind give me such a warning ere I put foot to floor," Nigel said, smiling faintly.

"Ah, true, but the mind is a contrary thing. It doesnae always lead us in the right direction or tell us the truth. And, no matter how sharp-witted we are, we can often allow it to lead us astray. Surely ye have thought of things that were neither wise nor safe and, worse, acted upon them."

"Oh, aye, and one's cursed mind doesnae have the courtesy to let ye forget such blunders."

Maldie's laughter caught in her throat as she became aware of the fact that the body she was washing was not as completely drained of strength as she had thought. There was certainly one part of Nigel's body that revealed no difficulty at all in standing. She had suspected that Nigel desired her, but seeing the stout proof of that tightening the front of his braies left her feeling embarrassingly flustered. She stood there, staring, unable to decide what to do next. There was only one thing she was sure of, and that was that she had just lost all chance of pretending that she had not noticed anything.

"Weel, 'tis some comfort to ken that I havenae been completely unmanned," Nigel drawled.

That piece of impertinence was just starting to pull Maldie free of her shock when she had the damp rag yanked from her hand, and a familiar deep voice said, "I believe the time has come for another to assume the duty of washing my brother."

Balfour nudged Maldie away from the bed. "I am sure Mistress Kirkcaldy can find other things to do."

"But, Balfour, the lass and I were just having a fascinating discussion about how one should always heed what one's body tells it."

Maldie heard Nigel grunt with pain, but could not see around Balfour to judge why. She was tempted to tell Balfour to go away, irritated by the way he was shoving her aside and taking over her duties, as well as telling her what she could or could not do. Then wisdom prevailed over pride. Nigel desired her and was obviously well enough to reveal that with more than a look or weak touch. It was undoubtedly best for both of them if she ceased to take care of any of his personal needs now. Bathing him could easily lead to a confrontation she would prefer to avoid.

"I will go and fetch his meal," she murmured and made a quiet, somewhat hasty retreat from the room.

The moment the door shut behind Maldie, Balfour tossed the rag aside and glared at his brother. He struggled to control his anger, one he knew was born of an unreasoning jealousy. When he had entered the room and seen Maldie bathing Nigel, he had felt the usual pang of envy. The moment he had seen Nigel's blatant arousal and the seductive look on his brother's face, it had taken all of his willpower not to throw Maldie out of the room and undo some of her fine work in healing his brother.

"Ye have a rough touch, brother," Nigel said, warily eyeing his scowling elder brother.

"Mayhap I am just disgusted that ye would try to seduce the wee lass who has worked so hard to keep ye alive," Balfour snapped as he moved to pour himself some wine, inwardly cursing the temper he could not seem to control.

"And why should that trouble ye so much?"

"She is but a poor, fatherless lass and was it not ye yourself who warned me against being blinded by a bonny face? Was it not ye who said that she held too many secrets?" He looked straight at Nigel, a little discomforted by the considering look on his brother's face, one that told him he had probably revealed too much of his feelings.

Nigel nodded slowly. ''I did and I still do. Howbeit, I now think those secrets have naught to do with us, are no threat to us. She is, as ye have just reminded me, a poor, fatherless lass. She has led a hard life and feels deeply about the shame her mother suffered and the way her father cast her and her mother aside. Her secrets are about herself and her past, about shames, hurts, and trials that she rightfully feels are none of our concern.''

''Mayhap.'' Balfour prayed that, if he shut his mouth now, Nigel would let the subject lag, but a moment later he knew that was a vain hope.

''I dinnae think ye are angry because I was succumbing to a lass ye mistrust.''

''These are troubled times. One should be cautious.''

Nigel ignored his words. ''I think ye want the lass yourself and ye thought I was stealing her away.''

''And I think ye have lain abed so long that your wits have become as weak as your body.''

''Nay. I am right. Ye cannae insult me out of my belief. Ye want the lass. I saw it when we found her on the road, but chose to forget that. I think I have chosen to ignore all signs of your desire for her. 'Twould interfere with my own plans, wouldnae it? Just how badly do ye want the lass?''

Balfour briefly considered heartily denying Nigel's assumptions and then making a hasty, cowardly retreat from the room. Then he shook his head. It would only gain him a small respite. His brother would never let the matter rest until his curiosity was satisfied. An honest answer now might silence Nigel. To his utter disgust, he found himself wondering if it would also make Nigel back down and leave Maldie alone. He hated to think he was that uncertain of his ability to woo and win a woman, especially one Nigel had also set his eye upon.

''Badly,'' he finally replied. ''At times I think my wits have been scattered to the four winds.''

"Aye, those green eyes can do that to a mon. So can a hearty lusting."

" 'Tis more than lusting," Balfour reluctantly admitted.

"How much more?"

There was an odd look on Nigel's face, intent yet somehow unreadable. It was as if Nigel was trying very hard to hide something. What if Nigel was also captivated? What if his brother also had feelings for Maldie, ones that went far deeper than a natural, manly lusting for a pretty woman? Balfour realized that he did not want to know, no matter how selfish that was. He did not want to feel obligated to give Nigel a fighting chance. If his brother was hurt by whatever happened between himself and Maldie, Balfour decided he would deal with that later.

A small, jealous part of him muttered that it would do the bonny Nigel some good to lose a woman. Balfour swore that he would do something to finally kill that still bitter, hurt young man inside of him, the one that had watched too many women turn from him to Nigel and obviously still resented it. He had not realized how deep that sense of injury had gone, not until Maldie had walked into their lives.

"I dinnae ken," Balfour replied quietly. "That 'tis more than passion is all I am sure of."

"And how does she feel?"

"She wants me. That I am certain of. She fights it because she believes passion destroyed her mother. Maldie doesnae want to repeat her mother's follies. 'Twas when I saw that I no longer feared I was about to repeat our father's mistakes that I was sure I was being driven by more than desire." He shrugged, a little disgusted by his own uncertainties. "I just cannae say how much more. 'Tis a fierce thing, but 'tis also a puzzling thing."

"Then have her, brother. She is yours. I withdraw from the field. What with your fears, confusions, and desires and her fears and passions, the field is too crowded anyway."

Before Balfour could ask what Nigel meant, Maldie returned. The cross look she gave him as she set a tray of food on Nigel's lap made Balfour fear she had overheard his talk with Nigel. He quickly discarded that concern. If Maldie had heard anything, she would have been a lot more than cross. Balfour knew that, to anyone idly listening, it would have sounded as if he and Nigel were callously deciding who would bed her. He doubted that his confession about the depth and confusion of his feelings would have wrung any sympathy from her either. Maldie was clearly just annoyed at his interference and the way he had ordered her around.

"Am I allowed to help him eat his food?" Maldie asked, frowning when Balfour grinned.

Balfour wondered fleetingly why he should be so inordinately pleased that he had not only guessed her mood, but the cause of it. "I should have thought that he was recovered enough to feed himself."

"Aye, he would be, if he hadnae got up and skipped about the room."

"I didnae skip," muttered Nigel, whispering a curse when he had to have Maldie cut his bread for him.

"And why shouldnae he be trying to walk?" asked Balfour, frowning a little when he suddenly became aware of how pale his brother was. "His fever has been gone for a week or more, and his wounds arenae in danger of opening."

"True, but he must now regain all the strength he lost. He must take his first steps with the utmost care, especially since one of those deep wounds was to his leg. I can understand what sets his mind to such foolishness," Maldie added, watching Nigel closely as he took a drink of cider. "Lying abed, rested and with a full belly, one isnae always aware of one's weaknesses and has no patience for caution. Howbeit, to do too much too fast could leave him with a stiffness in his leg he would never be rid of."

The firm tone of her voice told Balfour she spoke the truth, and he looked at Nigel. The tight, almost sullen look on his brother's face said that Nigel also believed her warnings. Once Nigel's fever had passed, Balfour had considered his brother healed, that the man only needed rest and food. He realized that he had been as foolish as Nigel. He could also see that Nigel was going to require a great deal of very close watching.

"How goes the plan to free Eric and make Beaton suffer?" asked Nigel as Maldie took the meal tray away.

"Slowly." Balfour leaned against one of the tall, thick posts at the foot of the bed and crossed his arms over his chest. "We ken verra little about the mon or about Dubhlinn. I have set a mon within the heart of the enemy's camp, but 'tis difficult for him to send us any information. Even the simplest thing could aid us, but we dinnae e'en have that yet."

"When ye say simple, do ye mean such things as when they open and close the gates?" Maldie asked as she poured herself a goblet of cider.

"Aye, e'en something as small as that."

"Weel, they open them when the sun clears the horizon, and shut them at twilight."

Maldie nearly flinched beneath the brothers' stares. The hint of suspicion in their eyes was justified, but that did not make it any less unsettling. In her eagerness to help defeat Beaton in any way she could, she had not considered how such information would be viewed. Nor had she considered the need to devise a very clever explanation for possessing such knowledge about their enemy. The truth, that she had learned all she could about Beaton so that she could more easily kill the man, would be viewed by the Murrays with distrust and, quite possibly, distaste.

"How do ye come to ken that?" demanded Balfour.

"I was searching for my kinsmen in and around Dubhlinn."

"Ye are the kinswoman of a Beaton?"

The way Balfour said that, as if she had just told him that she had the plague, reaffirmed Maldie's decision to never tell him her true parentage. "Nay, my kinsmen are minstrels. I had followed their trail to Duhblinn and lingered in an attempt to discover which way they had traveled upon leaving the place. The Beatons who kindly took me into their home were an aging couple in the village."

"Why did ye say naught? Ye kenned that we were fighting Beaton."

"I am no warrior, Sir Balfour. I didnae ken that ye would be interested in what little I saw or heard. I wasnae there when your young brother was taken, either."

Balfour sighed and ran a hand through his hair, then tried to rub away the sudden stiffness in the back of his neck. "I beg your pardon, Mistress Kirkcaldy. I didnae mean to insult or accuse you. With each day that Eric lingers in that mon's hold, I grow more concerned for his safety and, aye, mayhap see betrayal where it doesnae exist. Even now, I have found myself wondering how the mon kenned where and when to wait to capture the lad, and that has made suspicion set itself deep in my heart."

"No need for such a humble apology," she said. "Ye are at war and I am a stranger."

"Balfour," Nigel drew his brother's attention away from Maldie, "do ye really think someone has betrayed us? That someone here actually helped Beaton gain hold of Eric?"

"Aye. I wonder that I ne'er thought of the possibility before," Balfour replied.

As the brothers discussed who could possibly have betrayed them and why, Maldie idly tidied the room. She was heartily relieved that Balfour's interest in her and what she knew had been diverted. She had spoken too quickly, without thought. Minstrels, she decided, were a good choice of kinsmen, however, for few knew many by name, and their wandering ways meant that even fewer could be expected to know where they were. All she had to do was think of a name for them. There was a good chance that Balfour would never ask, but she wanted to be prepared with an answer.

The tangle of lies had begun to twist around her. It both alarmed and dismayed Maldie. She had rarely lied before. It was apparent that she had some skill in the art, but she felt no pride in that. Even though she did not want it to be true, she had to admit that lying to Balfour was especially painful. That he accepted her lies without question, even apologized for having reasonable suspicions about her, only made her more disgusted with herself. Deceiving someone was not something she liked to do. She was sure that deceiving someone who had taken her into his home and easily trusted her was a sin that could well stain her soul for a long time.

Maldie was pulled from her dark thoughts by the stealthy entrance of Grizel. She would not have known the woman was even in the room except that she was in between the ill-smelling woman and the tray she had been sent to retrieve. As Grizel brushed by her, Maldie had to clench her hands against the urge to wipe herself off. It was as if that light, swift touch had left her soiled, almost as if some of Grizel's filth and smell had clung to her. Maldie noticed that the moment she had looked at Grizel, had acknowledged the woman's presence, she had ceased to move so quietly. The two men talking so intently about forthcoming battles and possible betrayals were still completely unaware of the woman.

Grizel picked up the tray, turned to leave, and glanced toward the two men by the bed before marching out of the room. Maldie shuddered, chilled by the look on the woman's face as she had watched Balfour and Nigel. It had been a look of pure hate, a feeling so strong that it had briefly touched Maldie, leaving a sour taste in her mouth. She tried to tell herself that she was being foolish, that she had simply been infected by the brothers' talk of betrayal, but she could not make herself believe that. Even though she did not know the Murrays very well, she could think of nothing they could have done to inspire such hatred. But she could not ignore or deny it, either. Grizel loathed the brothers. Maldie wondered if she had just found their traitor. She then wondered if she could make them see it.

"Ye look weary, Nigel," Balfour said. "Rest. We but talk round and round and find no answers. I at least have the comfort of kenning that ye share my suspicions about a traitor at Dunncoill."

" 'Twould be better if we kenned who it is," Nigel murmured as he slumped against his pillows.

" 'Tis Grizel," Maldie said, deciding that the simple truth

was not only the easiest way, but nice to indulge in for a change. It was hard, however, not to take a defensive step backward when both men suddenly stared at her.

"What is Grizel?" asked Balfour. "Was she just here?" He grimaced slightly. "God's teeth, I think I can smell her."

"Ye may do so. I keep these chambers verra clean. 'Twould be easy to smell such filth when it enters now."

"Are ye saying that my chambers werenae clean before? I am wounded to the heart," Nigel jested weakly.

"They are but much cleaner than they were," she said. "Howbeit, I wasnae speaking wholly of Grizel's dirt or odor, just her hate. 'Tis so strong I could taste its bitterness." She smiled briefly at their identical looks of confusion. "Grizel hates ye and Nigel, Sir Balfour, truly loathes you."

Balfour rubbed his chin as he carefully weighed her words. "I ken that the woman is ill humored and appears to deal weel with no one here, mon, woman, or beast. 'Tis a long stride from that to hatred. And of what worth is it to me if she does hate me or Nigel?"

Maldie shook her head. "Thus speaks a mon raised in the palm of wealth and ease. Those surrounded by ones who serve them are oftimes too blind to see either their worth or their threat. Ye both feel certain that someone had to have aided Beaton in the stealing of your brother, yet can think of no one with a reason to betray you. Weel, I give ye a good reason— hatred. Ere ye dismiss Grizel as a threat, mayhap ye should ponder what might have caused her hatred. Therein may lie the answers ye seek."

"Our father bedded her once." Nigel shrugged gently, still favoring his wound. "She was fair, and cleaner, once, years ago."

"And your father cast her aside?" Maldie asked, fighting not to let her distaste for such behavior divert her.

"Aye, when he fell in love with Eric's mother. I fear Grizel's fair looks swiftly left her so, e'en when his new lover died, our father felt no desire to return to Grizel's arms."

"So, Grizel was once the laird's leman and fair of face. Then she is cast aside for a new lover, watches that woman's child raised as the laird's son, and watches her beauty fade. Not only do I see a verra good reason for the woman to hate Murray men, but a verra good reason indeed for Grizel to wish to harm Eric.''

'' 'Tis certainly enough reason to watch her more closely,'' Balfour said as he moved toward the door. ''I will do so. I need more than words and suspicions to call Grizel a traitor. She has been at Donncoill since her birth. Her kinsmen helped mine gain and hold this land.'' He paused in the open doorway and sighed. ''Although they have naught to do with her nor she with them, she does have kinsmen here. I need hard proof of her betrayal. And, now, I need ye to ready yourself to come to the great hall and dine with me.''

''But Nigel—''

''I will send Jennie up to tend to him.''

He was gone before Maldie could offer any further argument, and she cursed. For one brief moment she considered simply ignoring his command, then sighed. He would just come and fetch her, she was sure of it. It was going to be a long meal, she mused, as she found a brush and began to fix her hair.

Chapter Six

Balfour bit back a smile as he watched Maldie enter the great hall. She wore a dark blue gown, worn, carefully mended in a few places, and just a little too small, hugging her lithe body in a way he truly appreciated. Her thick, unruly hair was held back by a strip of leather, several heavy curls already slipping free to tumble around her small face. He stood up and waved her toward a seat on his right.

"This is too high a place for me," Maldie softly protested, hesitantly taking the seat he offered her. "I should be below the salt, as I have neither title nor proper birthright."

"Ye have saved Nigel's life," he replied as he sat down and signaled a page to pour her some wine. "That deserves a place of honor, more so than any title or weighty purse."

"He was wounded and I had the skills needed to help him." She shrugged. "I did as anyone would."

"Not anyone." He tried not to stare at the amount of food she was piling on her plate. It was obviously not a lack of appetite that kept her so slender. "Ye have acted with dedication and kindness, yet have asked for nothing."

"I have a soft bed, a roof o'er my head, and all the food I need or could want. 'Tis payment enough."

He said nothing, just watched her eat for a while. Although it amused him to watch such a tiny woman eat so heartily, it also pained him. There was the faint hint of hurried greed to her manner of eating. It was plain that she had often gone without, and he hated to think of how many times she must have gone to bed hungry. He realized that he had rarely thought of how hard life must be for those lacking the blessings he had been born with. At times he had savored a sense of pride over how well he cared for the people of Donncoill but, aside from the occasional giving of alms to the poor, he had never tried to extend that largesse to others. It shamed him to think that, for the lack of a helping hand, people like Maldie suffered. He knew his sudden concern for the plight of the poor was born of his feelings for Maldie, but he swore to himself that he would no longer be so blind to the needs of others.

"Mayhap ye would like a new gown," he suggested, then inwardly grimaced when she slowly turned to look at him with narrowed eyes. He should have weighed his words more carefully, for it was clear he had just delivered an insult.

"If ye find my gown too poor, I can return to dining in my room," Maldie said, a little surprised at how cold her voice was. If what he had just said was an insult at all, it was a small one, yet even the hint that Balfour might not approve of her attire struck her to the heart.

" 'Tis a lovely gown and ye look verra bonny in it," Balfour said. "Methinks ye take offense too swiftly, m'lady, that ye see insult where none exists. My words were but clumsily said. And I think ye have wit enough to ken I would be speaking pretty lies if I cried your gown the bonniest I have e'er seen. I ken naught about the fashions of ladies, but I can see that ye have but two gowns and have had them for many a year. There is no shame in that. I but searched for some way to reward you for Nigel's life, and thought ye may need or just wish to have a new gown."

Maldie sighed and smiled crookedly. "Ye are right. At times

I can bristle like a wee hedgehog, hearing what hasnae been said, sensing scorn behind the most innocent of words. I thank ye for your kind offer, but I must refuse it. Aye, these gowns are old and much mended, but I cannae accept gifts for doing something I would have done for anyone. God granted me the skill to heal people. It doesnae seem right to accept payment for doing his work.''

Balfour decided not to press the matter. He would speak to Una, the finest seamstress in the clan. That woman could make a gown for Maldie and had the wit to do so secretly. He would not ask Maldie what she wanted for a gift, for a small reward for all her work, but simply present her with one. Maldie had clearly been raised as a gentlewoman despite her poverty, and courtesy alone would make her accept it.

''How long were ye lurking about Dubhlinn?'' he asked.

''I wasnae lurking and I was there for little more than a fortnight,'' she replied, ignoring his grin.

Maldie had expected the questions, but they made her uncomfortable. More lies, she thought with a touch of despair. He was right to use the word lurking, too. That was exactly what she had done, grasping each and every opportunity to spy on the Beatons. She might still be there except that too many men had begun to take too strong an interest in her. She still felt guilty about leaving the old couple who had befriended her, stealing away in the dark of night with no word of farewell or, worse, gratitude.

Suddenly she was angry at her mother. Maldie wondered if her embittered parent had given any thought to what sins she would have to commit, what low trickery she would have to stoop to, to fulfill the vow of vengeance she had been made to swear. Then she felt swamped with guilt, silently cursing herself yet again as an ungrateful child. Her mother had shamed herself time and time again just to keep food in their bellies. That sad circumstance had been brought about by Beaton's cruelty. Was it really asking too much to want the man to pay for his heartless desertion, to expect her only child to extract that debt? A small voice in her head said *aye* but Maldie stoutly silenced it.

"Ye have grown most solemn," Balfour said quietly, lightly touching Maldie's tightly clenched fist where it rested upon the table. "Did ye have some trouble at Dubhlinn?"

"Nay. I but realized that, by aiding you, I could weel be endangering the kindly old couple who sheltered me." She smiled as she thickly spread honey on a slab of bread. "Then I recalled the old woman complaining about how Beaton ne'er waits for the ones in the village to seek shelter at the keep. The minute the mon thinks there is some danger approaching he shuts the gates, and cares nothing for who is left outside. She claimed he would lock his own mother out if the woman wasnae quick enough. She also said that the people in the village dinnae e'en try to run to the keep anymore. They hide and pray that whoever has come to kill Beaton willnae come hunting for them."

"Ye may ease your mind about them. I am nay planning to slaughter the Beatons. All I wish is to bring young Eric home and seek a reckoning from their laird." He shook his head as he mopped his plate clean with a piece of bread. "Mayhap the clan will live better and more peacefully without that fool leading them."

He said no more but became intent upon swishing the half-eaten piece of bread over his already clean plate, and Maldie wondered what odd mood had suddenly seized him. Then she realized that he was covertly watching something at the far end of the great hall. Carefully, she followed his gaze and was not overly surprised to see Grizel. The woman crept along in the shadow near the tapestry-draped walls until she reached the men at arms, and then sat on a chest near the wall. Although she appeared busy with her mending it did not take too long a study to see that the woman was listening to everything Balfour's men were saying. It was there to see in the way Grizel leaned toward the men, one ear cocked in their direction, and how she kept glancing at them. She even occasionally sent Balfour a nervous look, but did not seem aware of how closely he was watching her. Maldie decided that Grizel was not partic-ularly skilled at spying, had simply succeeded because no one paid her any heed. It was also possible that the ease with which the woman had accomplished her treachery thus far had succeeded in making her careless.

"I cannae believe I havenae seen it before," muttered Balfour, revealing that his thoughts echoed Maldie's.

"Ye rarely e'en saw the woman until now," Maldie said, and saw by the scowl that darkened his face that her words had not comforted him at all. "And, as ye have said, she and her family have been with the Murrays since the beginning. She would be the last one ye would suspect."

"Which is why she was such a good choice. Yet, I should have wondered. Ye are right. She hates us. I can see it clearly now. And she has reason to do so. My father treated her poorly as, I fear, he treated many women."

"Nay. That isnae enough reason to betray one's clan, one's family, and one's ancestors. Aye, hurt the one who has hurt and shamed you, but not all who are his blood or his clan, and that is what helping Beaton will do. I begin to feel most sorry for poor Eric."

"Aye, it cannae be easy to be Beaton's prisoner."

"In truth, I was thinking of how Beaton hated him when he was born and tried to kill him. Now there is Grizel who also hates him and doesnae care if the lad lives or dies. Both acted upon anger over sins that poor lad had naught to do with. It must be hard for him to ken that, simply by his birth, he has made two strong enemies. Aye, and now the verra mon who tried to kill him wants to call him son. Your wee brother must think the whole world has gone mad or, worse, he has."

Balfour grimaced and slowly nodded. He hated to admit it, but he had not given much thought to how Eric might be feeling. His concern had been to free Eric, to get the boy away from the danger Beaton wanted to thrust him into and the poison the man could whisper in his ears. Maldie was right, however. The boy had to be finding it all very hard to understand and could easily be wondering what it was about him that drew forth such hatred and trouble. Although Beaton now tried to claim Eric as his son, Balfour doubted that the man's hatred or anger had lessened. Eric was very quick-witted, probably the smartest of them all, yet he had to be confused. Such confusion, the inability to understand, was one of the few things that could unsettle the usually calm, sweet-natured boy.

"Aye, poor Eric must be near to pulling his hair out," Balfour said, and smiled faintly as he thought of the boy. "Young Eric loathes it when he cannae understand something. If Beaton hasnae told the lad much, at least not enough for Eric to sort this tangle out, the boy is probably ready to kill Beaton with his bare hands. What Beaton has done will make no sense to the lad and, if he is given the reasons for it all and they match what we believe, Eric will see it as a verra dull-witted thing to do. That will certainly irritate him."

"Ye make the lad sound as if he has little tolerance," Maldie said.

"Nay, 'tis not what I meant to do. Although, I would wager that Eric will ne'er have much patience for fools."

"That I can understand."

"Eric is a clever lad, sometimes frighteningly so, but he does understand that his quick, sharp wit is God's gift. He ne'er faults those who havenae been blessed in the same way. Howbeit, if he thinks ye ought to ken something and ye dinnae, and he thinks ye are acting foolishly when ye have the wit to ken the danger of it, he doesnae show much tolerance. That may be something he still needs to learn. I think 'tis his only fault." Balfour smiled crookedly. "In truth, Eric is even bonnier and sweeter of tongue and nature than Nigel."

"And therein lies a great danger for all of the lasses of Scotland."

She grinned when he laughed and nodded in agreement. It was clear that Balfour loved his half brother and was very proud of the boy. It touched her, said a lot about the man, yet, to her shame, it also stirred the faint hint of jealousy in her heart. Eric was a bastard, just as she was, yet he was loved by his father's family. That was something she had never known. No father, no family. Only her mother and, at times, Maldie had felt that her mother had not truly cared for her, had actually been angry that she was alive.

Maldie quickly shook away that thought. It hurt. She knew that the reason she found such thoughts so painful was because, deep in her heart, she knew they were the truth. It was better to turn her mind away from that truth before it made her bitter.

"Ye look sad, wee Maldie," Balfour said in a soft voice as he gently covered her clenched hand with his. "Dinnae fear. We shall win this battle and bring young Eric home to Donncoill."

"Aye, I am certain ye will."

She turned her attention to finishing her meal. He began to talk of defeating Beaton and gently prying information out of her. Maldie told him all she had learned, but was cautious in answering. She knew she needed to let him think she was unaware of the importance of what she knew, that it was simply his skillful questioning that brought forth such useful knowledge. There was some pleasure in knowing she was helping to bring Beaton to his knees, hopefully to his death, but that pleasure was severely depleted by the trickery she needed to employ to accomplish it all.

When Balfour signaled James to join them, Maldie inwardly grimaced. That man watched her, closely and often. The way his dark eyes were fixed upon her as she answered Balfour's questions began to make her uneasy. James was not as trusting as his laird. The more the man watched her, the more unreadable his expression became, the more nervous she got. If he mistrusted her he could easily arouse Balfour's suspicions. Unless she told the full truth, something she could not do, she could be seen as a spy, as someone working for Beaton and not against him. The very thought of that made her shiver, as much from distaste as from fear.

"Ye look weary, Maldie," Balfour said as he stood up and held out his hand. "Come, I will walk ye to your bedchamber."

It was on the tip of her tongue to say she was quite capable of finding her own way, but Maldie quickly bit back the words. That would begin a discussion that could last a long time, and she was suddenly eager to escape James's steady gaze. It could also be to her advantage to pull Balfour away from James while that man's suspicions were still so sharp. Given a little time to think things over, James's suspicions could ease. At least she prayed they would, Maldie thought as she allowed Balfour to escort her out of the great hall.

For a moment she felt trapped, pressed from all sides by the corner she had backed herself into. There was no place at Donncoill where she could completely hide from James's watchful eye. Balfour was increasingly underfoot, clouding her mind and confusing her heart with passions neither of them seemed able to control. The only place she could go to escape Balfour and James was to the tiny bed she had slept in since arriving at Donncoill, a tiny bed tucked in the corner of Nigel's room. Yet another place where she was constantly under the watchful eye of a Murray. There was no chance of escaping a Murray that she could see. That made lying and keeping secrets all the harder, and very tiring.

Balfour paused in front of a doorway across the hall from Nigel's bedchamber and opened the door, watching her closely. Maldie was in a strange mood, one moment smiling and talking, the next lost in thoughts that, judging by her dark expressions, were not particularly pleasant ones. Balfour was not certain how she would respond to the news that she had been removed from Nigel's room.

Nigel no longer needed Maldie's constant care, but Balfour knew that was not the reason he had given Maldie her own chambers. Nigel's blatant interest in Maldie had been what had driven him. He just hoped she would not guess that, for it could easily insult her and his lack of confidence embarrassed him.

"This isnae my room," Maldie said, trying and failing to break Balfour's firm grip on her arm.

"Aye. Now it is." He tugged her into the room, shut the door, and leaned against it.

"Nigel shouldnae be left alone. He may do something foolish."

"He willnae be left alone, but he doesnae need ye at his side day and night any longer."

"Then, mayhap, 'tis time for me to be on my way."

She felt her heart jump painfully at the thought that he might agree. That made no sense. Although she was careful to lie as little as possible, the half-truths she was telling were becoming so complicated, so twisted, that she was in real danger of tripping over them. Balfour desired her, and she was sure she lacked the will or strength to resist him for very long. Nigel desired her, something she could easily resist, but could also stir up trouble between the brothers and catch her firmly in the middle. James did not trust her. It would be wise to just leave before any or all of these complications caught her too firmly in their grasp. Yet, she stood tensely waiting for Balfour to give her a reason to linger at Donncoill. To her utter disgust, she knew it would not have to be a good one.

"Nay, ye should stay. Nigel still has need of your skilled care," Balfour said, reaching out and catching her by the hand. "As ye say, he could do something foolish. He is also still bedridden, weak, and must take care not to damage himself. Your skills kept him alive. I now need them to get him back on his feet, walking as straight and strong as he e'er did."

Maldie offered no resistance as he slowly pulled her into his arms. "And ready to draw his sword."

"I will need him at my side when I ride against Beaton. Aye, I need him ready and able to wield his sword in the fight." He pushed her thick hair back over her shoulders and touched a kiss to the hollow at the base of her ear. "Eric needs both of his brothers fighting to free him." He gently nibbled on her silken earlobe and delighted in the way she softly trembled in his arms.

"Eric is most fortunate in the family fate has chosen for him."

Maldie slipped her arms around his neck and lifted her face up toward his. It was a silent, shameless request for a kiss, but she did not care. His kisses made her feel good and she was hungry for them. One kiss could push all the troubled thoughts from her mind and all the fear from her heart. She even craved the way the touch of his lips sent warmth flowing through her body, making her tremble and her breath quicken. Maldie inwardly smiled as she admitted to herself that she simply liked the taste of him. She sighed and closed her eyes when he lightly ran his long finger over her lips.

"Such a bonny, tempting mouth," Balfour whispered.

His mouth was so close to hers she could feel the warmth of his breath, yet he hesitated to kiss her. Maldie partly opened her eyes, studying him from beneath her lowered lashes. She could see the passion in his dark eyes, but there was also a stillness to his expression that puzzled her. Try as she would, she could not clearly sense what he was feeling either. It was as if he had closed himself up, erected a barrier she could not penetrate, and, for reasons she did not really want to understand, that deeply troubled her. Was Balfour already sharing James's suspicions about her?

"I thought ye wanted to kiss me," she said, hating the touch of unsteadiness to her voice, for it was a sign of her uncertainty that he could easily read.

"I do," he replied, a little surprised that he had the strength to resist her obvious welcome.

"Yet ye hesitate. I havenae said nay."

"Oh, I ken that weel. Your *aye* is unspoken yet verra clear." He caressed her cheek with his fingers. "In truth, your invitation is such an exquisite mix of innocence and wantonness that I am fairly aching to answer it."

"But ye dinnae."

"Nay, for 'tis not just a kiss I need. Nay, nor even as much as we shared a week past in the shelter of the half-built tower. I have no patience for this game anymore. None. Aye, I should find it for ye are an innocent, but, mayhap, I am weak. Or mayhap I am just greedy and too selfish to tell myself nay."

"What are ye talking about?"

He framed her face with his hands, almost smiling at her expression. A beautiful myriad of emotions had put a flush in her cheeks and darkened her eyes to a rich, velvety green. She looked a delightful mix of confused, irritated, and nervous, but a hint of passion lurked behind all of those.

"I am trying to say that, if ye let me kiss you," he brushed his lips over hers, loving the way she briefly followed his mouth with hers when he pulled back, "if ye let me touch you, I willnae let ye run away this time. No retreat, no sudden crying of *nay* when every bonny inch of you quietly cries out *aye*. I will have it all, Maldie, or I will have none."

"Isnae that a wee bit unfair?" she whispered.

"Aye, that it may be, and probably not verra honorable either. But when I hold you, I fear my hunger for you devours all my guilt. So, what say ye?"

Maldie stared at him, knowing she ought to be furious about his all or nothing demand, yet understanding what pushed him to make it. If he suffered even part of the longing she did when she turned away from the passion they stirred in each other, she was surprised he had shown as much patience as he had. Looking into his dark eyes she knew that she had none left. She no longer wanted to just dream of all they could share. She wanted to know. If it proved to be a mistake, she would deal with the consequences later.

"Aye," she whispered.

Chapter Seven

Maldie stood tense and unsure as Balfour carefully released her and turned to bar the door. The taut look on his face and the way his eyes had darkened nearly to black told her that he had heard her soft assent. It also told her that, if she chose to change her mind now, he might not hear her. She had heard it said that a man could be blinded by passion. Maldie felt that Balfour was afflicted in that way. It did not frighten her, even though she knew it ought to, but she decided she was suffering from the same disease. Passion, she mused as he turned back to face her, could be a heedless thing. It was surely pushing her forward into what could become a very troublesome, complicated situation, and ensuring that she simply did not care.

"Say it again," Balfour demanded in a thick, husky voice as he picked her up in his arms and walked over to the bed. "I need to hear ye say it again."

"Aye." She gasped when he dropped her onto the wide, soft bed and sprawled on top of her. "I was certain ye had heard me the first time, for ye locked the door."

"I did, but hearing that one sweet word caused such a madness to flow o'er me, I decided I needed to hear it again. I feared I may have heard only what I wished to and not what ye had truly said.''

"If I had said *nay*, I wouldnae have stood there so quietly as ye locked the door."

He laughed shakily. "True. If I had the wit left to think clearly I would have kenned that. Are ye certain?"

"I may be innocent in body, my fine dark knight, but not in knowledge. I lived in a wee hovel with my mother and what grew to be a continuous line of men." She saw sympathy soften the passion tautened lines of his face and touched her fingers to his mouth. "Nay, dinnae speak your pity aloud. Sometimes a poor woman can do naught else to gain the food needed to keep herself and her bairn alive. Mayhap she had other choices, but she was gentle born and had little skill or knowledge. At times, I think most of the shame lies with those who ne'er helped her, ne'er lifted a hand to save her from the need to abase herself. I but speak of it so that ye ken I speak the truth when I say I ken what ye are asking of me and also ken exactly what I am agreeing to." She twined her arms around his neck and tugged his mouth closer to hers. "Now, I hadnae thought that ye were asking to talk."

"Nay. Howbeit, I do wish to say one thing, and that is to bless your mother for keeping ye from suffering her fate."

Maldie let his kiss silence any answer she might have been compelled to make. He did not need to know the full ugly truth, that it was she and not her mother who had preserved her chastity. From the moment she had changed from a child into a woman, men had tried to steal or buy her innocence. There had been times when her mother had been desperate enough to be angered by her stubborn refusal to accept any of the offers. Those were painful memories, and she was more than willing to let Balfour and passion push them from her mind.

"I wish I had the skill to caress you with bonny words," he said as he began to unlace her gown with unsteady hands. "'Twould be most fine to speak love words to you like some minstrel."

"I have no need for poetry and song." She grasped his hand

and pressed a kiss to his palm. "If words fail ye, speak with these." She touched a kiss to his lips. "And these. They and how they make me feel are what have drawn me here, nay pretty words."

Balfour groaned and hungrily kissed her, yanking the leather thong from her hair and burying his hands deep in its silken thickness. Her soft words made him half-mad with desire for her. They were a clear, sweet affirmation that she felt the same passion he did. He prayed that he could retain the will to go slowly with her, to help her feel the full reward of their desires despite it being her first time.

Maldie tried to pull his mouth back to hers when he ended the kiss, then murmured her pleasure as he covered her throat with fevered kisses. A small part of her was aware of the removal of her gown, but she simply lifted her hips to make it easier for him. She closed her eyes when she felt him tug off her shoes and begin to pull off her stockings, afraid that if she saw him removing her clothes modesty might make her hesitant. Maldie wanted nothing to interfere with the way he made her feel. The way he stroked her legs with his big, lightly calloused hands stole her breath away, making it very easy to think of nothing but him and the passion he ignited within her. When he returned to her arms, she clung to him, but his kiss was too brief to satisfy her greed.

She trembled as he unlaced her chemise, his long fingers brushing against her skin. When he kissed the space between her breasts, she gasped and clutched at his shoulders. He gently loosened her grip and she felt a brief coolness on her skin as he slipped off her chemise. She felt his fingers slowly trail across the top of her braies, and she cautiously peeked at him from beneath her lashes. He was staring at her braies as if he had never seen the garment before, and she suspected he had never met a woman who wore them before.

"Protection," she said, astonished at how thick and husky her voice was.

"Clever," was all he said as he began to take off his clothes. Without the touch of his hands or his lips Maldie had begun to feel her passion cool, enough so that she was becoming uncomfortably aware of her near nakedness. Watching him disrobe pushed aside that unease. She had to clench her hands tightly to keep from reaching out for him. His skin was dark and smooth, stretched taut over hard muscle. He had no hair upon his chest but small dark curls began just below his navel, the line broadening out to cushion his manhood. His legs were long and well shaped, lightly coated with black hair. She did not flinch away from the sight of him in a state of full arousal. It bemused her that she could suddenly find attractive something that had always frightened or disgusted her before. Passion, she decided, was a wondrous thing. It not only made one ready to cast aside all reticence, but could make what had always appeared ugly and threatening into something she not only appreciated but craved.

The odd smile on Maldie's face made Balfour uncertain as he slowly returned to her arms, shuddering with pleasure as their flesh touched. "I am verra brown," he murmured, sliding his hand up her rib cage and, almost reverently, moving it over her breasts.

"And I am verra thin," she said, her breath quickening as his touch restored the warmth to her body.

"Lithe," he whispered against her skin as he slowly encircled her breasts with kisses. "I but wondered why ye were smiling. It can make a mon uneasy when a woman smiles upon seeing him naked."

She laughed softly, then realized that he had mistaken the reason for her smile, that he had thought her amused by his appearance. It was increasingly hard to think clearly when each touch of his lips caused her insides to tighten with need, but she said, "I was but amused by my response to seeing ye naked and rampant. I have always seen that engorged staff as a weapon, ugly and threatening, yet I found myself pleased at the sight of yours. Passion, I thought, not only clouds one's thoughts, but one's eyes." He laughed softly against her skin and she could feel his relief, his joy at her approval.

"Pleased, eh?" He flicked his thumb over the hardened tip of her breast.

"Aye, pleased," she replied, surprised that she could still speak coherently.

"Nay afraid?"

"Nay, not at all."

"Losing your chastity willnae be painless, though I shall try to stir your passion high and hot enough to soften the blow."

"I ken it will hurt, but I am already caught in too great a fever to care." When he slowly drew her nipple deep into his mouth, teasing it with his tongue and gently suckling, she groaned and buried her fingers in his thick hair. "Aye, 'tis a verra great fever indeed."

Maldie shifted restlessly beneath his caresses, trying to press her body against his and clucking with impatience when he skillfully evaded her. Each tug upon her breast increased her need to move against him, to wrap herself around him, but he kept moving out of her reach. A slight coolness touched her skin as he tugged off her braies, but the warmth swiftly returned as he stroked her thighs and covered her belly with kisses. She gasped and started to pull away, shock breaking through passion's grip when he slid his hand up her inner thigh and caressed her intimately, but he held her steady until his touch stole away all resistance. Maldie opened to him, holding him tight as he returned his kisses to her breasts.

Soon she became so taut with a need she had no word for that she called out to him. In a heartbeat he was there, kissing her as he nudged her legs apart and eased his body down on top of hers. She shuddered, echoing his groan as she moved against him. Although she lacked the words to voice her need, her body knew exactly what it wanted.

As he slowly joined his body to hers, she could feel him watching her, but she kept her eyes shut. Maldie wanted nothing to distract her from all she was feeling, and she was sure that she would be captivated by the look in his dark eyes, so much so that she feared she might miss some small part of the experience. As his body united with hers she became acutely aware of all he was feeling. His passion, his need, and his taut anticipation matched and blended with hers, heightening them. There was a strong deep emotion inside of him as well, one she could feel within herself, but could not immediately recognize. Nor was she sure she could trust her judgment at the moment. Then he tore through her maidenhead and the quick, sharp pain pushed all thought from her mind. She heard herself cry out and Balfour grew very still.

Maldie waited a moment for him to do more than occasionally touch a kiss to her face, then cautiously opened her eyes. He was watching her intently. The taut lines of his face, the intensity of his dark gaze, and the flush upon his high-boned cheeks all told her that his passion was barely controlled, yet he did not act upon it. She slid her hand down his side and over his hip. He shuddered and closed his eyes, lightly touching his sweat-dampened forehead to hers.

"Why have ye grown so still?" she asked, hearing the same tremor in her voice that was washing over her body.

"I wished to let your pain ease," he answered, looking into her eyes and catching his breath when he saw the gleam of strong passion there.

"My pain?" She wrapped her legs around his lean hips.

"I heard ye cry out from it."

"Ah, and that soft noise brought ye to a halt?"

"Aye." His eyes widened slightly when she gave him a slow, distinctly sultry smile.

"Then do tell this poor wee innocent what noise she must make to get ye to continue."

He laughed unsteadily as he touched his lips to hers. "A wee moan of delight?"

Maldie complied, then gasped when he began to move inside of her. She clung to him, enfolding him tightly within her arms and her legs. He kissed her, his tongue mimicking the slow, deep thrusts of his body. The last clear thought Maldie had was that Balfour was still keeping a tight rein on himself, then she lost herself in a maze of emotion. Something inside of her grew taut, so taut it was almost frightening, and then it snapped.

She heard herself cry out even as she tried, nearly frantically, to pull Balfour more deeply inside of her. The way he suddenly began to move with more ferocity only enhanced the feelings bursting throughout her body. She cried out again, in fierce encouragement, when he grabbed her by the hips and plunged deep within her, groaning out her name as he shuddered. Maldie pressed her face against his strong neck, shivering with pleasure as she felt him empty himself inside of her.

For a long time Maldie continued to hold him close, fighting to cling to the feelings his loving had filled her body with. She savored the way he felt in her arms, the gentle touch of his hand as he stroked her side, and even the way their bodies still faintly trembled. When he began to move away she murmured her regret, hating the way he seemed to take all warmth with him. She closed her eyes, covering her face with her hands, when he returned to their bed with a damp cloth and washed them both off. By the time he crawled back into bed and pulled her into his arms, she was clearheaded again, thinking again, and she was not sure she wanted to be.

When Maldie said nothing, just curled up in his arms and frowned, Balfour began to grow nervous. He had pushed her into bed, had used her passion for him to get what he ached for faster than she may have wished to give it. It was not simply passion that had driven him, either. Nigel's blatant interest in Maldie had made Balfour desperate to mark her as his own. He could never tell her that. Nor could he tell her that his less than honorable plan had turned back on him. Not only had he marked her as his, or so he hoped, but she had innocently left her mark on him as well. He was hers. Completely. The moment their bodies had been joined as one, he had known it. All the feelings he had struggled to ignore or deny had been confirmed as truth. It was a grave revelation, one he neither wanted nor had the time to deal with at the moment. The longer Maldie remained quiet, the more he began to fear that she had somehow guessed what he felt. She had already revealed a true skill at sensing what others felt. He prayed that this was not one of those times.

"How fare ye?" he asked, tilting her face up to his.

Maldie stared up at him and idly wondered what would happen if she told him exactly what she had been thinking. She loved him. She had known it the moment their bodies had become one. If passion had not held her so tightly in its grip, she suspected she would have fled the room, perhaps even fled Donncoill. Balfour did not ask for love, only passion. That was all she had thought she wanted. She had successfully talked herself out of wanting, needing, or even feeling anything more—until now. It was hardly Balfour's fault that she was a fool, one who had lied to herself and not faced the truth until it was too late to turn back.

"I am fine," she replied. "Ye dinnae still fret o'er causing me pain, do ye?"

"Nay, yet ye were verra quiet. So quiet I feared something was troubling you."

"Not troubled really. Just thinking. I hadnae fully considered how final my decision was. I wasnae so slow-witted that I thought I could give away my maidenhead one night and grow a new one the next day. Nothing as foolish as that. 'Tis just that I cannae say *nay* again, can I?"

"Ye can cry *nay* whene'er ye wish to. This doesnae mean ye must now lie down with any mon." The mere thought of Maldie with another man made Balfour's chest tighten with anger and jealousy, but he fought to keep those emotions out of his voice. "I have ne'er believed that a maidenhead was all that decided a woman's honor or innocence."

Her eyes widened, not only because his opinion surprised her for it was one few people held, but because of the faintly sharp tone of his voice. She did not know how or why, but something she had said had angered him. "Ye have a generous heart, Sir Balfour. I didnae mean that I must now walk my mother's troubled path, just that I have now become your lover. That cannae be easily undone."

It could be, he thought, but bit back the words. If she thought that it could only work to his advantage and, guilty though it made him feel, he knew he would grasp the opportunity to keep her close. Maldie was too clever not to see the error in her thinking very soon, but her brief confusion would give him some time, time to strengthen whatever hold he had on her.

"Do ye have regrets now?" he asked, touching a kiss to her shoulder as he smoothed his hands over her slim back.

"I should, but I dinnae think I do." She idly trailed her fingers over his taut stomach, enjoying the way he trembled beneath her touch. It was comforting to see such proof that she was not alone in her weakness. "I always swore I wouldnae make the same mistakes my mother did, yet, when I try to brand myself with such a fault, I find I cannae believe this is the same as hers. Howbeit, that could just be some bold conceit I tell myself so that I willnae look too closely at my own weaknesses. 'Tis more comforting to think I have none."

"True, but this is a weakness I share."

Maldie laughed softly and smiled at him. "And that should make me feel less disturbed by it all, should it?"

Balfour smiled back and shrugged. "I could think of nothing else to say to soothe your troubled mind. As I have said before, I feared taking the same missteps as my father did. Yet, I too feel that this isnae the same. We both tried to fight what flares between us. My father ne'er even hesitated if he decided he wanted a lass."

She sighed and nodded in silent sympathy. "My mother ne'er hesitated either. Not when it was passion, not when it was coin. Since we are determined to delude ourselves, let us call our short time of restraint—"

"It wasnae that short a time. God's teeth, it felt like months to me."

" 'Twas little more than a fortnight. 'Tis no great show of restraint. Howbeit, we can console ourselves, and ease our doubts and fears, with the sure knowledge that the parents we so fear to emulate would ne'er have held steady for e'en that long. Do ye ken, 'tis most sad when ye can so clearly see the failings of the ones ye are supposed to honor and revere."

" 'Tis hard to remain blind to such things as one grows older and, God willing, wiser. That wisdom allows one to see those

faults and, if not understand them, at least forgive them. The
love I had for my father wasnae lessened by the discovery of
his weaknesses. He also had many strengths and skills.'' Balfour
started to grin. ''Aye. Mayhap if he hadnae been so *skilled,* I
ne'er would have discovered his weaknesses for the lasses and
neither would he.''

Maldie found it sweet that he could smile about his father's
follies even as he acknowledged the error of such ways. She
wished she could be so at ease about her mother's mistakes
and, the older she became, the more certain she was that her
mother had made some serious missteps. The sting of guilt she
felt when she thought such things, the sharp sense of disloyalty
that pained her at such moments of doubt, were growing fainter,
and that saddened her.

Deciding that she no longer wanted to think of her mother
for it only brought on pain and confusion, stirring up questions
she had no answers for, she smiled back at Balfour. Although
her body ached somewhat from its introduction to passion, it
was a discomfort she could easily ignore. The passion she and
Balfour shared was the first thing she had ever found that could
so completely clear her mind of any troubling thoughts and her
heart of all feeling save for the love she had for him. For a
time it even pushed aside the cold, bitter need for revenge that
had directed her every step for the last few months. Confident
that it would not take much to inspire him to give her another
taste of the blinding delight they could share, she slid her hand
down his back and caressed his backside, smiling wider when
he shuddered and instinctively pressed closer to her.

''Mayhap one shouldnae fault your father for his *skills,''* she
murmured, touching a kiss to the hollow in his throat. '' 'Tis
clear that he gifted his son with many of them.''

''Aye.'' Balfour closed his eyes and reveled in the feel of
her small, soft hand moving over his skin. ''Many women have
praised Nigel's skill as a lover.''

She felt a twinge of sympathy for all of the slights Balfour
must have suffered from foolish women blinded by Nigel's
beauty, then quickly pushed it aside. Although she was a skilled

healer there were some scars she could not mend. Balfour was the only one who could rid himself of such ghosts and finally recognize his own worth. The only thing she could do was let him know, by word and deed, that she was interested only in him, that her passion was stirred by his touch alone. She also decided that she would neither pamper nor pity his doubts and jealousies, for that could well extend their lives.

"Weel, I dinnae think I will test that opinion," she said sweetly as she slid her hand up his thigh and slowly curled her fingers around his erection. "I have all I need or want right here. I doubt I can find anything sweeter or fiercer. In truth, I dinnae want to, for I fear I wouldnae survive it."

Her intimate caress enflamed him so it made it difficult for him to speak. After but a moment he knew he would have to forego the pleasure of her touch or he would lose all control. He groaned softly, gently pulled her hand away, and rolled so that she was pinned beneath him. Balfour took a few, slow deep breaths to calm himself, then thought about what she had just said. He knew she was teasing him, yet the mere thought of her turning to Nigel made him both furious and terrified.

"Aye," he said, gently brushing the stray wisps of her wild hair from her face. "Ye may not survive bedding Nigel, but I dinnae think it is a fatal dose of passion ye should be afraid of."

Maldie stared at him, surprised by the hard chill in his voice. "Did ye just threaten me?"

"Nay. Warned ye." He sighed and touched his forehead to hers. "I fear I could lose all reason, and a mon who has had his wits stolen by anger can be a danger to all within his reach."

"True, but ye would regain your senses ere ye could hurt anyone too seriously."

"Ye sound verra sure of that."

"I am." She reached up to caress his cheek. "But it matters not, for it will ne'er come to pass. Ye are a great fool, Balfour Murray, if ye cannae see that I want only you."

Her words touched him deeply, but he knew it would take

time before he believed them without question. "So, ye say ye are mine."

"Aye, yours. Ye have marked me weel, my dark-eyed warrior."

"Good, for you have marked me too." He brushed his lips over hers. "Although, methinks it needs to be reaffirmed." He hesitated and watched her closely as he asked, "Do ye suffer any pain?"

Maldie curled her arms around his neck and tugged his mouth down to hers. "Mark away, my laird."

When he kissed her she gave herself over completely to the feelings he stirred within her. The final confrontation with Beaton would come all too soon, and with it would come some harsh decisions. Would she then tell him the truth? Would she try for more than passion? Would he even want her anymore once he discovered that she was Beaton's daughter? They were all questions she had no answers for, and she would not get her answers until she could tell Balfour all of her dark secrets. Even though she loved him, she could not tell him the truth. Not yet. So, she would have to keep all of her feelings secret as well, would have to accept that passion was all she could give or ask for until Beaton was defeated, and she was free of her vow to her mother. However, she thought with a shudder of delight as he began to cover her breasts with heated kisses, the passion they shared was so glorious she was sure it would be enough for now.

Chapter Eight

A huge yawn shook Maldie's body. She hastily glanced around her, pleased to see that none of the men guarding the high walls of Donncoill had seen it. They would easily guess why she was so tired, and she did not want to suffer that embarrassment. Then she smiled at her own foolishness. She and Balfour had been sharing a bed for a week and, even though she was sure everyone at Donncoill knew it, no one had done or said anything to embarrass her. Their acceptance of her as their laird's lover seemed to be complete and without condemnation. In truth, she was beginning to think that a lot of the people at Donncoill were pleased that their laird had a woman. Some were probably thinking their laird would soon marry her and finally beget himself an heir. Maldie hastily turned her thoughts away from that path. It was a tempting dream she could too easily become trapped in, and if in the end she was forced to leave Donncoill and Balfour, it would only add to her pain.

She stared down at the people coming and going through the thick gates of Donncoill, wondering if anyone would notice if she slipped away to rest, when something caught and held her attention. A bent figure, enfolded in a worn brown cape, was hurrying away from Donncoill. Maldie could not see the woman's face, but she knew in her heart that it was Grizel. She also knew that the woman was about to do something to help Beaton. Just as she wondered if she could find Balfour before all chance to follow the woman was lost, he stepped up behind her and wrapped his arms around her.

"I have been looking for you," he murmured, leaning forward to kiss her cheek.

"And I believe I ken why," she drawled, feeling his arousal as he held her close to his body. "Ye are insatiable."

" 'Tis your fault. Ye make a mon greedy."

"Ye make me feel verra greedy as weel. Howbeit, I think we must both forgo that pleasure for the moment." She pointed toward the cloaked figure scurrying along the road to the village. "I believe ye will gain as much pleasure if ye follow her."

Balfour frowned down at the person she pointed out to him. "Her? Who is it, and why should she claim my attention?"

" 'Tis Grizel. Aye, I ken that ye can see naught but a woman in a cloak, but trust me in this. 'Tis Grizel and she is hurrying away to betray ye again."

Even as he released Maldie and moved to stand against the wall, leaning forward a little and watching the woman closely, he asked, "Do ye have visions or the like? How can ye tell who that ragged figure is and what she is about to do?"

Maldie grimaced and shrugged. "I dinnae ken. I just do. Every bone in my body tells me that that is Grizel, and that she is rushing off to send word to Beaton. Please, just follow her. If I am right, ye will have the proof against her that ye have been seeking and can put an end to her treachery. If I am wrong, I give ye leave to hie back here and call me a fool."

"Being given leave to do so takes all of the joy out of it." He grinned when she laughed, then started down the narrow stone steps which were one of the very few ways a person could get up onto the high walls of Donncoill. "I will find James and we will set out after the woman. I just pray that he doesnae ask me why I insist upon creeping after that cloaked figure. I shall undoubtedly be deafened by his laughter when I am forced to reply that your bones told me to do it.''

She laughed softly, then quickly grew serious as she returned to watching Grizel. The woman needed to be stopped. There was no telling how much Grizel had learned before Maldie had turned suspicion her way, nor how much she had already told Beaton. Even now the woman could be hurrying off to tell a Beaton man something that could put Balfour's life in danger. Just the thought of such a thing made Maldie eager to run after Grizel herself. She was relieved to see James, Balfour, and two other men come out through the gates and set after Grizel, trying to be both swift and secretive. Maldie decided they were doing a very good job of both and she started to climb down off the wall. While Balfour was gone, spying on the spy, she was going to get some much needed sleep.

''*Now* will ye tell me why we are creeping after this filthy, ragged person?'' demanded James as he, Balfour, and their two companions slipped into the cover of the trees bordering the road.

''I think this is the one who has been helping Beaton,'' Balfour answered, proud of how quiet they all were as they moved through the brush, all of them keeping a close watch on the one they followed.

''I thought ye had decided that the traitor was that old, sharp-tongued sow Grizel.''

''It is.'' Balfour inwardly grimaced for he was being pushed to tell the truth about how and why they were all creeping through the wood. He was certain he could already hear the loud hoots of laughter. ''That is Grizel.''

''How in God's high name can ye be sure of that?'' James stretched his head forward as if that could make him see their quarry much clearer, then shook his head. ''Did ye see her ere she draped herself in that rag?''

''Nay. Ere ye can badger me to distraction with your questions, 'twas Maldie who said this was Grizel and that the woman is about to give us proof of her treachery.''

"Ah, Mistress Kirkcaldy sent ye chasing after Grizel. The same lass who told ye that Grizel hates ye and spies upon us.''

Balfour scowled at James, stung by the derisive tone in his voice. "Once Maldie made me look closely at Grizel, helped me to see the woman's hatred and ponder the reasons for it, it all made sense.''

"Weel, I may be willing to grant ye that truth, but this? Did the lass see the woman or hear Grizel speak of treachery?'' James cursed softly as the sharp branch of a dying tree dug a shallow furrow in his upper arm.

"Nay,'' Balfour muttered, signaling everyone to halt as they reached the edge of the trees beyond which lay the wide open fields at the far end of the village. "Weel, we have gone past the village so, mayhap, there is no traitor there. Mayhap Grizel is the only one.''

"Wait.'' James rubbed his long chin as he stared at Balfour. "Now, ye are my laird, but ye are also the lad whose arse I set on his first horse. That be the one I talk to now. Tell me what was seen or what was said. Tell me exactly why we are afoot, creeping about like thieves after a shrouded figure.''

As Balfour watched Grizel, waiting for the right moment to follow her, he softly cursed. "Nothing was seen and naught was heard. Maldie just kenned it. She said she felt it in her bones.'' One sharp glance was all it took to stop the chuckles of the two young men with them, then Balfour met James's steady gaze.

"She had a vision, did she?'' James drawled.

"Nay, just a feeling. Aye, this may be foolishness,'' Balfour ignored James's telling glance and began to watch Grizel again, "howbeit, what harm can come of it? We will either see betrayal or see naught. Although, I dinnae think that hunched, ragged woman is hurrying off to meet a lover.''

"Who can say? Passion can make anyone witless.''

Balfour decided to ignore James's muttered insult. He prayed Maldie was right, that this was Grizel and that the woman was about to prove herself a traitor. Although he hated the thought that one of his own people would help Beaton, even that distasteful situation was preferable to looking like a fool.

The moment he felt it was safe to continue on without being seen, Balfour left the shelter of the wood, his men quickly following. For almost a mile they followed their quarry before she stopped at a crumbling cairn near a small brook. Taking quick advantage of the heavy growth of shrub and grass, Balfour and his men hid themselves and waited. The cloaked figure sat down on a rock and shoved the hood of the cloak back, revealing Grizel's easily recognizable face. Balfour sent James a brief, triumphant glance.

"So the lass's tiny bones were right about *who* hid beneath the cloak," James said, grimacing as he tried in vain to get comfortable on the hard, rocky ground. "We have yet to see proof of any betrayal."

"I think that, too, is about to be revealed," said one of the two men with them, a burly, usually taciturn man named Ian. " 'Tis either Beaton treachery, or someone has finally decided to rid the world of that sour old hag."

Three men crept toward Grizel, cautiously looking around as they approached the woman. She looked their way with no sign of fear, only her usual expression of ill humor and impatience. What firmly caught Balfour's eye was the badge clearly visible on one of the men's dirty plaids. These were Beaton's men. It was all the proof Baltour needed. He signaled his men to begin to encircle the group by the cairn.

"Do ye intend to hold fast and try to hear what they say?" asked James.

"Should I?"

"Nay. 'Tis clear who the men are, and just as clear that they and Grizel are no strangers to each other."

"Try to capture one of Beaton's dogs alive," Balfour hissed as James began to move away, intending to come toward the traitorous group from the right. "Mayhap we can get him to tell us how badly Grizel has hurt us."

Balfour watched James nod before he disappeared into the

tall grass and scattered bushes. He prayed he could do as well as he began to creep toward Grizel. Although he could not defeat Beaton yet or rescue Eric, he now had a chance to hurt his enemy and he badly needed that small victory. He would steal away the advantage Beaton had gained from Grizel's betrayal of her clan.

When the time came to move against the group it all happened so quickly that Balfour felt somewhat disappointed. He and his men rushed in from all four sides. Beaton's men refused to surrender, tried to fight their way out of the trap they were caught in, and were swiftly killed. Grizel made no attempt to save herself, just sat there glaring at them all. Balfour could almost feel her hatred for them all as he wiped his sword clean on the padded jupon of the man he had just killed and slowly sheathed it. He wondered if the woman would now try to save herself by denying all they had just seen.

"So, the mighty laird of Donncoill has naught better to do than creep about after old women?" she snapped.

"Ye have shown yourself to be guilty of a grave crime, Grizel," Balfour said. "It would behoove you to speak with a little more humility, mayhap even express some regret."

"Regret?" She spat, smiling nastily when the men hastily stepped out of her reach. "I have no regrets."

"Ye have betrayed your clan, your family. Aye, and marked your kinsmen's name with a stain they may ne'er rid themselves of."

"I care naught for any of them. They spend their poor wee lives toiling for ye and yours. When I told them of how your father had shamed me and pleaded with them to fight for my honor, they refused. Let them save themselves, as I have."

"Ye havenae saved yourself, ye great fool," James said. "Ye have done naught but slip a noose about your own neck. And all this because a mon bedded ye once and chose ne'er to do so again? Ye had a place of honor amongst us, yet all the while plotted to stab us in the back?"

"A place of honor?" Grizel laughed, an ugly sound, sharp and heavy with her bitterness. "Ye mean the place our fine laird has given to his wee whore?'' She smiled when Balfour took a threatening step toward her, tightly clenching his hands as he fought the urge to strike her. ''Such a great honor to set myself in the path of every disease that crept into Donncoill, to rush to wipe the noses and the arses of the sick. There was only one thing I gained from that distasteful toil, and that was to get close to your father, Balfour. Aye, ye fools set his verra life in my hands and let me do as I pleased.''

''Ye killed him,'' Balfour whispered, shock stealing all the strength from his voice.

''Aye, right in front of your eyes. It took days, but I slowly robbed that bastard of blood until he had no more to give. And now I have given his cherished wee bastard to his worst enemy.'' She sat up a little straighter when Balfour drew his sword.

''Nay,'' said James, grasping Balfour firmly by the sword arm and halting his blow. ''That is what she wants ye to do. A quick, clean death by the sword is always preferable to hanging.''

''She killed my father. I thought it was God's decision or, at worse, the sad result of an inept healer, but she murdered him.'' Balfour took a long unsteady breath and slowly sheathed his sword. ''And we all stood by as she did it.'' He turned his back on her, not sure how long he could control his urge to strike her dead if he had to keep looking at her and listening to her. ''I cannae abide being near her. I will talk to her kinsmen when I can speak of this with some calm and reason. Bring her back to Donncoill and secure her,'' he ordered and did not wait to see his men carry out his commands.

Balfour used the long walk back to Donncoill to try and calm himself. He would need to be in control of his fury when he told Grizel's kinsmen of her crimes, and when he passed judgment on her. He could not perform either duty well if he let his anger rule him. His clansmen would not condemn him for that anger, but he knew it would be best if he could stand before them sounding calm, fair, and reasonable, especially since the judgment on Grizel would be death. That would gain him far more respect than righteous fury.

The moment he reached Donncoill he went directly to Maldie's room. He prayed she was there, for he lacked the patience to hunt her down. His need for her was strong and immediate. Instinct told him that she was exactly what he needed to help him gain some control over his emotions. It puzzled him that he could think the one who could so easily stir him to heedless passion was the same one he felt certain could help him regain his reason, but he could not shake the feeling.

Maldie woke with a start when the door to her room was thrown open, then loudly shut. She sat up and stared at Balfour, confused and a little alarmed at the look upon his face. It was a strange mixture of grief and deep, fierce anger. For one brief terrifying moment she feared that she was the cause of that anger, but then banished that fear. Balfour had not been gone long enough to have uncovered even one of her many secrets, and he had been busy hunting down Grizel. That furtive, shrouded figure had obviously been Grizel and the woman had proven herself a traitor. Maldie was both relieved that she had been proven right and filled with sympathy for Balfour, who did not deserve such betrayal.

"I am verra sorry, Balfour," she said softly as he moved to the side of the bed, taking his tightly clenched hand in hers when he sat down.

"Why?" He sighed and dragged his fingers through his hair before rubbing the back of his neck. "Ye were right."

"I had guessed that. What I am sorry for is that ye had to find out how bitter betrayal can taste. Ye did naught to the woman to deserve that."

Balfour lifted her hand to his lips and kissed her palm. "Your sympathy for my trouble is sweet and most welcome, but 'tis nay what I seek now." He smiled faintly when her eyes widened. "I ken that this isnae verra flattering, but I must clear my head, and I think that loving you will do it."

She laughed and pulled him down onto the bed. "I under-stand. First comes the passion which steals every thought from your head, then comes the sweet aftertime when your senses return and your body is at ease. 'Tis a perfect time to put some order into one's thoughts." She touched a kiss to his lips. "Just dinnae make it the only reason ye seek my bed, or I shall begin to feel like little more than a chamber pot."

"That will ne'er happen."

Maldie said nothing, just greedily returned his kiss. He made such vows because he thought he knew her. There was a good chance that he would never retrun to her bed once he found out the truth. He would feel betrayed, and the look she had seen on his face when he had entered the room told her how he felt about betrayal. The thought that he might soon cast her out of his bed, even out of his life, made her all the more greedy for his lovemaking.

Even as he tugged off her clothes, she hurriedly worked to remove his. When their flesh finally met she shivered with pleasure. Although she still sensed his anger he was not turning it against her in any way. She saw it as a challenge. It made her eager to see if she could stir his passion so high, make it so hot and fierce, that it burned all of that anger away, even if only for a little while. Maldie hoped that she could also soothe away some of the pain of betrayal.

Balfour grunted in surprise when Maldie suddenly pushed him onto his back, straddling him with her lithe body. Before he could say anything she began to stroke and kiss his body. He pressed his lips together, almost afraid to say a word for fear that it would cause her to stop what she was doing. When she began to cover his chest with soft, lingering kisses, occa-sionally teasing his skin with her tongue, he threaded his fingers through her thick hair and struggled to control his swiftly rising passion long enough to see how daring she would be.

That proved almost impossible when she began to intimately caress him, first with her small, soft hand, and then with her tongue. He shuddered beneath her caresses, fighting for the restraint needed to fully savor her loving. When she slowly

took him into her mouth, he cried out from the strength of the
pleasure she gave him. Too soon he knew he had to end it and
he pulled her up his body. She needed little direction, sheathing
him with a sultry skill that left him gasping for breath. He
forced her mouth down to his, kissing her fiercely as she brought
them both the release they ached for. When she collapsed in
his arms he clung to her, feeling an odd mixture of intensely
alive and as weak as a newborn.

It was not until Maldie eased the intimacy of their embrace,
hastily washed them both off, and then curled up at his side,
that Balfour was able to think clearly again. His first thoughts
were not of Grizel, Beaton, or traitors. Maldie had just made
love to him in a way few women knew, and in a way he had
never shown her or told her about. Recalling her innocence,
the proof of which he had seen with his own eyes after their
first joining, did little to still a growing unease. Such loving
did not steal a woman's maidenhead.

"How did ye ken what to do?" he demanded, looking down
at her and silently cursing his need to even ask the question.

Maldie sighed dramatically and cast him a mournful look,
pleased to see him flush guiltily. She knew she should probably
be highly insulted by the obviously unkind thoughts churning
in his mind, but she was not. She had just made love to him
in a bold way only the most experienced woman should know
about. Such skill in a woman he thought an innocent should
give him pause. The true insult would come if he did not believe
her explanation for, unlike some of the other things she told
him, it would be the truth.

"Did I nay clear your mind as ye wished?" she asked.

"Weel, aye, but . . ." He frowned in confusion when she
laughed softly and placed one long finger over his lips.

"Nay, I but tease you. My mother told me that men like
that. Was she wrong?"

Balfour was shocked, angry at her mother, and saddened by
this unhappy glimpse into her life. "Nay, she wasnae wrong
in what she said." Recalling the intense pleasure she had gifted
him with, he smiled and brushed a kiss over her mouth. "She

was wrong to tell ye about such things. Was she trying to—'' he stuttered to a halt, unsure of how to ask the question without delivering a grave insult to her mother.

''Was she trying to make me a whore?'' Maldie smiled a little sadly when he looked uncomfortable. ''Aye, at times I think she was. I could have earned a heavy purse for a few years, until my beauty and softness began to fade. Howbeit, I think that she often had naught else to talk about. Men and how to please them enough so that they would pay her weel was all she knew.'' She snuggled up to him. ''But let us talk about what made ye so angry.''

''I regret to say that I lost the chance to call ye a fool.'' He felt his anger return, but knew he could control it now. ''As I told ye, that ragged figure was indeed Grizel and she met with three of Beaton's men. I fear they refused to be taken alive. This small victory over Beaton would have been a lot sweeter if I had gained the chance to wring a few secrets out of one of his men.''

''Is Grizel still alive?''

''Aye, but she will tell me naught. If she kens any secrets about Beaton she will take them to her grave just to spite me. She made no attempt to save herself, just sat there and spit the ugly truth right into our faces.''

''Her hatred for you is even stronger than I had guessed if she will let it take her to her death.''

''Oh, aye, 'tis verra strong indeed. It turned her hand to murder.''

''Are ye certain?''

He nodded, idly rubbing her slim back and surprised at how simply touching her gave him the strength to control his grief and anger. ''She confessed to the deed. Do ye recall my speaking of our healer's use of leeches and bleeding when I first brought ye to Donncoill?''

Maldie felt a chill flow through her body, horrified by the thought forming in her mind, but knowing it was the truth, and her voice was softened by shock as she said, ''Ye told me that ye dinnae believe in it, not always, and that ye thought it had hastened your father's death.''

"It may have done more than hastened it. Grizel boasted of how she used her place of honor as our healer to kill the mon before our verra eyes. She said that she slowly bled him until he had no blood left to give. I ached to kill her, but James stopped me.'' He grimaced. "I had my sword drawn and was eager to cut down an old, bitter woman.''

"There is no shame in that. She killed your father, cruelly and with no remorse.'' She kissed his cheek. "Ye didnae kill her. E'en James couldnae have stopped you if ye truly wished to cut her down. Dinnae brood o'er what ye almost did. Think on what ye must do now.''

"I must tell Nigel and then I must speak to her kinsmen.'' He held her tightly for a moment. "I would prefer to stay right here.''

"Ye cannae. If ye wait too long to speak to Nigel and Grizel's kinsmen, they will hear it all from someone else. News this grave cannae stay a secret for verra long. The whispers have probably already begun.'' She smiled gently when he cursed and got out of bed. "Nigel must hear this from you, not through whispered rumor and half-truth.''

"I ken it,'' he muttered as he tugged on his clothes. "I but pray that I can keep a rein on my temper. It serves no purpose and will only feed his.''

Maldie turned on her side, tucking the sheet around herself, and she grinned at him when he turned to look at her. "Shall I wait here then, my laird?'' She was pleased when he laughed, glad that she could banish the sadness from his eyes if only for a moment.

Balfour kissed her, then gave one last adjustment to his plaid before moving toward the door. " 'Tis a verra tempting offer, lass, and I ache to accept it, but I think ye may be needed to tend to Nigel. He will be as mad with fury as I was when I first heard the truth.''

"Of course. Such anger could easily weaken him or make

him move too quickly. When ye are done telling him this sad tale, just rap thrice upon my door and I shall go to him.''

The moment the door shut behind Balfour, Maldie flopped onto her back and indulged in a hearty bout of cursing. This was Beaton's doing. He had used the hatred of a bitter, old woman to hurt Balfour and to steal a young boy from his home. The murder of Balfour's father may not have been done on his orders, but Beaton undoubtedly reveled in the deed and probably rewarded the murderer. Beaton was long past due for a harsh reckoning. The only question was who would get to him first—her or Balfour?

Chapter Nine

The sharp taste of the strong wine did little to calm Balfour, but he refilled his goblet anyway. He glanced around the great hall and saw few people even though the afternoon meal had been laid out for an hour or more. Balfour prayed that it was because no one had any appetite and not because he had just judged and hanged one of their clan.

He winced and took another long drink as he thought of the hanging he had just carried out. Grizel had been unrepentant at her brief trial, and had heartily cursed him and his family until the rope around her neck had cut off her bitter words. Balfour was not sure what troubled him most, her unwavering hatred and contempt, or the fact that he had carried out his first hanging as laird of Donncoill. Despite her crimes, he found no satisfaction in Grizel's death and certainly no pride in the fact that he had ordered one of the very few hangings of a Murray that had been held at Donncoill since the clan had first claimed the land.

"Come, laddie," said James as he sat down next to Balfour, his gruff voice soft with understanding. "Ye did what ye had to do. The woman condemned herself with her own words.

Mayhap ye could have excused the betrayal, but she killed your father, her laird.''

"I ken it." Balfour slouched in his chair. "And she gave my father neither a swift nor an honorable death, so 'tis only just that she didnae get one either. I have no liking for hangings and found the need to order one a distasteful duty. In truth, I am verra angry that the old woman forced me to do it.''

"Mayhap that was her last small act of revenge.''

"Aye, mayhap." He smiled crookedly. "It has been a verra long day e'en though 'tis but half-done. We found our traitor, judged her, and hanged her.''

"Aye, your wee lass's bones proved to have more wisdom than we did.''

"I think it will be a long time ere I can shake free of the guilt I feel o'er my father's death.''

"Guilt? Why should ye feel any guilt?" James helped himself to a tankard of wine.

"Because I stood there and watched that woman kill him. She made me an ally to her crime.''

"Nay," James said sharply, startling two young pages who lurked in the shadows near the wall waiting to see if they were needed to serve their chief. "Grizel was the clan's healing woman. Your father himself named her so.''

"But I was uneasy with the way she cared for him. I watched her bleed him again and again and thought it was weakening him instead of helping him, but I didnae stop her. It also should have occurred to me that a lover he had so coldly cast aside was not the right woman to tend to him.''

"Your father should have kenned that. He ne'er said a word and it was days ere he grew so weak he couldnae speak. I ken that my words willnae cure ye of your guilt, but believe me when I say, ye carry none for your father's death. None of us saw the crime; none of us suspected the woman.''

Balfour nodded, but he knew it would be a while before he could convince himself of that. It was hard to accept that he could have saved his father and had done nothing. Eric, too, might have been saved from the ordeal he was suffering if he

had just paid a little more heed. Grizel had been betraying them
for years, and it was hard to believe there had never been a
sign of her treachery, one he would have seen if he had just
been a little more alert. He shook aside those dark thoughts,
knowing they were futile for he could not change the past,
could not correct his mistakes.

"Weel, at least we now have proof that Maldie is no enemy,"
he said as he picked at the bread and cheese on his plate.

"Do we?" James murmured as he spread a thick layer of
brown honey on his bread.

"Aye. She was the one who showed us who the traitor was."

"That she did."

"Grizel was helping Beaton. If Maldie is also helping Beaton,
she wouldnae give us one of his spies."

"Why not?" James wiped his mouth on the sleeve of his
jupon and looked straight at Balfour. "What better way to
make your enemy think ye are their friend?"

"Nay, I cannae believe it."

"Ye dinnae want to e'en think it and I can understand.
Howbeit, we have just had clear proof of what can happen if
we dinnae look closely at everyone around us. Grizel was a
Murray, yet she murdered her laird and worked for her clan's
enemy."

"And Maldie isnae e'en a Murray," Balfour whispered.

"Aye. In truth, we dinnae ken who she is. She says she is
a Kirkcaldy, but we have no proof of that and cannae afford
to send men to the Kirkcaldys to test her claim. She has ne'er
told us who her father is either. Has she told you?"

"Nay."

Balfour inwardly cursed and pushed away his plate, his appetite completely gone. He did not want to listen to James, did
not like the taint of suspicion that was entering his heart. The
mere thought that Maldie might betray him cut him deeply. If
it was only his own life at stake, he was sure he would not
want to know, would rather go to his death in blissful ignorance.
Unfortunately, if he allowed her to lead him into a trap, a lot
of his clan would be right there at his side.

"I just ask ye to be careful," James said quietly. "Aye, she is a bonny lass and she seems all that is good. But Grizel was an evil-tempered woman who liked no one, and she fooled us. How much easier it would be for a sweet-faced girl to lead us to our deaths."

"Yet ye have found naught to accuse her with."

"I ken it. E'en so, she tells one little about herself and she simply appeared, walking into our lives out of nowhere. That alone should make us cautious."

"And she kens a great deal about Beaton and Dubhlinn. There is something to ponder. If she means to betray us, then why would she tell us so much that can help us?"

"It could also ensnare us. There is no kenning if what she tells us is the truth. I hear little from our mon at Dubhlinn. I am nay sure if he is even still alive. There is no way I can find out if what she tells us will help us save Eric and defeat Beaton, or if it is all some clever ruse meant to lead us down a path Beaton has chosen."

"Why would she save Nigel's life?"

"To make ye indebted to her and thus trust her."

"Why would she bed down with me?"

James shook his head. "Ye didnae need me to teach ye how weel a woman can use her womanly charms to make a mon stupid and blind."

"She was an innocent, James," Balfour said softly, not wanting anyone else in the hall to hear him. "I saw the blood that marked her so."

"There are ways a woman can trick a mon into believing she still has a maidenhead."

Balfour finished off his wine and abruptly stood up. He did not want to discuss the matter any longer. His mind still reeled from discovering all the crimes Grizel had committed and the hanging he had been forced to carry out. The very last thing he wanted to hear or be convinced of was that Maldie was also betraying him.

"Enough, James. Ye are right to try and make me open my eyes. 'Twas my blindness that allowed Grizel to do all she did.

Howbeit, I am unable to deal with the matter with a clear head and widely opened eyes. Later.'' He started toward the door, then hesitated, briefly looking back at a frowning James. ''I give ye leave to step in and stop me if ye can see that I am making a great fool of myself. Too many others could lose their lives if I am left to learn another harsh lesson on my own.''

All the way up to Nigel's room Balfour tried to push James's words of warning from his mind, but they refused to be dismissed. Grizel's betrayal had left him unsure of his own judgments. Just because he felt Maldie was not another Beaton spy did not mean it was so. He had thought Grizel was safe.

He stepped into Nigel's room and tried to return Maldie's welcoming smile. ''I can sit with Nigel for a wee while, Maldie. Go and have yourself something to eat.''

She nodded and walked out of the room, pausing only to squeeze his hand in a brief gesture of sympathy. The moment the door shut behind her he let out the breath he had not realized he had been holding. He needed to sort through James's suspicions and warnings a little before he faced her again. It would be too easy to give them away in word or deed and, if Maldie was a traitor, the worst thing he could do was warn her that he had guessed her game.

''The woman is dead?'' asked Nigel.

''Aye, Grizel went to her hanging as ill-tempered and contemptuous as she lived her life,'' Balfour replied.

''I wish I had had the strength to watch it.''

''Nay, ye would have gained little from seeing her die. I didnae. I cannae feel I avenged our father's death, for my guilt o'er that outweighs any satisfaction from finding his killer. And, when all is said and past, there sits the fact that she was just a bitter old woman, a lover cast aside. She did a lot of harm, but hanging her doesnae change that.''

Nigel grimaced. ''I ken it. It does stop it, however. She cannae hurt us or help Beaton anymore.'' He studied Balfour for a moment. ''Is it only your needless guilt o'er our father's death that has ye looking so troubled?''

" 'Tisnae needless. I could have stopped it."

"Since ye are determined to heft that burden upon your shoulders, I dinnae think I can change your mind. And ye didnae answer my question."

Balfour sighed and rubbed the back of his neck. "I find that I am willing to cast a suspicious eye on anyone now."

"And by *anyone* ye mean the fair Maldie."

"Aye, Maldie. Ye trust her."

"I do, and I dare not start to think of her as a possible traitor. Ye ken how I feel about the lass, and how I must feel now that ye have made her your lover."

"Did she tell ye that?"

"Nay, she said naught, but I am nay so weak-witted that I cannae guess why she didnae sleep on her wee bed in the corner last night. Ye move swiftly, brother."

He could feel the heat of a blush upon his face, but Balfour just shrugged. "I dinnae see why that should make ye reluctant to suspect her of anything."

"Trust me when I say that I couldnae do so fairly. 'Tis best if we dinnae discuss her at all."

There was a chill to Nigel's voice that surprised Balfour. His brother was jealous. He was certain of it. What he could not be certain of was how deep it went, how badly Nigel suffered from the loss of even a chance to hold Maldie. Balfour decided that Nigel was right. They should not talk about her. Nigel did not want to hear anything about what his brother was sharing with the woman he wanted, and Balfour did not really want to know how badly Nigel wanted Maldie.

Nigel cursed softly. "Does James feel she should be watched?"

"Aye," Balfour replied. "She is a stranger."

"Not to you," Nigel grumbled, then waved Balfour to silence when he started to speak. " 'Tis clear that James feels there is something amiss. Heed him. I willnae be a spy for you though. I cannae. As ye can tell, I am finding it hard to accept that I cannae just reach out and take the woman I want. I should like to think that I am a fair mon and wouldnae stoop to letting petty jealousies taint my thinking, but I would rather not be asked to test the truth of that. I owe the lass my life, and I dinnae wish to repay that with mistrust.''

"Neither do I.''

"I ken it and yet ye must. Ye are the laird and many lives depend upon you. And 'tis clear that ye would like to speak of this from time to time. Fine. I refuse to let a wee, green-eyed lass come between us. Talk if ye must.'' He smiled crookedly. "Just dinnae tell me what a fine time ye are having with her. Ye tell me what troubles ye and I will play her advocate. After all she has done for me, 'tis only fair that she has one.''

"James says that saving your life is a verra good way for her to win our trust.''

"I didnae ken that the mon could have such a hard heart. Aye, he is right. I hope ye will understand when I say that the reason why she saved my life doesnae matter. I still owe her.''

Balfour nodded and poured them both a tankard of cider. "She has told me nothing of herself. Just wee glimpses into her youth with her mother.''

"She has had a sad life. Mayhap she just wishes to forget it all.''

"True. She kens a lot about Dubhlinn.''

"She stayed there for a while and she has the wit to notice things.''

"Ye are a good advocate,'' Balfour drawled and was pleased to see Nigel grin.

For a while they continued in a similar vein, Balfour telling him things that could be suspect and Nigel pointing out how they could also be completely innocent. There were a few things Balfour did not tell him, cautiously avoiding any mention of the fact that he and Maldie were lovers and how good a lover she was.

Finally, unable to find any answers, he stood up. "Enough. We talk in circles. There is a good reason and a bad for every word she says and everything she does. I, too, dinnae wish to think ill of her, but I have no choice. I must try and look beyond what I feel and what I want to be the truth.''

"The curse of being the laird," Nigel murmured. "I have but one request."

When Nigel just scowled and hesitated, Balfour pressed, "What? I cannae grant your request if ye ne'er make it."

"If Maldie proves to be a traitor, a spy for Beaton, what will ye do to her?"

Balfour flinched away from the thought of her guilt and what he might be forced to do about it, then cursed his own cowardice. "I dinnae ken. I willnae hang her if that is what ye fear. We all owe her your life and probably the lives of some of the other wounded men who crawled back from Dubhlinn that day. What else I may choose to do with her, I just dinnae ken."

"Dinnae worry on it, Balfour. I just needed to ken that she would be safe. In truth, I dinnae ken why I e'en concerned myself with that. Ye would ne'er have the stomach to harm her. I dinnae think many of the men here would, not even James."

"Nay, not even James. I think all I will do if she does prove to be helping Beaton is secure her so that she can tell him nothing until this fight is over."

"Weel, I pray ye find nothing."

"So do I," said Balfour as he walked to the door, "if only because I will have a hellish time trying to make ye believe it."

He smiled faintly as Nigel's laughter escorted him out of the room. It was hard to accept that he was the one who would have to be suspicious of Maldie, have to watch her closely and weigh her every word. He would rather be in Nigel's position and be her advocate. He would even prefer to leave it all in James's capable hands as he had done at the start. He could do neither. He was the laird, and he could no longer shirk his responsibilities no matter how distasteful he found them.

There were many good reasons to at least be cautious around Maldie. In consideration for his brother's feelings for the woman, he had not told Nigel the one that weighed most heavily upon his mind. Maldie's skill at lovemaking troubled him, and there was no one he could discuss it with. It was almost funny, for Nigel was the one person at Donncoill who was the most knowledgeable about such things and could probably help either exonerate or condemn her. Maldie was passionate and free in the sharing of that passion, more so than he thought an innocent ought to be. The most disturbing thing, however, was the way she had loved him with her mouth. Her explanation had made sense and he desperately wanted to believe her, but it also stirred his doubt. It was almost easier to believe Maldie was some sly maid sent to seduce him into a trap, than to think that a mother would tell her daughter such intimate details on how to pleasure a man.

As he entered the bedchamber he and Maldie had shared for a week, he forced himself to return her welcoming smile. He wondered how much of his doubt about her was born of his doubts about himself, about his attraction to a woman, his appeal and his ability to keep a woman interested. He had never had such a beautiful, passionate woman give him a second glance, yet there sat Maldie, smiling as though she was truly pleased to see him and showing no interest in his brother. She was sharing his bed, yet all of his past experience said she should be curled up at Nigel's side.

"Ye look verra troubled, Balfour," she said quietly, holding out her hand and tugging him closer to the bed when he took it.

"I have no taste for hangings," he murmured as he sat down beside her on the bed. "I try not to watch them, yet I have just ordered one and stood there while it was done."

She slipped her arms around him and pulled him down onto the bed with her. "Ye had to. do it as I am sure everyone has told you." She began to follow the firm lines of his face with gentle kisses. "Ye must keep the law. What would happen if ye let her go, a traitor and a murderer? That would tell all who heard of it that ye have no stomach for righteous punishment. It would tell them that they could do as they pleased. I dinnae ken exactly what I am trying to say, except that ye had no choice. Ye didnae just punish her for what she had done, but to be sure that all ken they must hold to the law."

"Aye, I ken it. 'Tis a hard thing to say clearly, but 'tis something one just knows in their heart. Grizel couldnae be allowed to escape punishment for her crimes, not because she was old nor because she was a woman."

"Mayhap that is what troubles ye so, that she was an old woman."

"Aye, I think it is. I believe I shall pay closer heed to the women in my life. 'Tis clear that they can be as dangerous as any mon."

Maldie busied herself with the laces on the front of his shirt as she fought a sudden unease. She knew he did not have to be talking about her, that her guilt simply made her think so. He had just had to deal with Grizel, with her lies, her deceits, and her murder of his father. That was undoubtedly what he meant when he talked of the threat a woman could be. Maldie told herself not to be so afraid of discovery, that no one knew who she was, not even Beaton himself.

For one brief moment she considered telling Balfour everything. The need to weigh her every word and the constant fear that the truth would be uncovered before she was ready to tell it threatened to drive her mad. Then reason returned. She had to fulfill her vow—an oath made to a dying woman—or she had no honor. Once Balfour knew the truth, she might well lose all chance to do so.

"The pain of all ye learned today and what ye were forced to do will pass," she finally said. "And, if it has made ye more wary, is that truly such a bad thing?"

"Nay." He began to unlace her gown. "There is a lot of work I should be tending to." He kissed the hollow behind her ear.

"Aye, ye neglect your duties."

"Ah, weel, I think I have earned a moment or two of pleasure."

"Only a moment or two?" she whispered.

He laughed and kissed her. Maldie wondered if the strong need she had for him would ever fade, then prayed that it would. If she had to leave him she did not want to spend the

rest of her life aching for a man she could not have. The mere
thought that she might soon have to turn her back on the
pleasure he gave her made her want him even more, and she
hungrily returned his kiss.

She murmured her delight when he tossed aside the last of
their clothing and they were finally flesh to flesh. Maldie did
not think anything had ever felt so good. When he touched a
kiss to her breast she closed her eyes and combed her fingers
through his hair, determined to savor every kiss and caress.

Soon his hands and mouth seemed to be everywhere, and
Maldie found the hint of ferocity in his lovemaking exciting.
She shuddered as he dampened her inner thighs with kisses,
and fought to gain some control over her rising passion so that
she could enjoy his touch for as long as possible. Then his
mouth touched the heated softness between her legs and shock
stole away both her desire and her breath. She tried to move
away, to escape that intimacy, but Balfour kept a firm hold on
her. Her passion returned with a vengence a heartbeat later.
Maldie opened to his caress, crying out her pleasure. When
she felt her release near she tried to pull him into her arms,
but he ignored her, taking her to desire's heights with his mouth.
She was still shaking from the force of that ecstasy when he
began again, stirring her passion with a skill and speed that
was almost frightening. This time when she called to him, he
responded, joining their bodies with one hard thrust. She clung
to him and he kissed her, his tongue mimicking the strokes of
his body within hers. Their cries of release blended as they fed
their hunger as one, and Maldie held him close when he collapsed in her arms.

As her mind cleared, Maldie fought a sense of embarrassment. She may have been without skill, but she had knowledge and that particular manner of lovemaking was known to
her. Such intimacy was hard to accept, however, and she could
not stop herself from wondering if the great pleasure she had
found in such a caress was a sign that she had a whore's soul.
It certainly implied that she had little sense of modesty when
passion held her tightly in its grip.

"Dinnae frown so, lass," Balfour said, smiling faintly as he kissed the tip of her nose. " 'Tis no whore's game."

She grimaced, not sure she liked the way he so easily guessed her thoughts. " 'Tisnae always easy to ken what is or isnae a whore's game."

"True." He sat up and began to dress, laughing softly when she scrambled to pull the sheet around herself. "Ye will find those who say anything but a cold, quick rutting is a whore's game, and others who feel anything ye wish to do that gives ye pleasure is acceptable. I believe in something somewhere in between there." He winked at her. "And that made it all verra clear, did it not?"

She grinned and shook her head. "Oh, aye, verra clear."

He grew serious as he stood up and draped his plaid around himself. "We share a rare passion, lass, and I confess that I am more than eager to be daring. Howbeit, ye must tell me when I do something ye dinnae like."

Maldie blushed and was unable to look at him as she softly replied, "Be sure that I will. Just remember what my mother was and be patient with my uneasiness. I sometimes fear that if I like something we do too much it may be the mark of a whore."

He tilted her face up to his and kissed her. "A whore doesnae usually enjoy much of anything except for the coin it can bring her. Feeling passion doesnae make ye a whore, Maldie. 'Tis what ye do with that passion, how ye use it, that marks ye."

His words were comforting, yet there was an odd tone to his voice. She decided she was still feeling a little embarrassed and that made her hear what was not there. Balfour was not a man who said one thing but meant another.

"Go and do the work ye must do, ere the people of Donncoill think I have spirited ye away."

"I think I could be easily tempted to let you today. I am reluctant to face my people. There has been an unsettling quiet about Donncoill since the hanging."

"Of course there has been. Few people enjoy such a grue-

some sight. And they may be as saddened as ye are that one
of their own would commit such crimes against the clan.''

Balfour nodded, seeing the wisdom of her words. He left to
face his clan with a little more confidence. As he shut the door
behind him, he just wished he could regain the confidence he
had in her.

It hurt to even think she would betray him, and that angered
him. He had slipped beneath her spell with the blind speed of
an untried lad. She smiled a welcome and he came running.
Although he was sure no one else saw it in such a demeaning
way, it was still a little embarrassing. To taste such a sweet
passion, however, he ruefully admitted that he was more than
willing to endure a little embarrassment. It was past time to
harden his heart a little and open his eyes wider. He also had
to stop shying away from truth, or, at least, the quite probable
truth, like some child afraid he is about to have his hand slapped.
Maldie was a woman with too many secrets. He needed to
recognize the danger of that and start acting upon it. If she was
one of Beaton's minions, embarrassment would be the gentlest
of penalties he would suffer for being seduced by her.

Chapter Ten

James seemed to be everywhere Maldie turned, and she cursed as she hurried toward Nigel's bedchamber. It had been two days since the hanging. She had seen little of Balfour except when he slipped into her bed at night, but she had seen far more of James than she wished to.

The man had increased his watch on her, she was sure of it. It made her so uneasy her stomach ached. No matter how often she told herself that there was nothing he could know, no secret he could uncover unless she told him, she could not stop being afraid. Each time she saw him she waited for him to point an accusing finger at her and decry her as a spy and a traitor. Telling herself that she was being foolish, seeing trouble where there was none, did little to quell her fears.

"Ye look upset," said Nigel as he sat up in his bed, eager to practice walking some more.

"Nay, just feeling a wee bit harried." She forced herself to smile at him as she slipped her arm around his waist and they began to pace the length of the room. "There is a great deal to do here now that Grizel is gone. She may have been a poor healer, but she did tend to all of those wee aches and hurts so many suffer, thus giving me more time to tend to you. Now everyone turns to me.''

''Is there no one who could help you?''

''Nay, not yet. There is a woman who shows promise and interest in learning. She could easily become the next healing woman at Donncoill with but a little training.''

Nigel winced, the stiffness in his leg causing him some pain as he moved it. ''Doesnae it take years to become skilled at healing?''

''One can learn enough to help heal the small, common troubles if one has the wit. Grizel did, and she neither wanted nor liked the chore. This woman has the interest, the kindness Grizel lacked, and the wit. Ye will need to find her someone to finish training her though, for she will need someone who has more time than I do. She will do ye little good if her training ceases when I leave. In truth, one ne'er ceases to learn such things. There is so much knowledge, old and new, that it can take a lifetime.''

''When are ye planning to leave us?''

''When ye are weel,'' she replied, ignoring his frown over her vague answer.

''And where will ye go?'' He staggered, and only Maldie's strong hold on him kept him from falling.

''To find my kinsmen.''

Nigel cursed. ''Ye answer so freely yet say so little.''

''There is no more to say. I will leave when ye are hale again and thus my work here is at an end, and when I leave I shall continue my search for my kinsmen.'' She turned him back toward the bed. ''I think ye must needs sit down.'' She was relieved when he meekly did as she asked him to.

''But we have only circled the room a few times,'' he protested even as he sat down and used the sheet to mop the sweat from his brow.

''Aye, but 'tis for the fourth time today. Only yesterday we walked this room just three times. Your legs already begin to tremble.'' She poured him a tankard of sweet cider. ''That tells me that it may yet be too soon to try walking that often. We shall add the fourth turn about the room more slowly. After all, it does ye no good to add a fourth turn if it just makes ye so weak and destroys all the gains made in the first three turns.''

"Agreed," he muttered, accepting her judgment with sullen reluctance, but then he turned his full attention upon her. "Then, mayhap, ye will do me the courtesy of telling me the real reason ye looked so upset as ye entered my room.''

She glanced at him but was unable to hold his gaze. "I tol' you.''

"Nay, ye told me that Donncoill's people are keeping y busy mending their wee hurts and giving them potions for the many wee ailments. I ken that that is the truth. 'Tis just na the reason ye looked so upset." He just smiled when she gav him a cross look. "Is Balfour causing ye trouble?''

Maldie studied him for a moment, then carefully said, "Ma' hap I let vanity run amok, but I wouldnae have thought th ye would like to hear about me and Balfour.''

Nigel grimaced. " 'Tisnae vanity. We havenae and willnae speak upon it, but I think most of Donncoill has guessed how I feel. Mayhap I seek a vicarious pleasure in hearing that ye and my brother arenae happy." He grinned briefly, then grew serious again. "More so, 'tis because ye are alone. Who have ye to talk to? Besides Balfour, I mean. There has been neither time nor chance for ye to make friends here and there willnae be for several months, not until Eric is home and Beaton is dead. Everyone is consumed by the need to defeat Beaton and bring Eric safely back to Donncoill. And ye must needs spend a lot of time with me.''

"I dinnae mind," she murmured. "Healing is oftimes slow work, taking time and patience. 'Tis my duty as a healer to do all that I can do to help a mon.''

"How ye flatter a mon," he drawled, then chuckled when she blushed faintly. "Lass, if ye feel a need to talk, to say things ye may not wish to say to my brother, e'en to simply complain, I am at your service. After all ye have done for me, the least I can do in return is offer ye an ear, one that will hear your words without judgment or suspicion. Aye, and one who will hold fast to what ye say and ne'er repeat it unless ye give me leave to.''

It was a tempting offer. Maldie ached to have someone she could speak to freely. It was saddening that she could not do it with Balfour. She knew she could not do it with Nigel either. There were things she could tell no one at Donncoill, at least not yet. If there was even the slightest chance of a future for her and Balfour she was sure it would be severely threatened if he discovered that she had told Nigel secrets she had refused to tell him. Maldie did not want to put Nigel into the uncomfortable position of listening to her babble on about Balfour either. Even if she could do so without causing Nigel pain, she would still force him to have to compromise his loyalties to clan and kinsmen.

''Ye are most kind, Nigel, but it would be best for both of us if I refuse your generous offer,'' she replied. ''If there are things I cannae discuss with Balfour, my lover, I dinnae think I should then run and unburden myself to his brother. If Balfour discovered that I had confided in ye what I didnae or wouldnae confide in him, it could hurt him, or, at least, sting his pride. It could also place ye between the two of us, a place I dinnae think ye would like to be. It could e'en mean that, because of your promise to me, ye are forced to keep secrets from your brother, your laird. That must ne'er happen, especially not now when ye are soon to face your enemy at your brother's side.''

''I hate to see ye troubled,'' he said as she tucked him back into his bed. ''After all ye have done, ye deserve to be light of heart, to ken an ease of mind.''

''Weel, 'twill be many a month ere I can savor that sort of peace. Now, rest. I will send Jennie in.''

To be light of heart and easy in her mind was a dream Maldie dearly wished to see fulfilled. *If I survive,* she mused as she started out of the room. She needed to get away from Nigel, from the sympathy in his eyes, and from the comfort and understanding he promised her. It would be so easy to run to him with all of her troubles and fears, but, in the end, he could help her no more than she could help herself. In her heart she also knew that it could easily add to her troubles, dragging Nigel into the midst of them. She did not want or need the burden of guilt that would sit upon her shoulders.

As she stepped out into the upper hallway, she caught a fleeting glimpse of James and cursed. Maldie almost returned to Nigel, eager to complain, but swallowed the urge and headed down the stairs. Even if she could turn Nigel against James she would not, for she had quickly seen that both Nigel and Balfour looked upon the man as a second father. She sternly reminded herself that James was right to suspect her, to feel that she needed close watching, but that truth did little to soothe her. Justified or not, it was annoying to have one's every move keenly watched.

Instead of going to the kitchens to mix her salves as she had planned, Maldie strode out into the bailey. It was the one place where she did not see James's frowning face peering at her from around every corner. She knew that was because James was confident that the bailey was secure and that many another would keep a close watch on her, but Maldie decided that, at the moment, it was blessing enough to get out from beneath James's dark eyes.

She meandered around the bailey, peering in at the stables, exchanging a few words with the man who tended to the hounds, and even watching the armorer as he skillfully turned useless metal into a fine sword. Inwardly she smiled as she realized that what was only simple curiosity could easily appear to be spying to a suspicious person. James was a very suspicious person. She briefly considered a close study of a few of Donncoill's defenses to give James something to really fret about, then she allowed good sense to rule her. Doing something that could so easily make James feel his dark suspicions were justified was not the way to ease her burdens or lessen her troubles. In fact it could easily prove to be a dangerous game. Acting like an enemy spy when a clan was at war was, quite probably, an act of complete idiocy.

"Why are ye frowning so?" Balfour asked as he stepped up beside her, nodding a brief greeting to the armorer as he

tugged Maldie out of the man's work shed. "Did I startle you?"
He frowned when she briefly glared at him.

Maldie took a few deep breaths to slow the rapid beat of her
heart, even as she allowed him to pull her along at his side
while he began to walk. She knew that one of the reasons his
stealthy approach always scared her was because she was filled
with guilt over her deceptions. There was always that brief
moment of sharp fear that she had said something or done
something to give herself away. She knew she needed to control
that, for her unease alone could be enough to rouse suspicions.
James was probably whispering his doubts about her into Balfour's ears, and she did not want to do or say anything that
would add weight to the man's words.

"Ye should make some sound when ye approach someone,"
she said.

"There are times when that could get me killed," he replied.

"Weel, aye, but I am nay your enemy."

"Nay, of course ye arenae."

Balfour inwardly cursed when she glanced at him sharply,
the ghost of a frown upon her face. He was doing a very poor
job of hiding his increasing doubts about her. At times he
almost wished she would reveal herself, by word or by deed,
as a spy, one of Beaton's minions, for it would absolve him
of the terrible guilt he felt every time suspicion rose in his
breast. He detested the uncertainty he suffered. The pain he
sometimes glimpsed in her eyes, a look that told him she was
aware of his suspicions, tore at his heart one minute and angered
him the next. If she was innocent, then her pain was real and
he had inflicted it, but if she worked for Beaton, then it was
just another ploy to weaken him and to strengthen her power
over him.

He was sure that he loved her and that terrified him. He
wanted to tell her all that he felt and was afraid that she would
discover his weakness for her. He prayed that she was not on
Beaton's side, then wanted her to confess that she was. He
wanted her to go away and was terrified that she would leave.
He wanted her out of his bed even as he held her close through-

out the night. Balfour was so torn by conflicting emotions he feared he would go mad. The final battle with Beaton had to come soon, he mused, or he would lose his sanity and be incapable of leading his men.

"How go the battle plans?" Maldie asked, as they walked through the gates of the inner walls encircling the keep into the area where the half-built tower stood. "I hear little or nothing about it now, yet I ken the planning still continues."

"Weel, ye have been much occupied with Nigel, fighting to make him strong again."

"I just wondered why ye ne'er ask me any questions now. Do ye ken all ye need to about Dubhlinn?"

He leaned against the wall that joined the new tower to the old walls. "I think I have gleaned all I need to from you, all that can be of any use to me, leastwise. There are other ways of discovering what we must without pulling ye into the midst of a battle plan."

"I dinnae mind," Maldie said as she stood in front of him, desperately trying not to look as hurt and scared as she felt. "I should like to help ye as much as I can."

"Ye help me by tending to Nigel. Dinnae fret, sweeting, we have both eyes and ears where we need them."

"So, ye have heard from the mon ye have set within the heart of Dubhlinn."

"Come, we havenae seen much of each other in these last two days," he said as he reached out and pulled her into his arms. "Do ye truly wish to consume our time together with talk of battles and spies?"

Maldie wondered what he would do if she said yes, then bit back the word. She had sensed that she was being pushed out of all talk concerning Beaton, the coming battle, and the rescue of Eric. Balfour's evasive answers to her questions confirmed that. It was not only James who mistrusted her. That man had already begun to sway Balfour. She would hear no more about the battle.

Her first thought was that she should pull away from Balfour, far away. It was madness to remain his lover when he thought she was his enemy. It would taint every caress they exchanged. Then he pressed her closer to his strong, warm body and she felt her pride crumble. She felt something else as well. Balfour was as torn as she was. He had suspicions, but he did not want to. He still desired her despite those doubts. James had not yet won Balfour over completely. She and Balfour were not only well matched in their passion, she thought with a sad smile, but in their confusion as well. She could not know which would prove stronger, his doubts or his passion, but she decided to let fate lead her where it would. There might only be days left before they were forced apart, either by James's mistrust or the truth, and she did not want to lose one moment of that precious time.

"This isnae a verra private place," she murmured as she tilted her head back so that he could more easily tantalize her throat with soft kisses.

" 'Tis the perfect place from which to watch the sun set," he replied, savoring the taste of her as he gently nipped at her earlobe and began to unlace her gown.

"Is that what ye are planning to do?" When her gown fell into a heap around her ankles, she nimbly stepped out of it and kicked it aside. "Someone may see us," she added, as modesty briefly infected her.

"Nay. This is a favorite spot for lovers. Once we were seen to walk this way, all eyes were turned elsewhere."

"I am nay sure I like everyone kenning what we are doing here."

"They all ken that we are lovers. There are few secrets at Donncoill. But have faith, loving, no one will spy upon us, just as they would expect no one to spy upon them if they crept away for a tryst."

That was difficult to believe, but before Maldie could voice her doubt he kissed her, and she lost all interest in who might see them and what people might think. A small part of her was shocked by the brazen way she behaved as she matched Balfour kiss for kiss and caress for caress in the red glow of the setting sun. Their greed for each other held a hint of desperation, as if he also feared that their time together was coming to an end. It was not until they lay sprawled in each other's arms, exhausted from their frenzied lovemaking, that Maldie began to wonder if fate was leading her down the wrong path. Such heedless sensual gluttony seemed wrong, especially since neither of them spoke of love or marriage or of any future together at all.

"Ye shouldnae be so quick to condemn yourself when the loving has ended," Balfour said quietly, kissing her frowning mouth before rolling off her and reaching for his braies.

"How do ye ken what I am thinking?" She looked around for her chemise.

" 'Tis that solemn, almost angry look that comes o'er your bonny face when the flush of passion has left it."

A little unsettled by how easily he seemed to guess her thoughts, Maldie sat up with her back to him as she brushed the dirt from her chemise and prepared to slip it on. She tensed when he suddenly grabbed her by both arms, stopping her from covering herself. She could almost feel his stare burning into her back, and she knew exactly what he was looking at. Despite the fading light of a setting sun, Maldie knew the heart-shaped mark on the back of her right shoulder had to be easy to see. Until now she had been very careful to keep Balfour from getting a full, clear view of her back, the dim light in their bedchamber helping her. She kept very still, terrified that he recognized it as Beaton's mark. For more times than she cared to count she had cursed that clear sign of Beaton's siring her. Her mother had never let her forget that it was the mark of her bastardry, a clear sign that she was tainted by Beaton's blood. Now she feared that it could prove a threat to her life.

"Ye have a heart upon your back," Balfour said, his voice soft with bemusement.

She pulled free of his hold and yanked on her chemise. "I am sorry. I have tried hard not to offend ye with the sight of it."

"Sweet, wee Maldie, ye do hold some strange thoughts in your bonny head," he muttered, still frowning at her back as she hurriedly pulled on her clothes. " 'Tis no offense to the eye." He could tell from her quick, stiff movements that she was in no mood to be touched, so he began to get dressed.

"The way ye stared at it and e'en the odd way ye spoke implied that ye were shocked by the sight of it."

"And I was. I have been your lover for o'er a week now. I thought I had seen all of you." He grinned when she cast a quick glare his way. " 'Tis clear that I have been lax in my attentions." Balfour laughed when she leapt to her feet, then stood up to help her retie the laces on her gown. "Mayhap I must needs light a few more candles."

"Ye are trying verra hard to embarrass me." She tried not to be relieved that he had not immediately recognized the mark as one only a Beaton could carry. Maldie was sure that she was not out of danger yet, and she did not want to have her guard weakened by false hope.

"Nay, 'tisnae that hard to bring a blush to your cheeks."

"I am feeling verra eager to strike you."

"I am all atremble." He laughed and rubbed his arm after she lightly punched him there. "I think I may bear a scar there for all my days."

"Ye are in a humor to tease me, arenae ye," she said as he hooked his arm through hers and started to walk them back to the keep.

"Aye. I am also verra hungry now." He winked at her. "Ye have raised a powerful appetite in me, dearling."

She tried very hard not to blush again and hissed a curse when she felt the tingle of warm blood in her cheeks. It was good that he was in such high spirits, all of his doubts and suspicions gone for the moment. She just wished she had the skill to accept his teasing with no more than a calm, gently amused smile.

" 'Tis odd," he continued in a more serious tone, "but I have the strongest feeling that I have seen such a mark before, one of the same shape and set in the same place."

Maldie's step faltered as shock then fear rippled through her. She realized that despite her best efforts, his good humor had caused her to grow less wary. It took a moment for her to calm herself. She did not wish Balfour to guess how badly he had upset her. There was no possible way he could have seen that mark upon Beaton, but he could have heard about it. She shook away that chilling thought. Her mother had always told her that Beaton kept his mark well hidden, that the man considered it a stain set upon his skin by the devil himself.

"I have ne'er heard of anyone else bearing such a mark," she said, inwardly cursing herself for such a weak reply. "Ye didnae ken my mother, did ye?"

"Nay, of course not. Nor any other Kirkcaldy." He shook his head. "Yet, I still feel that I have seen such a mark before. Dinnae fret. 'Twill come to me."

Maldie sincerely hoped it would not as they entered the great hall. "Ye may mistake the shock ye felt for recognition," she said, desperately trying to dissuade him from thinking too long or too hard on the matter.

" 'Tis possible, but I can see that mark clearly, just not upon your fair skin."

It was as she sat down next to Balfour that a shocking conclusion began to form in Maldie's mind. She felt chilled to the bone. James sat across from her and she knew from his sharp look that she had let her shock show briefly in her face. Even fear of what he might think could not push away the idea forming in her head, however. No matter how hard she tried to deny it, she knew in her heart that there was only one other person, beside Beaton, upon whose back Balfour might have seen such a mark—on young Eric.

Eric was believed to be a Murray bastard, bred from the adulterous union of Balfour's father and Beaton's faithless wife. Balfour had said that Beaton might be able to convince people that Eric was his son by claiming that he had wrongly cast the child out while caught in the throes of a jealous rage. But what if that was the truth? There was still the possibility that Balfour's father had bedded the woman, but he might not have been the only one doing so. Her mother had told her how diligently Beaton worked to bear sons, often leaving her sore and exhausted. Until Beaton had discovered his wife's liaison, Maldie was certain that he had frequently bedded the poor woman. Eric could easily be the son Beaton so desperately wanted. Beaton may have actually tried his best to kill the one thing he truly craved.

There was a wealth of satisfaction to be gained from such a circumstance, but Maldie found herself unable to truly enjoy it. If she was right, and every instinct she had told her that she was, a great many people would be hurt, beginning with Eric, an innocent boy. It would devastate the youth to discover that he was not a Murray, that he was actually the child of the Murray clan's enemy. Such a hard blow might be softened if that father was one to be proud of, but Maldie sincerely doubted that Beaton had done one good thing in his entire miserable life. Eric would probably be as horrified as she was to claim Beaton as his father, but the boy would suffer far more from that than she ever had. Unlike her, Eric had savored the joy of a loving family. She had lost nothing by knowing who and what her father was. Eric would lose everything he knew and loved.

Balfour would also be deeply hurt, and Maldie fought to resist the urge to take his hand in hers and immediately convey her deepest sympathies. If nothing else, he would wonder how she could even think of such a thing, would probably demand some proof. The only way she could tell him the truth about Eric was if she confessed to her own parentage, and she was not ready to do so.

Maldie realized that she did not want to be the one to tell him such a hard truth. Nor was she sure it was her place to do so. She could see no gain in it either. The truth would only bring pain to a lot of people. In fact, it would deeply hurt everyone but Beaton. She had never seen the boy Eric, had never actually seen the mark upon his back that branded him as Beaton's son. Until she saw that proof with her own eyes, Maldie decided that it was best to say nothing at all. It should also be Eric's choice; it had to be Eric's truth to tell. She just wondered if such a young boy would have the strength to do so. As she heaped food upon her plate, she prayed that she would not be the one forced to expose that secret, that Eric would do what he must. She chanced a quick peek at Balfour and hoped that she could keep this secret as well as she had kept all of her own.

Chapter Eleven

"Malcolm is dead," James announced as he strode into the great hall.

Balfour nearly choked on the bread he was eating. "Dead?"

"Aye, he willnae be telling us anything more about Beaton or Dubhlinn. God's teeth, e'en if he had survived the beating they gave him, he couldnae have told us anything. Beaton had his tongue cut out."

"Are ye sure?" Balfour knew James would not repeat rumor, but he felt a need to have some hard proof.

"The bastards hung his broken body from a tree just outside of the village." James sat down and poured himself a tankard of wine, then took a long drink of it before continuing, "At first we didnae ken who it was, he was that badly beaten and I think the carrion birds had been nibbling at him. Howbeit, once we kenned that it was Malcolm, we also kenned who had murdered him. So, too, did it explain why his body had been left where it was."

"It was meant to be a gruesome taunt."

James nodded. "As was the hard, ugly way he was killed. They not only wanted us to ken that they had found our spy but set the fear of God into our men, making it verra hard for us to find another willing to slip inside of Dubhlinn. We have already cleaned Malcolm's body and readied it for burial, and there are signs that he was cruelly tortured.''

"Any word from our other mon, Douglas?''

"Nay, but I would guess that he still lives or he would have been swaying in the breeze next to Malcolm.'' James shook his head. "I thought ye foolishly wasted your time when ye took so long and worked so hard to find two Murray men who had the skills ye needed and who didnae ken each other, not e'en by sight. Such care shows its worth now. By the looks of Malcolm's battered body he spent many long hours in hell, and probably would have told Beaton all he could.''

"Mayhap. Although Malcolm was a fine, honorable mon. He wouldnae have sent another mon to his death.''

"Not willingly, but if he was tortured, as I believe he was, he may have been too blinded with pain to think of the consequences of what he told Beaton. He would have been able to think of only one thing—making the pain stop.''

Balfour took a steadying drink of wine. "I realized I could be sending those men to their deaths, but I ne'er gave a thought to how hard, how lacking in honor, those deaths might be.''

"Why should ye? Ye would ne'er deal with a mon in that way, no matter what he was guilty of.''

"Should I bring Douglas home?''

"Nay. If Beaton hasnae found him ye could weel put him in danger by trying to get word to him. I didnae ken Malcolm weel, he was your cousin Grodin's mon, but I do ken Douglas. A good mon, brave and steadfast. He is also a clever mon. If he thinks he is in danger of suffering Malcolm's fate, he will flee Dubhlinn. Douglas will have the wit to ken that it wouldnae be cowardice to do so, that he can be of no use to you dead, for ye will not only lose what knowledge he has gained, but a good sword arm as weel.''

"Good. I dinnae want another mon's death upon my conscience.''

"Malcolm's death isnae your fault. He kenned the risk he

was taking, and ye warned him many times that he would die
if he was caught. None of us could foresee the way the poor
bastard would die. If we had, ye would ne'er have sent him
there. Ye cannae take on the burden of every death. Aye, ye
are too quick to let guilt take hold of ye. Ye have ne'er caused
a death out of arrogance, anger, pride, or even simple carelessness. We are at war with Beaton and Eric's life is in danger.
Ye shouldnae be surprised if men die. They will continue to
do so until Beaton is dead.''

''And so ye must cease pouting o'er it,'' Balfour added,
smiling faintly as he repeated one of the phrases James had
often flung at him and his brothers during their training.

James returned his smile. ''Aye. Wise words ye should heed
more often. Now, what is of greater importance than even
Malcolm's death is how Beaton discovered the mon.''

''Mayhap Malcolm made a mistake, revealed himself in some
way.''

''Mayhap, but I find that hard to believe. He was a clever
lad from what little I learned of him. Certainly clever enough
to ken if he had erred, and flee ere he could be caught. Ever
since this cursed trouble began, years ago, we have had a mon
inside of Dubhlinn, yet none was ever discovered. Beaton has
proven again and again that he pays little heed to those who
work to protect him and keep him in comfort. Once accepted
by the people working within and without Dubhlinn, a mon
was ne'er e'en looked at by Beaton. There is another possibility
ye must consider.''

''Someone within Donncoill told Beaton who Malcolm
was.'' Balfour disliked the turn the conversation had taken, but
knew he would be putting his clan in danger if he did not
consider all possibilities. ''It could have been Grizel.''

''Grizel has been dead for a fortnight. And we killed the
men she had gone to meet.''

''Before that?''

''Possible, but, nay likely. Beaton wouldnae have waited for
so long to catch and torture a Murray. If one of the men Grizel
had gone to meet had escaped us, I could believe it was her

who pointed the finger at Malcolm. Malcolm might have survived torture for a fortnight, although I pray to God he didnae have to endure for that long. But, nay, Beaton learned who Malcolm was after Grizel died.''

''We have yet another traitor at Donncoill?''

''Or one of Beaton's spies.''

Balfour knew who James suspected. The man's mistrust of Maldie was so complete that it had begun to infect him. It was hard to believe that she could send a man to his death, however. And if she was one of Beaton's minions, she would have to know what a slow, torturous death it would be. Maldie was a healing woman, one whose patience, skill, and gentleness were already legendary at Donncoill. Such an act should horrify her, should be something she could never willingly do. Balfour also hated to think that he could be so fooled by such a woman, that he could ever desire her.

''I ken who ye think it is,'' he finally said.

''Aye, and ye think so, too, although ye are working yourself into a sweat trying to push the thought from your mind. Aye, Malcolm could have done something foolish that got him caught, something he didnae realize he had done, or was seen and acted upon so quickly he had no chance to flee. Howbeit, 'twould be a grave mistake to ignore the possibility that someone slipped word to Beaton that one of our men was in his camp.''

''I ken it,'' Balfour snapped, then he sighed and rubbed the back of his neck. ''I ne'er told her Malcolm or Douglas's names, only that we had a mon within Beaton's camp.''

''Beaton wouldnae need a name, only to ken that one of the poor souls laboring for him was one of our men. Did ye tell her that we had two men at Dubhlinn?''

''Nay. And, ere ye accuse me of it, I am nay allowing my heedless passion for the lass to taint my thoughts, or turn me from the truth. Mayhap my heart, but nay my loins. I just dinnae want to believe I could care for and desire a woman who could send a mon to such a horrible, painful death. And, she is a healer. Ye but need to watch her tend to the ill or injured once to understand how difficult I find it to believe that such a woman could do such a cruel thing.''

"I am prepared to believe that she wouldnae do it willingly, that Beaton holds some sword at her throat which forces her to act on his behalf. The why of it doesnae really matter to me now, only in that it would make ye feel less pained if she was being forced to be Beaton's spy. I just want her power to hurt us taken away from her.''

Balfour lightly drummed his fingers on the thick wood of the table. James was right. If there was even the smallest chance that Maldie was slipping information to Beaton, she had to be stopped, deprived immediately of any opportunity to see anything, hear anything, or get a message out to Beaton. He would have to confine her, keep her under close guard, until he was able to uncover the truth. If she was guilty she would accept such a gentle penalty for her crimes. If she was innocent he was going to hurt her, deeply insult her, possibly beyond her ability to forgive him. Balfour realized that his choices were few and grim. If Maldie was guilty and he let her run free, she could cost him the victory he needed and many of his clansmen's lives. If he treated her as a spy, confined and guarded her, it could cost him Maldie.

"I face a loss no matter which way I turn," he muttered.

"Aye, ye do," James agreed, reaching out to briefly clasp Balfour's shoulder in a gesture of understanding and sympathy. "But think on this for a moment. Either way ye turn ye could lose the lass. If she is a spy, she will flee or ye will be forced to hang her, but a lot of Murrays will have died needlessly, fighting in a battle she has made sure they can ne'er win. If she is innocent, ye may send her fleeing your side hurt and angry. I fear that trusting her will cost ye the most."

"It will." Balfour finished his wine and abruptly stood up. " 'Tis always best to get the most distasteful chores done quickly. I will go and confront her at once.''

"She may confess all, e'en tell ye why she works for Beaton, and it may be a reason ye can understand.''

"She may, but I dinnae think wee Maldie will be that forth-coming."

Balfour made his way to the bedchamber he shared with Maldie with the slow heavy tread of a condemned man. His mind filled with the heated memory of their wild lovemaking by the tower only two nights ago, and he grimaced. He had walked away from there feeling at ease, confident, and light-hearted. Maldie had grown quiet, and he had begun to think that she was keeping something from him. He did not want to think that she was hiding the fact that she had just sent a man to his death. Balfour dreaded the thought that he could be such a fool.

As he stepped into the room Maldie turned and smiled at him from where she sat by the fire, brushing her newly washed hair. She was beautiful. He wanted her and he loathed himself for that weakness. He even loathed her a little. Balfour knew that if she proved to be guilty of aiding Beaton, he would be far more than hurt. He would never again trust in his feelings for a woman.

Maldie frowned as Balfour said nothing, just stared at her as he shut the door and leaned against it. He was very tense, his arms crossed over his chest and his hands clenched tightly. There was a hard, cold look upon his face that made her very uneasy. She tried to reach out to him, to find out what emotions made him look so stern, but she could feel nothing. His face was alive with emotion, yet somehow he had closed himself off from her. That made her feel afraid. Suddenly she did not know the man standing by the door.

"What is wrong, Balfour?" she asked, her growing fear clear to hear in her trembling voice.

"Malcolm, our mon in Beaton's camp, was found hanging from a tree outside of the village." The shock on her face appeared real, but Balfour knew he could no longer afford to trust in what he saw, heard, or felt.

"Oh, Balfour, I am so sorry," she said, standing and moving toward him.

"Why? Didnae ye expect Beaton to kill him?"

She stoppd so quickly she stumbled, and she stared at him in confusion. "Why should I ken what Beaton was going to do to the mon?" Had Balfour suddenly discovered who she was, she thought, fighting the urge to flee from the cold, angry man she faced.

" 'Tis but passing strange that Beaton has ne'er found one of our men, not in thirteen long years, yet suddenly he discovers poor Malcolm." He watched the color fade from her face and struggled against the urge to comfort her, to take back his harsh words.

"Ye think *I* am aiding Beaton? Could not Grizel have told him?"

"Grizel has been dead for a fortnight, and the men she went to meet also died, so they could tell Beaton nothing. If she had told Beaton sooner, then Malcolm would have been dead sooner. Nay, it had to have been someone else."

"And ye believe that someone else is me," she whispered, barely able to speak over the knot in her throat. She did not think she had ever been so hurt.

"Can ye make me believe elsewise?"

Maldie swayed a little, his words striking her heart like a sword blow. She had expected this, or so she had thought. Since her arrival at Donncoill she had feared discovery, but that had been about her parentage. Once it was discovered that she was Beaton's daughter such mistrust was only to be expected. This accusation was coming without that knowledge behind it.

The only reason for this accusation was that she was not a Murray. Grizel's betrayal had obviously not been enough to make them see that even their own could sometimes turn against them. Maldie found her hurt swiftly turning to anger and insult. She may not have told them all they wished to know about her, but that was not reason enough to think she would send a man to his death.

"My word is not enough?"

"Nay, I cannae allow it to be." He sighed and shook his head. "Ye have cloaked yourself in secrets, yet expect blind trust. We dinnae ken who ye are, where ye have come from, or what ye were doing on that road, yet ye want us to believe that ye are our friend.''

"I have been more than a friend to you." She was pleased to see him flush, for it meant he still had some doubt about her guilt, felt some reluctance about what he was doing to her.

"Can ye nay see how e'en that can make ye suspect?"

"Passion is a crime now, is it?"

"Maldie, just tell me something, anything, about yourself, something I can have a mon test the truth of.''

"And why should I?''

"Why willnae ye?''

"Who I am is nay your concern, nor is where I come from, where I am going, nor anything else about me. Ye want me to give ye proof that I am not a spy? Weel, where is your proof that I am?''

Balfour grew angry again, infuriated by her stubbornness. He was not asking anything that should be difficult for her to give. All he wished was a little information about her, the sort of information most people would give without hesitation. All anyone at Donncoill knew about her was that she was a skilled healer, her mother was dead, she was a bastard, and she sought her kinsmen. Considering how long she had been with him that was precious little.

"Can ye nay see why I do this? I am at war. My brother is being held by my enemy. I cannae afford to simply trust a person because they say they are innocent. I need more than that, Maldie, or I must treat ye as the enemy ye could weel be.''

"Then I suggest ye cease berating me for crimes I havenae committed and seek out the true traitor.''

"As ye wish. Ye will be confined to your chambers, allowed only to go and tend to Nigel.''

"Are ye sure ye wish one of Beaton's dogs to touch your fair brother?''

"Ye have had ample opportunity to do the mon harm and havenae. Also, Nigel may not be strong enough yet to ride to

battle, but he is certainly strong enough to defend himself
against a wee lass. Mayhap some time alone will make ye see
that this isnae the time to hide behind your pride. Surely a little
truth isnae too much to pay for your freedom.''

He left the room, barring the door from the outside. He was
saddened, angered, and confused by the confrontation. At first
Maldie had looked stricken to the heart, then she had grown
furious. That seemed to indicate that she was innocent, that
she was being falsely accused. Yet, she offered no defense
other than denial.

''Is it done?'' asked James, moving to stand by Balfour.

''Aye.'' He nodded at the man James had brought to guard
Maldie's door and started toward the great hall, James at his
side.

''I dinnae suppose she confessed and begged forgiveness.''

''Oh, nay, Maldie wouldnae have done that even if she was
guilty.''

''Ye still dinnae think she is?''

''I dinnae ken what I think. The way she reacted to the
accusation was the way an innocent person would, but she
could just be skilled at playing a part. Yet, she offered no
defense except to say she was innocent. I asked for some
information, something she could tell me about herself that we
could verify and she told me to go and look for it by myself.''
As they entered the great hall, he caught a fleeting look of
amusement on James's lined face and scowled. ''Ye think that
is funny?''

''Aye, I fear I do.'' James shook his head as they sat down
at the head of the largest table and poured themselves some
wine. ''In truth, it makes me think she may be innocent. Aye,
or far more clever than we are.''

''I have just accused my lover of a heinous crime, of sending
a mon to a gruesome death, and now ye say she may be innocent?''

''I have always thought she might be, have ne'er found
anything to show her guilt. Howbeit, ye would ne'er have acted
against her if I had told ye that. I am nay so old that I cannae

be swayed by a bonny lass with green eyes, but I am nay blinded by the beauty of them either. One of us had to harden his heart and look at all the possibilities.''

Balfour cursed and stretched, trying unsuccessfully to ease the tension in his body. ''She will ne'er forgive me for this.''

''If she doesnae care enough for ye to see that ye do what ye must, then ye wouldnae have held her verra long anyway. 'Tis odd that she would still tell ye nothing about herself. I fear one must ask what the lass is trying to hide.''

''Aye. She does have a lot of secrets, and we can no longer let her roam free hoping those secrets arenae ones that could hurt us. I ken that I have done what I had to do. I just wish that doing the right thing felt better.''

Maldie stared at the locked door for several moments before she could make herself move. She staggered to the bed and threw herself on it, staring blindly up at the ceiling. So many emotions tore through her that she found it a little hard to breathe. The one thing she did not want to do was cry, but the choking lump forming in her throat told her that she would not get her wish. Softly cursing Balfour, she turned onto her stomach and gave in to her tears, letting them rule her for a while.

It took longer than she liked to gain control of her emotions again, but as her crying shuddered to a halt, Maldie decided it had served a good purpose. She was tired, but she was clear-headed. Now she could think about what had happened even though she wished she could just forget it all.

The fact that she had been accused of spying for Beaton was not what bothered her the most. She had been expecting it for a long time. It was that Balfour had accused her of it without knowing the one thing that made her look guilty—the name of her father. He had no proof that she was any more than she appeared, an orphan wandering the country seeking out her kinsmen, yet he was able to believe her capable of sending a man to a horrible death. That Balfour could even consider such a thing was a hard blow.

In a way, she mused, it was almost funny. If she was not in so much pain, she might even muster up a chuckle over the irony of it all. She was there because she wanted to kill Beaton, wanted to help Balfour and the Murrays destroy the man, yet she was being held prisoner—suspected of helping him! Somehow she had erred, had left herself vulnerable to such suspicion, but she could not see how. Balfour spoke of how secretive she was, but Maldie could not believe that was all of it. Did everyone who passed through Donncoill sit down and recite their lineage?

She cursed, got up, and poured herself some wine. There were no answers. He could not understand why she would not tell him everything about herself, and she could not understand how that reluctance could be turned around to get her accused of helping Beaton, of taking part in the death of a man. She and Balfour were never going to come to a meeting of the minds on this. He was, after all, proud of his family, his heritage. It would probably be impossible for him to understand how someone else might just want to forget that she even had a family.

What she had to consider was how to get out of the mess she was in. She still needed to fulfill her vow to her mother, and she could not do that while confined to a bedchamber in Donncoill. Maldie ambled over to the door and tried to open it, not at all surprised to find it barred from the outside. She had heard Balfour slide the bar into place. There was undoubtedly a big, sword-wielding Murray standing out there as well. The straightforward way was definitely not the way to get free.

There was the choice of telling Balfour what he wanted to know. She could tell him a great deal without revealing who her father was. However, if he sent a man to her old home to ask about her, that truth could easily come out. Her mother had not been reticent about the man she blamed for all of her misery. Maldie was also sure that some of the townspeople would gleefully tell some tales that would not make her look like an innocent, honorable, and trustworthy person. There had been a few things she had done out of a need to survive that she was not particularly proud of. She had also made little effort to endear herself to the sometimes irritatingly pious people of town.

Simple, foolish pride kept her from telling the man anything anyway. It obviously annoyed Balfour that she still refused to answer all of his questions and, at the moment, that was a small, satisfying punishment for his accusations that she was not inclined to give up. That left her with little more to say in response to his accusations than she was innocent and he was a fool. That was not enough to get her free. She was not in fear of her life. Balfour was not a man who would hang someone simply because he thought she might be guilty of something. As he had with Grizel, he would wait until he had overwhelming proof and, since she was innocent and there was no proof to be found, she was safe.

There was really only one thing she could do and that was to get out, free Eric, and prove that she had never helped Beaton. This whole matter with Beaton had to be resolved. She realized that even as she was proving her innocence she would be revealing the whole truth about herself, a truth she was sure would send Balfour fleeing her side, but that did not matter. If he chose to hate her because her father was William Beaton, that was his weakness, but she would not sit idly by and allow him to think her a traitor to her friends and a murderer.

Maldie suddenly laughed. Her amusement was enhanced by the soft sound of movement outside her door for she knew the guard was frowning at it, wondering if she had gone mad. There was a small chance that she had. Her lover, the man she loved to desperation, thought her such a low creature that she would aid his enemy and hand a man over to the bastard to be slaughtered without a qualm, yet she knew she could come to understand why he had been forced to do it. If that was not madness, what was? *Probably deciding that the perfect solution to my difficulty is to escape, hie to Dubhlinn, and rescue Eric,* she mused and giggled again.

She was locked in a room at Donncoill, a strong keep, and well guarded. The only place she would be allowed to go to was Nigel's room. If she did escape and it was discovered quickly, she would have half the Murray clan chasing her across the countryside. At Dubhlinn she would have to be very careful, for they would all be wary of any stranger now. As she closely watched her own back she had to find Eric, then free him. Finally she had to get herself and the boy safely out of Dubhlinn and back to Donncoill.

"What could be simpler," she muttered as she set her cup down and sprawled on the bed.

It was impossible and she should not even consider it, but she did. It was the only plan she had and it would require a great deal of thought. Turning her mind to such a mad adventure was far preferable to sitting alone in her room with her pain.

Chapter Twelve

"What are ye plotting, Maldie Kirkcaldy?" demanded Nigel as he eased his aching body down onto the bed.

She turned from the tiny window she had been staring out of and looked at him. For three days he had been her only companion, unless she counted the silent guard who walked her across the hall. Neither of them had talked about the things she had been accused of, and they had done a good job of ignoring her imprisonment as well. They had just worked hard to improve his ability to walk again, something he was doing very well at. She had begun to think that that was his only interest. It was clear that Nigel was still keeping a close watch on her, however.

"Why should ye think I am plotting anything?" she asked as she moved to the bed and poured him a tankard of cider.

"Because my fool brother has made ye a prisoner?"

"I thought we were ignoring that wee difficulty."

"When ye said naught the first time ye came to my room after he had committed this folly, I decided ye didnae wish to speak of it. Weel, mayhap ye dinnae, but I find it hard to ignore such an insult."

She smiled, for he looked so outraged. It was nice to have someone who believed in her, but she knew a lot of that was because he felt he owed her his life. There was even a chance that he was so outraged and felt indebted enough that he would help her escape, but she would not ask it of him. This was her problem and she would solve it herself.

"I but wonder how long it will be ere Balfour realizes the error he has made."

"Ye speak of it so lightly. Dinnae ye see the insult he has dealt ye?"

"Clearly. At times 'tis most difficult to look beyond it. Howbeit, when I dinnae feel like impaling him upon some spike," she grinned when he laughed, "I can also see that he had little choice."

"There is always a choice."

Maldie shrugged. "Mayhap, but sometimes all of them are distasteful. Someone told Beaton that Malcolm was a Murray and that got the mon killed. Never before has a Murray mon been caught slinking about Dubhlinn. Now, either Beaton has grown very clever, which I dinnae think anyone would consider, or someone told him about Malcolm. Grizel is dead and so it couldnae have been her. So Balfour looks about trying to see what has changed at Donncoill, and what does he see? Me. I am the reasonable choice of suspect."

"Nay, ye arenae," Nigel snapped.

"Dinnae judge your brother too harshly," she said. "He is the laird, responsible for all who live on his lands. That sometimes calls for hard decisions. There is also a wee bit more to it all than simply blaming the stranger for all that has gone wrong. And, to be fair to Balfour, he doesnae fully believe it all himself, but, with a battle drawing nigh he cannae chance that his trust is misplaced. He did give me the opportunity to defend myself."

"And ye didnae?" Nigel frowned. "Why wouldnae ye?"

"I got angry. Pride reared its witless head." She took his empty goblet from his hand and set it on the table next to the bed. "I decided my word should be good enough. He asked

me questions, asked me to give him some tiny piece of information that he could send a mon to verify, thus proving my
innocence. I told him that if he was so eager to find out something he had best get busy and look for it.'' She found that she
was able to smile faintly when Nigel laughed.

"That pride could get ye hanged,'' he warned, all signs of
good humor abruptly leaving his face.

"Nay,'' she said without a hint of doubt. "Not with Balfour.
He needs hard proof ere he sentences anyone to death.''

"Aye, ye are right. Balfour is a merciful and just mon. 'Tis
sad that he is also a fool.'' He grinned when she giggled, then
grew serious, watching her closely as he said, "That leaves ye
but one choice. Ye must escape Donncoill.''

She was proud of how carefully she controlled her expression
and her emotion, especially the quick flash of fear that her plans
had been uncovered. Nigel could not possibly have guessed her
plans, for they were too wild. After all, the Murrays also planned
to rescue Eric and they felt they needed a whole army to do
it. No one would think a wee lass would even consider trying
to do it on her own. That he suspected she had cherished a few
thoughts of escaping was no surprise and no threat to her.

"Of course. Fleeing would certainly prove my innocence,''
she drawled.

"Ye shouldnae have to be proving your innocence, curse
it.''

"Nay, but running away like a thief in the night will not
help me. I will be fine, Nigel. Truly. Aye, I am deeply hurt by
all of this, but I am alive and the truth will out. I but need to
wait.''

"If I can be of any help—''

She held up her hand to stop his words. "Dinnae e'en say
it, Nigel. 'Tis best if ye stay right out of this. Ye believe in
me and that is enough. Anything else and ye risk disobeying,
or worse, betraying your laird.'' The door opened and Maldie
saw Jennie standing there, the guard looming behind her. '' 'Tis
time to return to my room. Rest, Nigel. Ye grow stronger and

can walk longer and more steadily every day. 'Twill be more
tempting now than e'er before to try and do too much.''

"I ken it. Ye have proven right in all ye have advised me
to do so far. I see no sense in closing my ears to your advice
now.''

Maldie slowly walked out of the room. Jennie averted her
eyes, blushing as Maldie walked by her. Everyone knew why
Balfour had confined her to her bedchamber, and Maldie knew
that what trust and respect she had begun to build was probably
all destroyed. That was very hard to bear because she had begun
to feel she belonged at Donncoill, that she was accepted, even
liked. It was the first time in her life she had ever felt such
things, and she was devastated by their loss.

The door was shut behind her and she cringed as she heard
the bar slide across. She hated being locked in. She had always
been free to come and go as she liked, many said too free. It
had only been three days that she had been confined, but she
was beginning to feel chokingly trapped. Maldie took a deep
breath to calm herself and walked to the small window. A few
slow, hungry breaths of the warm, fresh air eased the growing
sense of panic she had begun to feel. She could at least see the
outside and she was grateful for that. Balfour could have easily
confined her to the dark cells deep in the dungeon beneath
Donncoill.

"But then, he shouldnae have locked me up at all," she
muttered as she strode back to her bed.

She fought the urge to sit there and cling to her anger and
hurt. As she had for the last three days, she turned her mind
to her plan to get free and save Eric. It was the only thing that
had kept her from becoming trapped in her own misery and
pain. It was almost complete, but the last part of it was the most
difficult. She had thought of a way to get inside of Dubhlinn, a
way to find out where Eric was hidden, and even a way to get
him out of there with little chance of being seen. Maldie doubted
there was any complication she had not considered and made
a plan for, from how to slip around guards to the possibility

that she and Eric might have to run for their lives. The only thing she had not yet figured out was how to get out of Donncoill.

There were several ways she could get away, but none of the opportunities she needed had yet presented itself. No one had called for her healing skills, thus getting her out of the small area she was confined to. The guard never took his eyes off her or left the door unlocked. No one even came to visit her.

Suddenly she had an idea, one that was so simple she was astonished that she had taken so long to think of it. All she needed was a reason to get one of the maids to come in to help her. If she claimed it was some female trouble none of the men would demand much of an explanation, would probably shy away from hearing even that much. The only part of her plan that would be really difficult was that she would have to hurt the maid, not badly, but enough so that the woman was unconscious and would stay so long enough for her to get off Donncoill lands.

A soft rap sounded at the door and for one brief moment she thought luck was with her, that she might not even have to lie to get a maid to her room. Then Balfour stepped in and she inwardly cursed. Seeing him was going to stir up all the feelings she had been working so hard to bury. Maldie could already feel her hurt and anger stinging the back of her throat.

"If ye havenae come to beg for my forgiveness then ye might as weel leave," she said, sitting so straight on the edge of the bed that she could feel a twinge in her back.

Balfour sighed and dragged his fingers through his hair. He was not sure why he had come to see her again. It was doubtful that anything would be changed, yet he felt a real need to give her one last chance to defend herself, one last chance to give him something that would allow him to let her go. After several days of being locked in a small room, her only respite a short walk across the hall to Nigel's room, he had hoped that she would feel more inclined to cooperate with him. Her greeting and the stubborn look upon her face told him that had been a foolish hope.

He had missed her and not just in his bed, although the loss of her curled up at his side had made it nearly impossible for him to sleep. Balfour found that he missed seeing her, even in passing, and talking to her. While he understood the stance she had assumed, it angered him for it kept them apart. He began to think that she did not find that as intolerable as he did, and that hurt.

"I came to give ye another chance to tell me the truth," he said.

"I have told ye the truth." Maldie decided that the reason that lie did not bother her was because she was so angry at him.

"Mayhap, but there has been little of it. The more I have thought on the matter, the more I have come to realize that, although we are lovers, ye are still a stranger to me. I ken none of all the little things one usually learns about a lover."

"And I have ne'er met people who are as concerned about such things as ye Murrays are. I am what ye see. What else matters?"

"When ye stand accused of helping our enemy, of even aiding in the murder of a good mon, a great deal more is needed than *I am what ye see.* Can ye nay see the danger ye are in, lass?"

"Do ye mean to hang me then?"

She was pleased to see him pale. It meant he was not without some feeling for her. His accusations and his absence had made her begin to wonder if he had lost all interest in her. Since she would soon leave Donncoill and probably him as well, it was a foolish thing to worry about, yet this sign that he still cared for her in some way, no matter how small, was comforting. It also made her more confident in her judgment that she would face no punishment until he had irrefutable proof of her guilt, something he could never get for it did not exist.

"Nay, of course not. If naught else, ye havenae actually killed anyone with your own hand, as Grizel had. But why willnae ye try to prove my suspicions wrong?"

"Because they are insulting and unfounded and dinnae

deserve my time or my interest. If I proceed to try and prove my innocence, then I justify your accusations and I refuse to do that.'' She crossed her arms over her chest and coldly stared at him, silently challenging him to continue the argument.

''Ye are a verra stubborn woman, Maldie Kirkcaldy,'' he said and shook his head. ''Mayhap 'tis justified. I dinnae ken anymore. But, ye might take some time to consider how dangerous blind pride and stubbornness can be. I pray it willnae come to it, but silence in a matter such as this could cost ye dearly.''

The moment the door shut behind him, she collapsed on the bed. His last words had been a threat, but Maldie felt no fear. Balfour would not harm her. And if by some chance she was letting her heart lead her astray in her judgment of the man, there was always Nigel to turn to. That man would never let his brother harm her. She had been determined not to get Nigel mixed up in the troubles between her and Balfour, but if her well-being or her life was in danger, she would not hesitate to pull him in on her side.

Balfour's visit had shown her one thing, however. It was time she got out of Donncoill. She did not think she could endure one more time of hearing the man she loved demand that she give him proof of her innocence. No matter how well she understood the awkward position he was in, how he had to do just what he was doing, that hurt.

He was right to warn her about the folly of too much pride and stubbornness. She did have too much pride and many thought it was sadly misplaced. After all, they would mutter, what did she have to be so proud about? She would not, however, swallow that pride just to soothe his groundless suspicion.

Maldie was just not sure how long she could hold to that determination. When she saw him she wanted to do whatever he asked, so that they could be together again. She wanted to be back in his arms, back at his side, and back in his confidence. She knew that, if she did not flee Donncoill soon, that want could grow too strong to resist.

She waited for one full hour, hoping that Balfour would then be too busy or too far away to come to her, then started to groan. It only took three hearty groans to bring the guard to the door. She knew he was listening because she heard his sword thump against the wood. One more loud groan opened the door. Maldie fought not to smile at the look of extreme concern on the man's scarred face. She clutched at her stomach, rocked back and forth on the bed, and moaned softly.

"What is wrong with you?" the guard demanded, edging into the room.

"I need a woman's aid," she replied, pleased with the unsteady, raspy tone of her voice.

"Ye are ill?"

" 'Tis a woman's ailment and I need a woman to help me, ye great oaf," she yelled, then moaned, acting as if simply raising her voice was enough to increase her great pain. "Get me one of the maids."

He quickly backed out the door and barred it. Maldie allowed herself a brief grin over his swift retreat. Just as she had suspected the words *a woman's ailment* had silenced all questions. They could put the fear of God into even the bravest of warriors, men who would not even blink as they looked upon the most gruesome of battle wounds or inflicted them. When she heard footsteps hurrying back toward her door, she quickly returned to clutching herself and groaning. It was a little hard to keep up the pretense when poor Jennie was shoved into the room and the door barred behind her. The guard was clearly desperate not to learn any more about it all, did not even want to accidentally overhear anything.

"What ails ye, mistress?" Jennie asked as she moved to the side of the bed and placed a comforting hand on Maldie's arm.

Maldie cursed Balfour as she looked into the young, brown-haired maid's soft blue eyes. It was his fault that she was going to have to hurt Jennie. Even though she had no intention of doing the girl any real harm, she hated the thought of hitting her. Jennie did not deserve it, nor did she deserve the trouble she might get into for letting the prisoner escape.

"What ails me is that I am locked away like a mad aunt,"

she muttered, then swung her fist, hitting poor Jennie square on the jaw.

It greatly surprised Maldie when Jennie was felled by the first blow. She had expected a little bit more of a struggle. Then she grew concerned and quickly looked the young maid over, relieved to discover that the girl was alright. Despite having had little practice at knocking someone down, she had obviously hit Jennie in just the right place with just the right amount of strength. She felt a brief surge of pride, then was angry. Balfour was the one who deserved to get punched in the jaw, not poor shy little Jennie.

As she hefted the girl onto the bed, Maldie hoped that Jennie would not suffer too lurid a bruise or ache for too long. She gently tucked the girl up in her bed, pulling the covers up high to hide her lighter hair. The guard would probably not step into the room, afraid he would somehow become involved in female problems, Maldie thought with a faint sneer, but he would still be able to see the wrong color of hair from the doorway.

She softly cursed as she tried to hide all of her hair beneath the linen scarf she had taken from Jennie. It was a little warm for a cloak, but Maldie put one on, pulling the hood up to further hide her hair and her face. If Grizel could get all the way out of Donncoill and to the other side of the village so often with no one paying her much heed, then it ought to work for her. Maldie stepped up to the door, took one last look toward Jennie to reassure herself that nothing could be seen, and softly rapped.

Her heart stood still as she stood in front of the guard, fighting to keep her face averted, and her voice slightly higher, as Jennie's was. ''I need to go into the village for a few rags and—'' She choked to a halt when the guard tugged her out of the room and nudged her down the hall before locking the door again.

''Just go, lass,'' he muttered. ''I dinnae need to ken the what or the why.''

Maldie tried not to let the ease with which she walked away from the guard make her too cocksure. It was a long way to

the front gates. If too many people spoke to her, or someone
found Jennie, she would never make it. With every step she
took, Maldie prayed that she would not meet up with Balfour,
James, or anyone Jennie was close to.

As she neared the gates, Maldie had to fight the urge to run.
That would certainly draw attention to her. Out of the corner
of her eye she saw Balfour and James talking near the stables
and she took the chance of slightly quickening her step. It was
not until she was yards away from the high walls of Donncoill
that she released the breath she had been holding. Her body
was soaked in sweat and she knew it was not all because she
wore a dark, heavy cloak on a sunny day. She was not surprised
that she was already exhausted. Keeping her cloak clutched
tightly around herself, she began to walk faster. Until she was
on the far side of the village there was still a chance that
someone could discover her.

The moment she stepped into the thick wood bordering the
village fields, Maldie flung off her cloak. She allowed herself
a brief respite to dampen her linen scarf in the cold water of
the brook which meandered along the edge of the wood and
bathe the sweat from her face. Since it was already late in the
afternoon, she knew she would not make it to Dubhlinn before
the sun set. She would have to spend the night in the forest.
That did not frighten her as much as the possibility that Balfour
would be hunting her down. Maldie doubted she would get
much sleep. She would either be listening closely for sounds
of pursuit or running from it.

"And once I am within the walls of Dubhlinn I will be safe
from Balfour," she said, then grimaced. "I will only have to
protect my back against the Beatons who live there. I surely
have gone mad if I thought this would work."

She cursed and flopped onto her back, wishing she was in
the mood to enjoy the shade and the cool grass. For a moment
she decided she was safe enough. She could rest for a little
while and try to think. The wisest thing she could do was get
as far away from Donncoill and Balfour and Dubhlinn and

Beaton as she possibly could. Maldie told herself that again and again, but herself was not feeling inclined to listen.

It was vitally important to her to prove her innocence to Balfour. She was not sure if that was because of her strong pride, or her deep love for the man. Whichever emotion pushed her, she knew she could not and would not leave until the matter was resolved. Either she gave Eric back to the Murrays and proved her innocence that way, or she got caught, Beaton killed her, and the Murrays realized through her death that she had been falsely accused.

There was one other thing that prompted her to continue with her plan. Eric could well be her half brother. If he was a blood relation, then she had a duty to try and rescue him. She also had a deep need to see the truth with her own eyes. If she fled now, ran away from it all, she might never know.

Maldie stood up and brushed herself off. It was clear that she did not want to listen to the voice of wisdom. She started the long walk to Dubhlinn. The gates would be closed tight long before she could get there, and that left her with two choices. She could sleep on the hard ground and pray that it did not rain or grow too cold, or she could return to the tiny cottage of the kindly old couple who had first taken her in and hope that they would do so again. Maldie decided to try her luck with the old couple, although she hated herself for using them.

Life, she mused, had become far too complicated since arriving at Donncoill. She had walked away from her mother's grave with but one plan, to get to Dubhlinn and kill William Beaton. Now she was accused of helping the very man she wanted to kill, had one brother not so secretly in love with her and one who was her lover, and the boy they all fought so hard to save from Beaton's clutches could well be her half brother. If she tried to tell someone about all of this, Maldie was sure that he would never believe her.

Her thoughts turned to young Eric as she walked through the thickening trees. No one at Donncoill had ever had a bad word to say about the boy. She wondered sadly if that admiration and love would continue if he did prove to be Beaton's son. It was one of those secrets that would be best kept, one that should die with anyone who knew it. Unfortunately, she herself was the reason it would soon no longer be a secret. Balfour had seen the mark upon her back, soon he would learn that she was Beaton's daughter, and thus he would learn the truth about the boy he had called brother for so many years. Beaton, she thought angrily, had a true skill at destroying people's lives. She swore that, if Eric was left alone, cast out by Beaton and Murray alike, she would take him with her. It was the least she could do for inadvertently causing his life to shatter, and it would be nice to have family again.

It occurred to her that she had lost that blind need to kill Beaton. Maldie suspected that her hatred for the man still rested in her heart, for it had been nurtured within her by her mother from the day she had been born. It could probably flare up in a blinding glory if she set eyes on the man, but it was no longer the only thing in her heart or her thoughts. Even now, as she marched straight toward the lion's den, she barely thought of revenge at all. It was Balfour and an undoubtedly frightened boy named Eric who held all of her attention. She found it a little strange that thoughts of Balfour, which caused her a deep pain, were more welcome than ones of a well-earned and long overdue execution.

"Weel, mayhap fate will smile upon me," she muttered as she climbed over a moss-covered, fallen tree limb. "Mayhap I will not only free Eric and thus prove my innocence, but be able to rid this land of the curse of William Beaton as weel." She grimaced and softly cursed as a branch tore a small hole in her skirt. "All I must do is get to Dubhlinn in one piece."

Chapter Thirteen

"Where is she?" Balfour yelled, then cursed as the trembling maid grew as pale as the fine white linen sheet she was sprawled on.

He could not believe that Maldie had slipped away beneath their very noses, but that appeared to be exactly what she had done. Intending to speak to her one more time, and ruefully admitting that he simply wished to see her, he had brought her her evening meal. When the guard had told him that she had fallen ill, he had been concerned. But, as the man unlatched the door, he complained about how Jennie had never returned with the things she had rushed away to get, and Balfour's concern had turned to alarm. He was infuriated but not completely surprised when he had entered the room to find a barely conscious Jennie sitting up in bed and clutching her head. He had bellowed insults at the guard, then bellowed for James, and was now bellowing at the poor terrified maid. His lack of control was getting him nowhere and he waved James over to the side of the bed.

"I am about to scare the child to death," he said, stepping

back and letting James take his place. "Ye tend to her and see what ye can find out."

"Aye, ye need to calm yourself," agreed James as he checked the bruise on the girl's jaw.

"What has happened?" demanded Nigel from the doorway.

"Beside some fool dragging his crippled arse across the hall?" Balfour grumbled as he quickly moved to help Nigel over to a chair set next to the fireplace. "Maldie has slipped away."

"Ah, so the lass did escape ye." Nigel could not keep his pleasure over that out of his voice, and he shrugged when Balfour glared at him.

"Did ye ken what she was planning to do?"

"Nay, I but suspected it, and, unlike you, I dinnae act upon suspicion alone."

"Ye didnae want to. Weel, this proves all of my suspicions."

"Does it?"

"She has fled. She would only do that if she was guilty."

"Aye? Mayhap she did it to get away from you." Nigel smiled coldly when Balfour paled slightly. "Ye accuse her of spying and murder without proof, and expect her to linger here to see what madness will next sieze you? Nay, she did what any other person would do—ran as fast as she could. After all, if ye accuse her and imprison her without proof, might ye not hang her next?"

"I would ne'er have hanged her. Nay, not e'en if she had proven to be guilty," Balfour said quietly. "Maldie should have kenned that."

"After the way ye have behaved these last few days, I think the lass felt that she didnae ken ye at all." Nigel looked at James when the man stepped over to them. "Did Jennie finally find her tongue?"

"Aye," James replied. "It seems that Maldie feigned some woman's illness and sent for the lass. Then, when Jennie came in to tend to her, Maldie hit her. The poor maid recalls naught after that."

"What about Duncan, that fool of a guard I set outside of

the door?'' Balfour asked, briefly looking around for the man only to find that Duncan had slipped away the moment James had finished speaking with him.

"He says he let Jennie in and thought he had let Jennie out." James shook his head and laughed softly. "The poor mon was so afeared that one of the lasses would say too much about a *woman's ailment* that he didnae pay much heed. Once pressed he realized that Jennie wasnae wearing a cloak when she went in, but she was when she came out. Maldie was a clever lass. Ere Duncan had a moment to look closely at her, she spoke of needing things for a woman's bleeding time. He didnae let her say much but nearly pushed her down the hall.''

Balfour stared at Nigel and James, aghast when the two men laughed. They seemed uncaring or unaware of the consequences of Maldie's escape. If she was guilty of all he had accused her of, and he prayed he was wrong, she was headed straight for Dubhlinn to tell Beaton the wealth of information she had gathered. If she was innocent, she was out there roaming the countryside, alone and with little or no provisions. Neither circumstance was something to laugh about.

"I am pleased that ye can find enjoyment in Maldie's cleverness, but have ye thought of what happens now?" he finally demanded.

"We search for her or we leave her be," James replied.

"If she is the spy we feared she was, she is running for Dubhlinn to fill Beaton's ears with who kens how many of our secrets." He nodded when James grimaced.

"She is no spy," Nigel snapped.

"She came from nowhere, she told us nothing, and she was verra interested in our fight with Beaton. Too interested," Balfour said.

"Aye, laddie," James agreed. "She left too many questions unanswered."

"Mayhap the answers werenae any of our business," Nigel said. "She is a bastard and her mother was obviously a whore. That is not a life one wishes to talk about."

"I ken it," Balfour said, rubbing the back of his neck. "I

wasnae asking for every sordid detail. All I wished was some tiny bit of information that I could have one of my men go and affirm. Some little thing that would prove she was what she said she was, who she said she was.''

''And if she was who she said she was and so was her mother, what do ye think the people in her village would say about her? Do ye think they would just say aye, she lived here and it sounds as if ye hold the Maldie we kenned? Nay, if her mother was what she said she was, those people would have talked our mon's ear off, filling it with poisonous gossip and righteous indignation over the low morals of some people. Ye ken what village people can be like. Mayhap she just didnae want us to ken the whole ugly truth, or hear the vicious lies that would be told.''

Balfour sighed and nodded. ''I had wondered on that, but such proof was needed. Do ye really think I wanted to lock her up? Aye, or really wanted her to be one of Beaton's minions working to destroy us? 'Tis the verra last thing I wished, yet I had to consider it. The last time we stood against Beaton we lost good men to his trickery. I couldnae afford to ignore this, to just hope that I was right to trust her.''

''Ye are blinded by your debt to her,'' James said gently.

''A debt ye should share. 'Tis nay only my life she saved either. A few of the men she tended to could easily have died from their wounds or, as we now ken, from Grizel's murderous attentions. She *heals* people,'' Nigel stressed. ''She oftimes worked until she was exhausted to help people o'ercome their wounds or illnesses. How could ye think that she could show such compassion if she was working for Beaton?''

''There is no gain to be made in discussing this any further,'' Balfour said. ''We will ne'er agree. Howbeit, innocent or not, the lass is out there in the dark alone and without any provisions.''

''Are ye sure she has no provisions?''

''Aye, for she had no opportunity to gather any and I dinnae think she would have risked staying here long enough to grab some once she got out of this room.''

"Which means that she is already far away, so why bother trying to catch her?"

"Because until I have proof that she is not working for Beaton, I cannae let her run about free with all she kens about us and Donncoill. If she takes such information to Beaton, we will not only lose the battle to free Eric, but we could lose our lands as weel. Until this is all over and Eric is safely home, I must ken where Maldie is and that she is securely locked away, deprived of any chance to tell that bastard anything."

"Weel, we cannae begin the search for her now," James said when Nigel fell into a sullen silence. "We must wait until full light before we hie after the lass."

"Just promise me that ye willnae hurt her," Nigel asked, looking from James to Balfour and back ayain.

"I would ne'er hurt Maldie," Balfour swore. "And whate'er men join in the hunt for her, they will be told that she isnae to be hurt, not e'en bruised."

"Weel, then, go run after her and drag her back here, but ye will pardon me my smugness when she proves to be innocent and ye prove to be a fool."

Balfour leaned against the parapet and stared at the sky, impatiently waiting for the sun to rise. He had not slept and had had very little to eat. His emotions were too fiercely confused for him to rest. He was terrified that Beaton would soon know enough to totally defeat them, and that Maldie was out there wandering the land with no food, no water, no blanket, and no protection. Even now he could not make up his mind if she was guilty or innocent.

What troubled him most was that, even if he found her and brought her back to Donncoill, he could never hold her again. If she was innocent, he had shown her that he could not trust her, and that would surely kill any feeling she had for him. Maldie was a very proud woman and he had treated her as if she was the lowest sort of traitor, implying that she was little more than a whore using her body to pry secrets out of the enemy. If she was guilty, he could never trust her again, could not allow her to stay near enough to him to sway him again.

"Laddie, ye shall wear that wee brain out if ye continue to spend all your hours thinking o'er things that have no answer," James said as he moved up next to Balfour, yawned, and scratched his stomach. "Ye havenae slept at all, have ye?"

"Nay. I paced the floor and stared at the walls of my bed-chamber. Now I stare at the sky and curse the sun for being such a slow-moving fellow."

James laughed and shook his head. "Ye should have rested, for we may have us a verra long day."

"Weel, aye, there is a lot of land to search and Maldie is a wee lass. She may not be so easy to find."

"There is that. There is also the fact that we may have to rush to battle."

"Why should we?"

"Why? Ye clearly havenae been spending all night thinking thoughts to help your clan or save your brother." James reached out and patted Balfour on the arm when the man flushed guiltily. "Nay, dinnae take that as a rebuke. I understand how such a bonnie lass can consume a mon's thoughts."

"Aye, she did, although I doubt I can recall half of what I thought or if it would make sense if I did, for I am verra confused. Did she flee because she is guilty or because she is furious? Is she running to Beaton or to somewhere else, to those kinsmen she ne'er told us about? Is she the worst sort of whore whom I must toss aside, or will she toss me aside because I have so gravely insulted her it cannae be forgiven? Question after question and no way to answer them, for I dinnae have the most important answer of all—is she working for Beaton?"

"And that is the most important question of all at this moment. There is no way of kenning the truth, but we can no longer wait until we have it. Aye, let us see if we can catch her, but nay for long. And, e'en as we hunt our men should be preparing to march upon Dubhlinn."

"Nigel isnae ready to go to battle."

"He can drag his pretty arse up onto a horse and be at your

side to offer his advice. He shouldnae go at all, but I have allowed him that much for he willnae stay here as he should unless we tie him to his bed. Think, laddie. If that wee lass is a Beaton, she will soon be telling our enemy all of our plans. We must march against him by first light tomorrow if we are to have any hope of catching him by surprise. I would prefer to march ere the sun rises today, but I am nay sure we can be ready so soon."

Balfour slumped against the wall. James was right. They had no more time to plot or ready themselves. If they did not act quickly, they would have to start all over again. By the end of this day, if Maldie was one of Beaton's spies, the man would know all about them and almost all about their battle plan. He had already told her more than he should have before he had begun to have doubts about her. Then he frowned, and an idea began to form in his tired mind.

"Nay, we will not march on Beaton yet."

James gaped at him. "I ken that ye dinnae want the lass to be guilty of what we have accused her of, but ye must at least consider the possibility that she is. If we wait, Beaton will have time to act upon what she will tell him. He will ken all we have said and he will slaughter us."

"He nearly slaughtered us last time because we tried to throw ourselves against his cursed walls. E'en if he hasnae done all he must, he will certainly close his gates and have his men ready to greet us. Trying to breach those walls will kill us all, or at least cull our numbers so badly that he can then come and take Donncoill."

"Weel, aye, mayhap." James grimaced and rubbed a hand over his graying hair. "What choice do we have?"

"We wait and we make a new plan. And I think I already have a good one. I may be verra tired, but it seems like a clever idea. There is one thing Maldie told me—"

"Ye cannae trust what she said, or, rather, ye shouldnae trust in it too much."

"I ken it, but she didnae tell me this in the way that she told us other things about Dubhlinn. This slipped out as she told me another tale, something humorous that had happened to her on a market day at Dubhlinn. I really dinnae believe she was saying it to trick me into anything. 'Twas just talk. Market day at Dubhlinn is three days from now.''

"And how will that help us?"

"By simply waiting three days, we will already have unsettled Beaton. He will expect us to act immediately when Maldie tells him of how we had suspected her. When we dinnae come racing to his gates he will wonder if what she said was true, or if she even understood what she had heard. Beaton has ne'er had much faith in the wit of women. A market day brings a lot of people to a town, a lot of strangers," he added, nodding when James's eyes slowly widened.

James cursed softly and paced the wall for a moment, muttering to himself and rubbing his chin as he thought. "We could slip a lot of men into Dubhlinn, at least into the town and the surrounding area, without Beaton suspecting anything."

"So, ye think it is worth a second look? That there is a plan to be made there?"

"Oh, aye. It may e'en be a better one than we had. Now, let us go and find that lass if we can. This new idea of yours would work e'en better if she hasnae gotten to Dubhlinn to warn Beaton that we plan an attack. Aye, much better indeed if he isnae alert and watching for us."

"Did ye find her?" Nigel demanded, sitting up in bed as Balfour entered his room.

"We saw her," Balfour replied as he poured himself a large tankard of hearty wine and took a deep drink.

"What do ye mean—ye saw her?"

"Just that. We saw her—running straight for Dubhlinn."

"Nay." Nigel vigorously shook his head. "Nay, I willnae believe it."

"Do ye think *I* want to believe it?" Balfour snapped, then took another drink to try and calm the emotions raging inside of him.

"Ye already did or ye wouldnae have locked her up."

Balfour sighed and shook his head as he sat on the edge of Nigel's bed. "I dinnae ken if it is because ye dinnae listen or ye dinnae want to, but I did what I had to. Somehow Beaton was discovering our little secrets, and since Grizel was no longer able to tell him anything, it had to be someone else. Maldie was the only other one it could be, or, at least, there was a verra strong possibility that it was her. I simply couldnae risk trusting her, no matter how dearly I wished to. Yet, in my heart I prayed that I would be proven wrong. It gives me no pleasure at all to be proven right."

"Nay, she wouldnae take Beaton's side."

"Nigel, she ran straight for Dubhlinn. Three men saw her. More men than that found her tracks leading that way. She left here and walked directly to Dubhlinn. What else can it mean?"

"I dinnae ken," Nigel snapped. "I just cannae feel that she would e'er have anything to do with a mon like Beaton. There is too much kindness in her."

"So I thought."

"There could be an explanation. Aye, it does look as if she is helping Beaton, but we dinnae ken how much and we certainly dinnae ken why. Until I have learned all the reasons, I cannae believe, nay, I *refuse* to believe that the woman who healed me was nay more than a traitorous whore."

It made Balfour wince just to hear the words, even though he had thought them when his men had returned and told him what they had seen. That had been three hours ago. It had taken him that long to calm down enough to come and tell Nigel the bad news. He had not expected Nigel to be so adamant in his refusal to believe it. What made it all the more difficult to listen to him was that he desperately wanted to believe Nigel was right.

"I am eager to feel as ye do, brother, but I dinnae think it would be wise. It is hard enough to think that I have been made a complete fool of. I refuse to hold on to any hope so that she can make me look an even greater fool."

"She cared for you, Balfour. I am sure of it."

"Nay." Balfour jumped to his feet and began to pace the room.

The nearly crippling pain he had felt when his men had told him what they had seen was still there, tearing at his heart like some carrion bird. He knew that, if he allowed it to, this betrayal could destroy him. He did not want to talk about her, did not want to discuss any possibility that she may yet prove innocent even in some small way. He did not want to even think about Maldie, although he suspected that could prove to be impossible. There was a part of him that hated her, hated her for making a fool of him, hated her for betraying him, but especially hated her for making him love her. He still loved her, and he wanted to bury that feeling so deep that it would never be able to rear its head and blind him again.

"I would prefer to talk about the coming battle," he finally said.

"Ye are still going to battle? Hold," he held up his hand when Balfour began to speak. "Now, I dinnae want to believe the lass is working against us, but this news has at least made me see the wisdom of your argument. One has to consider the possibility. If she is with Beaton, she is telling him all of your plans at this verra moment. If ye ride out to battle ye will be slaughtered, for he will ken your every move and be ready for you."

"He will be ready for what I *had* planned to do, but nay for what I am now planning to do."

"There is a new plan?"

"Aye, and e'en James thinks it has an excellent chance of success."

"Do I have a few more days to gather my strength and ride with you?"

"Three. Weel, we will ride out on the morning of the third day, today being the first of the three." Balfour smiled faintly, able to be pleased with his plan despite the pain he was in. "We are going to market, Nigel."

It took Balfour over an hour to explain it all to Nigel, but his brother's enthusiasm for the plan had been uplifting. He felt more confident of victory as he made his way to the great hall. The only dark cloud on his horizon was that Maldie was somewhere inside of Dubhlinn. Balfour prayed he did not find her on the day of the battle. It would be best for all of them if she fled and never returned to the area.

"Nigel didnae want to believe it," said James as Balfour sat down next to him and helped himself to some food.

"Nay. Does that surprise you?" Balfour asked.

"Not as much as it should." He shook his head. "I had hoped that he would see reason now. He has been most unforgiving about how ye treated the girl."

"Oh, he is more understanding of that, does in truth see the need to be cautious now, that one cannae always rely only on what one feels. Now all he prays for is that there is a good reason for what she has done, one that will allow him to forgive her."

"Is that what ye hope for?"

"I dinnae ken. Mayhap. At the moment I am trying verra hard not to think of the lass at all. Thoughts of her only rouse my fury and remind me that she has played me for the greatest of fools."

"Then I will say only one last thing about her. Try to calm that fury ere we go to battle. There is a chance ye will see her at Dubhlinn, and it would be unwise to act with heedless anger. Not only will ye then be distracted from the battle, which could prove fatal, but ye may do something ye will later regret."

"Are ye also about to tell me that there may be a good reason for what she has done?"

"There could be. Aye, she ran to Dubhlinn, but we dinnae yet ken exactly why she did that. I but wish ye to nay leap to judgment. If ye allow yourself to think that there may be some reason, some opportunity for forgiveness, then ye willnae go into a rage if ye see her at Dubhlinn."

"Ah, I see. Ye are afraid that, if I see her, I will hie after her, leaving my men leaderless. That I will run her down and cut her down in some vain attempt to restore my monhood and bruised pride."

James shrugged, smiling faintly at the sarcastic tone of Balfour's words. "Aye, mayhap."

"Weel, dinnae fear. Fool that I am, e'en now I ken that I could ne'er hurt one unruly hair on her head. What I am hoping is that she really does have the strong instinct of survival that I think she has, and will be off and running the moment the battle begins."

"And speaking of the forthcoming battle, what did Nigel think of the new plan?"

"He thought so weel of it that I left his room feeling quite confident of success."

"Not too confident, I pray," James drawled.

Balfour laughed softly. "Not heedlessly so. Nay, I just feel that, for the first time in thirteen long, bloody years, we have a chance of ending this feud."

"Then, at least one good thing will come out of this mess. That and having wee Eric back with us."

"Aye," was all Balfour could say, and he turned his attention to his meal and talk of the battle ahead of them.

It was not until he was alone in his room that he allowed himself to think of Maldie. In truth, he had little choice, for she pushed her way into his mind as brazenly as she had stepped up to him on the road to Dubhlinn. He sank down onto the edge of his bed and buried his face in his hands.

He felt as if someone had died, so powerful was his grief. In a strange way, he realized, it was as if she had died. The woman he had thought she was had never existed. It had all been a lie. He had been taken for a fool, shamed by his own trusting nature. What he had seen as the great love of his life had been no more than a well-played act by a skilled whore in Beaton's service.

Chapter Fourteen

Maldie cursed as she felt the thorns of the bramble thicket she hid in poke into her. It was already the middle of the day and she still had not reached the village outside of Dubhlinn. For hours all she had been able to do was scurry through the wood and low brush for a few yards, and then quickly hide again. Murrays were everywhere she looked. She could not believe they would come so close to Dubhlinn. It was clear that Balfour truly thought she was one of Beaton's slinking dogs, and that hurt. She was also furious at him because his groundless suspicions were the reason that she had spent so long in a slow torturous crawl toward Dubhlinn.

She looked toward Dubhlinn and recognized the line of trees mere yards away. They marked the far end of the fields around the village. Instinct told her that the Murrays had gone as far as they would go in their search for her. They were already risking being seen by a Beaton, any closer and that risk became a certainty. All she had to do was get to those trees, and she would be safe.

For a little while longer she watched the three Murray men who had sent her diving into her extremely uncomfortable hiding place. They rode back and forth, never crossing some line that only they could see. Maldie knew that that was the point where they would go no further. Cautiously, she began to inch her way out of the bramble thicket. She could run fast; all she needed was a minute when they were not looking in her direction.

There was, she admitted, a problem or two with her plan. She could never outrun a horse if they decided to risk it all and run her down. A skilled archer could easily stop her, although she could not believe that Balfour would order her killed. Then again, she mused as she crouched behind the thicket waiting for her chance to run, Balfour had done several things lately that she had not thought him capable of, so she should probably not be so confident in her opinion of him. The final problem was that she would be seen to be running straight for Dubhlinn. The men searching for her already suspected where she was going or they would not be there, harassing her every step of the way, and she was sure that she had not covered her tracks very well. Once they saw her, however, they would have proof and so would Balfour, she thought sadly. She quickly pushed aside that moment of sadness, telling herself that she was going to enjoy proving them all wrong, as she bolted for the trees.

The cry of discovery that cut through the air sent her heart into her throat. For a brief moment she heard the pounding hooves of horses in pursuit and feared that she had been wrong, that the Murrays were indeed willing to risk all just to stop her. Then there was a lot of shouting and the sound of a hard chase came to an abrupt halt. She waited in cold terror for an arrow to slam into her back, but it never came. Once inside the trees she stumbled to a halt, clung to a tree as she struggled to catch her breath, and looked toward the Murrays. For one long, silent moment, she stared at them and they stared at her, while she waited tensely to see if they would do anything. Then they turned their horses sharply and galloped back to Donncoill.

"And back to Balfour," she whispered, slumping against the rough bark of the tree for a moment.

She was exhausted and she had barely begun her adventure. Ahead of her lay the hunt for Eric and trying not to be discovered while doing it. Then she and the boy had to escape and get all the way back to Donncoill without being recaptured. As she started toward the village, Maldie wondered why her obviously disordered mind had not given her a less impossible way to prove her innocence.

"Lassie, what has happened to ye?"

Maldie smiled wearily at the tiny gray-haired lady who stood in the low doorway of her tiny wattle and daub cottage gaping at her. Eleanor Beaton was clearly shocked by her tattered, muddy condition, but there was no condemnation in the woman's light gray eyes. Concern softened the woman's lined face as she tugged Maldie inside and, although she needed the help, Maldie felt like the basest of traitors. She was there to help destroy the woman's laird, to throw Eleanor's tidy little life into complete chaos.

All the while Eleanor helped Maldie clean up and put on the gown she had left behind the last time she had fled Dubhlinn, the woman kept up a constant stream of talk. By the time Maldie found herself seated at Eleanor's tiny, well-scrubbed table, she was sure she had heard every tiny scrap of gossip about Dubhlinn and all of its people. When Eleanor sat down across from her, her work-worn hands clasped on top of the table and her bright eyes fixed firmly upon her, Maldie had to laugh.

"Ye are fairly bursting with questions, arenae ye?" she asked, grinning at the little woman.

Eleanor grinned back briefly and nodded. "Aye, but I ken that ye like to keep your own counsel."

Maldie sighed and tried to put some order into her thoughts as she chewed on the bread Eleanor had given her. "I am verra sorry that I just left ye without even a word of thanks."

"What else could ye do, dearling, with those men chasing after ye like starving hounds after a hare?"

"Ye kenned that?"

"Aye. These eyes may be old, but they still see a lot. I just prayed that wherever ye had run to, ye were safer than ye were in this sad place." Eleanor shook her head. "Matters worsen here by the hour. I begin to think the laird has truly lost his mind, that mayhap the disease which twists his body has twisted what little wit he had too."

"I didnae e'en ken that he was ill."

" 'Tis kept a verra close secret, lass. The mon fears all who live around him, and with good reason. There are many who hunger after this land."

Maldie wondered how Nigel had found out about the man's illness if it was so secret, then decided it was probably best if she did not know, for it undoubtedly concerned a woman. "What has your laird done?"

"Stolen a child from the Murray clan. As if that isnae shameful enough, he has stolen the verra child he set out upon the hillside to die years ago. The Murrays have already tried to take him back, but, alas, they failed." Tears sparkled in the woman's eyes. "I lost my beloved Robert on that sad day."

"Oh, Eleanor." Maldie reached out to clasp the woman's hands in hers. "I am so verra sorry. He was a good, sweet mon. The Murrays?"

"Nay. 'Twas a Beaton mon who cut him down. Those low hirelings our laird surrounds himself with dinnae ken who we are, cannae tell a Beaton from a Murray. My mon saw the Murrays retreat from the field and was walking back to our wee hidey-hole to tell me it was safe, when one of our laird's dogs saw him. They cut him down ere the other villagers could stop them. Robert was an old, crippled mon who had no sword, and yet they killed him. I curse them all. I ken we have been told that the Murrays are our enemy, heartless bastards who wish to steal all we own and leave none of us alive to squawk about it, but I cannae believe that they would have killed my sweet Robert."

"Nay, never." Maldie realized she had spoken with a suspicious firmness when Eleanor's eyes narrowed.

"Lass, ye arenae a Murray, are ye?"

"Now that is a question I can answer with complete honesty—nay. I am truly a Kirkcaldy, although ye may find it difficult to get one of them to admit kinship to this bastard child. But, dinnae fear, ye arenae harboring one of the enemy."

Eleanor shrugged her thin shoulders. "I wouldnae care, but I would be afraid for meself and all of my kin. Our laird found a Murray mon in the keep and killed him. He has since hanged two other men because he thought they, too, worked for the Murrays. If ye e'en look at the mon wrong ye risk a hanging or, God forbid, the horrible death that poor Murray fellow endured. Some of the villagers swear that they could hear his screams in the night." Eleanor shivered and rubbed her thin arms.

"This may not have been a good time for ye to return here, lass," she continued. "A dark cloud hangs o'er us and the wolves are drawing near. I swear our laird makes a new enemy with every word he spits out of his rotting mouth. And, now, this madness. Trying to claim as his son a child he tossed out years ago, threw aside like scraps he feeds his hounds? He claimed far and wide, and verra loudly, that his wife had betrayed him with the old laird of the Murrays and that the child was a Murray bastard, fit only to feed the wild beasts that roam the forests. Now we are all to believe that this poor lad is his heir. That sad child willnae live one day past the laird's death, and I am fair sure of that."

"What has he done with the boy?" Maldie asked, fighting to keep any hint of her keen interest out of her voice.

"Sorcha, who works in the kitchens at the keep, says that the laddie was too spirited for Beaton's liking, and so has been thrown into the dungeons until he comes to his senses." Eleanor's voice dropped to a whisper of amazement. "She said the boy laughed when Beaton tried to call him his son, said that he would rather be the spawn of the devil hisself. Beaton then said something insulting about the old Murray laird, and the boy attacked him. I fear the laddie suffered a beating for that."

Inwardly, Maldie grimaced. That did not bode well for how the boy would take the news if he did prove to be a Beaton. "But the lad is alright?"

"Aye. Beaton certainly doesnae want the lad crippled or dead, just quiet and tame. Why are ye so interested in the boy?"

Maldie shrugged and busied herself trying to cut a neat slice off the block of hard cheese on the table. "One cannae help but feel some sympathy for the boy."

"I may be old, lassie, but my wits are still sharp. Aye, and my nose is sharp enough to smell out a lie when it wafts by." Eleanor held up her hand when Maldie started to speak. "Nay, dinnae tell me a thing. Just answer me one wee question— should I be making sure that my wee hidey-hole is clean and comfortable?"

"Aye." Maldie smiled sadly. "I will take a risk and tell ye one other thing. Make sure that all the ones ye can trust and care about are ready to flee to their little warrens at the first alarum. Aye, at the verra first hint of trouble."

"The Murrays are going to try and get that boy back again."

Maldie smiled. "I thought ye didnae wish to hear about such things."

Eleanor chuckled. "Nay, I dinnae, but, being the curious old woman that I am, I also want to hear it all. Ignore this old fool. If I pester ye with questions just remind me that, sometimes, 'tis far safer to ken naught."

"I will, for I dearly wish ye to stay safe and alive. Now, I have only one question, but ye need not answer if ye feel it will put ye in danger in any way. Where is the dungeon inside of Dubhlinn? When last I was here I ne'er did find that out."

"The door to it is in one of the walls of the great hall, set just below a large shield with a rampant boar on it."

"How apt," Maldie drawled, and Eleanor giggled.

Suddenly the woman took Maldie's hands in hers and gently squeezed them "Be careful, lass. Be verra, verra careful. Ye are a brave lass, far braver than any I have met before and I have met a lot of women in my long life, but bravery cannae stop a sword or a fist. Walk softly, keep your bonny head down, say little, and ne'er look a mon in the eye.''

An hour later, all the way to the gates of Dubhlinn, Maldie carefully repeated Eleanor's advice. It was very good advice, she could see that clearly, but she was not sure she would have the wisdom to make use of it, not unless she thought about it carefully. It was all completely against her nature. Eleanor was telling her how to be totally self-effacing, and that was something Maldie had never done.

Not look a man in the eye? She would not hesitate to spit in it if he deserved it. Keep her head down? After a brief attack of shame at a young age when she had first discovered what her mother was, she had been cowed, but she had quickly refused to ever bow her head to anyone again. As far as saying little, she had always had a problem keeping quiet, especially when she felt something needed to be said. Eleanor was a dear woman who cared about her and had given her some very sound advice, but Maldie suspected that the only piece of it she would be able to follow was the one that told her to walk softly.

''Weel, my bonny lassie, where have ye been?''

Maldie cursed softly as she heard that chillingly familiar rasping voice. A fat-fingered and very filthy hand was curled around her arm and the man turned her around to face him. Maldie wondered yet again where, in all of Scotland, Beaton had found such an ugly, squat man. She was not one to judge a person by appearance alone, but she knew from sad experience that this man was ugly all the way through. He was one of the reasons she had fled Dubhlinn long before she had wanted to.

''I am a healing woman,'' she replied. ''I go where I am needed, and sometimes it takes a very long time for someone to mend.''

''I had wondered if ye had run away from me.''

''Nay, I run away from no mon.'' She inwardly cringed when he rubbed his hand up and down her arm.

"Oh ho, a spirited lass. I like a wee bit of fire in my women."

She tried to pull her arm free of his hold but he just tightened his grip, smiling at her and revealing a mouthful of rotting and broken teeth. "I havenae time to flirt with ye, sir. I came to Dubhlinn to see if anyone has need of my skills."

"I do."

The sharp-nosed woman who spoke tried first to just push the man away, but he would not let go of Maldie's arm. Clenching her hand into a fist, the woman brought it down hard on the man's wrist. He bellowed in pain and released Maldie. The way the man looked at the woman before he stomped away made Maldie shiver. She hoped the woman had the sense to watch her back.

"I dinnae think it was wise to make that mon angry," she murmured, feeling a need to warn the tall, thin woman.

"George will do naught to me unless he can catch me alone in a dark corner, and I will be certain that he ne'er does. He is afraid of my mon." The woman stuck out one long, boney hand. "I am Mary, Mistress Kirkcaldy."

Maldie shook her hand. "What do ye have need of me for?"

"My son is ill." Even as Mary replied she began to drag Maldie along toward the keep.

Maldie carefully questioned the woman as they made their way to the rear of the keep. It sounded as if her child had little more than a mild chill and a touch of the wind, so Maldie allowed herself a small twinge of satisfaction. The need to tend to the child would give her a good reason to come and go from the keep. She did not need to worry the woman by treating the child as if he was close to death either. All she needed was a few close looks at the great hall to see when it was most in use and by whom, just enough to tell her when she could slip down to the dungeon unseen and, if not immediately free Eric, at least visit with him.

The woman's small son was huddled in a small alcove at the back of the huge kitchen. Maldie dosed him and calmed him, knowing that sleep was really the best and only cure for what ailed him. Nevertheless, sometimes a small taste of medicine made the one who swallowed it think they were being healed. The little boy's stomach pain began to ease very quickly. The way Mary and her son stared at her with such open admiration made Maldie feel uncomfortable, especially since she was using them to get what she needed. Maldie silently promised that she would find a reason to send Mary and her child to Eleanor in the village as soon as she found out what she needed to know. With a battle coming they would be a great deal safer there.

After accepting a gift of food from Beaton's larder, Maldie slowly made her way out of the kitchen. A lot of people greeted her, some thanking her again for healing their ills or injuries, and some just wished to gossip with someone who had traveled outside of Dubhlinn. Maldie quickly realized when she had first arrived at Dubhlinn, that, as a healer and a woman, she had been considered no threat and had been allowed a great deal of freedom in and around the keep. It still angered her that she had been driven away by foolish, lustful men before she had learned all she needed to. This time would be different. She had no intention of leaving until she had found Eric and rescued him from Beaton.

A very young maid walking to the great hall heavily ladened with food gratefully accepted Maldie's offer of help. Only half-listening to the girl's chatter, Maldie looked over the huge room very carefully. She also noticed that, as soon as the food began to be laid on the tables, the hall filled with people very quickly. The time around and during a meal was obviously not a good time to slip down to the dungeon unseen.

As she walked back to Eleanor's cottage, Maldie briefly felt overwhelmed. The task she had assumed was a huge one and the chance of her succeeding was very slim. She straightened her shoulders and pushed aside the encroaching sense of failure. Eric was in danger, and the boy could easily prove to be her half brother. If Balfour truly believed that she was a spy for Beaton, then he would also assume that she had told the man everything she knew about the battle plans of the Murrays and quickly change them. That meant that she did not know when, how, or where Balfour and his men would come for his brother. Eleanor had said that Beaton did not want Eric badly hurt or killed, but the woman had also said that her laird was going mad. She could not leave the boy's fate in Beaton's hands. There was also the matter of her innocence, which she had to prove.

"Child, I began to worry about you," Eleanor called from her doorway, pulling Maldie back from her dark thoughts.

"I am fine, Eleanor," Maldie replied. "There was a young boy who needed some tending to. He had the wind and a tiny touch of the ague," she continued as the old woman pulled her inside of her home.

Eleanor nodded as she began to set out the evening meal. "Ye have the touch, lass. 'Tis truly God's gift to you."

"So I have been told." She set the small bag of food Mary had given her down on the table. "And here is a gift from the lad's grateful mother."

Maldie smiled at Eleanor's delight over the cheese and the slab of salted pork. Beaton's larder had been full to overflowing with such riches, so many that he would have to have a grand feast every night for months before he used it all. Maldie suspected that there was a lot lost through spoilage. The man obviously had a deep fear of being starved out of his keep during a long siege, but it seemed a heartless crime to let food rot when his people could use it.

"Did ye find out how that boy fares?" Eleanor asked as she reverently placed the food in a small chest set near the alcove that Maldie slept in.

"He is still locked up tightly in Beaton's dungeons, still refusing to calmly accept Beaton as his father and the Murrays as—how does Beaton word it?—oh, aye, as low, thieving, fornicating bastards."

Eleanor giggled and nodded. "Aye, I have heard that one. The mon should be verra wary where he points his filthy finger and attempts to act more pious than they. Beaton used to mount any poor lass who couldnae run faster than he did. Now e'en I can run faster than the mon, and I am nay sure his wee pintle is working as it should.''

"Eleanor," Maldie gasped, amused and a little shocked by the old woman's words.

"Weel, 'tis true. Some folk think that whate'er the disease is that is rotting him away, it is a punishment from God. 'Tis a puzzle to me that ye havenae been called to go and have a wee look at him. He has tried some verra foul salves in a vain attempt to stop or cure his ailment. He should have learned that ye are a healing woman by now and wished to see if ye have anything he hasnae yet smeared upon himself.''

"Nay, he hasnae called me to him at all, not once since I have been here or when I stayed here before. Either no one has thought to tell him about me, or he took one look at me and decided I was not what I say I am. I have had a lot of trouble with that sort of thing happening to me of late," she muttered, thinking of Balfour and then quickly pushing him from her thoughts.

"Weel, ye do look like a child, dearling. Tiny and delicate. Ye have to forgive people if they sometimes dinnae think ye have the years in ye to have learned so much.''

"I ken it. And I still have a great deal left to learn." She stretched and stood up. "I think I must go bed. I am verra tired. The journey here wasnae an easy one, and it wore me out more than I realized.''

Maldie was startled when Eleanor suddenly stood up and embraced her, clinging to her tightly. She patted the woman's back and felt the woman's fear. It was so strong that it even overpowered her grief for her beloved Robert.

"What is wrong? Why are ye frightened?" she asked.

Eleanor stepped back a little and smiled faintly. "Ye always ken what I am feeling. Methinks ye have more gifts than your healing touch. At times, 'tis as if ye can see into a person's heart.''

"Aye, I do seem able to sense things. Howbeit, it takes no

great gift to ken that ye didnae answer my question. Ye are
frightened, Eleanor, verra frightened. Why? Have ye heard
something, some warning of trouble? Mayhap I can help.''

''What I am frightened of is what ye are about to do.''

Maldie tensed and knew the fear she now felt was her own.
She had thought she had been careful, measuring her every
step and watching her every word so that she would not give
away any hint of what she was about to do. Somehow Eleanor
had guessed something, and if *she* had, someone else might
have, too.

''What I am about to do? I dinnae ken what ye mean.''

''Ye dinnae have to tell me and ye can cease feeling so
uncertain. I really dinnae ken much, just that whate'er ye are
here for, it has to do with that poor wee lad that Beaton has
locked away. Ye do what ye must, lass, and be assured that I
will ne'er betray ye by word or deed. All I ask is that ye be
verra careful.''

''I am always careful, Eleanor,'' she said gently.

''Nay, dinnae just mouth words to soothe me. I mean this.
Be verra careful. I have an uneasy feeling about all of this. I
have suffered enough grief this year, losing my beloved Robert
as I did. Please, I cannae bear to lose ye, too. Ye are like my
own child.''

Maldie was deeply touched and hugged the woman. She
loved the little old woman and was pleased to discover that
she was cared for in return. It was sad that, after such a short
time, she could share a bond with Eleanor that she had never
shared with her own mother. The difference, she realized, was
the kindhearted Eleanor. Eleanor knew how to care about people, even ragged young women who showed up at her doorstep
with little more than the clothes on their backs.

Margaret Kirkcaldy had truly cared about no one, not even
her own daughter. It was a hard revelation to accept, but Maldie
forced herself to look at it. If her mother had any feelings, they
were for the various men in her life, all of whom had treated
her shabbily. Maldie was no longer sure even that those times

her mother had been crying about loving some heartless man had been real. What Margaret had always craved, the only thing that had given her any pleasure, had been the attention given her by men, the flattery and the gifts.

There had always been a bitterness in Margaret, the first seed undoubtedly planted by Beaton. As the years had passed and her health and beauty had begun to fade, the flattering lovers slowly becoming just men with an ache in their groins and a few coins in their pockets, that bitterness had become deeper and harsher, possessing Margaret completely. Maldie could not help but wonder if she had been sent to murder Beaton not to avenge lost honor, but stung vanity.

She hastily shook those thoughts away as she kissed Eleanor on the cheek and went to her bed. Her mother may well have been at fault for a lot of the things that happened to her after Beaton had deserted her, but it was still Beaton who set her mother on that path of debasement and destitution. If he had not seduced Margaret away from her family, she would have probably been married off to some laird and suffered her unhappiness within the holy bonds of matrimony, all her children legitimate, and with no need to sell her body just to have enough food to survive.

There was a part of Maldie, a large part, that wanted to confess everything to Eleanor. She really needed someone to talk to, to discuss it all with, from her growing doubts about why her mother had sent her on a mission of vengeance to her concerns about young Eric. Maldie knew that Eleanor would listen with sympathy and understanding, but she had to fight the temptation. If anything went wrong, if she was captured by Beaton either trying to save Eric or trying to fulfill her vow to her mother, she wanted Eleanor to be able to honestly swear that she knew nothing about it.

Although she was so tired her whole body ached, Maldie found sleep slow in coming. She knew that the dawn would mark an important day. She could not shake the conviction that tomorrow she would act. She was just not sure if it was going to be against Beaton or for Eric, or even if that was one and the same. As she closed her eyes she wished that the insight which was making her so certain of these things would give her some hint as to whether she would face victory or bitter defeat.

Chapter Fifteen

Inside of the huge kitchens of Dubhlinn it was hot, and the air was choked with the smell of cooking food and unwashed bodies. Maldie wiped the sweat from Mary's little boy's forehead and frowned darkly. She had expected to see far more improvement in the boy. Little Thomas was not so desperately ill he was in any real danger, but he would not get better quickly under such dire conditions. She had already decided to send Mary and Thomas to Eleanor for safety, and Eleanor was more than willing to take them into her tiny, clean home. Now she knew she could tell them that it was for the health of the little boy with complete honesty.

"He isnae going to die, is he?" Mary whispered as she wrung her hands and looked at her child with tears clouding her eyes. "He is my only bairn. God has already chosen to take three to His bosom. I pray He hasnae chosen this one, too."

"Nay, he isnae going to die," Maldie reassured her. "I am verra sorry that my frown has alarmed you. I wasnae scowling o'er his ill health, but o'er the ill surroundings he must lie in.

Ye need to get him out of here, away from the smothering heat and the smells.''

"But where can I take him? This is where I abide near all the day and night.''

"I have a friend in the village, Eleanor Beaton, a recent widow.''

"I ken the woman. Nay weel, but I have spoken to her a few times.''

"She will take ye in until the boy is strong and hale again. 'Tis a nice, clean wee cottage with a wee bit of land, so that the boy can sit out there when God blesses us with a wee bit of sun.''

"That would be lovely and most kind of her.'' Mary lightly ruffled the boy's soft chestnut curls. "Ye are verra certain that she willnae mind?''

"Verra certain,'' Maldie replied. "Ye take the laddie there as soon as ye can and I promise ye, he will begin to look hale and happy in a verra short time.''

Maldie smiled as the woman immediately picked her child up, muttered a brief but heartfelt thank you, and left. The health of her only child was obviously of far more importance to Mary than any of the other duties she had. It was nice to see such maternal love, and Maldie was a little ashamed of the brief twinge of jealousy she felt. As she left the heat and stench of the kitchen she decided that she needed to stop grieving for what she had never had and learn to control her childish envy.

When Maldie caught sight of George just outside of the doors to the great hall, she cursed and pressed herself into a tiny shadowed alcove cut into the wall beneath the stairs. The man had been lurking around every corner since the moment she had arrived at the keep. After two long hours of trying to elude him and his unwanted attentions, she was tempted to do him some serious harm.

"Why are ye cowering in the shadows, lassie?'' asked a soft deep voice to her left.

She cursed under her breath again and looked at the man who slouched against the wall next to her. This man was at least pleasant to look upon, she mused, being tall, lean, with long brown hair, and soft brown eyes that painfully reminded her of Balfour's. Maldie was swiftly growing to dislike men, however. She had very important things to do and lusty men seemed to be impeding her at every turn. Dubhlinn clearly needed some more women.

"I am hiding from that foul-smelling lump of a mon down there." She nodded toward George.

"Ah, George. Aye, he is hard on the eyes and the nose. I am Douglas." He thrust out his hand.

"And I am Maldie." She briefly shook his hand. "Now, I should like to continue with these idle pleasantries and say that I am pleased to meet you, but, today, that would be a lie. I havenae been here verra long, little more than a day, and I am already sick to death of men, false flatteries, and guiling smiles."

He grinned but did not go away, ignoring her blunt invitation to leave her alone with high good humor. "I havenae flattered you."

Maldie was surprised into a laugh. "And, thus, with but a few words, he delivers the fatal blow to my poor wee vanity." She looked back toward George and muttered a few harsh insults. "Doesnae he have any duties to perform?"

"Aye, he bellows and waves his sword about whene'er our laird feels threatened."

"Ah, the laird. I havenae set eyes upon the mon yet. Not the last time I passed this way or this time."

"He doesnae show his face verra often. 'Tis for the best, I am thinking."

"Oh. So, he *is* verra ill. There have been whispers about it. Mayhap I can help him. I am a healer."

Douglas nodded. "I have heard that. A good one, too, so all say. The mon is beyond healing, lass. About all the good one can say is that he isnae a leper, although he looks as poorly as any I have e'er seen." He grimaced. "Ye cannae stomach looking at the mon when his skin is at its worst. Then it eases away for a wee while. But it always returns and is usually worse than before. 'Tis as if he rots from the inside. He willnae survive much longer. Weel, now that I think on it, none who kenned of his illness thought he would live this long, either.''

"How long has he been ill?"

"Three years."

"Then, mayhap, he just has some ailment of the skin." She smiled slightly when his eyes widened. " 'Tis nay only lepers who suffer such things, although I believe theirs is much more than an illness of the flesh. Believe me when I tell ye that I have seen some stomach-turning skin ailments. If your laird had something that was truly fatal, I think he would have died by now, dinnae ye?''

Maldie felt a little relieved and was briefly afraid that some blind, foolish part of her actually cared for the man. She looked deep into her heart and, although there was the stirring of distaste over her plan to kill the man, there was certainly no sense of kinship with him. The relief she felt was because, if she got a chance to fulfill the vow she made to her mother, she would not be killing a man who was already dying, one who might even be too frail to defend himself against anyone. From the moment she had heard talk of Beaton's serious illness, she had feared that she would face the hard choice of killing a man on his deathbed, or breaking the oath she had sworn to her dying mother.

"Why are ye so interested in our laird's health?" Douglas asked.

"I am a healing woman. Ye are a warrior, are ye not? Do not all battles and weapons stir your interest, and nay just the ones ye have fought in or owned?"

"Aye, but heed me weel, lass. This is nay a good time for anyone to be asking too many questions at Dubhlinn, not even a wee bonny lass such as yourself.'' He nodded toward the doors of the great hall. ''Your besotted courtier has left.''

She nodded and quickly left the man, glancing back only once to see that he was gone. In truth, he was gone from sight so swiftly and so completely that she wondered if he had been there at all. Maldie shook away that fanciful thought. His warning against showing too much curiousity had certainly been real. There had been no hint of a threat in his voice, but she took it as one. Douglas might not have any intention of harming her for simply asking a few questions, but others would willingly do so.

As she walked by the heavy doors of the great hall, she looked inside and her heart skipped with a mixture of hope and anticipation. The great hall was dark, every window draped with a heavy cloth. It was also empty. Maldie could not believe her luck as she slipped inside. For hours she had practiced her explanation in case anyone asked why she was descending into the dungeons, but it did not appear that she would have to use it.

It was not until she touched the latch of the door which would lead her down to Eric that Maldie realized she had erred. A great hall had many shadowy corners and she should have peered into them harder. A few soft whispers were her first sign of trouble, then light filled the room as someone yanked down one of the cloths hiding the windows.

"Ah, 'tis the wee healing lassie from the village," drawled a deep hoarse voice. "I dinnae believe I called for ye to go and tend to my prisoners."

Very slowly, Maldie turned and looked around the great hall. A tall, lean man stepped out of one of the still darkened corners of the room and started to walk toward her. Behind him walked an even taller, even leaner man, but aside from a quick look at that man's too narrow features, Maldie had no interest in him. It was the first man who held her gaze, and from the way he had spoken she guessed he was Beaton.

Her mother's description of her seducer was almost useless, Maldie decided as the man stopped in front of her. The woman had recalled the man of twenty years past, and Beaton had not aged well. Maldie knew that some of what made him appear to be such an ugly old man was the disease that left his skin raw, open and scabbed-over sores interspersed with skin stretched so tight that it had a shine to it. The bonny blue eyes her mother had claimed had captured her heart were trapped between deep red lines and were rheumy. The thick brown hair she had sighed over was no more than a few filthy wisps of white hair poking out of his head at odd angles.

Only Beaton's form was still as her mother had described it, holding both strength and grace. Whatever was destroying the man's skin was not yet harming his body, although Maldie suspected it could cause him great pain at times and even steal his strength when it was at its worst. It was probably then that his body became twisted, as Eleanor had claimed it did. And maybe Eleanor was right when she said that Beaton was rotting, his evil manifesting itself upon his body so that all who looked upon him could clearly see what he was. Maldie just wished that she was not looking upon the man now, not when she was so close to helping Eric.

"I had heard that a lad down there had required some discipline," she replied, fighting to keep her voice calm and sweet, to not reveal in any way the anger and hatred she felt churning to life inside of her. "That can sometimes leave a lad with a few small injuries and I thought I would see if he needed or wanted some salve."

"Such kindness." He leaned closer to her and frowned. "Who are ye, lass?"

"Maldie Kirkcaldy." She held her breath when he spoke, for the stench of rotting teeth was almost too strong to stomach.

"Why are ye here?"

"I am a healing woman, my laird. As the minstrels do, I travel about to do my work. They soothe the ears and troubled hearts with their music, and I soothe the pain of illness with my salves."

"I have ne'er liked the whine of minstrels. Kirkcaldy? I believe I have heard that name before. Where are ye from?"

Rage tightened Maldie's insides. The man did not even recognize the clan name of the woman he had seduced and abandoned. Margaret had never forgotten him, but Maldie suspected Beaton had forgotten her mother the moment the woman had born him a girl child.

"Kirkcaldy of Dundee," she said, realizing the anger she

could not control had begun to seep into her voice when the man with Beaton tensed and watched her with narrowing eyes.

There was a chance that Beaton's companion recognized her name. He was obviously the man who stood firmly at Beaton's right hand. If he had done so for a long time he could well recall a lot more about Beaton's past than the man himself did. That would be necessary if he was to know who all of his laird's enemies were. Sometimes the person one considered the least-important could become his deadliest enemy. Maldie also recalled her mother speaking of a thin, long-faced man who shadowed Beaton's every step. She was sure that this was the man.

And that made him the one to watch, she mused, struggling not to let anger steal away all caution and good sense. Maldie suspected there was little chance that she would even get to see Eric now, at least not today. What she needed to do was to get out of the great hall alive and without having roused any dangerous suspicions about herself. The sharp look upon Beaton's companion's face told her that it might already be too late to avoid the latter. The heedless, fierce rage churning inside of her told her that she would have to work very hard not to do something that would only get her killed.

"I have been to Dundee, havenae I, Calum?" Beaton asked his companion, all the while keeping his gaze fixed unwaveringly upon Maldie. "Years ago?"

"Aye," replied Calum, with a deep voice that one would never have expected to arise from such a thin chest. "Twenty years past, mayhap longer. Ye lingered there for a wee while."

"Ah." Beaton gave Maldie a nasty smile. "Are ye one of my bastards then?"

Maldie saw no reason to deny it now, for it was clear that Calum knew exactly who she was. "Aye, begot off of Margaret Kirkcaldy, a gentleborn lass that ye seduced and abandoned."

"Margaret, eh? I have kenned many a Margaret. But, aye, the longer I stare at ye, the more I begin to recall. Ye have the look of your mother, I suspect, and 'tis why ye stir a memory or two. A verra dim memory, for I have yet to meet a woman who deserves more than a good rutting and a hasty fareweel.''

It took all of her willpower not to strike the sneer off his face. With the sad condition of his skin she knew that even a light slap would be an agony for him, and she ached to give him that pain. She did not think she had ever been so angry or so filled with hatred. A small voice in her head told her that he was simply not worth such strong emotion, that the only one who would suffer from any sort of confrontation with Beaton was herself, but she found it hard to listen to. The violent nature of her thoughts both alarmed and appalled her, but even that did not calm her down. Her mother had wanted the man dead, but Maldie wanted him to suffer the agonies of hell first.

"So speaks a mon who thinks only with his pintle, which usually means that he ends up sadly lacking in wit."

Calum moved to strike her, but Beaton halted him with one sharp gesture of his hand. "Did ye come here looking for money? To try and fill your wee purse with my coin simply because we are related by a blood kinship?"

"I wouldnae touch your coin if I was naught but starved flesh hanging off brittle bone and groveling on my belly in the foulness that fills the gutters. And there simply isnae enough coin in your chests to pay for all of your crimes."

"Oh, aye, there is. One can solve many a trouble and wave aside most difficulties with money."

"Not this time."

"Nay? Your mother was willing to take my coin, like most whores are."

"My mother was no whore when ye lured her away from her kinsmen. Ye destroyed her. Ye lied to her, made promises that ye ne'er meant to keep, and then left her, shamed and penniless, when she didnae give ye the son ye wanted."

Beaton shook his head. It was something Maldie decided he should not do very often, for it made the scattered clumps of white hair upon his head flop around in a most unattractive way. She was almost pleased to see how ugly he had become.

Not only did she consider it to be God's justice, but it made it a lot easier to keep her distance, to think of him not as her blood father, but as just a man, a sick old man. Except in spirit this was certainly not the man her mother had so often described, not the man Margaret Kirkcaldy had loved and bedded.

"I fear I have a hard truth to tell ye, lass," Beaton said.

" 'Ware, Beaton," she murmured in a cold voice, knowing that she was near to losing control completely. If he continued to belittle her mother, Maldie knew she could easily forget that she had wanted to get out of Dubhlinn alive. "Ye have no right to say such things about my mother. I willnae allow ye to spit upon her memory."

"*Ye* willnae allow it?" Beaton laughed, a broken, raspy sound that briefly became a hacking cough. "Ye dare to threaten me? My heart fair leaps with fear."

"Ye havenae got any heart. Only a truly heartless mon would treat my mother as contemptuously as ye did."

"I treated your mother just as she deserved. She was a lass with warm blood and little wit. I cannae be blamed for her foolishness. If she told ye that she didnae ken that I was married, didnae ken the difference between sweet words said in the fever of passion and the truth, then she lied to you."

Maldie shook her head, appalled when she actually considered his words for a moment. "Ye didnae tell her."

"Nay, why should I? Howbeit, I ne'er offered her marriage, but she left her kinsmen and came with me. Oh, she may have been untouched ere I had her, but she was still a whore in her heart. She gave up her maidenhead for no more than a few gifts and sweet words. And she enjoyed the giving of it. I swear I have rarely bedded such a greedy lass." His eyes narrowed and he watched her closely as he continued, "I would wager that she didnae grieve for me verra long ere she wrapped herself around another mon. She loved a rutting too much to go without for verra long. Believe what ye wish, lass, swallow your mother's lies if it makes ye happy, but dinnae come blaming me for all of your troubles. If I am at fault for anything 'tis just

for showing your mother what she truly was—a whore, and a
hungry one at that.''

Her dagger was in her hand before he finished speaking.
Maldie did not long consider the fact that she was one tiny lass
with a small dagger facing two belted knights with swords. All
she could think of was that she wanted Beaton dead. The
demeaning way he spoke of her mother demanded that she do
something. Such insults could not go unpunished. He tried to
wash his hands of his own guilt by blaming Margaret for all
that had happened to her. A still sane part of her whispered
that one reason she was so enraged was because Beaton had
put into words things that she had already thought of herself,
fleeting ideas that had caused her to suffer guilt and shame.
She pushed that realization aside as quickly as she had all those
other traitorous thoughts and, raising her dagger, lunged at
Beaton.

She screamed in frustration when he knocked her back.
Calum tried to grab her, but she neatly eluded him. Her dagger
still clutched tightly in her hand, she faced the two men. Beaton
looked amused. Calum stood just slightly in front of his laird,
ready to take the next blow for the man. She was amazed by
such loyalty. Beaton did not seem to be the sort of man who
either deserved it or rewarded it. One look into Calum's
unblinking black eyes told Maldie that there was no weakness
there to play with.

It was hopeless and she knew it. Her rage had made her act
without thinking of all the consequences, made it all too easy
to push aside the one brief moment of sensible hesitation she
had felt. Now she was as good as cornered. Even though both
men had suspected she would strike out, they had not known
exactly when or how she would. That small chance of surprise
had given her an edge that could have given her what she
wanted—Beaton's death. All that was gone now. She could
try to kill Beaton again or she could surrender. Either choice
would surely get her killed.

''Ye have my spirit, lass,'' Beaton said. '' 'Tis almost a
shame that ye are a lass.''

"Oh, aye, I was yet another failure for ye in your never-ending search for a son. And ye always blamed the woman for that lack, didnae ye? Did ye ne'er think that it was ye yourself who was failing? That mayhap your seed is too weak to produce the heir ye so hunger for?"

As Maldie had hoped, that enraged Beaton. She thought it was all nonsense, even deeply insulting to imply that producing a girl child was a sign of weakness, but had guessed that Beaton believed such a thing. The rage that transformed his ravaged face told her clearly that he had suffered such doubts about his manhood.

Maldie braced for Beaton's charge, but still only barely escaped the full brunt of it. She struck out with her dagger as she stepped aside, leaving a long gash upon Beaton's arm. His scream of pain and fury as he fell to the floor was still ringing in her ears when Calum grabbed her. She tried to stab him, too, not wanting to kill him, just desperate to make him let her go so that she could flee. He got a tight grip upon her wrist and squeezed, twisting her wrist slightly at the same time, until the pain pulsing through her arm made her release her weapon. Calum only eased his grip slightly as he yanked her closer to Beaton. Two armed men stumbled into the great hall, drawn by Beaton's screams, and Maldie felt all emotion leave her in a weakening rush. She stood, numbed, waiting to die as she watched Beaton stand up in front of her.

"Ye have just made a verra foolish mistake, lass. A fatal one," snapped Beaton, his voice hard and cold, holding a hint of the strong, imposing, and cruel man he had once been. Now he was just cruel.

"My only mistake was in putting my dagger in your arm and not burying it deep into your black heart."

"Ye would kill your own father?"

He asked the question without shock or horror, just simple curiosity, and Maldie found that chilling. In fact, the emotion Maldie sensed behind the question was admiration. From the moment her mother had pulled that oath from her she had been torn by the horror of the crime she was being asked to commit against the man who had sired her, and a sense of justice long overdue. Beaton clearly saw nothing wrong with trying to kill one's own father. She briefly wondered how his own father had met his death.

"Aye. I gave my mother a promise while she lay wracked with pain on her deathbed. I swore an oath that ye would finally taste the justice ye have eluded for so long."

Beaton almost smiled. "As I said, 'tis a shame that ye are a mere lass."

"Can ye turn your twisted wee mind to naught but sons and heirs?"

"A mon needs a son."

Maldie shook her head, realizing that Beaton would never understand the cruelty of his behavior. He would never know how deeply he had hurt the women he had used, and the children he had cast aside as worthless simply because they were females. If he were not so ill, she suspected that he would still be doing so, still bedding any woman who did not have the sense or the speed to get away from him, and then deserting her when she did not bear him his son. For that alone he deserved killing, but she had lost all chance of delivering the retribution he so richly deserved.

"And, so, desperate for what ye couldnae produce with your own indiscriminate rutting, ye stole a son from the Murrays." She laughed, a short, harsh sound. "Do ye truly think that the world and its mother will believe he is yours?"

"They will. He was born of my wife. And now I ken why ye were trying to creep down to see the lad. Ye are working for the Murrays against me, arenae ye? Was this betrayal part of your revenge?"

"Ye are a fine one to speak so disparagingly of betrayal. 'Tis the verra air ye breathe. Ye have dealt in it so often that it has become a habit for you. If ye werenae so sick, ye would still be betraying woman after woman and feeling no remorse for your cruelty."

"Ye set too much worth upon what is merely the folly of

passion. But what I may or may not do in the days to come isnae going to be your concern for verra much longer.''

His smile was chilling, and Maldie had to struggle to hide her fear and maintain her look of calm disgust. "Nay? Are ye going to become a monk then?''

Beaton chuckled. "Nay. Your executioner. At the end of market day ye will hang.''

"Ah, ye dinnae think that the jongleurs and minstrels will be amusement enough for your clansmen.''

"We will see how weel your spirit and that sharp tongue of yours endures when a noose is slipped about your bonny, wee neck. Now, since ye were so eager to see my son Eric, I will grant your wish. Calum, take my wee murderous bastard down to the dungeons and set her in Eric's cell.''

Maldie did not struggle as the cold-faced Calum led her away. There was no chance of escape, so she decided to try and go to her prison with dignity. Even as Calum pushed her ahead of him, down the dark, steep steps that led to the dungeons of Dubhlinn, she prayed that she was wrong about just when Balfour would attack again. Market day, she thought as the iron door of Eric's cold cell was shut behind her, would be a very nice day for Balfour to ride to his desired victory over Beaton.

Douglas cursed and edged away from the high doors to the great hall. Maldie had roused his curiosity, and now he knew why. She had come to kill Beaton. He had not been able to believe his eyes when he had looked into the great hall just in time to see her attack Beaton. Douglas wished he could have heard more of what she and Beaton had said to each other, but he had been too far away to catch more than the occasional small piece of their conversation. The girl could have her own reasons to want the man dead or she could be working for one of Beaton's many enemies, including the laird of Donncoill.

After only a moment of considering that possibility, Douglas shook his head. Balfour would never send a woman, especially not a wee, bonny lass, to kill his enemy for him. Nevertheless, Douglas was sure that this was something Balfour needed to know, and it was far too important to entrust to the tangled and often very slow line of spies and messengers Balfour had established between Donncoill and Dubhlinn.

As he slipped out of Dubhlinn, Douglas knew that it was time to leave anyway. Since Malcolm had been discovered and killed, it had become dangerous for anyone to ask even the most innocent of questions. Douglas suspected this would be the last piece of information he would gather from Dubhlinn. It and all the other scraps he had been unable to send home had to be given to Balfour before the man tried to rescue Eric a second time. All the way back to Donncoill, Douglas found himself hoping that they could find some way to rescue the young woman who had so valiantly tried to kill Beaton.

Chapter Sixteen

"Douglas?" Balfour paused in wiping down his horse, an activity that often calmed him as much as the long hard ride he had just indulged in, to stare at James in surprise. "What is Douglas doing here? Was he discovered by Beaton?"

"I havenae had the chance to talk with the lad all that much," replied James, as he led Balfour out of the stable and walked toward the keep. "He arrived but moments ago, dusty, exhausted, hungry and thirsty. I swear to sweet Jesu, Balfour, the lad looks as if he ran all the way here from Dubhlinn. I told him to go to the great hall and get himself a drink, mayhap something to eat, and that I would fetch you. He is most anxious to speak with you."

Balfour softly cursed. "I pray that he isnae about to tell me something that will destroy all of our plans for the morrow."

"Nay, for they are good ones, holding a fair hope for success."

They were, and Balfour was hungry for a victory, even a small one. From the moment James had told him that Eric had been taken, it seemed as if nothing had gone in his favor. There had been misjudgments, betrayals, and failures. Even though he was still reeling from Maldie's betrayal, he saw a chance to win against Beaton and he dreaded the thought that Douglas was about to steal that away from him.

The moment he stepped into the great hall, Balfour saw Douglas. It was hard to miss the big handsome man. Douglas paced back and forth next to the head table, taking long drinks from a heavy silver goblet. The man did look as if he had suffered a long hard journey. He was covered in mud and dust, and, despite his agitated pacing, he looked battered and exhausted.

"Sit down, Douglas," Balfour said, as he moved to his seat at the head of the table. "By the look of ye, ye should be most weary of walking."

"So weary that I fear if I sit down I will fall asleep ere I can tell ye what I must," Douglas said, even as he sat down on a bench to Balfour's right, immediately across from James. "I ran more than I walked. My innards told me that I had little time left to reach you, and I dinnae ken where that fancy came from."

"Do ye think Beaton had guessed who ye are?" asked James.

"Weel, there was no sign that he had," replied Douglas. "He moved verra quickly when he discovered who Malcolm was. If he had guessed who I was, I dinnae think I would have been given time to think about what I should do. Nay, I would have been fighting for my life every step of the way."

"Aye, Beaton's dogs would have been yapping at your heels all the way to these gates," muttered James.

"So, what did ye feel was of such great importance that ye had to bring the news to us yourself, and at such a speed?" asked Balfour.

"To begin with, Beaton may not be dying, so, if ye had thought to just wait until the mon breathed his last foul breath, ye may have a verra long wait." Douglas reached for the jug of wine, hesitated, then refilled his goblet with sweet cider.

"But everyone has said that he is verra ill. The rumors of his impending death have been so often repeated that they have to have some truth in them, dinnae they?"

"Oh, aye, but e'en though the mon looks as poorly as any I have e'er seen still walking, what ails him may not kill him. Once I was recalled to the fact, I realized that he has been dying for three years or longer! This lass I met is possessed of a healing touch, and she seemed to think that, if he truly had a killing disease, he should be dead by now. She said it was probably just some ailment of the skin. It does lessen and worsen as some ailments of the skin are apt to do."

Although Douglas's news that Beaton could still live for many years was not welcome, Balfour was far more interested in the lass he had mentioned. "Ye met a lass there who has the healing touch?"

"Aye, a bonny, wee lass."

"With unruly black hair and green eyes?"

Douglas frowned slightly as he stared at Balfour. "Ye describe this lass as if ye have seen her."

"I think I have. Her name is Maldie Kirkcaldy."

"Weel, I didnae ask her her clan name, though that sounds right. Others kenned it and I think I heard the name a time or two. All she told me was, '*I am Maldie.*' I had heard about her healing skills, that this was her second visit to Dubhlinn, and that she stays in the village with an old woman who was newly widowed. Curious that ye should ken this lass."

"Oh, aye, I ken her. She stayed here for a wee while, then went running back to her master, Beaton."

"Her master? Why should ye think Beaton is her laird and master?"

"She stayed here long enough to learn all about us then, once we had guessed her game, she went racing back to Dubhlinn. The lass appeared on the road to Dubhlinn as we crept away from our loss, kept her own counsel verra tightly, had no answers or explanations when I presented her with my growing suspicions, and then fled to Beaton."

"And ye believed she told the bastard all she had heard and seen?"

"Aye, what else was I to think?"

Douglas shrugged. "Just what ye did, I am thinking. How-beit, ye are wrong. That lass is no ally of Beaton's."

"How can ye be so certain of that?" Balfour tried not to be too hopeful for, knowing how desperate he was to learn that Maldie had not betrayed him, he was too eager to accept any other explanation for her actions.

"Oh, aye, verra certain. That lass wasnae at Dubhlinn to help old Beaton. She was there to kill him."

Balfour was so stunned that he could not speak for a moment. It was an effort to stop himself from gaping at the man. A quick look at James gave him some comfort, for that man was looking equally as shocked.

"Did she tell ye that was why she was at Dubhlinn?" Balfour finally asked, his voice roughened by his lingering shock.

"Nay, she did more than that. I saw her trying to stick a dagger in his heart with my own eyes."

"But why?"

"That, I fear, I cannae tell ye. I was peeping in at the doors of the great hall, and she and the old mon were at the far end. All I caught was a few words and I dared not draw any closer. There was something about how cruelly he treats women, talk of betrayal, a few weel-said insults by the lass, and a few mentions of how long overdue he is to taste some weel-deserved justice. I wondered which one of his enemies had sent her, e'en considered the possibility that ye might have, but now I think it was some personal vengeance."

There was one question that Balfour had to ask, although his fear of Douglas's answer made him hesitant. "Is she dead?"

"Not yet," replied Douglas, and then he yawned so widely that his body trembled.

"She tried to kill the mon. I would have thought that she would have been killed right there, right then, by Beaton himself or one of his men."

"I think Calum, Beaton's most faithful cur, would have cut her down without hesitation, but he didnae. As I said, 'twas hard to hear from where I stood. Howbeit, one thing was said verra clearly and loud enough for all to hear. Beaton evidently has a liking for using a loud, kingly voice when he pronounces a judgment. The lass is to hang at the end of market day on the morrow. I was hoping there might be something we can do to help the lass.''

''There may be,'' Balfour forced himself to reply, fighting the urge to ride for Dubhlinn immediately. ''We plan to attack Dubhlinn on the morrow.''

''Then I am even gladder that I left that muck heap when I did. I may have some information that will aid you.''

''I am sure that ye do, but go and bathe, then rest.''

''There isnae much time left.''

''There is enough for ye to steal a few hours of much needed sleep. 'Twill make your mind clearer.''

The moment Douglas left the great hall, Balfour poured himself a large goblet of strong wine. It took several deep drinks before he felt calm enough to think straight. The mere thought of Maldie being led to the scaffold made him desperate to ride to her rescue with no hesitation or plan, and he knew that would be utter folly. He had a plan of attack, a very good one, and it could easily accommodate the need to rescue Maldie.

He suddenly cursed and shook his head. ''I forgot to ask Douglas where Maldie had been put to await her hanging.''

''There is a lot ye forgot to ask the lad, but dinnae fret,'' said James. ''We have time to let Douglas rest and to find out all he learned while at Dubhlinn. Ye were right when ye told him he needed to get some sleep. He was so weary he could easily have forgotten to tell us something of great importance. A mon that tired cannae think too clearly. Aye, and he needs to be rested so that he can ride with us on the morrow.''

Balfour nodded. ''And, when I told him of our plan to ride against Beaton in the morning, he gave no hint that he kenned anything which could prevent that.''

''Aye, and that he would have remembered no matter how blind-weary he was.''

''Good.'' Balfour rubbed the back of his neck and grimaced. ''I fear my wits fled me when he told me that Beaton means to hang Maldie. One moment I believe that she has betrayed me, the next I discover that she is to hang for trying to murder Beaton. Why should the lass try to kill the mon?''

"Only she can answer that question. There could be many reasons why, and we but waste time trying to guess which one put that dagger in her hand.''

"I just fear that it may have been me.''

"Ye? Ye didnae ask the lass to go to Dubhlinn and try to stick her dagger into Beaton.''

"Nay, but I accused her of betraying me, of working for Beaton against us. Mayhap the lass thought this was the only way to save her honor, to prove her innocence.''

"That lass is no fool. There are many less risky ways for her to prove her innocence.''

Balfour smiled faintly. "The lass may be clever, but she isnae so clever or so perfect that she is free of all wild ideas or plots or ne'er acts without thinking everything through most carefully.''

"Mayhap, but that leaves us with no reason why she stayed at Dubhlinn for a fortnight ere she came here,'' James pointed out. "There is more to all of this than we can understand ere we speak to the lass.''

"Aye, so we had best succeed on the morrow. Not only must we free Eric from Beaton's grasp, but free Maldie from the hangmon's noose. I but pray that they are both in the dungeons of Dubhlinn for, unhappy a place as it is, 'tis the safest when the battle starts.''

Maldie cautiously felt her way along the wall of the dark cell until she touched the edge of a cot, and then she sat down. It took another moment before her eyes adjusted to the dim light provided by one smoking torch set in the wall outside of the cell. She felt Eric before she saw him, felt his fear, his anger, and his curiousity.

"How are ye, Eric?'' she asked. "Has Beaton hurt you?''

"How do ye ken who I am?'' the boy asked as he edged nearer to her.

"Ah, weel, I have just arrived here from Donncoill."

"My brothers sent a lass to aid me?" His voice held the hint of shock as he warily sat down next to her. "Nay, they would ne'er do that. Mayhap ye are some trick played by that bastard Beaton. He means to use ye to turn me to his side."

"Nay, ne'er that. He but felt that I might like to meet you ere I hang on the morrow." Just saying those words made her shiver, but she fought against giving in to her fears. Eric needed strength and calm now.

She studied Eric for a moment as he stared at her wide-eyed with shock and disbelief, clearly struggling to think of what to say next. He was indeed fair of face. His features still held the softness of a child, but there was already the hint of the handsome man he would become. His hair was a very light brown, and she suspected it would be even lighter if they were not sitting in the near dark. There was a brightness to his eyes that told her they were not brown like his brothers. In truth, the fine lines of his face did not remind her of any of the Murrays. They did not really remind her of Beaton either, so they had to be a gift from his mother. It would be easier to make up her mind about his blood heritage if she could see him in the bright light of day, but she knew she would have to depend upon the mark. If he carried the same one she did, there was no doubt about who had fathered him. Maldie was just not sure she ought to tell the boy.

"Why are they going to hang you?" Eric finally asked.

"Because I tried to kill Beaton."

"Why?"

"I promised my mother that I would as she lay dying. She made me swear an oath that I would find him and make him pay with his life for the harm he did her. The mon seduced her, and then deserted her, leaving her alone and penniless with his bairn at her breast.,

"Ye are Beaton's bairn?"

"Aye, one of what is said to be a large horde of daughters he didnae want. Ah, I see I have shocked you," she murmured as he gaped at her. " 'Tis a shocking thing to try and kill one's own father, but, in truth, I have ne'er seen the mon before today, so I have no true feeling for him. There is no more bond between us than a tiny little voice in my head that tries to remind me that his seed made me. I didnae listen to it, I fear.''

''Aye, 'tis shocking that a child would try to kill her father, but that isnae what shocked me the most. As ye say, ye dinnae e'en ken the mon, have ne'er e'en set eyes upon him. Nay, what shocked me to the heart was that your own mother would ask ye to do such a thing, to commit such a sin for her.''

''Weel, she had been terribly wronged by him. She told me so quite often as I grew. She was a gentleborn lass, and he should not have shamed her that way.''

''True enough, but the crime was *hers* to avenge. She shouldnae have asked ye to swear to kill your own father, to set that black sin upon your soul. I am sorry if ye see this as an insult to her, but 'tis what I truly think. She must have grown verra bitter to e'en think on such a thing.''

''She had,'' Maldie said softly, saddened by his words for they were the stark truth. ''From the earliest time that I can recall she talked to me of how I was to cleanse her name of the shame he had blackened it with.''

''She raised ye to kill the mon?''

Maldie winced. The boy meant no disrespect. He spoke with the blunt, sometimes painful, honesty of the child he still was. His direct question pounded in her mind, however, demanding an answer. The one that formed was enough to sicken her.

He was right. With one simple question he had exposed the truth she had fought so hard to ignore. As she sat in a Dubhlinn dungeon awaiting a hanging, she no longer had the strength or the will to ignore that truth. Her mother had raised her from the day of her birth to be the sword of vengeance she herself was too cowardly to wield. It would be kinder to think that Margaret Kirkcaldy had never thought of the consequences of that, of the danger she would be putting her only child in, but Maldie could no longer deceive herself even that much. Her mother had been so eaten up with her hatred of Beaton, that she simply had not cared what happened to her daughter so long as Beaton suffered some punishment. Whether her daughter failed and died or succeeded and blackened her soul forever with the sin of killing her own father, had not mattered to the woman.

"Aye," she whispered, too hurt to even cry. "She raised me to kill the mon."

"I am sorry," Eric said softly, resting his long-fingered hand on her shoulder. "I did not mean to speak of things that hurt you."

"Ye didnae hurt me, laddie. My mother did. All I suffer from at the moment is the fact that I am too weary and too close to death to keep lying to myself. In my heart I have kenned it all along. I was just verra good at ignoring it. And, aye, mayhap I ached to kill Beaton simply because he had left me with her, or because I wanted to blame him for what she was. Then, too," she forced herself to smile at him, "he is a mon that sorely deserves killing."

Eric grinned, then plucked at the torn back of her gown. "Ye fought hard, did ye?"

"Not hard enough."

She knew the moment he saw the mark on her back, its shape and size visible beneath the torn back of her gown even in the dim light. He tensed, then shuddered. Maldie inwardly sighed, for there would be no hiding the truth now. From all she had heard, Eric was far too clever to miss the implications of sharing a birthmark with her.

"Ye have one of those too, dinnae ye?" she asked softly, her voice weighted with sympathy.

"Aye, I thought it was from my mother."

She could tell from the unsteadiness of his voice that he was not going to take the truth well. What sane person would wish to discover that he was the son of a man like Beaton, and not one of the clan that had lovingly succored him his whole short life? Maldie took his hand in hers, knew he wanted to cry but fought the tears, and wished there was something she could say that would ease his pain.

"I am sorry."

"I would prefer to be a Murray," he whispered, his voice thick with the tears he refused to let fall.

"Ye still can be. They dinnae need to ken this. Only one person has seen my mark, and he didnae recall where he had seen it before, only that it looked a wee bit familiar. So, there is a chance that ye can keep this a secret. Especially if that person ne'er kens who I really am."

"And would that person be my brother Nigel?"

"Nay, Balfour," she muttered, then scowled when she felt his surprise. "Balfour isnae a bad-looking fellow, ye ken."

"Oh, aye, I ken it. 'Tis just that the lasses dinnae often ken it." He sighed and buried his face in his hands for a moment. "Of course, he isnae really my brother anymore."

"Weel, nay. 'Tis probably nay the time to say this, 'tis too early for ye to gain any joy in the irony of it all, but Beaton thinks he has stolen his wife's bastard and must hoist a lie upon the world when, in truth, he has taken back the only legitimate child he has ever sired."

"Aye, 'tis too early for me to enjoy that sad jest. I dinnae want to be his son. The mon is a swine, a cruel, heartless boor. He wishes to twist me into the same sick mon he is."

"Ye could ne'er become like him."

"Who can tell? If he makes me watch the death of another mon the way he made me watch Malcolm suffer, I may lose my wits enough to be quite like him."

Maldie put her arm around the boy, horrified by what Beaton had done. She had heard about the torturous death Balfour's man Malcolm had suffered. To make a young boy watch such a thing was cruelty indeed. Eric might be right to think that Beaton meant to twist him into the same sick man he was. How many times could a boy be subjected to such horror before he did begin to change, to begin to gain that particular type of cold heartlessness that Beaton had perfected in himself?

"I must tell Balfour and Nigel the truth," Eric said, sighing heavily and slumping against the damp stone wall of their cell.

"As I said, ye dinnae really have to," she said, respecting

his honesty but wondering if he understood how much pain it could bring him.

"I really have to. I couldnae look them in the eye if I held this secret in my heart. I wish I could get word to them now ere they risk Murray lives to try and rescue me. 'Tis nay right that any Murray should die trying to save me, a Beaton, from my own father."

"They would still save ye from Beaton," she said, but his quick, crooked smile told her that he had heard the doubt in her voice. "I feel that they willnae be able to hold this against ye, but then I recall how long the feud has gone on, how deep the hatred goes, and that confidence wavers. I am sorry."

"Why? 'Tis the truth. One should ne'er be sorry to tell the truth."

"Aye, one should if 'tis a truth that hurts someone. Your honesty is most admirable, but ye will soon learn that not everyone wants to hear the truth either. Some people will be made quite angry by it, some will be quite hurt. One shouldnae lie, but then sometimes one shouldnae be so quick to tell the whole truth, either. Weel, it may not seem of much value to ye at the moment, but, if the Murrays cannae look beyond the blood that runs in your veins, ye will still have me. We are brother and sister."

He laughed shortly and shook his head. "Oh, aye, that might help except that ye are about to die." Eric gasped and clutched at her hand. "Oh, sweet Jesu, I am so sorry. I allowed my own hurt to kill all my wits. I should ne'er have said such a cruel thing."

"Dinnae fret so." She took a deep shaky breath to calm the sudden attack of fear his words had infected her with. "I dinnae plan to die on Beaton's scaffold."

"Do ye have a plan of escape?"

"Nay. I did until I was tossed in here, but now I must think of a new plan."

"I dinnae intend to sound boastful, but if there was a way out of here, I think I would have found it by now."

"Mayhap. Howbeit, I got myself out of a locked, guarded

room at Donncoill. I walked out, walked through the keep, and straight out of the gates with nary a soul stopping me. I may yet think of a way to get us out of here. The hardest part will be thinking of a way to get this door unlocked.''

"The large number of weel-armed Beatons between us and freedom being but a small concern, of course.''

"Of course.''

"Might I ask why my brother had put ye in a locked room and set a guard there?''

"Ye might.''

He grinned briefly. "But ye might not answer, either, eh? How about a simpler question then—who are ye?''

"She is Maldie Kirkcaldy,'' said a hoarse voice that sent shivers down Maldie's spine and she wrapped her arms around Eric, not sure if she were trying to protect him or comfort herself as they both looked at Beaton. "How touching,'' Beaton said as he leaned against the bars. "It seems my wife's bastard and my own have bonded together against me. Weel, 'twill be a short friendship.''

"Ye cannae hang her,'' Eric said, pushing Maldie back so that his body was between hers and the bars Beaton peered through.

"Oh, aye, laddie, I can.''

"She is but a wee lass.''

"Who wields a verra sharp dagger. She tried to kill me, laddie, tried to kill her verra own father. Why, e'en the church would approve of her hanging.''

Maldie wriggled free of Eric's light, protective hold. "As if ye care what the church thinks. Ye should have been excommunicated years ago. Ye must be verra generous to the church for them to continue to grant ye absolution.''

"Dinnae fear for my soul, daughter. I have done my penances and confessed all my sins.''

"I pray that isnae enough, for ye are surely one who has earned the tortures of hell.''

"Ye shall be tasting them before me. Did ye forget that ye should have absolution ere ye die?'' He smiled when she paled.

"For one who nearly committed such a grave sin as killing one's own father, absolution may be all that saves ye from hell's fires. 'Tis a pity that I havenae been able to find ye a priest."

"Then ye had best hope that all your confessing and false piety wins ye the favor ye seek, for I will be waiting for ye in hell, Beaton. Aye, waiting and eager to make ye suffer for all of your crimes."

"Beaton, ye have to get her a priest," said Eric. "She is your own flesh and blood."

"Aye, and much like her father, though methinks she would be loath to admit it. Howbeit, she would need more time than she has to be as good as I. I didnae fail when I went after my father," he said, smiling coldly at their shock, then turning and walking back up the stairs.

"He killed his own father," Eric said after Beaton left, shock stealing all the strength from his voice.

"I had wondered on that, for he showed no real disgust or shock that I had tried to do so," said Maldie as she slumped against the wall.

"God, how I loathe that mon, more so now that I ken he is my blood father. 'Tis odd. I dinnae feel any different. I still feel like a Murray, nay a Beaton."

"And I feel like a Kirkcaldy, nay a Beaton. Dinnae fret on it, lad. Just be grateful that ye werenae raised by that mon. The Murrays did weel by ye, and mayhap ye can soon do weel by the clan Beaton has ground beneath his boot for so long."

"Maldie, I am nay sure I will be made laird here after Beaton dies. Aye, I am his son, but all ken me as a bastard of his wife, e'en him. I dinnae think I have any proof that I am his son, either." He sighed and shook his head. "And now I am not e'en a Murray. I am without kin, and mayhap without friends."

"Cease this bemoaning of a fate that hasnae e'en happened to ye yet," she scolded gently as she put her arm around his slim shoulders and briefly hugged him. "And, ne'er forget, ye have me. As I said, I have no intention of gracing Beaton's gibbet, so I shall be here for you for many a year. And dinnae forget that ye had a mother, too. There is all of her kin. E'en if they dinnae believe that ye are Beaton's true heir, no one has e'er denied that ye are your mother's son.''

"I shall try. It willnae be easy, for my head is filled to overflowing with thoughts of how I was a Murray, how I have always been a Murray, and how do I stop being a Murray now?''

"Is it such a bad thing to always be a bit of a Murray?''

"Nay, not a bad thing at all, not e'en if they cannae accept me as a Beaton. Of course, all of this worry may be for naught, as we are still stuck here. For Balfour and Nigel to ken the truth, I must speak to them, and I dinnae see that I will be doing so verra soon.''

"Have faith in your new sister, Eric,'' she murmured as she watched the guard take his seat outside of their cell. "I have nay been raised as gently as you, and I have a few sly tricks up my ragged sleeve.''

"Can I help?''

"Aye, ye can pray verra hard that I think of a clever and successful plan, or that your brothers decide that now would be a verra good time to come to your rescue.''

Chapter Seventeen

"Market day at Dubhlinn draws a comfortingly large crowd," Balfour said, cautiously adjusting his sword beneath the cloak he wore as he looked around the crowded streets of the town.

They had left Donncoill before the sun had risen and reached Dubhlinn before the heavy mists of the morning had been completely burned away by the sun. Balfour had been concerned that the hard, swift journey would leave his men too exhausted for battle, but they were still as eager as he was to repay Beaton for the humiliation they had suffered at his hands the last time they had marched to Dubhlinn. Nigel and a large group of his men waited in the hills just beyond Dubhlinn and would slowly inch forward, waiting for the signal to attack. Another group wandered about dressed in ways that disguised their clan association as well as their purpose. That had been the slowest part of his plan to implement, for they had all had to arrive a few at a time and blend with the villagers and travelers in small enough numbers not to raise any suspicions. They would all slowly make their way into the bailey until enough of them had gathered to hold the gates. Once they held the gates of Dubhlinn, the rest of his men would rush in and Beaton's reign would be brought to a swift bloody end. So far, all had gone as they had planned, and Balfour prayed that their good fortune would continue.

"Aye, 'tis a busy and profitable marketplace," agreed Douglas as he stepped up on Balfour's left. "Dubhlinn's fields and pastures produce weel."

"Yet his people dinnae look plump and happy."

"Weel, I didnae say the bastard shared it, did I," drawled Douglas, then he frowned and pointed at an old woman walking through the market stalls with a younger woman and small boy at her side. "That is the old widow Maldie stayed with. I dinnae think she will grieve her laird's death too long, for 'twas his blood-hungry dogs who killed her poor old cripple of a husband."

"Mayhap we shouldnae speak of Beaton's impending death too freely," murmured James from Balfour's right, as he warily watched the crowd milling around between them and the road to the keep.

"Nay, we should just continue to slip up the road to the keep," agreed Balfour. "Can ye see if our men are drawing any closer to those open gates?"

"Nay," replied James and he smiled faintly. "And that is a good thing, laddie, for if I could see them then, mayhap, so could one of Beaton's men."

"Of course." Balfour laughed softly and shook his head. "I am as nervous as a page following his laird to his first battle."

Before James could say anything, Balfour stopped dead in his tracks. There, set upon a small rise at the far end of the village, was the scaffold. There, if he was not successful, Maldie would soon hang. Balfour had to take a deep breath to quell the urge to go and tear the thing down.

The thought of the danger Maldie was in had tormented him since Douglas had first told him of her fate. He could not stop himself from wondering if he was somehow at fault for her being there, for her attempt upon Beaton's life, and, ultimately, for the death sentence she had been given. Nothing James or

Nigel had said had eased that fear. Neither of them had been able to explain her actions to his satisfaction, in a way that made him certain he was not to blame in any way. There seemed to be no other reason for her to have done what she did than to prove her innocence. Balfour knew he was doing all he could to get her out of Beaton's grasp, but that was not really enough to ease the guilt he felt. Only Maldie's forgiveness could do that.

"Come, laddie," James said quietly, taking Balfour by the arm and tugging him in the direction of the keep. "The lass willnae suffer that fate if we all keep our heads."

"I ken it. 'Twould be folly indeed to expose us all by tearing that down, and it wouldnae save Maldie for more than a day or so, only for as long as it took them to build a new one."

"Nay," murmured Douglas, "not even that long. 'Twould only save her for as long as it took them to find a tall tree." He shrugged, but took a cautious step away when Balfour glared at him. "Beaton wants her dead, and when that mon wants someone dead he isnae in the humor to let a broken scaffold deter him."

"Ye are a true comfort to a mon, arenae ye, Douglas," said James, unable to fully suppress a chuckle.

"I dinnae think Maldie's impending execution is a matter for laughter," said Balfour, scowling up toward the keep.

"Cease your fretting, Balfour. The lass will come through this day hale and saucy."

"How can ye be so sure of that, James? Have ye suddenly been gifted with the sight?" Balfour inwardly winced, knowing James did not deserve his sarcasm, but even his confidence in his plan did not ease the worry that knotted his stomach. That fear of failure and of how dearly it could cost him made his temper short.

James ignored Balfour's ill humor. "Nay, I just ken the lass. She has wit and, though she be of gentle blood, she is as crafty as any city wench. She will keep herself safe. If she is with the lad, she will keep him safe as weel. And this is a sweet plan, one that probably couldnae fail e'en if we were all drunk and stumbling. So, rest easy and keep your mind on getting inside those gates ere the alarum can be sounded.''

"That old woman is watching us," hissed Douglas, glancing furtively behind them.

"What old woman?" asked Balfour, more interested in trying to see which of the many figures on the road were his men, but they were all so well disguised he could not tell them from the villagers and people of the keep.

"That Eleanor woman the young lass abided with for a while. She watches us."

"Do ye think Maldie told her something?"

"Mayhap. If the lass suspected ye would attack, she might have told the old woman to watch and hie for safety if she guessed that something was afoot. Maldie would ken that the woman couldnae look to her laird for protection. In truth, most of Beaton's people already ken that."

"Curse it, do ye think she will sound an alarum?" Balfour risked a glance behind him and saw the old woman, her gaze fixed firmly upon him and his companions even as she wended her way through the many people trying to sell their wares.

"Not to warn Beaton and his men," Douglas said. "I told ye, they murdered her husband and Beaton has done little to win the love of his people. The ones who fight for him are mostly hired swords. Nay, the only thing that could cause us some difficulty is if she has told too many others. Beaton could get a wee bit suspicious if the whole village suddenly took to the trees."

"Oh, aye, just a wee bit."

Balfour inwardly cursed. He could understand if Maldie had wished to warn her friend of approaching danger, but he prayed she had chosen well in giving her warning. If Eleanor had the wit to tell only a few people and to slip away quietly, they could still be successful. If the old woman had indeed told the whole village, they could easily find the gates slammed in their faces, for even Beaton's hired dogs, who were obviously heartily enjoying the drink and whores that accompanied market day, would guess that something was wrong if all the villagers disappeared.

He tensed as they drew near to the gates, increasingly afraid that they would be discovered and he would have to watch all chance of victory slip from his grasp. There was no cry from behind as they stepped through the gates and no guard confronted them. Beaton's men had obviously failed to notice that the whores they gathered round were strangers, and that many of them were very reluctant to sell their wares.

It had been Nigel's idea to use the women to help distract Beaton's men, ensuring that Beaton's guards were too busy to watch who came and went from Dubhlinn. The idea had been sound, but Balfour had been reluctant to use it, not wishing to put women in danger. Once it had been presented to the women, however, they had had no lack of volunteers. Several of the women were ones who had had their men killed or wounded by Beaton in past battles, and they were eager to help in his defeat. It was obvious that the plan was a good one and was working well. Balfour just prayed that the women they had recruited would not pay too dear a price for their aid.

"We can begin," whispered James.

"All of our men are gathered?" asked Balfour even as he prepared to throw off his cloak.

"All that are needed to hold the gates so that the rest may rush in."

"Shall we begin quietly or with a roar?"

"Oh, aye, let us roar. I want Beaton to hear his death approach."

Balfour grinned as he threw off his cloak and drew his sword. The women clustered around Beaton's guards were watchful and were already hurrying out of reach of the men when Balfour sounded his clan's war cry. James and Douglas heartily echoed it and quickly struck down the Beaton men closest to them. As Balfour began to fight his way to the keep itself, he saw the bailey fill with his men and felt the first sweet taste of victory. He fixed his mind on finding Eric and Maldie, knowing that any victory would never be satisfying unless he got them both back to Donncoill safe and unhurt. He prayed they had the sense to stay out of the midst of the battle until he could lead them to safety.

Maldie covertly watched the guard watch her. There was a dark, hungry look on his pockmarked face that she easily recognized, but his lust did not frighten her. No man at Dubhlinn would touch Beaton's daughter, and she was sure everyone knew who she was now and what she had tried to do. Such news would have spread through Dubhlinn so fast it would have reached the village by the time the cell door had shut behind her. Even though Beaton intended to hang her at the end of the day, in a strange way he was also protecting her. Maldie was just not sure if it was fear of Beaton himself that made his men just look but not grab, or fear that she might carry the seed of the disease that had so ravaged their laird.

Eleanor would have heard what had happened to her, too, she thought, and sighed. Maldie hoped that the woman was not too worried and did not do something foolish to try and help her. She wished she had had the time and opportunity to explain things to Eleanor, to tell the woman the truth. It was probably for the best, she decided, for it would have made the woman uneasy to know that she sheltered one of Beaton's bastards, one with murder on her mind. Maldie just hoped that Eleanor could forgive her.

She looked at Eric, who dozed on the filthy cot she sat on. They had talked until the early hours of the morning, until neither had the voice left to speak and their exhausted bodies had forced them to go to sleep. Eric was still heartbroken, still found it difficult to think of himself as a Beaton and not a Murray. He was also deeply afraid of how the men he had called brothers for all of his life would treat him once they discovered that he was the son of the enemy. There was nothing she could do to ease that pain and fear, but she knew that Eric now saw her as family. More than blood bound them now. If the boy was set aside by the Murrays—and she did not want to believe that Balfour could be so cruel—he knew that he would not be alone. Maldie just hoped that that would be enough.

All the flattering things she had heard about Eric were true, she mused, and gently brushed a stray lock of hair from the boy's brow. He was clever, sweet of nature, and loving. She was proud that they were related by blood. One could not have asked for a better brother. Maldie prayed that Beaton and Nigel would feel the same.

Those concerns had to be set aside for the moment, however. Their most important and immediate need was to get out of Dubhlinn. Maldie was disappointed in herself, for she had not thought of any new, clever plan to get away. Instead, she was going to use the same ploy she had used to flee Donncoill. Instinct told her that the scowling man Beaton had set in front of her cell would be as offset by talk of a female's various ailments as Balfour's man had been. She wondered briefly if she should warn Eric of what she was about to do, then decided that he would probably behave more appropriately if she did not. Later, when her plan showed signs of succeeding, she would tell him, for she would need his help. She hoped he would forgive her trickery.

After taking a few deep breaths to steady herself, she clutched her belly and groaned as she bent over double. Eric immediately woke, his face paling as he sat up and put an arm around her. The fear on his young face made her feel very guilty, but she just groaned louder.

"What ails the lass?" demanded the short, heavy guard as he stepped closer to their cell.

"I dinnae ken," Eric replied. "Maldie, are ye in pain? What is wrong with you?"

" 'Tis my woman's time and it comes on hard," Maldie said, rocking back and forth and moaning. "I need a maid's help."

Blushing furiously, Eric looked back at the guard. "Ye must bring a woman to help her."

''Why?'' the guard snapped even as he backed away, staring at Maldie as if she had caught the plague.

''Because she is in pain, ye great fool. Why, she might even die if she doesnae get some help.''

''What matter that? The lass is for the scaffold in but a few hours.''

Maldie inwardly cursed. She had not considered that complication. At Donncoill no one had wanted her harmed, so they had been more than willing to get her all she needed to stay hale and happy. Here everyone knew she was soon to hang, that she was as good as dead, and a dead woman did not need any pampering. Then Eric began to speak in a cold, commanding voice, and she decided she needed to have more confidence in the boy.

''I think Beaton would want her to still be alive when he hangs her,'' Eric said. ''Aye, alive and fully aware of her impending death. He wants to send her to hell and he willnae be verra pleased if he learns that ye sat by, idle and uncaring, whilst she took herself to that blighted place. If ye value your ugly hide at all, ye had best fetch her a woman to tend to her.''

Maldie heard the guard curse, then hurry away. She waited a moment before looking to be sure he had gone. When she finally looked straight at Eric his eyes widened as he stared at her. She knew she would not have to waste much time in explanations.

''I am not ill, Eric,'' she reassured him, watching and listening closely for the guard's return. ''This is how I got out of Donncoill. He will be bringing me a maid in a moment and when he unlocks the door to let her in, we must be ready for him.''

'' 'Twill be two against two,'' Eric said, frowning slightly as he considered their chances. ''That is a verra big mon, and neither of us is verra large.''

'' 'Twill be us against him. The maid will do naught. All we must do with her is make sure that she doesnae get free and cry out an alarum. The guard must be rendered useless enough so that we can get past him, out of this cursed cage, and lock him up within it.''

"I understand.''

"Good, for he is returning.''

Maldie wished they had had more time to make a plan. Neither of them really knew what the other would do. It was going to take a great deal of luck to get free. She took another deep breath and firmly told herself not to worry as she returned to her act of being in severe pain. Eric was a clever lad. Even in the short time they had been together, he had proven that time and time again. She would put her trust in his instincts.

The door opened, Maldie heard the soft rustle of skirts move toward her, then heard the guard bellow. She looked up, saw that the plump young maid was not watching her, and moved quickly to take advantage of that. She grabbed the maid by the arm and, when the woman turned toward her, punched her. The woman grunted once and started to fall. Maldie shoved the maid toward the cot, let her slump over the thin, hay-stuffed mat, and then turned toward the cell door.

Eric was clinging to the guard's back like a tenacious child. His slim arms were wrapped tightly around the man's thick neck and his long legs encircled the guard's soft waist. Beaton's man was trying desperately to shake free of the boy, slamming him up against the thick iron bars and the stone walls and clawing at Eric's arms. One look at the pale, strained expression upon Eric's face told Maldie that the boy would not be able to hold on much longer.

It was not easy to get a clean swing at the man as he thrashed around the tiny cell, waving his arms to keep her at a distance and then trying yet again to loosen Eric's grip. Then the man began to stagger, Eric's tight hold on his neck finally making it too hard to breathe. The guard's eyes closed as he gasped for air and frantically tore at Eric's arms. Maldie made her move. She hit the guard on his very prominent jaw as hard as she could. She heard Eric curse as the man stumbled backward and hit the wall, but he did not go down. She hit him again, echoing Eric's curse as pain shot through her arm, but this time she succeeded. Eric barely got off the guard in time as the man took a few steps toward a rapidly retreating Maldie, then reeled and fell, banging his head on the filthy stone floor with a loud, sickening thud.

"Are ye alright, Eric?" she asked as she hurried to the boy's side.

"I dinnae think there is one part of me that doesnae ache, but 'twill pass," Eric replied, wincing as he looked over the torn sleeves of his shirt and his badly scratched and bruised arms. "Some clean water to wash in wouldnae be amiss, either."

"True, but that will probably be a long while in coming." Maldie gently flexed the fingers of the hand she had hit the guard with. It was going to be livid with bruising, but she was sure it was not broken. "He was a hard mon to knock down."

"Do ye think he is dead? He hit the floor dangerously hard."

Cautiously, Maldie approached the prone man and checked him for any signs of life, finding a strong pulse in his throat. "He still lives. Come, we had best get out of here."

Eric groaned softly as he followed her to the door, his body protesting every move he made. "Are we going to lock them in here?"

"But of course," Maldie answered even as she picked up the key the guard had dropped when Eric had jumped on him, then shut the heavy door of the cell. "We cannae be sure how long either of them will be *resting.*" She locked the door and tossed the key aside then looked up the steep, narrow stone steps that led to the great hall. "I just wish that we kenned another way to get out of here."

"There is probably some bolt hole only Beaton himself kens about," said Eric, as he crept up the stairs and listened at the thick oak door at the top. "I cannae believe the mon would leave himself without some way to escape his many enemies. I fear I havenae been able to learn of it, so we must take our chances this way."

When Eric suddenly tensed, then looked at her with wide

eyes, Maldie felt her heart skip with alarm and she hurried up the steps to stand behind him. "What is wrong?" she whispered.

"I think we may have more to worry about than who might be lurking in the great hall."

Maldie quickly became aware of the sounds coming through the door. Even muffled by the thick wood, the clash of swords and the screams of wounded and dying men were easily recognizable. "A battle, and 'tis within the keep itself. Do ye think it is Balfour?"

"We had best pray that it is, or we shall be in as much danger from Beaton's foes as from his followers."

Her heart pounding loudly with fear, Maldie squeezed past Eric and eased the heavy door open enough to peer inside of the great hall. No one was there, but the sounds of battle were certainly coming from some place close at hand. Then she heard a bellowed war cry and felt her heart stop briefly with hope and anticipation. She looked back at Eric and could see from the stunned look upon his face that he had also heard that exhuberant Murray yell.

She had asked Eric to pray that they could get out of their cell and that Balfour would choose today to attack, but the request had mostly been made in jest. Fate was clearly smiling widely on her and Eric today. Maldie tried not to grow too sure of success or safety for they were still within the keep and, although she could hear Balfour and his men and knew that they had a good chance of victory now that they had entered Beaton's very walls, they were nowhere to be seen. There was a lot of Dubhlinn surrounding them, and there might well be a lot of Beaton's men between the great hall and the safety of the Murray camp.

" 'Tis Balfour," said Eric as he followed Maldie into the great hall. "The Murrays have actually gotten within the gates this time. Victory is assured. We are free!" He hugged Maldie and laughed.

"I think I must ask ye to pray for things more often," she teased and returned his quick grin. "Hold," she ordered, and grabbed him by the arm when he started to hurry away from her.

"But 'tis the Murrays out there. We will be safe now."

"Aye, we will be once we can get to one who isnae fighting for his life and can set us somewhere safe. We must tread warily for now, however, for we dinnae ken what lies between us and them."

"Weel, now, everyone told me that ye were a clever lass," drawled a deep, raspy voice that chilled Maldie's blood, and she turned to face one very large, sword-wielding obstacle between her and Eric and the doors leading out of the great hall.

"It seems I should listen to ye more often," murmured Eric, "for 'tis clear that ye can often be right."

"Weel, this is one time I really wish I wasnae."

Chapter Eighteen

"Ah, 'tis George," Maldie said, and tried to smile at the scowling man. "Have ye come to surrender to us then?"

"Surrender?" George bellowed as he moved toward her and Eric. "I have come to kill you, ye black-haired bitch. This is all your doing."

"My doing? How can that be? I am but a wee lass, George. I cannae command an army."

"Nay? Ye arrive at Dubhlinn and, for the first time in thirteen long years, the Murrays get in through our gates. It all seems verra clear to me. This be all your fault."

Maldie wondered how long she could keep the man talking. His attention was fully fixed upon her, and she could feel that Eric was cautiously moving away from her side. As long as she could hold all of George's interest, Eric had a chance to do something to hinder the man's clear intent to kill her. Although she was not sure what a slender youth could do against a man the size of George, she was more than willing to give Eric a chance to try. And if they were truly fortunate, a Murray might just happen by to rescue them. It sounded as if there were plenty of them around.

"Now, George, I dinnae think that ye are seeing too clearly," she continued, catching a glimpse of Eric sidling toward the weapons still hanging on the walls, evidence that the Murrays had indeed caught the Beatons completely by surprise. "I was here once before, if ye recall, and the Murrays were soundly defeated, sent back to Donncoill like whipped dogs. If I was truly the one behind this defeat, why didnae I help the Murrays the last time they rode against you?"

George frowned and hesitated, then vigorously shook his head. "Nay. Ye try to trick me. Ye werenae here when the Murrays were beaten back. I ken it weel, for 'twas when we stole the laddie. Ye werenae here then, for I had been searching for ye the whole day. Everyone I asked told me that ye had gone away. Ye went away to help the Murrays."

A soft screech of surprise and alarm escaped her when George suddenly charged straight at her. She darted out of his way as fast as she could, but he was still able to slash at her skirts with his sword. Running was not the most clever of defenses but, since she had no weapon, Maldie decided it would have to do for now. Using the tables, chairs, and benches in the great hall, Maldie tried to always keep something between her and the heartily cursing George. Eric was still trying desperately to get a weapon off the wall that he could use, and she needed to gain him the time to do so.

Maldie leapt upon the huge head table and watched as George stood at the side of it, glaring at her and breathing heavily. She suspected it was not the safest place in the great hall, but she was also out of breath. She had already stumbled twice and knew that a fall could prove fatal. Each time she had tried to get to the doors, George had been between her and them. Each time she had tried to reach one of the weapons on the wall, George had been there. For just a moment she needed to stand still. If she watched him closely, she was sure there was enough room upon the table for her to elude his sword.

"Ye should be out there with the others trying to save Dubh-linn," she said, "not in here chasing a wee lass and a young boy."

"I am nay interested in the lad," George replied. "He is Beaton's brat. If a Beaton sword doesnae cut him down to keep him from gaining Dubhlinn, then as soon as the Murrays ken that he is a Beaton and not one of their own, one of them will end his life. And this battle has already been won by the Murrays. Once they got within the gates, Dubhlinn was doomed to fall. I will linger here only long enough to kill you, and then I shall search for safer lands."

It took Maldie a moment to grasp the full importance of what George had just said. "Ye ken that Eric is Beaton's child?"

"Aye, he carries the mark."

"How would ye ken that? Were ye his nurse or midwife?" She quickly pressed her lips together. It was not wise to insult a man with a sword.

"I was one of the men told to leave the bairn on the hillside to die." He shrugged. "I kenned that Beaton had a mark and was curious to see if he was right about the child."

"But Beaton doesnae ken the truth."

"Nay, the fool. He was too enraged to e'en look at the bairn. Once he kenned that his wee whore of a wife had bedded down with the old Murray laird, he was blinded to the truth. Ere Beaton took it into his head to claim the lad as his own, even a whisper about the boy could get ye killed. I decided to hold fast to what I had learned. Only the lad's mother kenned the truth, and mayhap the midwife, but neither of them lived long enough to tell anyone. Beaton made verra sure of that."

"Of what use is it to ken such a truth and keep it to yourself for all these years?"

"I was waiting for that bastard Calum to slip from favor with our laird, and then I would have used it to take his place. Now, it doesnae matter. 'Tis useless. Both Calum and our laird will soon be dead, and I shall be back to selling my sword to whoever has a wee bit of coin. I had a good life here, and ye stole it all away from me, ye bitch."

He swung his sword at her and Maldie barely escaped having her feet cut off at the ankles. As he prepared to strike at her a second time, she did the only thing she could think of. She kicked him as hard as she could, bringing her foot up under his chin. George screamed, dropping his sword as he clutched at his jaw. Blood trickled out of the corners of his mouth, and Maldie wondered if he had lost a few of his teeth or even a bit of his tongue. She kicked him again, full in the face.

George was thrust back by the force of the blow. An odd look of horror and surprise crossed his face, and he looked down at his chest. Maldie followed his gaze and gasped. The tip of a sword blade was protruding from his thickly padded jupon. He started to fall forward and she heard a soft curse from behind him. The sword point disappeared and George fell to the floor. Behind him stood Eric, pale, wide-eyed, and holding a bloodied sword in his two hands.

"Oh, Eric," she murmured as she hopped down from the table and took the sword from his hands.

"He was going to kill you," Eric whispered, wiping the sweat from his brow with a shaking hand.

"That he was. Now, set that truth firmly in your mind and ye willnae suffer for doing this." She started to gently pull him toward the doors, eager to escape the great hall before anyone else arrived.

"I shouldnae suffer at all for killing one of the enemy. I am to be a knight when I am one and twenty. I believe they must kill the enemy from time to time."

She was glad to hear that hint of his sharp wit, even though there was still a tremor in his voice. He would recover from the horror of killing George. It was a shame that he had had to kill his first man before he had even really begun his training as a knight, but there had really been no choice at all. George had seen that all he had built was falling down around him, and he had decided she was the reason he was losing everything. He had needed someone to blame, someone to pay for that loss with blood. If Eric had not killed the man, George would have killed her. She was sorry for the shock and pain Eric was suffering, but not for the fact that he had killed that man.

"Beaton killed my mother," Eric said quietly.

"So George said," Maldie answered, keeping a close watch for any armed Beaton as she headed for the iron-studded door that led to the bailey.

"And George was the one who left me out to die."

"Aye, on Beaton's orders." She knew he was simply saying aloud all of the reasons why it was simple justice to kill George. "And George did it even after he learned that there was no reason to, that ye really *were* Beaton's son."

Eric grunted as, once outside of the door, Maldie shoved him up against the wall. She was sorry to add to the many bruises he had, but the bailey was crowded with fighting men and, until she could see a clear path to the gates, she wanted the youth protected and unseen in the shadows near the high walls of the keep. After only a moment of watching the battle, one the Beatons were clearly losing, she decided that there was no safe way to get to the gates. They could not continue to cower near the door either. She cursed.

"What is wrong?" asked Eric, looking around the bailey and trying to see if there was anyone he recognized and could call out to. " 'Tis nay easy to ken who is who in this melee, is it?"

"Nay. 'Tis nay easy to see a clear and safe path to the gates either."

"We cannae stay here."

"I ken it. It may be sheltered now, but with so many armed men about, ones who are eager to kill and others who are desperate to flee the killing, it willnae be safe for long."

"Then we had best run for our lives."

Before she could stop him, Eric darted around her, grabbed her by the hand, and ran toward the gates. Maldie held tightly to the sword she carried and prayed she would not be forced to use it. It was madness to run straight through the heart of a fierce battle, but she had had no choices to give the boy, and no time to think of any. She noticed that they were not the only ones fleeing either.

When Eric abruptly halted, she bumped into his back and cursed. They were only feet from the gates, but set firmly between them and freedom stood a bloodied Calum. He smiled and she felt her blood run cold. Ignoring Eric's sharp protest, she yanked on the boy's arm and set herself between him and Calum.

"I am no coward to hide behind a lass's skirts," Eric muttered.

"This lass holds a sword and ye are unarmed," she said, not taking her eyes off Calum.

"Ye can barely lift the weapon, child," Calum said. " 'Twill be too easy to cut ye down and then the boy."

"If it will be so easy, then why do ye hesitate?" she asked, aiming the sword at him and feeling the weight of it all the way up her arms. Maldie was not sure she could even swing such a large weapon, and the coldly amused look in Calum's eyes told her that he did not think so either.

"Am I to just rush forward and impale myself?"

" 'Twould be justice if ye did. Where is your laird? I didnae think ye were able to walk or talk without him."

"My laird faces Balfour Murray. Since this battle is lost, I saw no gain in standing with him."

"And so ye slink away like the adder ye are."

"Beaton was right. 'Tis a shame ye are a lass. Ye would have made him a fine son."

"I dinnae see that as any great flattery. Now, my brother and I have many things to do, and ye and I dinnae really have anything to say to each other, so, shall we just finish this dance?"

Calum laughed, a soft chilly sound that made Maldie very uneasy. "Are ye that eager to die, lass?"

"Nay, that eager to kill you."

Even as she prepared to meet his strike, another sword appeared between hers and Calum's, taking the blow meant for her. Eric grabbed her and pulled her away as Calum turned to meet this new challenge. Maldie looked at the man who had taken her place and decided that she might have been mistaken while she was at Donncoill. At times it could be very nice to see James.

"Ye ken James far better than I do," she said to Eric, neither of them taking their eyes from the two men fighting in front of them. "Do ye think he can win against Calum?"

"Aye, without e'en sweating," Eric replied, his voice full of pride.

"Such faith in the mon."

" 'Tis deserved."

Maldie saw the truth of that a moment later. Both men were bloodied, filthy with the dirt of battle, and Maldie knew James had done as much fighting, if not more than Calum, but it was Calum who wavered first. James smiled faintly when the man faltered, leaving himself open for the death blow James quickly delivered. She stood quietly by as James wiped his sword on the dead man's padded jupon, then turned to look at her and Eric.

"We had hoped that ye would have the sense to stay in the dungeons where ye would have been safe from all of this," James said, taking the sword from Maldie's hand. "Ye should have picked a smaller one, lass."

"Ah, weel, I lacked the time to choose carefully," she said.

" 'Tis good to see ye, laddie," James said, giving Eric a brief hug. "Come with me. I will take the two of ye to where the pages and the wounded wait with the horses. Ye will be safe there." He looked at Maldie as he led her and Eric out through the gates. "And ye will stay there."

"Where would we go, James?" she said sweetly and smiled when he scowled at her.

"Are ye weel, laddie?" James asked Eric as he slipped an arm around the boy's shoulders and saw him wince faintly.

"A wee bit bruised, but no more."

"Beaton beat ye, did he?"

"Some, but the bruises I carry were not all from him. Our escape from the dungeons wasnae as easy as we had hoped for."

Maldie walked quietly beside them, only partly listening as Eric told James all they had done. The boy revealed a pleasant touch of modesty as he described his part in it all. The way

James kept glancing at her made Maldie a little uneasy. It was hard to tell if he was angry or surprised.

James left them with the horses and hurried away to find Nigel. As Maldie sat down on the hillside next to Eric, she wondered what had possessed Nigel to ride to this battle when he was not fully healed from the last one, then sighed and shook her head. Men being the odd creatures that they were, she suspected some twisted ideas of honor and pride had made him come. James was clearly keeping a close watch on the man, and that had to suffice.

"I found it verra hard to accept James's hearty welcome," Eric murmured.

"Why?" she asked.

"Because 'tis a lie. I am not the lad he thinks I am."

She smiled gently and patted his hand where it rested on the grass. "Ye are the same lad who rode by his side ere Beaton had ye taken from Donncoill."

"Mayhap inside, but I am now a Beaton, not a Murray. James greeted a Murray, one he thinks is one of his clan. I ached to tell him the truth right then." Eric began to agitatedly yank the grass out of the ground. "He is a good mon and deserves to ken the whole truth."

"If ye are going to tell him, then ye shall have to tell them all. That should be done when they are all together, so that they hear it together."

"Oh, aye, and so that they all then spit on me together."

"I dinnae think they will spit on you," she said, pained by her inability to ease his fears. "They have cared for ye for thirteen years, Eric. I dinnae think that can change so verra quickly."

"Mayhap not." He gave her a crooked smile, a little embarrassed by his own foolishness, then sighed heavily. "It will change though. It has to. They may have cared for me for years, but they have also loathed and fought the Beatons for years as weel. 'Tis hard to explain. 'Tis just that I feel things must change. How can they not?"

"I fear I have no answers to give ye, Eric. I dinnae ken your

clan as weel as ye do. James, Balfour, and Nigel all seem to
be good, fair men. Aye, and they all possess some wit. It would
seem to me that it should make no difference in how they feel
toward you. After all, ye havenae lied. Ye also thought ye were
a Murray. They told ye that from the day ye were plucked off
that hillside and brought to Donncoill.

"There is one thing ye must do, however. Dinnae let this
change you. Dinnae let it poison your heart so that ye see hate
and mistrust where it doesnae exist. Aye, it can be painful to
hope all will be weel, then find out that it will not be. But, if
ye make yourself believe that they must dislike and mistrust
you, ye will become a different mon, not the one they have
known for so long."

"Ye are saying that if I continue to believe the worst, then
the worst may just happen. I will make it so."

"Aye, something like that. Now, ready yourself, for I see
your foolish brother Nigel limping his way up the hillside."

Eric laughed and eagerly accepted Nigel's hug. Nigel collapsed on the grass by his side and Eric was soon relating the
tale of their escape all over again. Maldie felt someone staring
at her and looked up to see that James was standing before
her. Her eyes widened a little when she saw how uneasy he
looked, as if he was a little embarrassed.

"I said I would stay here," she said, smiling a little as she
tried to ease some of the awkwardness he so clearly felt.

"Aye, I suspect ye will." James cleared his throat. "I but
wished to apologize for my suspicions."

"Ye dinnae need to," she replied, wishing she could stop
his unnecessary apology. "Ye had a right to suspect me. If
naught else, I was the only one ye didnae ken weel, and I
arrived at your gates at a verra suspicious moment."

"That is nay good enough. I had no proof that ye were a
Beaton spy. None at all. I should not have let my concerns
make me unfair in my judgments."

"Ye did what ye had to. I feel no ill will."

He nodded, then frowned slightly. "Ye didnae happen to
find out how Beaton discovered who Malcolm was, did ye?"

"Nay, I didnae talk long with Beaton and he wasnae of a mind to confide in me."

"I think I may be at fault for that," said Eric.

"Nay, lad. Ye would ne'er betray your own," Nigel said, patting his young brother on the back.

"Not on purpose, nay. But, I think I may have revealed in some small way that I recognized him. He came down to the dungeons with Beaton the day after I was tossed down there. I was verra surprised to see him standing there at Beaton's side. That may have shown on my face, and it was all Beaton needed."

"Nay, he would have needed more than that, I think," James said.

"Mayhap Malcolm was seen when he came to visit me later, alone," Eric continued. "I think he hoped to rescue me. 'Tis what he spoke to me about."

"That would be the mistake that got him killed."

"Aye," agreed Nigel. "It would have been. Beaton would have had the dungeons carefully watched. Aye, the wrong glance from you may have stirred a suspicion or two, but they would have died away. Malcolm acting so quickly to try and set ye free would have made that brief glance of recognition far more important than it needed to have been. None of us will e'er ken what Malcolm was thinking, but by showing so much interest in you, he gave himself away. That is what got him murdered."

Eric shivered and, wrapping his arms around himself, rubbed his hands up and down his arms in a vain attempt to remove the sudden chill that had run through his body. "And it was a slow, brutal murder, too. I dinnae want to see such cruelty e'er again. For that alone Beaton should die a hundred deaths."

"Ye saw Malcolm murdered?" demanded James, his voice hard and cold.

"Beaton thought it would harden me to see how traitors are treated." He shook his head. "Malcolm suffered for days, but he ne'er told Beaton a thing, whispered not one secret about the Murrays. He was a verra brave and loyal mon. I dinnae think I could have held firm throughout such agony. Nay, not when it went on for days."

"No lad should have had to see that."

"I suspect Beaton saw such cruelty at a young age," murmured Maldie. "From all Eric told me, the mon seemed to think the lad needed such training, needed the hardening it would bring. Aye, sometimes men like Beaton are born mean, but sometimes such men are made, the evil in them nurtured and strengthened throughout their younger years."

"Ah, so ye mean to say that since Beaton's father was a cruel bastard, that made Beaton a cruel bastard, too," said Nigel, and Maldie nodded. "Sad, but it willnae save him from the killing he deserves."

"Nay, and I wouldnae suggest that it did. In truth, I think Beaton would welcome death if he wasnae so terrified of the judgment he will face. And I believe Beaton's father may have been crueler than we can e'er imagine. 'Twould be one understandable reason why Beaton killed him and seems to suffer no guilt for having done so."

"Beaton killed his own father?" James asked, his voice softened by the horror of such a crime.

"Aye, he told me so himself."

"He killed my mother as weel," said Eric, pulling the men's attention his way.

As Eric explained how he had gained that piece of information, Maldie took the moment to try and gather her courage. Eric would soon be telling his brothers and James the whole truth about himself. That meant she would have to be truthful as well. James's reaction to the news that Beaton had killed his own father told her that at least some of her truths would not be accepted. It was indeed a grave sin to murder one of your parents, but she had never allowed herself to think about that for long. She had the sick feeling that she would soon see just how unacceptable it was to everyone except men like Beaton.

Beaton's opinion that she was more like him than she would like to be stuck in her mind and made her inwardly cringe. She did not want that to be true, but she had to wonder on it. If she had been quicker and Beaton and Calum had been slower, she would now have the blood of her own father on her hands. The truly upsetting thing about it all was that Beaton, foul work of a man that he was, probably had far more justification for killing his father than she had for trying to kill hers.

Deep inside of her brewed a hard anger at her mother. The only thing that kept it locked within her heart was that right beside it was a pain she was not sure she could deal with. If her mother had loved her at all, the woman's bitterness had eaten it all away. No truly loving mother would do to her daughter what Margaret Kirkcaldy had done to hers. Margaret had raised her only child to go and kill a man, and not just any man, but the one whose seed had made her, and she had not once cared what that might do to her child.

Maldie wondered how much else Beaton had said might be true, and feared that a great deal of it had been. Margaret had not wanted Beaton dead because her heart had been broken, or even because she had been left poor and shamed, but because her soaring vanity had been stung. It was a horrible thing to see in one's own mother, but the more Maldie considered it, the more it tasted like the truth.

Whenever Margaret had spoken of love and broken hearts, the woman had often sounded as if she quoted some minstrel's lyrics. There had always been a faint ring of falseness to her protestations of love lost, but Maldie had tried to tell herself that it was simply a reticence to speak of such personal things. However, other things her mother had said when speaking of Beaton had clearly concerned her badly stung pride, the insult she felt over being cast aside like some common whore, and they had always sounded sincere. Even when her mother had been dying and demanding that Maldie swear a blood oath to kill Beaton, the woman had spoken of her injured pride, of the outrage she still felt that the man would do such a thing to her. Maldie realized that it was only when she had hesitated that her mother had even mentioned her broken heart. She also realized that not once had her mother spoken of the man's crime in deserting his child. That had always been her own grievance, and she had just assumed that her mother had shared it.

When Eric nudged her to draw her attention to him, she welcomed the interruption in her thoughts. All the pain and anger she held inside were rising up, choking her, and now was not a good time to face them or any of the other hard truths she had ignored for so long. Eric was like a salve on her sore heart. He cared for her and she had no doubt about that at all. The youth did not have a false bone in his body. She prayed that that would never change.

"Are ye tired, Maldie?" Eric asked.

"Aye, weary to the bone, but I will be fine," she replied. "This will all be over soon." She looked toward the village, pleased to see that there was little fighting there. "I hope my dear friend Eleanor got safely away."

"The old woman ye stayed with?" asked James.

"Aye, how did ye ken that?"

"Douglas told us."

Maldie briefly gaped at James. "Douglas is a Murray mon?"

"Aye, always has been. When ye tried to kill Beaton and were sentenced to hang for it, he came back to Donncoill. Too much had changed and he was gaining little knowledge. As he said, to act even a little curious about the laird and his doings was enough to get ye killed."

"It was," agreed Eric. "Beaton hanged several men simply because he thought they *might* be guilty of treason against him. From what little I heard they had committed no crime save to ask the wrong question or hear some small thing Beaton felt they shouldnae have. Most people kept their distance from the keep and from Beaton. Few people e'en dared to open their mouths. Douglas was wise to get away while he still could."

"Ye saw the old woman Eleanor, did ye?" Maldie asked, regaining James's attention.

"Aye, and she saw us," replied James. "Ye warned her, didnae ye?"

"I did. I hope she heeded it and did so without harm to your cause.'' She smiled crookedly as she looked at the smoke rising from within the walls of Dubhlinn. '' 'Tis clear she didnae hurt ye at all.''

"Not at all, and I feel sure she got to a safe place. There is nary a doubt in my mind that she had guessed we were not here for the wares of the marketplace.''

"Good. She is a sweet, kindhearted woman and I was afraid for her.''

Despite all of her efforts not to, Maldie realized that she could not stop herself from continually glancing toward the waning battle. She knew she was looking for Balfour, and the hint of amusement in James's eyes told her that he knew it, too. It made no sense, for anything she might have shared with the man would soon be brutally ended. Yet she was hungry for the sight of him, wanted to see with her own eyes that he had survived the battle and was able to enjoy a well-deserved victory.

"I am going to go and find that fool laird of ours," James announced, pointedly glancing at Maldie. "I cannae believe there are any Beatons left to fight.''

"Calum said he left his laird facing yours," Maldie told him.

"Weel, that confrontation should be over by now," James muttered, frowning slightly as he hurried back toward the keep.

"Balfour wouldnae lose to Beaton, would he?" Eric asked Nigel, his voice softened by concern.

"Nay," Nigel replied without hesitation.

"If Calum spoke the truth, then the fight between Balfour and Beaton has either lasted a verra long time or—"

"There is no *or*, lad. Balfour will defeat Beaton. Mayhap he plays with the mon. Mayhap Calum lied. Mayhap Balfour and Beaton had a lot to say to each other ere they truly began to fight. The length of time one takes to fight an enemy doesnae determine who wins or loses. Believe me, lad, Beaton doesnae stand a chance against our brother.''

Maldie watched James disappear through the high gates of Dubhlinn and prayed that Nigel was right. Eric's worry was her own. Beaton should have been defeated by now, and yet there was no sign of Balfour. She felt sure that, after today, she would never see Balfour again, but she did not want that to be because Beaton had killed him.

Chapter Nineteen

"Murray, ye bastard," yelled a raspy voice, and Balfour tensed.

He easily recognized the voice. It was the same one that had taunted him from the walls of Dubhlinn the last time he had tried to rescue Eric and failed so miserably. Beaton was approaching him from behind and Balfour felt alarm ripple through him.

Balfour quickly turned, his sword at the ready. He was surprised that Beaton had even spoken, had not simply crept up on him and stabbed him in the back. It should have been Beaton's first thought upon finding him without a man to watch his back, but Beaton was obviously too enraged to think clearly. It was understandable for the man was seeing everything he had built be cut down before his eyes, but it could prove to be fatal.

Beaton stopped but feet from him, ripped off his mail cowl, and Balfour gaped, unable to control his expression of shock. The last time he had seen the man Beaton had been high up on the walls of Dubhlinn, and Balfour had not been able to see the way the man's disease had ravaged his face and body.

Although he could only see Beaton's face, it looked as if the man was rotting away. Balfour's first instinct was to back away, to put as much distance as he could between Beaton and himself for fear of catching whatever ailed the man, but he resisted that urge to give into his fear. No one else at Dubhlinn seemed to be suffering the same affliction, even though Beaton had been fighting it for at least three years. That indicated that it was not something one could just catch. He also trusted in Maldie's knowledge of such things. She had told Douglas that it was just some affliction of the skin, and would have quickly warned the man and everyone else she could if it was one a person could catch. Since she had not issued such a warning, Balfour decided that what Beaton suffered was his own private torment, something that could not be healed or inflicted upon others.

"I have come for my brother," Balfour said, watching Beaton closely since the man had a reputation for fighting in less than honorable ways.

"Ye mean my son?"

"My father's son. Ye cast the lad aside as if he were no more than scraps from your table. Ye have no claim to him. Ye denounced that years ago."

"A serious lack of foresight that I now intend to correct."

"No one will believe it." Balfour then shrugged, having espied Calum slipping away and leaving Beaton alone to face his fate. "It doesnae matter anyway, for ye will soon be dead."

"This slow rotting ye see hasnae killed me yet."

"Nay, but I dinnae intend to leave ye alive now that I have found you. Ye have committed your last outrage against my people."

Balfour knew the moment that Beaton realized he was alone. The slight loss of color the man suffered when he saw that Calum had deserted him made Beaton look an even more sickening gray. For one brief moment he wondered if it was right to fight with the man. It seemed somewhat dishonorable to take up his sword against such an obviously sick knight. Then he watched Beaton move and realized that, no matter how bad the man looked, he still had his strength and probably some of his former skill. Beaton still had the ability to kill him, and that was all he needed to know.

"Arenae ye going to ask about your wee whore?" Beaton taunted him as they began to slowly circle each other.

"If ye try to enrage me with your insults about Maldie, I would save your breath, especially since ye willnae be enjoying it for much longer. Ye willnae cause me to act foolishly. Ye will just be giving me more reason to kill you."

"Mayhap, my boastful enemy, I shall kill you."

"Face to face with no one to aid ye? I think not. Ye have let others do your fighting for you for too long, Beaton. Aye, either that or done your killing treacherously in the dark, and from behind. A mon can lose his skills quickly when he doesnae keep them honed."

Balfour realized that Beaton was not keeping the same control over his emotions that he was. The man's face flushed a deep red, accentuating the sores and seared skin grotesquely. Beaton was clearly too lost in his fury and sense of defeat to realize the weakness he was revealing. As plainly as if he had spoken the words aloud, he told Balfour that he could be taunted into acting rashly and that could make him easier to kill.

"Ye may have won this battle, Murray, but I intend to see that ye ne'er survive to enjoy the sweet taste of victory. Aye, and neither will the two ye have come to save."

It was hard, but Balfour ignored the man's threat, Beaton's not so subtle claim that Eric and Maldie were about to murdered. Fear for them was a hard knot in his belly, however, as he met and parried Beaton's first, somewhat frantic strike. The power of the blow was enough to tell Balfour that he needed to keep all of his attention upon Beaton. The man's skill may have slipped due to high emotion and lack of use, but he was still a serious threat. All he could do was pray that Beaton lied, or, if he did not, that he could reach his brother and his lover before whatever murderous plan Beaton had made was enacted.

The battle was fierce and silent. Balfour was grateful for the fact that Beaton needed all of his strength to fight him and had none left for any taunts. He was proud of his control over his emotions, the way he had concentrated all of his feelings and attention onto one goal, killing Beaton, but Balfour knew his grip was a tenuous one.

It did not take long for Balfour to know that he would win the fight with Beaton, unless some horrible twist of fate or one of Beaton's men intervened. The man still had some skill left and strength, but that strength was waning. Whether it was because of the illness or too long a dependence upon others to do his fighting, Beaton tired swiftly. His sword thrusts became more erratic, and he began to stagger when he avoided Balfour's attacks.

The end came in an almost disappointing way. Beaton stumbled even as he tried to parry a blow by Balfour, and left himself open for a swift, clean death stroke. Balfour did not hesitate to take full advantage of that, thrusting his sword deep into Beaton's chest. As he watched the man fall, Balfour felt little more than relief that it was over, and that now he could find the two people he had come to save. Beaton had been their enemy for so long, Balfour was surprised at how little he felt over the man's death, but decided that he did not have the time to sort out his own vagaries.

He wiped his sword clean on Beaton's jupon, idly noting that Beaton's armor was old. Although the man had been accumulating wealth off the backs of his people for years, he had clearly not spent much on weaponry and armor to protect them. Beaton had evidently depended mostly on hiding behind Dubhlinn's high, strong walls. It explained the ease with which the battle was being won once they had gotten within those walls.

"Weel, now ye are the corpse ye have looked like for so long," he muttered as he stood up and looked around.

The few remaining Beatons who were still fighting had either seen or already heard of their laird's death. A cry had gone up as soon as the man had fallen. Balfour doubted they would continue to fight, at least not for Beaton. Since so many of Dubhlinn's men at arms were hired swords, outlaws, and outcasts, there might be some who feared capture more than death. The battle, however, was as good as finished.

As he strode toward the keep, Balfour paused by one badly wounded Beaton man lying in the mud, bent down, and grabbed him by the front of his tattered jupon, lifting him off the ground slightly. "Where are the prisoners?" he demanded, wanting to make sure that matters had not changed since Douglas had fled Dubhlinn.

"Which ones?" the man asked, his voice weak and hoarse with pain, but still holding a thread of defiance.

"The lass Beaton meant to hang and the boy he tried to claim as the son he couldnae make for himself," Balfour snapped, gently shaking the man.

"Jesu, cannae ye let a mon die in peace?"

"Nay, and, if ye die before ye tell me what I wish to ken, I will follow ye to the gates of hell to throttle the answer out of ye."

"In the dungeons, curse ye." The man groaned when Balfour let him go and he fell back down on the ground.

"Who is with them?" Balfour felt a brief touch of guilt over his rough treatment of a wounded man, then looked more closely and decided that, although the man was badly wounded, it was probably not fatal.

"One guard."

Balfour stepped over the man and walked into the keep. He held his sword at the ready, but met no one who challenged him. In fact, he met no one at all, and realized that his surprise attack had been more successful than he had hoped, so complete that no one had had time to set up a defense within the thick, sheltering walls of the keep. Stepping into the great hall, Balfour saw the door Douglas had told him about, and all of his fears for Eric and Maldie rushed up to choke him. Without any thought for his own safety, he ran straight for it, flung it open, and hurled himself down the steep stairs.

* * *

As he slumped against the cool wall of the great hall, Balfour wiped the sweat from his face with his sleeve. He had fought his way to the hall and heedlessly rushed down to the dungeons only to find a frantic maid and a groaning guard. They told him that Eric and Maldie had knocked them out, locked them in, and fled. Balfour had left the two there, ignoring their colorful aspersions upon his, Eric's, and Maldie's characters as he raced back up the dark stairs. Once back in the great hall, however, he had come to a halt, unsure of where to go and what to do next. He had been so sure that he would find Eric and Maldie that he felt rooted to the spot with the weight of his disappointment.

He did not know where James was, or Douglas, or Nigel. Once the battle had begun he had paid little heed to anything except getting to the great hall, to the dungeons where everyone had said his brother and Maldie were being held. Cursing softly under his breath, he started out of the room, knowing to his disgust that he could well have passed within feet of them, may have even missed them by minutes. The only comfort he could find was that, if Beaton had planned their murder, they had escaped that. He just did not know when, where to, or if they had been successful. Trying to flee in the midst of a heated battle was not easy.

Suddenly, he saw the dead man sprawled beside the head table, and he tensed. Balfour realized that he had become so consumed with finding Eric and Maldie that he was not keeping a watch on the enemy. This man was dead, but he still should have at least noticed the body, been aware of the implications. For all that it looked deserted, the inside of the keep was obviously not completely safe. Balfour wondered who had killed the man and prayed it was neither his young brother nor Maldie. Neither of them was hardened enough to accept killing a man as necessary, as simply a part of battle and survival. And they should never have had to, he thought with a strong wave of self-disgust, for he should have been there to protect them.

"Balfour," cried a deep familiar voice from the doorway.

"James, I dinnae think I have e'er been so glad to see you," Balfour said as James walked up beside him and stared down at the dead man.

"Yours?"

"Nay. I was just hoping that it wasnae Maldie's or Eric's." He frowned when James grimaced. "Have ye seen them? I went racing down to the dungeons only to discover that they had already let themselves out."

"Aye, they have and aye, this death came at their hands."

"They are unhurt?"

"They are. Calum tried to see that they didnae leave Dubhlinn, alive, but I ended that threat." James suddenly grinned. "I came upon them by accident. Your wee lass was standing there trying to lift a sword that was bigger than she and keeping herself between Eric and Calum. For a wee lass she has a lot of courage."

"She tried to fight with Calum?"

"She was just trying to get herself and the lad to safety. Have ye seen Beaton or has that slinking coward managed to avoid the judgment he so richly deserves?"

"I just sent Beaton to the devil."

"So that is why the fighting has all but ended."

"Then I need not return to it. Good. Where are Eric and Maldie?"

Balfour was eager to see his brother and Maldie, eager to see with his own eyes that they were unharmed. Until he did, he knew he would not be completely at ease, would not be able to fully believe that he had won. If nothing else, it had all gone too well, been too successful, and he found such ease of victory a little hard to believe in.

"They should not have had to do this," he muttered, nudging the dead man with his foot. "Maldie should ne'er have been forced to take up a sword."

"Lad, ye cannae be standing guard over everyone all the time," James said. "Ye would die from lack of sleep."

Balfour smiled briefly. "I am not completely guiltless in all of this but, aye, ye are right. I cannae watch everyone all the time or ken every danger that may lurk about the next corner. Dinnae fret. I am nay donning a hair shirt, just feeling a wee pinch or two of guilt.''

''Then let this victory soothe it.''

'' 'Twill be better soothed if I can see my brother and Maldie.''

''Follow me, laddie. I set them with the pages and the horses, safe upon the hillside. I put your fool of a brother Nigel there, too.''

''He is alright?'' Balfour asked as they stepped out into the bailey.

''Aye, just weary. He still doesnae have the strength needed to endure a full battle. Once his men no longer needed his direction, once it was clear that only God could snatch this victory from our hands, I took him out of the fighting.''

''I suspect he wasnae too pleased.''

James just smiled, and Balfour turned his attention to what was happening in the bailey and beyond. The battle was indeed over. His men were disarming the ones who had surrendered and the women and children were already appearing in the bailey. They meandered amongst the dead and wounded, looking for their men. The sharp sounds of grief were already welling up and Balfour inwardly grimaced. Beaton had left him no choice, but he did feel for the women and children who had lost fathers, sons, husbands, and lovers. There was a good chance that their lives would be better now that Beaton was dead, but he knew they would draw no comfort from that for a long while.

''There is naught ye can do for them,'' James murmured as they started to walk up the hill, at the top of which was Maldie and Eric.

''Aye, I ken it. It ne'er fails to steal some of the glory of victory, however. I also wonder what will happen to them now. We cannae take these lands. There are too many other claimants, and some in far more favor with the king than us.''

''It cannae be any worse for them than what they have already suffered under Beaton.''

"It may be one of Beaton's kinsmen."

"I should like to believe that all Beatons arenae as poisonous as that one."

Balfour just nodded, for his full attention was on the small group of people at the top of the hill. In but a moment he would see Maldie again. The last time he had seen her he had accused her of being a traitor, of being one of Beaton's curs. He still wondered if that was why she had come to Dubhlinn to kill Beaton. It was hard to guess why she had done it, or why she did anything. Balfour knew that he understood very little about Maldie, and knew even less. He was sure of one thing, however, and that was that she would not be welcoming him with open arms.

Somehow he had to get her back to Donncoill, he decided. He needed time to soothe the insults he had delivered, time to try and win back her favor. He could not let her go. She was too important to him, to his happiness. If he had to, he would tie her up and drag her back, holding her until she consented to hear him out.

Maldie watched Balfour climb the hill and felt weak with relief. He had finally won his fight against Beaton and lived to enjoy it. She heartily wished she could savor it with him, share in his pleasure. Instead, she was about to tell him things that would definitely steal some of that joy away. It seemed very unfair. No one had deserved death as much as Beaton did, and Balfour should be proud of the fact that he had rid the world of such a man. Maldie hated herself for what she was about to do and how it would taint all of that. She felt Eric touch her hand and looked at the boy.

Eric looked as despondent as she felt. She took his hand in hers. She was about to lose the man she loved. Eric was about to lose a lot more. Maldie knew she had to be strong for him.

"We have to tell him," Eric whispered, not wishing Nigel to overhear the conversation. "I dinnae think it can wait."

"Probably not," she agreed. "He just looks verra pleased,

and he has just beaten the mon the Murrays have been plagued by for thirteen years.''

"Aye, and this news willnae let him enjoy that for long. Nay, 'twill steal it all away. In a way, it will show that this long, bloody feud was based on a lie, that many a Murray had died for nothing. Howbeit, that will be the way of it no matter when we tell him. And if we wait too long, it may be worse.''

"I ken it. He will then wonder why we didnae tell him when 'tis clear that we had to have gained all this knowledge during our stay at Dubhlinn.'' She grimaced. "At least, the knowledge of who ye really are. I have held to my truth for a long time, even lied to hide it.''

"Mayhap we dinnae need to tell him all of your secrets.''

"As I told ye before, we must. Ye didnae learn about your birthright from the fairies. Once Balfour learns how ye ken who your father is, he will look to me. The mark we share not only proves we are bound by a blood kinship, it reveals my lies. And I am weary of telling them. Nay, it all has to be told. If we tell only a part, Balfour has the wit to figure out all the rest, and then we shall both be liars in his eyes.''

Eric smiled fleetingly, his expression weighted with sadness. "In truth, I would prefer it if we both speak the full truth. After all, if I am to be cast aside because of my parentage, 'twould be nice to have ye cast out with me. 'Tis nay verra good of me to think such a thing, but I fear I do.''

She briefly squeezed his hand in a gesture of understanding. " 'Tis no great sin. No one likes to be alone. Trust me in that, for I have been alone for most of my life.''

"No longer,'' he said firmly.

Maldie felt deeply touched, for she knew he had just made a vow. No matter what happened when the full truth was known, she would not be alone. He knew exactly who she was, had learned most of her sad past, and was fully aware of the sin she had come to Dubhlinn to commit, but he remained faithful. In her heart she knew he would always be there for her, always be her family, yet it was going to take some getting used to.

Such kindness, such steadfastness, was not something she was accustomed to.

"What are ye two whispering about?" asked Nigel.

"Just wondering what has happened to Beaton," replied Eric, unable to meet Nigel's eyes.

"Since our brother marches toward us looking verra much alive, then I must assume that Beaton is dead," Nigel drawled, smiling briefly at Eric. "Are ye sure ye werenae hurt?" he asked when Eric still did not look at him.

"Aye, Maldie and I are both weel."

" 'Tis glad I am to hear it," said Balfour as he finally reached them.

Balfour spared one brief glance for Maldie, then swept Eric up in his arms. Maldie could feel the wealth of confused emotion seizing Eric as he returned Balfour's hug. The boy loved his brothers, still felt a deep kinship with them, and knew that he was about to tell them a truth that could destroy all of that. This could well be the last time he enjoyed such open, easy affection from the men who had raised him, and Maldie shared his grief. She had to fight the urge to weep, not only for the pain Eric was in, but also for the pain the others would soon suffer.

She began to wonder what Balfour's furtive glances toward her meant. It was impossible to sense what feeling was behind those almost nervous looks her way. She did not even bother to try to reach out to him with her senses. She was bound too tightly to all Eric was feeling, and her own emotions were in such turmoil she felt almost nauseous. Even if she could sense what was going on in Balfour's mind and heart, she doubted she would have the clarity of mind to understand any of it. Considering all she was about to tell him, she was also sure she would not want to sense any of the feelings those truths would stir. It was safest to close herself off from the man.

"Are ye alright, Eric?" Balfour asked as he set his young brother down and studied him.

"I am fine. I am but a wee bit bruised," Eric answered,

pulling away from Balfour and standing next to Maldie, who slowly rose to her feet and took him by the hand.

Balfour frowned at the pair standing before him and began to feel a little uneasy. Eric looked almost tormented, as if he steeled himself for something distasteful. Maldie looked sad. He wondered how much she had told the boy about what had passed between them. Eric had a keen sense of justice and might well be very angry about the accusations his brother had flung at the young woman.

"I saw the man ye had to kill," he said, suddenly anxious to talk about something, anything, other than what Maldie and Eric appeared prepared to say. "I am sorry ye had to endure that. I should have been there to protect you."

"Ye cannae be everywhere, Balfour," Eric said kindly. "And, 'twas no glorious battle that felled that mon. In truth, he backed into the sword I held."

"The first time one spills another's blood is always hard."

"I ken it, but dinnae fret o'er me. I also ken that he was going to kill Maldie and a skill with words was not enough to change his mind about that. 'Twas her or him and I am truly glad that it was him."

"So am I," Balfour said quietly, looking at Maldie and feeling very uneasy when she could not, or would not meet his gaze. "Why was the mon so eager to kill you?" he asked Maldie.

"He blamed the defeat he faced upon me," she replied. "He decided that the only way ye could have gotten within the walls of Dubhlinn was if I had been helping you, spying for you."

Balfour winced. "Ye have suffered greatly from wild accusations, havenae ye."

Maldie shrugged. "I try too hard to be a stranger. One must expect such things when one does that. Ye won the fight with Beaton?"

"Aye, the bastard is dead."

"Then justice has been served," she murmured.

He grimaced and dragged his hand through his sweat-soaked

hair. "I begin to think that I am the only one who kens that we have won this battle."

"I ken it," said Nigel, even as he stood and moved next to Balfour, but his gaze was fixed upon Maldie and Eric and he frowned. "Methinks what ails these two has naught to do with this battle."

"There are some things we must tell you," Eric said, standing straight and finally meeting the gazes of both men directly.

"They can wait, laddie," said James. "We will be riding back to Donncoill soon. There we can have us a fine feast, and ye may talk all ye want."

"After I tell ye what I must, ye may not wish to share bread with me."

"Now, Eric, if ye still fret o'er Malcolm's death, I told ye that ye were not at fault," Nigel said, trying to reassure the boy and frowning when it did not lighten Eric's solemn face at all. "He fears he revealed that he kenned who Malcolm was with a look, but I said that wasnae enough, that 'twas Malcolm's attempts to rescue the lad that got him killed."

"Nigel is right," Balfour said, but he knew concern over any possible complicity in Malcolm's death was not what troubled the boy.

"'Tis nay Malcolm or his death that troubles me," Eric snapped, his brief flare of temper causing Balfour, Nigel, and James to stare at him in surprise. He sighed and rubbed the back of his neck.

"Ye begin to worry me, laddie," Balfour said, trying to smile and knowing he failed miserably. "Come, what can ye have to tell us that could be so verra bad."

"I am not a Murray," Eric announced in a clear, hard voice. "We have all been wrong for thirteen long years. Ye see, your father may have bedded Beaton's wife, but he didnae beget me. I am a Beaton."

Chapter Twenty

Maldie did not think she had ever seen men look as stunned as Nigel, Balfour, and James did. They obviously wanted to cry out a denial, but some small part of them held them silent. She wondered if they hesitated because they thought there was some truth to what Eric had just announced, or if they feared that the boy had been driven to madness during his captivity. It soon became clear that they would prefer to believe the boy had lost his senses.

"Nay, laddie, that is what Beaton wished ye to believe," Balfour said. "If he was to get the rest of the world to heed his claim about you, then he certainly had to have ye believe it, too."

"I am no witless child," Eric said.

"Nay, of course not. Howbeit, ye were in that mon's hold for a verra long time. Even the most clever of men can eventually believe something if it is repeated often enough. Aye, especially if there is no voice of truth to counter the lies."

"Ye are trying so hard to turn what I am saying into no more than a Beaton lie, and that is making it all the harder to tell ye the truth. I can see all too clearly that it will be most unwelcome and mayhap so will I.''

"Ye could ne'er be unwelcome," James said.

"I am a Beaton. Believe me when I say that I wish with all my heart that it wasnae true, but it is. Look at me. I carry no look of the Murrays. We have all assumed that I but looked like my mother, but it always struck me as curious that no hint of our father was in me. I am fair and ye are all brown. I am small and none of ye are.''

"That could still be all from your mother. Not every child takes from both parents," Balfour said.

There was a tightness to Balfour's voice that made Maldie look at him closely. He believed. She wondered if he had always had questions, but had preferred to shrug that doubt aside. If that was the case, she prayed it was because of love for Eric.

"Aye, but I was right to think there should be some touch of my father in me," Eric said. "Mayhap it was foresight upon my part. I dinnae ken and I really dinnae care. I found that mark.''

Balfour suddenly looked at her, and Maldie knew he recalled hers and how it had looked so familiar to him. "Aye, *that* mark.''

"Ye are a Beaton too?''

"Aye. Beaton was the mon who bedded and deserted my mother, who brought her down into the mire she died in.''

"But ye were going to kill him.''

"Aye, that is why I came here. To my shame, that is even why I allowed myself to be taken to Donncoill. I had lurked around Dubhlinn for weeks and ne'er gotten close to the mon I swore to kill. Ye wished him dead as weel and I thought I could use ye and yours to get closer to him, to get that chance I had failed to get upon my own.''

"But, lass, why should ye wish to murder your own father?" asked James when Balfour said nothing, just stood there staring at Maldie, then Eric, and then Maldie again.

"Because my mother made me swear to do it, made me give

her a blood oath on it.'' She smiled coldly at their shock. ''My mother had hated Beaton since he left her. 'Twas all vanity and stung pride. I used to think it was love or shame, but 'twas not. One thing I did gain from my brief sojourn in Beaton's dungeons was a clarity of mind, painful though that clarity is. My mother raised me to be her weapon against the mon she felt had slighted her.''

''Other men had slighted her, had they not?'' Nigel asked, his gaze soft with sympathy, one she wished she could see in Balfour's eyes, but his were black and empty.

''Aye, they had, again and again until she looked only for the coin. I will probably ne'er understand why she felt Beaton was worse than all of the others, but she did. And I was Beaton's child. She probably felt that there was no better weapon to use against him than his own flesh and blood. Mayhap she even wished to punish me for the sin of surviving my birth.'' Maldie shrugged. ''It doesnae matter much now. I buried her and came straight here to kill my father, as I had vowed I would do. And I do ask your pardon for it, but I did try to use all of you to help me.''

''I fear I was the cause of that painful revelation,'' Eric said, gently squeezing her hand. ''As is my habit, I had a question or two and simply asked them, not caring what they might pull forth.''

''The revelation was long overdue,'' Maldie whispered. ''All ye did was make me look at the truths I had fought so hard to ignore. I believe the truth I gave you was harder to bear.''

''What is this mark?'' asked Nigel. ''Many of us has a mark or two upon his body. It doesnae need to mean there is a kinship.''

''This mark is too clear, too distinct, and unique to argue with,'' Eric said, even as he yanked off his jupon and showed the men the heart-shaped mark upon his back. ''Maldie kenned who she was and who had left that mark upon her skin. Her mother was quick to tell her that much truth. There is no denying what it says.''

Nigel grimaced, casting a worried glance at a still silent

Balfour. "Mayhap your mother was distant kin to Beaton, and ye gained the mark through her and not Beaton."

"If I was the only one who carried it, aye, that would do to soothe our fears, but that doesnae explain where Maldie got hers then, does it? Nay, 'tis proof that I am Beaton's son, his legitimate heir, although that shall take some proving. And that mon we killed also kenned it."

"Did Beaton?"

"Nay, or he wouldnae have taken so long to grab me, would he? George, that mon I killed, said that he was the one who left me out to die. Howbeit, he took a wee peek to see if I carried the mark he kenned Beaton carried upon his back. He always kenned the truth but held fast to it, hoping there would come a time when it could gain him something. When one thinks of how eager Beaton has e'er been to beget a son, it shouldnae be a surprise that he bedded his wife frequently. And when one thinks of how cruel he was, it shouldnae be a surprise to learn that she couldnae stop him from doing so. Thus I was conceived."

Eric took a deep steadying breath before continuing, "I also discovered that Beaton himself killed my mother and the midwife who brought me into the world. He didnae want them about as reminders of what he saw as his shame. That was fine with old George, for it also meant that there was no one to tell Beaton the truth, except him. So, not only must I learn to accept that I am not a Murray but a Beaton, but that my father killed my mother and tried verra hard to kill me."

"Beaton was a bastard who clearly spread misery where'er he went," said James as he stepped forward and hugged Eric, briefly reaching out to clasp Maldie's shoulder in a gesture of sympathy. "It seems he had old Grizel kill your father as weel. Ah, your foster father then."

"The men are gathering and must wonder why we linger here," said Nigel as he looked around, then he grabbed Balfour by the arm and shook him a little. "We should return to Donncoill."

"Aye, we should," agreed Balfour and, after stiffly hugging Eric, he moved toward the horses.

"*All* of us," Nigel called after him.

"Aye, quite definitely *all* of us."

"Nay," said Maldie, shaking her head. "I think it would be best if I went in another direction."

" 'Tis too late in the day for ye to go anywhere, and ye have no supplies," argued Nigel as he pulled her toward his horse.

"But after all I have just told ye, I dinnae think ye wish much of my company."

"Nay, ye dinnae think that sulking knight riding off will wish to share your company," Nigel nodded toward the rapidly retreating Balfour as he tossed Maldie up on his saddle, "but he isnae the only one who resides at Donncoill." He mounted behind her and cast Eric a brief smile, as he and James rode up beside them on the same horse.

"I dinnae feel right about this, either," said Eric. "Balfour didnae spit on me, but he didnae welcome me back, either."

"Nonsense, lad," said James. "He hugged ye."

" 'Twas like being shrouded in ice. He hasnae accepted this, hasnae settled it in his mind. Mayhap me and Maldie should linger here."

"Nay. If naught else ye should be close at hand so that Balfour can speak with ye when he overcomes the shock he has suffered."

"That seems to be a verra good reason *not* to be within his reach," muttered Eric.

Nigel smiled and reached out to ruffle the boy's thick fair hair. "The mon was deep in shock. Now, I dinnae ken why this news should hit him so much harder than it did us, although I have a wee idea or two, but he will come to his senses."

"Even if he does, it willnae change the fact that I am a Beaton, not a Murray."

"Ye are a Murray. Mayhap not in blood or in name, but in all else," Nigel said firmly, and James nodded his hearty agreement. "We raised ye as one of our own for thirteen years. Did ye really think we could just cast that aside? And ye are still the wee bairn James found cast on a hillside to die. Ye are still the child of a woman our father loved, as much as our father loved any woman leastwise, fickle rogue that he was. None of that changes. And did ye not think that once in all these years it might have occurred to us that ye were not our father's bastard?''

''Ye ne'er said a word to me.''

''Of course not. The thought, when it came at all, was but a fleeting one and of no great importance.''

''Then why is Balfour so upset?''

''That, I fear, has little to do with ye, lad,'' Nigel murmured.

Maldie flushed when all three men glanced at her. Such interest was one reason why she did not want to go to Donncoill, but Nigel was right. It was too late in the day to go anywhere else. It would be nearly dark by the time they reached Donncoill, and that was closer than any place she had to go, except Eleanor's, but that would probably not be safe for a while. The grief of those who had lost a loved one would have to ease before they could look at one of those they felt responsible for their defeat without hatred. And, if she was going to journey anywhere, she did need a few supplies. It was probably not right to take anything from the Murrays after she had deceived them so badly, but she would. A little loss of pride would be easier to bear than hunger and cold.

All the way back to Donncoill there was no sign of Balfour. When they reached the keep, he had already retreated to his bedchamber. To Maldie's dismay she was led to the same bedchamber she had fled from by a painfully quiet Jennie.

''I am verra sorry I hit you,'' Maldie said as she stepped into the room then turned to face the young maid. ''I had to get away from here.''

Jennie sighed, stared up at the ceiling for a moment, and then finally met Maldie's gaze. ''It hurt, ye ken. I still have a wee bit of a bruise.'' She pointed at the yellowing bruise on her small chin. ''And poor Duncan hid from our laird for two days. I think he might still be trying to stay out of the mon's sight.''

"I had to get out of Donncoill." Maldie sighed and shook her head. "Ye will hear all of it verra soon, I am certain. And I dinnae think it will make ye think much better of me than ye did when all thought I was betraying the Murrays. Howbeit, please believe me when I say that I am verra sorry I hit ye."

"Weel, I suppose. Howbeit, if ye decide ye have to leave again, dinnae call for me."

Maldie winced when the young maid left, shutting the heavy door behind her with a distinct thud. She moved to the bed and flung herself onto it, staring blindly up at the ceiling. Even though she was probably not going to stay at Donncoill for very long, she had a feeling that it was going to feel like years.

Balfour giving her this room again could mean several things and she knew she ought not to think on it very much, but her mind refused to be stilled. Perhaps he did just need time to think. She had told him some things that were very hard to accept. Nigel and James apparently accepted and understood, so perhaps Balfour would after he had had a little time to ponder it all. He had put her in this room so that, after he was done thinking, he could come to her. When her heart started to pound with hope and anticipation, she decided she should think of something else. Balfour could have had her put in this particular bedchamber because it was the only one he had free.

She hurt, and she knew it was not simply because of the ordeal she had been through in the last few days. Her body was badly bruised, but most of her pain was from within. In a way she had lost her mother, the truth she had had to face about the woman stealing away the last of her self-deluding lies. She had never really had a mother, had simply lived with a woman who had grudgingly fed and clothed her while raising her up to kill a man. Maldie supposed it would have devastated her more if she had not already suspected it.

Then there was the matter of her father, a man she had planned to kill. Although she was very glad she had not stained her hands with that sin, she was content about his death. Her mother had always spoken of the man as a deceiver and deserter, but he was far worse than that. He had deserved killing for far more reasons than Margaret Kirkcaldy's stung vanity. It had been hard to finally meet him, however, to see with her own eyes the evil that had spawned her.

Deep in her heart she was afraid that some of that evil was within her. Maldie suspected that Eric suffered from the same fear. She knew it would be a long time before she stopped questioning every action she took, stopped wondering if some small taint from Beaton was making her think a certain way or do a certain thing. No matter how often she told herself that she did not have to grow to be like her father—that just because his seed had made her it did not mean she had to be like him in even the smallest way—it would be a very long time indeed before she could believe that completely.

And then there was Balfour, she thought, tears welling up in her eyes. Or, rather, there was not Balfour. She would wait for a little while, but she felt sure it would be a sad waste of time. He would never return to her bed, probably never even wish to see her from a distance. She had not betrayed him in the way he had thought, but she had betrayed him in some ways. She had lied to him and, at first, had planned to use him to gain her own ends. Maldie was sure that was not something such a proud man could easily forgive. She would wait, however, right there in the room where they had shared so much, for hope was a hard thing to kill.

Even the soft light of dawn hurt Maldie's eyes as she peeked out of the window. She had not slept at all, merely dozed from time to time throughout the long night. Balfour had not come to her. The only person she had seen had been a sullen Jennie, who had delivered her evening meal and hastily left. That she had been served in her room and not invited to dine with the others in the great hall had been telling in itself, but she had still waited. There was no point in waiting any longer.

Slipping on her cloak and picking up the small bag she had packed during the long night, Maldie slipped across the hall to Nigel's room. She was not surprised to find a sleepy-eyed

Eric there sharing a very early breakfast with an equally tired-looking Nigel. They did not seem particularly surprised to see her either.

"Ye are giving up faster than I thought ye would," murmured Nigel.

"I am not one to beat my head against a stone wall," Maldie said.

"Maldie, but wait a little longer," urged Eric.

"I cannae."

"Why? Is not Balfour worth a little patience?"

Maldie could tell that Nigel had told Eric everything, more than she had, and far more than the boy ought to know. She cast one sharp glance at Nigel, who just smiled faintly and shrugged. It had been her plan to simply come and say a quick farewell, but she realized that had been a failed plan from the start. Nigel and Eric thought she ought to stay, and they would never keep that opinion to themselves and simply let her walk away. She set down her bag, nudged Eric to the side, and sat down, helping herself to a piece of the bread he and Nigel devoured.

"If ye mean to talk me to death, I will help myself to a last meal," she muttered.

Eric rolled his eyes and took a long drink of cider. "This is cowardly, ye ken."

"So, I will just add that to my many faults. I can be a coward as easily as I was a liar."

"Maldie, ye had no choice but to lie. If ye had told everyone the truth from the beginning, ye would have spent all this time sitting in Donncoill's dungeons. No one would have listened to ye and no one would have believed you, no matter how often ye told them that ye would never help Beaton. Ye are his daughter. That is all that would have been considered. To a Murray, I fear the idea that ye wouldnae help your kinsmen, that ye might even want him dead as much as they did, would simply have been unbelievable."

"So, my lies can be explained. It really doesnae matter. 'Tis clear that they cannae be accepted. I cannae be accepted."

"Nay, I will nay believe that." Eric briefly clasped her hand in his. "I have been accepted. Everyone kens now that I am Beaton's son and, aye, there was shock, but nothing else. Ye were right. To all here I am still just Eric. As James said, I just went from being a blood son to a foster son. 'Twasnae a big change in most people's minds."

She kissed him on the cheek. "I am glad for you. Howbeit, our situations are a wee bit different. I wasnae raised here. I havenae been one of the family for thirteen years. I but appeared on the road to Dubhlinn and hid the truth for my own purposes. And, when ye recall that my purpose was to murder my father, 'tis nay a very laudable one."

"That may be hard for some to understand, but, considering the mon Beaton was, I dinnae think ye will be condemned for that," Nigel said. "And ye went to save Eric. Ye did save Eric."

"Nay, once the battle began there was little chance that he would be harmed. In truth, I put him at more risk by taking him out of the dungeon than by leaving him within. Any danger to him would not have come until the battle was over and, if, by some miracle, the Beatons had won but their laird had died. Beaton wanted Eric alive, and all of his men kenned that."

"Ye are too modest. Mayhap that is why ye are so quick to believe no one can forgive ye for what are truly verra small wrongs."

"Small?" She laughed and shook her head. "Nay, not small at all. Ye ken better than I that your brother values the truth above most anything else. I rarely told that mon the truth. Nay, not e'en when he asked me directly, tried to get me to say something to help him set aside the suspicions he had. He wanted to believe me, poor mon, and I gave him nothing."

"If ye truly believe that your crimes are so vile, then why do ye think he should come to some decision on them in but one night?"

"Oh, there is a clever question," she said as she stood up and picked up her bag. "Mayhap, Eric is right. Mayhap I am naught but a coward. I was able to brave one night of waiting and I cannae brave any more. The longer I must wait for him to speak to me, the more I think I willnae be able to bear what he has to say.''

Eric hugged her. "Please, Maldie, give it but one more night."

She briefly ruffled his thick curls, then gently pulled free of his hold. "Nay, not even one more hour.''

"Ye are a stubborn lass," said Nigel.

"Verra stubborn.''

"Where will ye go?" asked Eric.

"I am nay sure.''

"Go to your kinsmen," advised Nigel.

"The Beatons?" she asked.

"Nay, fool," he said and laughed softly at her scowl. "The Kirkcaldys.''

"Oh, nay, I cannae go there.''

"And why cannae ye? Ye have ne'er met them, have ye?''

"Weel, nay, but I have heard all about them," she said, starting to feel a little uneasy, suffering a growing suspicion that there was something she had not considered, and that Nigel was going to show her what that was.

"Aye? And who told ye all about them?''

"My mother," she whispered.

"I have no wish to add to your pain, lass, but this time it may be for your own good. Your mother lied to ye and used ye. Is it nay possible that some of those lies she told ye were about her own family? Mayhap she saw things in them that arenae there. And, mayhap, she told ye they were all unforgiving bastards who would make your life a pure hell because she did not want to go back and face them herself. What better way to make ye cease to ask about them than to make ye think they are all hateful?''

Maldie felt the start of a throbbing in her head. She rubbed at her temple, and tried to think through what Nigel had said without adding to her growing headache. It was odd how she got one each time she tried to think of her mother and all the things the woman had done.

Nigel was right and she knew it. She really did not have to consider it long to know that. What angered her was that she had not thought of that herself. She obviously still had a very large blind spot when it came to her mother and all of the woman's duplicity and cruelty. It all made a horrible sense. Her mother felt she had been shamed, and her pride would not let her family see that. She chose poverty and degradation for herself and, to some extent, her child, rather than go back to her own family.

"There may have been some truth in what she thought," she finally said. "Bringing home a bastard child is not always a welcome thing."

"Nay, true enough. But ye will never ken for sure until ye go and see them for yourself, will ye? Now, I dinnae ken the Kirkcaldys, but then I have ne'er heard anything verra bad about them either. I think ye owe them a chance, dinnae ye?"

"I suppose," she admitted grudgingly. " 'Tis at least a destination and I didnae really have one when I came here."

"Good. I think it willnae be as hard as ye think."

"Nay? If they do welcome me, then I shall have to tell them about their kinswoman. 'Tisnae a pretty story. Nor is my own. Ye are asking me to prove that my mother told me yet another lie and then to have to go through the ordeal of telling all those distasteful truths again. I think that could prove to be verra hard indeed."

"As I said, ye willnae ken all of that for certain until ye go."

"Ye do have a choice," said Eric. "Ye could stay here."

Maldie shook her head. "And such a choice that is. Nay, I will go to the Kirkcaldys."

"And ye will send us word of how ye fare?" asked Eric.

"Aye, I will send ye word and, trust me, Nigel Murray, if ye are wrong, 'twill be a harsh word I send."

He just laughed. Maldie hastily said her goodbyes, kissing each of them on the cheek and slipping out of the room. The walk to the gates of Donncoill was a torturous one. Each step of the way she feared meeting with Balfour, seeing the cold hate she was sure he now felt for her. When she finally stepped through those gates without being stopped she thought it odd that she did not feel any better, did not feel relieved or even free.

"And where are ye off to, lass?"

That deep voice startled her so much she nearly dropped her pack. Fighting to calm herself, she turned and scowled at James, wondering where the man had come from. She had kept a close watch for him or Balfour, but had seen nothing.

"My grave if I get too many frights like ye just gave me," she snapped.

James just smiled and asked again, "Where are ye going?"

"To see the Kirkcaldys."

"A good choice."

"What? No attempt to make me stay?"

"Weel, I figured that ye arenae in the mood to be dissuaded, if Nigel and Eric couldnae stop ye."

"Ye ken that I was with them? Ye are a verra sneaky mon, James. Verra sneaky indeed."

"Go on, lass, and take care. I dinnae like the thought of ye wandering about alone, but ye have been doing it for a verra long time so I shall try not to worry about ye. Ye need to see the Kirkcaldys, I am thinking, more than ye need to stay here."

"Mayhap ye are right, James." She gave him a kiss on the cheek and smiled when he blushed. "Take care."

"God be with ye, lass."

As Maldie started on her way she tried not to think too much on how easily everyone was letting her go. It may be exactly as they said, that they felt she really needed to see her Kirkcaldy kin, and not that they believed she had no chance with Balfour. Or worse, she mused, did not want her to be there so that she could even try to win the man back.

She shook that thought aside. It was unkind and possibly very unfair. No one save Balfour had shown any difficulty in accepting the truth about her, and understanding and forgiving it. They could just as easily be sending her on her way so that she did not linger at Donncoill and face further heartbreak at Balfour's hands.

It was going to be hard to try and push Balfour out of her mind and heart. She loved him, more than even she could understand. Simply walking away from Donncoill and possibly relinquishing all chance of being with him again was killing her, but she could not turn back. If Balfour truly wanted her, he would not have to work too hard to find her. She briefly wondered if that was why James, Nigel, and Eric had all steered her toward the Kirkcaldys, then told herself not to be a fool. There was only one thing she had to think about, and that was getting to her kinsmen safely and as quickly as possible. There would be time enough in the days and years ahead to deal with her pain.

Chapter Twenty-One

"Where is she?" demanded Balfour of the trembling guard at the gates of Donncoill.

Duncan groaned and rolled his eyes. "Ye have lost her *again?*" He took one long look at the dark expression on Balfour's face and swiftly took a few steps back. "I dinnae ken," he muttered, then turned and hurried away. "I havenae seen her."

Balfour cursed and dragged his hands through his hair. Poor Duncan was soon going to refuse to stand guard over anything. Even when the man was not guarding Maldie herself, he found himself the object of his laird's fury when the girl disappeared. This time Balfour had no idea of why Maldie was nowhere to be found, did not even know whether to be angry or afraid. It appeared that she had walked away from him yet again, but why?

He turned and walked back into the keep, then headed straight to Nigel's bedchamber. It hurt, but Balfour knew that Maldie still felt more comfortable talking of some things with Nigel and now Eric than she did with him. He had spent one very long night and nearly all of the day thinking on all she had

told him. Now he was ready to talk to Maldie about it all.
Balfour began to fear that he had waited too long, that Maldie
had decided she no longer wished to discuss it with him. Or
maybe telling him the full truth and walking away had been
her plan from the very beginning.

The moment he entered Nigel's bedchamber, Balfour knew
there was something he needed to do first, even before he gave
another minute of thought to Maldie. Nigel was sprawled on
his bed talking quietly with Eric who sat on the end of the bed,
his back against one of the tall posts. The wary looks both of
them sent his way made him feel somewhat ashamed of himself,
a feeling enhanced when, after that first glance, Eric just stared
at his hands.

Balfour knew that, selfishly, he had given little thought to
the boy while he had been sunk deep in his own misery. Everything Eric had believed in, everything he had come to depend
upon, had been taken from him. He needed to know, without
doubt, that his parentage made no difference. Balfour knew
that stiff hug he had given the boy just before fleeing Dubhlinn
and all the ugly truths Maldie had told him, was simply not
enough. Eric needed a great deal more assurance of his acceptance than that. Balfour walked to the end of the bed and
put his arm around the boy's slender shoulders, regretting the
stiffness he could feel in Eric and hoping he could talk it away.

"It seems that we were both cursed in our fathers," Balfour
said.

"Your father just cuckolded men. My father killed them,"
Eric said, but he relaxed a little.

"Lad, no clan and no family is without its bastards. Ye ken
better than most that the Murrays have had their share. Ye
have heard all of the stories. Every now and then someone or
something twists a person, pulls the darkness up from deep in
his soul until it poisons his every act and thought."

"A bad seed."

" 'Tis what some people call them. I suppose there can be
such a thing. Most evil men are made. We all ken who made
Beaton."

"His father." Eric grimaced. "And Beaton killed him for it, didnae he?"

Balfour was so shocked he stepped back a little. "Beaton killed his own father?"

"I am sure Maldie and I said so." Eric shrugged. "Mayhap not to you though. I cannae recall."

"And mayhap I just didnae hear it. I didnae hear much at all after I was told that Maldie was Beaton's daughter and that ye were his son." He frowned. "And that Maldie tried to kill her own father."

"So, like father, like daughter? Nay, Maldie rather proves your feeling that someone or something twists a person, doesnae she. With Maldie 'twas her own mother. She isnae like Beaton," Eric said firmly.

"I ken it, lad, and I could tell her that if I just kenned where she was." Balfour tensed when both Nigel and Eric suddenly averted their eyes. "Where is she?" he demanded.

"Why should ye think that we would ken where she is?" asked Nigel, crossing his arms behind his head.

Balfour moved to stand at the side of the bed and scowled down at his aggravatingly calm brother. "Where is she?"

"And I have a question for you. Why do ye wish to find her?"

"To talk to her, of course."

"Ah, of course. It took ye a full night and a day to think of what to say. I hadnae thought ye were so slow of wit, Balfour."

"Nigel," Eric murmured, watching the two older men nervously. "I dinnae think this is a game ye ought to play."

"Ye would spoil my fun, lad?" Nigel asked, smiling faintly at the youth.

"Aye, this time I would."

"She has fled Donncoill again, hasnae she?" said Balfour, suddenly feeling exhausted and defeated.

"Aye," replied Nigel. "She fled from here this morning. She has gone to meet with her Kirkcaldy kin."

"But she has always said that they dinnae want her."

"So her mother said, but 'tis clear that her thrice-cursed

mother wasnae much concerned with the truth. Maldie decided to go to her mother's kinsmen and try to find out what that truth is.''

"So, 'tis over," Balfour whispered, desperately wishing he was alone, but knowing that he could not simply run away. That would tell his brothers far too much about the feelings he had for Maldie. He suspected that they had already guessed the sad state of his heart, but he saw no reason to give them hard proof.

"Over?" Nigel sat up straight, rubbing his leg when the abrupt movement brought him a twinge of pain. "The lass has gone to see her kinsmen and that tells ye that it is over?"

"And what else am I to think?"

"That she grew weary of waiting for ye to decide whether or not ye liked what she had told you?"

"No one could *like* what she told me."

Nigel cursed softly. "A poor choice of word. Accept, forgive, understand? Do they sit better on the tongue?"

"I needed time to think. Why is that so difficult to understand?"

"We didnae need more than a few minutes. What do ye think it told her when ye needed so much longer? Ye love the lass, but ye dinnae really ken much about her, do ye?"

"And how was I to ken much about her when she told me nothing? Aye, and what little she did tell me was a lie."

"Not all," said Eric, rising quickly to Maldie's defense.

Balfour sighed and rubbed the back of his neck. He really did not want to talk about this. His emotions were strong and sharp and causing him a great deal of pain. He wanted to go and hide in his room like a chastised child and nurse his injuries.

"The lass has made her choice. One night was not much to wait if she truly cared what I thought or felt. If naught else, she could have come to me to tell me that she was leaving if she was so deeply interested in my feelings. She didnae. She just slipped away." He started toward the door. "Ye asked what I thought my long silence told her? Weel? Ye are a clever mon, Nigel, what do ye think her leaving ere we could talk about all of this tells *me?*''

Eric winced as the door slammed shut behind Balfour. "Is that it then?''

"Nay," Nigel answered. "That just means that it will be a wee while and take a wee bit of clever talking ere he hies out after her.''

"Do ye think Maldie will wait for him?''

"Aye." Nigel's smile was a little sad. "For far longer than she might want to.''

"Weel, I hope we have guessed right about the Kirkcaldys. Maldie will need their acceptance, their welcome, to ease the pain of waiting for Balfour to come to his senses.''

Maldie clutched her bag tightly and looked around the great hall of the Kirkcaldy keep. Walking through the high gates of her mother's old home had been the hardest thing she had ever done. Now she stood terrified that, in but a few moments, she would be tossed back out through them.

In her heart she knew there was every chance her mother had lied about her kinsmen, just as she had lied about so much else. Either that or Margaret had been looking at them in the same twisted, incomprehensible way she had looked at so many other things. There was also the chance that, for once in her life, Margaret had been completely honest. It was the last possibility that had Maldie trembling where she stood.

The men at the gates had stared at her so hard it had made her nervous. They had not hesitated to honor her request that she speak to the laird. That, she knew, was a little odd. Someone should have at least asked what she wanted to talk to the laird about. She wondered if the ease with which she had gained a private audience with the laird was because she had the same green eyes and black hair so many others had. When she had seen the similarities between herself and several of the guards at the gates, she had experienced a sense of coming home. Maldie had killed that as quickly as she could. Until she spoke to her mother's brother, she dared not think of such things. If she was cast out as her mother had said she would be, it would only add to her pain if she had tasted the brief joy of kinship.

A tall man walked into the great hall, watching her closely as he moved to his seat at the head table. He only had one man with him, a shorter, thinner man, whose hand never left the hilt of his sheathed sword. More green eyes and black hair, she mused, as she obeyed the tall man's silent gesture to move closer to the table.

"Ye are a Kirkcaldy?" the tall man asked.

"Are ye the laird of this clan?" She tried to stand straight and steady, to hide her fears.

"Aye," he answered, smiling faintly. "I am Colin Kirkcaldy. Am I the one ye seek?"

"Ye are. I am Maldie Kirkcaldy, the bastard daughter of Margaret Kirkcaldy."

The only thing she was sure of was that she had deeply shocked them. Both men stared at her with faintly agape expressions. Colin had paled ever so slightly. He looked around quickly before fixing his gaze on her again.

"Where is Margaret?" he asked.

"She died during this last winter."

"Ye have the look of her, of a Kirkcaldy."

"I have the look of a Kirkcaldy because I am one."

"And your father?"

"Beaton of Dubhlinn, and ye willnae be seeing him, either. He died a few days ago at the hands of Balfour Murray, laird of Donncoill."

To her surprise, Colin chuckled. "Ye have the bite of a Kirkcaldy, too. Sit down here, lass. On my right. Thomas, fetch us some wine," he ordered the man with him.

"Are ye sure?" Thomas asked. "Ye would be alone."

"I think I can defend myself against this wee child," Colin drawled, then looked at Maldie as soon as Thomas had left. "Ye havenae come to kill me, have ye?"

"Nay, though, if what my mother said about all of ye is true, mayhap I should consider it."

He leaned back in his huge, ornately carved chair and rubbed his chin. "And what did my sister say about us?"

After taking a deep breath Maldie told him everything Margaret had said about her family. The fury that darkened her uncle's handsome face made her a little nervous, but it also told her that her mother had lied again. Her uncle did not only look angry, he looked hurt and deeply insulted. When Thomas returned with the wine and saw how upset Colin was, he glared at Maldie.

"Easy, laddie," Colin said, tugging Thomas down into the seat on his left and pouring them all some wine. He quietly repeated what Maldie had said and Thomas looked equally as furious. "It seems Margaret was true to her ilk to the day she died," Colin murmured. "If ye believed all of that, then why are ye here?"

Maldie took a long drink of wine to steady herself. Something in the way Colin had spoken of Margaret being true to her ilk told her that the man had few delusions about his sister. What she was about to tell him, however, were not simple errors of thinking or the follies of pride. She could not even guess how the man would react or if he would believe her at all. It was tempting to just say nothing, but Maldie knew to her cost the problems brought on by hiding the truth or telling lies. This time she was going to start and finish with the truth, the whole ugly truth. Taking a deep breath she told him everything.

It was a long time after Maldie finished speaking before Colin could speak. "I cannae say which makes me angrier or sicker at heart, the way she lied to ye, the way she treated ye, or that she actually tried to get ye to kill your father. Aye, mayhap the latter, for the rest was hurtful, but that could have cost ye your verra soul."

Maldie shrugged. "I didnae do it."

"Ye tried."

"Aye, I tried." She grimaced. "I am nay sure I was doing it for her though. But it doesnae matter now. The mon is dead, as he deserves to be, and it wasnae by my hand. I will do a penance for the thought."

"The one who should be doing a penance is, sadly, beyond all chance of redemption. I ne'er understood my sister, ne'er understood where that vanity came from. She was beautiful and mayhap too many people told her so. I dinnae ken."

"I am finding some comfort in telling myself that sometimes people just do things that no one will e'er understand. It keeps me from fretting o'er it all too much."

He reached out and took her hand in his. "There is one thing ye must ken. We would ne'er have thrown ye out into the cold. If my sister had bothered to pay heed to something other than her looking glass, she would have seen that we are not without our fatherless children, and few are faulted for that. Certainly not the poor bairns who had naught to say about the circumstances of their birth."

"Aye, but those bairns didnae have Beaton as their father."

"Who your father is matters naught to us. He didnae raise ye. Aye, and despite the fool of a woman who did, ye seem to have grown into a sensible lass."

Maldie laughed. "Sensible? I have just spent months running about trying to stick a dagger into my own father."

"Ah, weel, we all have our wee moments of folly."

She shook her head. "I have had more than a few wee moments," she murmured, thinking of Balfour.

"Weel, ye can tell me all about it now that ye have returned to where ye belong."

"Are ye sure? Ye only have my word that I am Margaret's daughter."

"All ye have said sounds just like my sister, sad to say. The tale of how ye came to be also matches all we ken. And there is the final proof. That is what my eyes tell me. Ye are Margaret's daughter. Is she not, Thomas?"

Thomas nodded. "There is no doubt."

"So, lass, welcome home."

Maldie sighed and stared blindly out over the high walls of her uncle's keep. She had been fully accepted by her new family, joyously so. Despite her past, despite all she had done or tried to do, the Kirkcaldys were honestly happy to have her with them. She had been surrounded by comfort and kindness for two weeks. She should be the happiest she had ever been, but she was not. The moment she left the warmth of her family, the moment she was alone with her own thoughts, she grew sad, and all the pain she had tried so hard to ignore swelled up inside of her. Yet she continued to try and find moments where she could be alone, and that made no sense at all to her.

"Who are ye yearning for, lassie?" asked her uncle as he walked up and leaned against the wall at her side.

"And why should ye think I am yearning for anyone?"

"I am five and thirty, lass. I have seen a wee bit of yearning in my time. E'en suffered it myself for my wife, may God cherish her dear soul. Ye are yearning. Now, if I was a wagering mon, I would wager that ye are yearning after the laird of Donncoill."

Maldie tried not to look as surprised as she felt. She tried to think over all she had told her uncle to see where she may have given herself away, but it was impossible. She had been talking for almost two weeks. It was possible that she had somehow given herself away simply in the way she said Balfour's name. It was also possible that her uncle was just guessing.

She sighed again. It did not matter if he knew. In fact, she was hungry for someone to talk to. Although she had been alone for most of her life, had sorted out all her problems by herself and mended all of her own hurts, this was something she seemed incapable of dealing with.

"Mayhap I am," she finally said, "but it doesnae matter."

"Are ye sure?" he asked gently.

"He isnae here, is he?"

"Nay, but that need not say anything of importance. How did matters stand when ye parted?"

"Not weel."

He patted her on the shoulder. "Why dinnae ye just tell me it all from the beginning? Sometimes that can give the teller a clarity of mind. I may even be able to see what ye cannae, simply because 'tis your heart involved.''

There was enough truth in that to inspire Maldie to confess everything. If there was even the smallest chance that her uncle could help, she was willing to risk his censure over the way she had behaved. As she finished her tale, however, she saw the hard look of fury on Colin's face and wondered if she had just killed the joyous welcome she had been enjoying for the last fortnight.

''I suppose I have followed in my mother's footsteps,'' she murmured. ''I am sorry that I have disappointed you.''

''Nay, that is not why I am angry. I was just wondering how soon I could reach Donncoill and kill its laird.'' He watched Maldie closely as she paled.

''Nay,'' she cried. ''Ye cannae do that.''

''Why not? He has dishonored ye, hasnae he?''

''I would rather not think of it as dishonored,'' she said, wincing slightly even as she said the word, for she knew that would be the way everyone else saw it. ''I just thought I could be—''

''What? A mon? That ye could taste your pleasures where ye wished and walk away?'' He smiled crookedly, taking a few slow, deep breaths to get his anger at Balfour under control. ''Ye may have more spine than many a mon I ken, but I fear ye havenae become a mon. Fair or not, a lass cannae just go about bedding any mon who stirs a heat in her. Nay, not if she wishes to hold to her good name. And, if she isnae a whore at heart, she cannae do it without cost to herself, without hurting herself. And that is what ye did, isnae it?''

''Weel, aye, I may have a wee bit.'' She scowled at him when he laughed. ''Oh, all right then, without a lot of pain. Aye, I foolishly thought I could just enjoy the passion and then leave.'' She blushed a little. ''It was a verra strong passion, ye ken, and I decided why not? It felt verra good and I was weak enough to want to enjoy feeling verra good for a wee while.''

He briefly hugged her. ''No one deserved it more than ye.

I just wished ye had thought a wee bit more of the consequences.''

"I did think of the consequences, but at the time I was also still thinking of killing Beaton. I was beginning to think that I wouldnae survive the fulfillment of my vow to my mother, so what did consequences matter? 'Tis not Balfour's fault that I felt more than passion," she added softly.

"Nay, but 'tis his fault that ye were given a taste of that. Ye couldnae feel it on your own. He saw it in you, he kenned that ye felt it, and he helped himself."

"Nay, it really wasnae like that." She told him about Balfour's fears of acting like his reckless father. "He was as unsure as I. I had just hoped that more would come of it, and that was my own foolishness. Balfour is a mon who believes deeply in the truth, and I didnae deal in the truth verra often while I was at Donncoill."

"It sounds as if ye dinnae expect the mon to come after ye."

"I dinnae. What I hoped is that ye might be able to tell me how to stop looking for him."

Colin smiled and shook his head. "That is something ye must do yourself. 'Tis a cure that is hard to find and 'tis one that is hidden inside of you. There is no salve for a broken heart."

"They say that time can heal it."

"Aye, but I often wonder if *they* have e'er suffered one."

Maldie smiled. "Ye arenae helping."

"There are only two things I can think of to do for ye. One is to kill the bastard, and the other is to go and fetch him and drag him here to wed you."

" 'Twould hurt me more if he was killed, especially if he was killed by my kinsmen. And I want no mon who has to be dragged to the altar by force. I only want one who sets himself there willingly."

Colin slipped his arm around her shoulders and started to lead her down the steps and off the walls. "I could go and talk sense to the lad."

"Somehow I think that would be much akin to dragging him back here at swordpoint."

"I am sorry, lass."

" 'Tisnae your fault. 'Tisnae Balfour's either. Fate decided that I must give my heart to a mon who cannae abide a liar at the verra time I was sunk in lies. Nay, I must accept that I lost this gamble. That even though passion became love for me, it remained only passion for him."

"Then he is a fool."

"Mayhap I will soon think so, too, and I am sure that will help cure me of yearning for him. 'Tis hard to ken that ye could love someone so much and they dinnae feel the same, mayhap ne'er can. 'Tis even harder when ye ken that it may weel be all your own fault."

"Your sins werenae that big, lass. If the mon loves ye, he will forgive the wee lies ye told. If he doesnae forgive, then ye are better off alone. And although I have only kenned ye for a fortnight, I can say without hesitation that he will be the one who loses the most."

She stood on her tiptoes and kissed his cheek. "Thank ye. I will nay waste away hoping for him to come for me. Dinnae fear for that. My mother may have been a poor mother, but she did teach me one thing, how to survive. 'Tis one thing I can do verra weel indeed and even Balfour Murray, fine, handsome knight that he is, willnae defeat me. It may take me awhile, but I will push that mon out of my head and my heart."

"If ye dawdle about much longer, that lass will have cured herself of wanting ye," said Nigel, sitting on Balfour's bed and watching the man pace his room.

"And what makes ye think that she still wants me?" Balfour asked as he stopped and stared at Nigel.

He had tried very hard in the last three weeks to get Maldie out of his head and out of his heart, and he had failed miserably. Worse, everyone seemed to know that he had. Eric and Nigel never lost an opportunity to try and persuade him to go after

Maldie. They had no sympathy for his fears, for the terror he felt over the chance that he would go to her only to be pushed away. Even James had muttered a suggestion or two. Balfour was beginning to wonder if they were right and he was wrong.

"And what makes ye think that she doesnae?" asked Nigel.

"Oh, mayhap the fact that she isnae here."

Nigel swore softly. "She wasnae going to wait for ye to decide what ye did or didnae feel about what she told you. The fact that ye said nothing for so long made her sure that whatever ye might say would be all bad. How many times does that have to be said before ye understand it?"

"Ye make her sound like a timid lass, one who would run at the fear of a harsh word. Maldie is nay a timid lass."

"She didnae run from fear of *any* harsh word, but from fear of *yours*. That should tell ye something. What I begin to wonder is what are *ye* running from?"

Balfour sighed and sat down on the end of his bed. "A hard question."

"But mayhap one ye should ask yourself. Aye, and mayhap one I should have asked sooner."

"I dinnae wish to ride there and present myself, heart in hand, only to discover that she left because she was done with me. I have wronged her so many times from accusing her of crimes she hadnae committed, to killing her father."

"She was intending to kill the mon herself," Nigel said, nearly shouting as he fought the urge to shake some sense into Balfour.

"Aye, because she gave her mother her oath. Weel, I robbed her of any chance to fulfill that oath."

"Which is a good thing."

Balfour nodded. "I think so, but will she?"

"I think so, but ye will have to ask her."

"Ye willnae leave it to rest, will ye?"

"Nay."

"I would have thought that ye would prefer me and Maldie not to wed," Balfour said quietly, watching Nigel closely.

"Weel, I willnae dance at your wedding, but I do want ye

and her to be happy. Even though I may wish it to be otherwise, that will only happen if the two of ye are together. I kenned that early on. Ye are mates. Fate chose weel when she sent Maldie to you.''

''Do ye think she is still at the Kirkcaldys?'' He frowned when Nigel looked a little guilty. ''Ye have heard from her, havenae ye?''

''Weel, Eric and I have heard from her. We asked to ken if all went weel with the Kirkcaldys. Our reason was twofold. If it didnae go weel, we hoped she would tell us where she would go next. After all, we needed to ken where she was so that we could send ye in the right direction when we finally talked some sense into you. And it seems that her mother didnae tell the truth about her kinsmen, either.''

''They would have taken her in?''

''Willingly, happily. That mother of hers denied her a far more pleasant childhood than she had. There was no need for her to have lived fighting to eat and watching her mother become the whore of Dundee. And she would have had people to give her the caring her mother was incapable of.''

Balfour cursed and rubbed the back of his neck. ''The lass has had more than her share of misery, and I didnae do much to ease that, did I? And, now, from what ye tell me, if I go to her, I will have to meet all of them as weel.''

''Dinnae try to use that as a reason to linger here and be miserable.''

It surprised him a little, but Balfour laughed. He wondered if, by deciding to take the risk and go after Maldie, he had somehow freed himself of the grief he had suffered since she had left. There was still a chance that he had lost her as he feared he had, but, somehow, the thought of going and trying to woo her gave him back a little of the hope he had lost. Balfour doubted he could hurt any more than he did now. And if he did go after her, he could at least cease to torment himself with questions about what would happen if he did. Good or ill, he would finally have some answers to all of his doubts and questions.

"I will leave for the Kirkcaldy keep on the morrow," Balfour announced, and ignored Nigel's exaggerated sigh of relief.

"Do ye want me to ride with ye or will ye take James?"

"I will go alone."

"Alone?"

"Aye, alone. If Maldie can do so, then so can I. And if all she does when she sees me is spit in my eye and wish me straight to hell, I would prefer to suffer that humiliation alone."

Chapter Twenty-Two

Balfour inwardly cursed and took a deep drink of the spiced cider he had been served with reluctant hospitality. He had had a long, tiring journey to get to the Kirkcaldy keep, and all he wanted to do was find Maldie and drag her back to Donncoill. Instead, he sat in a very clean, tapestry-draped great hall surrounded by what appeared to be dozens of Maldie's kinsmen. If that was not discomforting enough, they were all staring at him as if he was a threat to her, and many of them had the same striking green eyes that Maldie did. The most imposing Kirkcaldy was their laird and Maldie's uncle, Colin, a huge man with bright green eyes and the same thick, unruly black hair his niece had. He looked as if he would like nothing more than to run a sword through his heart, and Balfour wondered just how much Maldie had told the man.

"I thank ye for the drink," he said as he set his empty goblet down on the well-scrubbed oak table. "It has washed the dust of travel from my throat. Now, if ye would be so kind as to tell me where I might find Maldie, I should like to speak with the lass."

"About what?" demanded Sir Colin Kirkcaldy, rubbing a

hand over his broad chest as he stared hard at Balfour. "Ye have held the lass at Donncoill for months. I am thinking ye had more than enough time to say whate'er ye wished to her. Aye, and more than enough time to say some things ye should ne'er have said at all."

"Mayhap, sir, while she was there, I didnae ken exactly what I wished to say."

"And, mayhap, now that she has been returned to her kinsmen, she doesnae wish to hear it."

"Aye, true enough. But what harm in letting me speak my piece? I believe wee Maldie has the spine to tell me *aye* or *nay* or bluntly wish me gone from her sight."

"The lass has more spine than some men I know." Colin frowned at Balfour and softly drummed his long fingers on the table. "The child has had a hard life and I dinnae think she will e'er tell us all she had to endure. She was cast aside by her father, though that was truly for the best, and treated poorly by her mother. My sister had more pride than wit. She should have brought herself and that wee bairn home, not hidden herself away from us until we all thought her dead. An even larger crime to my way of thinking was how she raised that child to believe that we all wished for such a separation."

"Nay. The woman's worst crime was raising Maldie to be her sword of vengeance." Balfour smiled coldly when Colin and some of the other Kirkcaldys stared at him in surprise.

"Ye ken that, do ye?" Colin refilled Balfour's goblet, watching the man closely as he did so.

"I should like to boast that I guessed it all upon my own, that my wits were that keen. Howbeit, they arenae, and I was too all-consumed with Beaton, with stopping his constant crimes against my clan and with retrieving my brother Eric."

"Maldie's brother."

"Aye, *and mine.* Ye cannae cast aside thirteen years of fostering a child, of calling him brother and believing it, just because his blood proves to be of another clan."

Colin scratched the gray-spattered beard stubble on his chin.

''Ye didnae say that when ye were first told the truth. I was told that ye didnae say much of anything.''

Balfour leaned back in his chair and felt his confidence slowly return. Colin Kirkcaldy was willing to give him a chance, to hear him out. He briefly wondered why Colin needed to know anything about his relationship with Eric, then inwardly shrugged. In some ways Eric's future and well-being could be of interest to the Kirkcaldys, since the boy was blood kin to Maldie. The way the boy was treated now that all knew he was Beaton's son could also tell the man something. And although he could rightfully declare such things a private matter, Balfour certainly had nothing to hide and did not want the Kirkcaldys to think he did.

''I rode up to Eric and Maldie heady with the sweet taste of victory. Ere I could speak I was told that not only is the lass I want the daughter of the mon I had just killed, but so is the boy I have called *brother* for thirteen years. Mayhap I am not as quick of wit as others, but I found such news enough to steal away both speech and thought. Aye, especially since the reason for the long, bloody feud was that all thought my father had bedded Beaton's wife and got her with child, and now Maldie was telling me that it wasnae true. Weel, not all of it leastwise. She then added to my shock by telling me the true reason she had been on the road to Dubhlinn, that she had come to murder her own father. Aye, and she added that she had planned to use me and mine to achieve that vengeance. I needed time to think o'er all I had been told and she gave me none, fleeing Donncoill ere we had cleaned our weapons of the blood of the Beatons.''

''That was nearly a month past, my friend. 'Tisnae that long a ride from Donncoill to here.''

''I have slow horses,'' Balfour drawled, then inwardly cursed when Colin just grinned while a few of the many other Kirkcaldys crowding the hall softly chuckled. ''She gave me no reason for why she was leaving. She just left. No fare-thee-weel, no explanation, not even a *thank ye for helping me exact the revenge I sought*. I was left to find my own answers for all she had done, for why she had fled, and none of them suggested that she would wish me to follow her. If naught else, I had just killed her father.''

''She cared naught for the bastard.''

''So she said. So everyone kept reminding me. But even if that were true, then there remained the fact that I had robbed her of the revenge she had been seeking for so long. She had made a deathbed vow to her mother, a blood oath, and I had just stolen all chance for her to fulfill it.''

''If that had troubled the lass, ye would have kenned it. She wouldnae have quietly slipped away. Nay, though I have kenned the lass for less than a month, I can say with confidence that she would have let ye ken she was angry.'' Colin crossed his arms over his chest. ''Do ye ken what I think? I think ye were sulking. Did ye really expect our Maldie to sit about and placidly wait for ye to decide what ye did or didnae feel about all she had just told you? Or what ye did or didnae feel about her?''

''I felt she should have given me a day or two to swallow all she had told me. 'Twas a belly full. My lover was my enemy's child, my brother wasnae my brother, a long, costly feud had been based upon a lie, a bairn had nearly been cruelly murdered because of that lie and might still be deprived of his birthright because of it, and the lass I trusted admitted that she had lied to me from the beginning.''

''Ye didnae trust her the whole time she was there.''

''Ye seem to have won the lass's confidence,'' Balfour murmured, a little surprised that Maldie had told the man so much. ''Nay, I didnae, and in the end it was revealed that I was right to wonder what game she played. She had a lot of secrets and she had lied to me. I but guessed the wrong game. Now, although I can understand your concern for your niece, our discussing all of this only keeps me from seeing her. I have told ye all I mean to. Whate'er else needs to be said must be between me and Maldie.''

''She is on the east side of the loch.''

Balfour tried not to gape at the man as he slowly stood up.

''That is it? No more questions? Ye arenae e'en going to ask me what my intentions are?''

Colin just smiled. ''I feel they must be all that is honorable or ye wouldnae have chased the lass down. Ye certainly wouldnae have sat here trying to patiently answer my questions, some of which were most impertinent. And if ye just mean to further shame the lass, ye will ne'er leave my lands alive. Now, see if ye can get the fool lass back here for the evening meal. She hasnae been eating as she should.''

Balfour almost laughed as he stared at the man. ''Maldie may not have been raised amongst her kinsmen, but I begin to see what is meant when people say blood will tell.'' He could hear Colin laughing as he strode out of the great hall.

As soon as he mounted his horse it took all of his willpower not to gallop out of the Kirkcaldy keep and race for the loch. The thought that Colin might see him or hear of his haste and have a hearty laugh gave him the strength to act as if he felt no real urgency. Balfour also suspected that approaching the loch at a headlong gallop could easily warn Maldie, giving her time to hide or flee. The last thing he wished to do was to spend more precious time hunting her down. It was past time she ceased to guess at his thoughts or feelings and sat still to listen to what he had to say.

Maldie sighed, baited her fishing line, and dropped it into the water. Since arriving at her kinsmen's lands she had spent many days lying in the soft grass at the loch's edge, pretending to fish. A few times she had actually caught something, but it had been by accident. She only claimed to be fishing so that she could be alone. Her uncle Colin was a very clever man and she suspected he had guessed her game, but he said nothing. At times she caught a fleeting glimpse of one of her many kinsmen so she knew she was being watched, but she did not really mind. The guards her uncle set around her never disturbed her solitude, so she felt no urge to complain.

Most of her was still delighted beyond words to have found

her family and be warmly accepted by them. There was a small part of her, however, that found such a large family very difficult to adjust to even after a month of trying. She was accustomed to being alone, to having no one save her mother to speak to and, quite often, her mother had been either sullenly silent or sharp-tongued and angry. Those ill moods had grown so frequent in the last year of Margaret's life that Maldie had rarely spoken to the woman. Now, suddenly, she was surrounded by people who loved to talk, boisterous, friendly people. There were times when she had to escape to the quiet of the loch, had to steal a moment to be alone with her thoughts.

"Although why I should continually seek that when they arenae verra pretty ones, I dinnae ken," she muttered to her reflection in the still, clear water. "I should be running away from the cursed things."

Balfour still remained prominent in her thoughts and that angered her. It had been a month since she had seen him, longer since she had been kissed or held by him. He should not be haunting her, not so strongly or frequently. She loved him but that love had not been returned, had not even been acknowledged by either of them, and it had not been strengthened by word or touch or even sight of the man in weeks. Maldie did not understand why her stubborn heart was so reluctant to let the man go.

It hurt, and she could almost hate him for that, except that she knew it was not Balfour's fault, not completely. He had made her no promises, never once speaking of anything but the passion they shared. She had tried to talk sense to herself time and time again, but her heart simply refused to listen to reason. It had decided that it wanted Balfour Murray despite her better judgment, and it now refused to let him go.

A soft noise in the grass pulled her from her dark thoughts and she looked behind her, gaping up at the man standing there. As she stumbled to her feet she wondered wildly if her mind or her heart was playing tricks on her. She then thought of running, but sternly told herself not to be such a coward. Maldie straightened her shoulders and tried to calm the rapid beating of her heart.

"Why are ye here?" she asked, inwardly cursing the tremor in her voice, for she did not want Balfour to guess how tumultuous her emotions were.

"I have come for you," he said, stepping closer and effectively trapping her between him and the loch. "Ye left without saying fareweel, sweet Maldie."

He watched her closely but, except for a darkening of his fine eyes, she could not read his expression. To her astonishment she could not sense any emotion in him at all. It was as if he had shut himself away from her completely. Maldie wondered when and how he had gained that skill. It was a very inconvenient time for him to learn how to shield himself. She shivered, feeling chilled by the loss of her ability to touch him in that way.

"No one likes the bearer of bad news," she muttered. "How is Eric?"

"The lad is hale. All of his bruises have healed. What did ye think I would do to him?"

"Nothing bad. Truly." She dragged her fingers through her hair and grimaced. "I was just worried about him. He had suffered an ordeal. All he had once thought was true had been shown to be a lie. A mon he had been taught to hate, a mon who had tried to cruelly murder him ere his life had truly begun, was shown to be his true father. Aye, and although he told me that all was weel, I did wonder how ye and the others might truly feel about that."

"Eric is my brother." He shrugged. "I cannae change what I have felt and believed for so many years simply because I have discovered that the lad and I dinnae share a blood kinship. Until Eric told me how the truth had been revealed, I did, for a brief time, wonder how ye could have been so cruel as to tell him something he didnae need to know, something that could only hurt him. After all, the mark ye two share isnae one all can see with ease. It has to be uncovered. Then, all I had to try and understand was why ye had lied to me, and why ye lacked the courage to stand and face me.''

"I didnae think ye would wish to see me again after I had deceived you."

Balfour reached out and took her by the hand, tugging her into his arms. "Did ye not once think that I might wish to hear the why of it all?"

"I told ye the why of it after the battle." She tried to remain taut, to resist the allure of being back in his arms, but it had been too long. Slowly she rested against him, encircling his trim waist with her arms. "I told ye everything."

"Oh, aye, and ye started with the worst news, the most shocking. After ye told me that ye were Beaton's daughter, that your own mother had made ye vow to come to Dubhlinn and kill your own father, and that my brother wasnae truly my brother, can ye be so verra surprised that I wasnae listening too closely to anything ye said after that?"

She looked up at him and tried to think back to the day of the battle. It was hard, for what she wanted to do was savor the beauty of him, kiss those firm lips, and roll about on the soft grass in naked passionate abandon. Maldie pushed those thoughts aside, certain they would return with a vengeance, and relived the moment she had told him the whole ugly truth. She had thought the still, wide-eyed look upon his face had been shock and anger, but now realized that he had been stunned. The truths she had told him had hit him like blows to the head, each one scrambling his wits until he simply heard no more. She had not actually felt anything from within him, had not really been aware of his emotions at all. Maldie realized that she had decided how he would feel, and had never looked any further. She had also been too concerned with her own turbulent emotions, desperate to keep them tightly controlled, to even try to touch upon what Balfour had been suffering.

"Weel, it doesnae really matter how ye have or havenae accepted the truth, for one thing hasnae changed," she said, not fully meaning what she said. It did matter. She was just not sure she wanted to know how he felt about it all, for the truth could easily add to the pain she was already suffering. "I am still Beaton's daughter, the spawn of your greatest and oldest enemy."

"My greatest and oldest enemy is the English."

Balfour almost laughed at the way she stared at him somewhat stupidly. Many men would hold her bloodline against her, but he did not care what it was. He knew some of that was because he had come to know her before he had discovered who had sired her. There had been time to learn about her, time to see that she carried none of Beaton's taint. It was not going to be easy to convince her of that, however. Even after staying with her Kirkcaldy kin for a month, Maldie was obviously still deeply concerned about carrying Beaton's blood in her veins.

There was also the fact that he did not feel much like talking. It had been too long since he had held her, too long since he had kissed her, and far too long since their bodies had been joined. He touched a kiss to the top of her head, breathing deeply of her scent as he smoothed his hands down her slim back. She trembled, and he felt his desire leap to life in response to that sign that she might still share his hunger. Balfour knew they had a great deal to talk about, but, as he tilted her face up to his, he decided that talking could wait.

Maldie only briefly considered refusing his kiss. There was so much they had to say. She did not even know why he had come after her. It had to have been for far more reasons than to say he understood why she had done what she had. Then he touched his lips to hers, and she decided that none of it mattered. If he had only come for another taste of the passion they could share it would hurt her, but she doubted her pain could be any worse than it had been since leaving Donncoill. At least she would have one last sweet moment of passion to add to her memories of him. She heartily returned his kiss, greedily drinking in the taste of him.

"We should talk," she said, making one last weak attempt to grasp at reason even as she tilted her head back so that he could more easily kiss her throat.

"We will," he said, unlacing her gown as he pulled her down onto the soft grass.

"But not now?" Maldie murmured with a pleasure she could not hide as he stroked her body with his big hands even as he continued to loosen her clothing. She was starved for his touch and did not have the will to hide it.

"I find that I am too distracted to talk." He tugged her gown down to her slender waist and gently nibbled the hardened tips of her breasts so prominently visible beneath her thin chemise. Her soft groan made him tremble. "A wee respite will clear my head."

"Only a wee respite?" She grasped him by his taut buttocks and pressed him close, the feel of his hardness almost enough to satisfy her need it was so strong and heedless.

"I fear I am too starved for ye to linger o'er this much missed feast."

"Dinnae fear. 'Tis a feeling I ken all too weel. Ye will hear no more argument from me, though I may be compelled to urge ye to hurry."

"Nay, I think not. Not this time, loving."

Even as Balfour hurriedly removed her clothes, Maldie used an equal haste to pull off his. They both cried out with delight as their flesh touched for the first time in too long. Maldie could not get enough of the feel of his strong body pressed against hers, his warm skin beneath her hands, and the touch of his mouth as he feverishly covered her body with kisses. She tried to return each caress but their lovemaking soon grew wild, their desperate need for each other stealing away all ability to linger in the heady time that comes before the culmination of their desire.

When he finally joined their bodies, Maldie clung to him with all of her strength. She tried to pull him ever deeper within her, meeting each of his hard thrusts with a ferocity of her own. Even as her body convulsed with the power of her release and she called out his name, she felt him shudder with his own, his cry blending with hers. She closed her eyes and held him close, fighting to cling to the pleasure they had just shared, that blinding delight that could so easily disperse all fear and uncertainty.

With the return of her senses came an awareness of the chill in the late afternoon air. Maldie also became painfully aware of her nakedness. She hastily sat up and tugged on her chemise. For the first time since they had become lovers, Maldie felt the harsh sting of embarrassment. They had truly let passion rule this time, allowing it to hurl themselves into each other's arms while there was still so much left unsaid between them, so many troubles unsolved and questions unanswered. She recalled that she did not even know why he had hunted her down. Now that her blood had cooled, she feared she had made a grave error in judgment. One last taste of passion would not be enough to ease the pain of being a fool and, if Balfour had come only to bed her, that was exactly what she would be.

"Ye are thinking the worst of me, arenae ye, lass," Balfour said as he sat up and wrapped his plaid around himself. "Trust me when I tell ye, loving, that I wouldnae ride so long a way just for a wee tussle upon the grass, sweet as it was."

"Sorry," she murmured, casting him a weak smile. "As always I acted upon what I wanted, then, after I rushed ahead and was beyond redemption, I paused to wonder if I had done the right thing or the wise thing." She laughed, a short, self-abasing laugh. "I ne'er do the right thing."

Balfour pulled her into his arms. "Oh, aye, ye do."

"I betrayed you," she whispered.

"Nay, although I did see it as such for a wee while. I wish I could find the words to tell ye how verra sorry I am for any pain I caused ye with my mistrust, but what ye did wasnae betrayal. Ye told no one my secrets and helped no one to harm me in any way. Ye didnae act against me or my clan in even the smallest way. Ye just lied."

She stared at Balfour in surprise. "*Just* lied?"

"Aye, and ye did a poor job of it, too. Ye twisted your tongue into knots trying not to tell me the truth, yet not tell too big a lie. 'Twas mostly half-truths or no answers at all." He idly began to try and tidy her hair, knowing it was useless, but enjoying the feel of her thick, soft hair too much to stop. "After I calmed enough to see beyond my anger and hurt, I looked more closely at all ye had told me. I thought o'er every talk we had shared and every answer ye had given to all the questions I had asked. What lies ye did tell me were ones meant to hide the truth. Ye didnae want me to ken who your father was. And ye were right to hide that truth from me. Once I kenned it I would ne'er have trusted you, ne'er have believed that ye would do naught to help him." He shook his head. "'Tis unfair to hold a child at fault for what was done by a mother, a father, or any other kinsmon. I ken it weel. Howbeit, learning that Beaton had sired you would have made me do exactly that."

"After all Beaton had done, ye cannae blame yourself for that." She reached up to stroke his cheek, delighted beyond words that he had forgiven her for her deception, that he even understood why she had deceived him. "I told ye so little about myself ye had naught with which to decide my guilt or innocence. And would ye have believed me if I had told ye that I ached to kill the mon, that I was there to fulfill a vow of revenge?"

Balfour grimaced. "Nay. 'Tis hard to believe that a child would kill her own father, bastard though Beaton was. 'Twould also have been hard to believe that a wee lass such as your own self would do so."

"I almost succeeded," she protested, her pride stung, then she sighed. "'Tis probably best that I didnae."

"Despite your vow to your dying mother and the fact that Beaton deserved to die, aye, 'tis probably for the best. Heartless filth though he was, that mon's death wasnae worth your immortal soul. For a time I wasnae sure which ye would find harder to forgive, that I had robbed ye of your vengeance or that I had killed your father." He fought the urge to heartily return her brief kiss, knowing that they needed to talk before they let passion rule them again, "I then began to hope that ye faulted me for neither."

"None of it troubled me." She snuggled up against him,

savoring the feel of his strong arms wrapped around her. "I had come to see the hard, cold truth about my mother. Margaret cared naught for me. From the moment I was born she had but one use for me—to avenge her lost honor. Aye, she would have also liked me to become a whore, so that she wouldnae have had to work so hard, but mostly she wished me to kill Beaton for her. I think I have always kenned the truth, but I pushed it from my mind for it was a painful one. E'en when I could no longer turn away from the truth, I struggled against thinking on it much for I didnae wish to let loose all the ugly feelings it stirred within me."

Balfour held her a little tighter, knowing there was nothing he could say or do to ease that pain. " 'Tis they, Margaret and Beaton, who lost the most, Maldie. They denied themselves the joy of a child, one who would have loved them weel and done any parent proud." He smiled when he saw her blush, even the tips of her ears turning a faint red. "I fear we cannae choose our kinsmen. 'Tis sad that ye were cursed with such a heartless pair, but ye rose from that mire clean and bonny, in soul as weel as in body."

"I think ye had better cease speaking so kindly," she said, her voice unsteady as she struggled to control a surge of emotion. " 'Tis odd, but I feel near to weeping."

He laughed and kissed her cheek. "I have no skill with flattery and pretty words and ye have no skill at accepting them. We make a fine pair." He slipped his hand beneath her chin and turned her face up toward his. "Now, 'tis past time I tell ye why I hunted ye down. Aye, especially since I begin to think of forgoing talk again."

"Why *are* ye here?" she asked, her heart beating so hard it pounded painfully in her ears. The soft look in his dark eyes held such promise she was almost afraid to look into them.

"For you. I have come for you." He touched his fingers to her lips when she frowned and started to speak. "Nay, let me say it all. Then all ye will need to say is *aye* or *nay*. There will be no confusion. I want ye to come back to Donncoill with me. Since ye left 'tis as if all the life has fled the place. I need ye there. I need ye at my side. I want ye to be my wife, to be the lady of Donncoill."

It took all of Maldie's will to stop herself from loudly crying out an immediate yes. He had said so much, yet not enough. He needed her, he wanted her, and he would marry her. She knew most women would think her mad to even hesitate, but she needed more. He was speaking of marriage, of being bound by law and God for life. She needed him to love her.

For a moment she wondered if she could make him say it before she had to, then decided that that could take a long time. Men were so reluctant to bare their souls to a woman that, even if Balfour *did* love her, she could be wedded, bedded, and the mother of three of his children ere he finally made mention of the fact. Although she dreaded baring her soul, she knew it was the only way. And, she mused as she steadied herself, he deserved the full truth. If they were to be married, it was also the best way to begin. She prayed that she was not taking too great a gamble with her heart. Once she had exposed all she felt for him, it would be that much easier for him to devastate her even if he did not want or mean to.

"I want to marry you," she began and, when he started to hug her, she placed a hand on his chest and firmly kept a small distance between them. "Howbeit, I may yet say no. Ye speak of need and want, and we both ken that our passion is weel matched. What ye cannae know, for I have worked hard to hide it from ye, is that I love you, Balfour Murray." She could tell little from the wide-eyed look upon his face and the sudden tautness in his body, so she doggedly continued, "I may love ye more than is wise or sane and have done so since the beginning. Mayhap it will make little sense to ye, but I cannae wed ye, cannae bind myself to ye for a lifetime, if ye dinnae feel the same." She cried out from surprise and some discomfort when he crushed her to his chest.

"Ah, my bonny wee lass, ye are such a fool. Or, mayhap we both are. Aye, ye will have love, possibly more than ye want at times."

"Ye love me?" she whispered, wriggling in his arms until

his hold loosened enough for her to look at him. Her heart was pounding so hard and fast she felt a little nauseated.

"Aye, I love you. I, too, think I fell in love the moment I set eyes upon you." He eagerly returned her kiss, gently pulling her down onto the ground. "Then your answer is yes? Ye will marry me?"

"Aye." She started to kiss him again, then frowned as a familiar sound cut sharply through the air. "Was that a hunting horn?" she asked as she sat up and looked around.

Balfour laughed, sat up, and reached for their clothes. "Aye, 'twas a hunting horn. 'Tis your uncle, Colin, telling us that we have been alone long enough and," he tossed her her gown, "if we dinnae appear before him verra soon, the hunt will indeed be on." He smiled at her when she frowned in doubt. "Trust me, lass. If we arenae dressed and walking back to that keep verra soon, we will be encircled by your grinning kinsmen."

Maldie grimaced as she got dressed. She was no longer alone in the world, able to do as she wished without answering to anyone. It delighted her, made her feel wanted and cared for for the first time in her life but, as Balfour paused for one brief kiss before walking her back to her uncle's keep, she began to see that a big family could also be a big problem.

"I think the days until we are wed are going to be long ones," she murmured.

Watching as nearly a dozen widely grinning Kirkcaldys appeared as if from nowhere and began to escort them back to the keep, Balfour nodded in heartfelt agreement. "Verra long indeed."

Chapter Twenty-Three

Maldie grit her teeth and tried to sit still as Jennie fought to comb the tangles from her hair. She cursed herself for forgetting to braid it last night, for her restless sleep had left it in a sadly gnarled mess. It was going to take a lot of work to make it look good for her wedding, or, at least as good as her thick, unruly hair could ever look.

Her wedding, she thought, and sighed. She found it odd that her stomach could churn with fears and nerves while her heart soared with happiness. It had been exactly one month since Balfour had told her that he loved her and asked her to be his wife. Aside from the time they had been apart and she had thought him lost to her forever, Maldie was sure that this had been the longest month of her life. Balfour and she had seen less and less of each other, as the days had slipped by and more and more Kirkcaldys had arrived for the wedding. It had quickly become clear that her uncle was determined to keep them apart until their wedding night. They had not even been able to steal a kiss in days. Worse, she had not been able to woo those three sweet words out of Balfour again, and she was beginning to wonder if she had actually heard him say that he loved her or had just dreamed it.

There was a sharp rap at the door and, even as she turned to bid the person enter, her uncle strode in. She frowned at him as he sat on her bed. He really was a fine figure of a man, tall and strong, his kind, good-humored nature clear to see in his handsome face. Maldie was continually amazed that her mother could believe such a man would turn her and her bairn out into the cold. That Margaret would deprive her child of knowing such a good man was something else Maldie struggled to forgive her mother for. She even appreciated the similarity in their looks, the same wild black hair and green eyes, for it gave her a sense of belonging. Colin's constant guard over her and Balfour, however, was not endearing him to her at the moment.

"I havenae hidden him under the bed," she drawled.

Colin laughed. "I ken it. I just saw the lad pacing his room."

"Pacing? That implies that he is troubled. Do ye think he has changed his mind?" she asked, cursing the uncertainty that made her even ask such a question. She knew it was unreasonable, but she blamed her uncle for that, as his efforts to keep her and Balfour apart had ensured that all of her fears were not soothed by sweet words of love from her betrothed.

"Foolish child," Colin scolded, but his smile was filled with gentle understanding. "Nay, he but suffers as all men do when they take a bride. Dinnae tell me that ye arenae uneasy, for I willnae believe ye."

She smiled faintly and shrugged. "I am, yet I dinnae understand it. This is what I want."

"Aye, and what he wants or he would ne'er have chased ye down." Colin shook his head. " 'Tis just the way it is. Ye have more than most couples who are oftimes set before a priest barely kenning each other's names. Makes no difference. Ye are swearing vows afore God and kinsmen. 'Tis a grave matter and no one should do it easily." He stood up and walked over to Maldie as Jennie helped her into her gown. "Ye go and help the women, lass," he told the maid. "I can help my

niece now." He began to lace up Maldie's gown the moment
Jennie left the room, pausing to touch the heart-shaped birthmark on her back. " 'Tis a bonny sign God set upon your
skin."

" 'Tis Beaton's mark," she muttered. "My mother often
pointed to it as a sign of the cursed blood I carry in my veins."

He turned her around to face him. "Your mother was a fool,
God bless her soul. A bitter fool. Did ye not stay with an old
couple, Beatons by blood, who were good and kind and held
no love for their laird? Who were, in truth, all the things Beaton
was not?"

"Weel, aye, but . . ."

"Nay but. The laird of Dubhlinn was a bastard with no heart
and no honor. That doesnae mean that all Beatons carry the
same taint upon their soul. Isnae the boy Eric also a Beaton?"

"Aye, 'twas the fact that he, too, carries this mark that told
him that sad truth, but ye ken all of this."

"I have met the lad and he is a fine boy who will become
a good, honorable mon. The Beatons of Dubhlinn will be weel
blessed if he can gain the right to be their laird. Are ye nay
proud to be a Kirkcaldy?"

"Of course."

"Weel, as I have said before, our clan hasnae been free of
sinners. We have had a traitor or two, murderers, thieves, and
men who wouldnae ken what honor was if it grew legs, walked
up to them, and spit in their eyes. Trust me, the Murrays, too,
have had and will have a bad seed from time to time. Ye cannae
fault a clan for wishing to keep such things a dark secret, but,
if ye shake the tree of any family, some rotten fruit will fall
out. Ye have grown into a fine lass despite your parents. Be
proud of that."

Tears choked her throat and a deep blush seared her cheeks
as she stared up at her uncle, deeply touched by the honest
affection she could see softening his eyes. "Thank ye, Uncle,"
she managed to whisper.

"Ye havenae been told your worth verra often, have ye,
lass," he said, shaking his head.

"It doesnae matter."

"Oh, aye, it does. A child needs to be told his worth from time to time if he is to grow up hale and strong, in spirit and in body. 'Tis that lack of deserved praise that makes ye so quick to fear that your big brown mon is about to change his mind about marrying you."

"My big brown mon?" she muttered, biting back a smile.

"Aye, I have ne'er seen so much brown on a mon. Brown hair, brown eyes, brown skin. I hope he doesnae wear something brown to stand afore the priest, or we might mistake him for a log."

"Uncle," Maldie cried, laughing as she lightly swatted him on the arm. "Be kind. He is a bonny mon."

He slipped his arm around her shoulders and started to lead her out of the room. "That he is, lass, and he has chosen himself a bonny bride. One of the bonniest in all of Scotland." He winked at her. "And ye shall have bonny brown bairns." He laughed when she blushed. "We had best step quickly now or your laddie will think ye have changed your mind or fled to the hills."

"She should be here by now," Balfour muttered as he paced before the small altar set up at the far end of the great hall.

Nigel rolled his eyes and leaned against the wall, crossing his arms over his chest. "Her uncle has gone to fetch her. He kens all that passed between ye and Maldie while she was here. 'Tis certain he willnae let ye or her flee this marriage."

"I wouldnae make any wager on that. She but smiles at the mon and he will probably allow her to lead him to the verra gates of hell." He smiled faintly when Nigel laughed, then grew serious again. "Whene'er I see her uncle look at her I wonder yet again how that fool of a mother of hers could keep her hidden from such a family. I have seen more of them than I have wished to in the last month and ne'er seen any of them show coldness or condemnation toward the lass because of her bastardry. How could a woman ken her own kinsmen so little, judge them so wrongly, that she would prefer to become a whore and try to make her child one rather than seek her family's aid?''

''Pride. Overwhelming pride from what little I have heard said of the woman,'' Nigel answered. ''It seems she found her sad life preferable to returning home shamed and carrying a bairn. She hadnae made herself weel loved amonst her kinsmen either, so mayhap that decided her. If ye have always acted as if ye are so much better than all around you, ye certainly dinnae want to let them see that ye are not. Let it lie, brother. 'Tisnae something ye or anyone else will e'er understand. Maldie survived her mother's pride and idiocy and survived it verra weel, too. Now, turn your attention to your marriage for here comes your bride.''

Balfour looked toward Maldie and sharply caught his breath. She wore the soft green gown he had had made for her. It fit her slender body perfectly and the rich color flattered her. Her thick hair tumbled over her shoulders, its soft waves decorated with green ribbons. There was a light flush upon her cheeks, and he thought that she had never looked so beautiful. Wondering yet again how he had won the heart of such a woman, he walked over to take her hand from her uncle's grasp.

'' 'Tis your last chance to consider the step ye take, Maldie,'' he said. ''Once the vows are said, there is no escape from this brown knight.''

Maldie smiled, remembering her uncle naming Balfour her big brown man. That made Balfour sound almost common and, as he stood there in his fine white shirt, draped in the plaid of his clan, he looked far from common. She wondered what madness had siezed her which made her think she could make such a fine laird content, then hastily shook aside that pinch of doubt. He said he loved her and she loved him. She would have a lifetime at his side. There would be plenty of time to learn all that could make him happy.

'' 'Tis your last chance as weel,'' she said, tightening her hold on his hand. ''Howbeit, if ye try to flee, do remember that I can run verra fast.''

He laughed and brushed a kiss over her lips before turning toward the young priest from the village. As they knelt before the priest, Maldie glanced around at the crowd in the great hall. Kirkcaldys were all mixed in with Murrays, and Maldie knew more then her marriage to Balfour would keep the two clans allied. Eric stood by her uncle and he grinned at her. She quickly grinned back, then found her gaze captured by Nigel. The smile he sent her was a sad one and she felt his loneliness. There was nothing she could do for him, however, and praying that he would overcome the ill-fated love he had for her, she turned her full attention back to the priest. Balfour was about to make vows to her before God and his clan, and she did not want to miss one tiny word of it.

Balfour was still laughing at Colin's nonsense when he turned and found Nigel at his side. A quick glance at Colin revealed that man discreetly slipping away, leaving him and his brother alone in the crowd of celebrants. The man had clearly guessed that all was not well between the brothers, and Balfour mused that Colin could be an uncomfortably perceptive man at times. There was a still, solemn look upon Nigel's face that made Balfour uneasy. He had hoped that Nigel would conquer his feelings for Maldie or, at best, learn to live with them, but he began to think that had been little more than a foolish dream. Balfour knew that, if he stood in Nigel's place, he would find the situation a pure torment.

"Congratulations, brother, and many good wishes." Nigel smiled crookedly. "And I do mean that."

"Thank ye, but that is not all ye wished to say, is it?" Balfour said quietly, tensing, yet not sure why he dreaded Nigel's next words.

"I am leaving."

"I havenae asked that of you."

"I ken it. I need to leave. I am truly happy for you, hold no anger toward ye or Maldie. Neither of ye has caused this trouble. 'Tis all my own doing. 'Tis clear to anyone with eyes in their head that ye love her and she loves you. I thought I could accept that, live with it, and get o'er it. I dinnae think I can do that if I must watch the two of ye together each and every day.''

Balfour briefly clasped his brother by the shoulder. ''The last thing I wanted to do was drive ye from your home.''

''Ye arenae driving me out,'' he said firmly. ''I swear it. I am taking myself away for a wee while. 'Twill be easier to cure myself of these unasked for and unwanted feelings if the one who stirs them isnae before my eyes. I dared not even kiss the bride. And, in truth, I fear what jealousy may drive me to do. I willnae allow this to come between us, to hurt ye or her. Both of ye have been more tolerant and understanding than I deserve, and I dinnae want to destroy that.''

''Where will ye go?''

''To France. The French are willing to pay a Scotsmon to fight the English.'' He smiled at the dark frown that crossed Balfour's face. ''And ye can set that thought aside, brother. I dinnae go to war seeking death. I may be in love with my brother's wife and, aye, 'tis torment, but I fear I love myself as weel. I go to kill the English and, mayhap, this cursed feeling that causes us both trouble. That is all.''

''Will ye stay for the morning feast?''

''I will leave at first light. There are a few Kirkcaldys who set out for France at dawn, and I will ride with them.'' He briefly hugged Balfour. ''I willnae be gone forever. I am nay a complete fool, one who will spend all his days yearning for what he cannae have. I will be back.'' He sighed and looked around at the crowd. ''And, now, I must go and tell Eric.''

Balfour watched Nigel disappear into the crowd and sighed. When Maldie stepped up beside him and took him by the hand, he held on tightly. She frowned up at him and he realized she did not know about Nigel yet. He knew how easily she could sense how he felt, and so he forced all thought of Nigel from his mind. Unwilling to steal any of the joy of their wedding day, he decided he would tell her the sad news later.

"Do ye think we can creep away unseen now?" he asked as he tugged her into his arms.

"I doubt it." She laughed softly and shook her head. "There are simply too many people here. We will have to nudge a few aside just to get to the doors, so I think all chance of slipping away unseen has been stolen."

"Aye." He grinned and picked her up in his arms. "So, let us make a grand show of it then."

Maldie laughed and buried her face in his neck as he strode through the cheering crowd. Some of the remarks hurled at them as they left the great hall made her blush. She recognized her uncle's voice bellowing out some of the more ribald suggestions, and swore she would make him pay for that. Getting out of the great hall did not end the gauntlet they had to walk through. There were people throughout the keep. They passed cheerful guests on the stairs and all along the upper hall. Maldie was almost surprised to find their bedchamber empty.

"One of us has too large a family," she said, then laughed as, after he had loudly shut and latched the door, he tossed her onto the bed.

Balfour sprawled on top of her and gave her a quick, hard kiss. "There was more than enough room here until Kirkcaldys began to swarm through the gates. Ye looked verra bonny in this gown," he murmured as he began to unlace it.

"Aye, I did." She exchanged a quick grin with him. "I do like it, so mayhap ye could be careful." Her words were muffled by the gown as he yanked it over her head and tossed it aside.

"I was careful. I didnae rip it off as I felt inclined to."

She curled her arms around his neck. "It has been a verra long time, hasnae it?" she whispered against his lips.

"Too long."

"But, 'tis our wedding night. We should at least try to control our greed."

She wriggled free of his grasp to kneel at his side, smiling sweetly at his frown. Her desire for him was so strong it made her weak, and she found that an amusing contradiction. Maldie was determined to gain some control over her passion, however.

This was her wedding night, a once in a lifetime event, and she wanted their coming together to be something special. The first time she and Balfour were joined as man and wife should not be some hasty, greedy, blind coupling. She knew she was too hungry for him to fulfill all of her fancies, but she was determined to at least try and fulfill one or two.

"I am feeling verra greedy indeed, lass." He muttered a curse when he reached for her and she gently slapped his hands away.

"As I am, but one of us must show some restraint and 'tis clear that that willnae be you."

"I am nay sure I like the idea that ye have some restraint to grasp," he grumbled, then murmured his pleasure as she slowly began to remove his clothes.

Maldie took every opportunity she could grasp to kiss him and stroke him as she tugged off his clothes. The way he trembled beneath her touch had her own passions soaring, and control grew harder to maintain. When he was finally naked she kissed him from head to toe and back up again, careful not to linger over the pleasurable chore, knowing his need was already at a painful height.

She straddled him, easing their bodies together. Maldie hesitated a moment to catch her breath, pleased to hear that Balfour was breathing as hard as she was. Grasping tightly at the few threads of control she had left, she smiled sweetly at Balfour as she slowly pulled off her chemise. She cried out in surprise, then gasped in pleasure when he abruptly sat up, held her close, and began to hungrily kiss her breasts. As she threaded her fingers through his thick hair, she decided that she had been strong enough.

His lovemaking grew fierce and Maldie reveled in it. Balfour grasped her by the hips and moved her slowly at first, then faster. He kissed her, the thrust of his tongue shadowing the movement of his body within hers. Thus entwined, he drove them to the release they both craved. Their cries blended perfectly as they found that release as one.

"Ah, Maldie, my wild temptress," he murmured a long time

later, as he eased the intimacy of their embrace and held her close. "I had thought to love ye slowly, to make our first time as mon and wife a long, sweet loving. I had planned for hours of reveling in our passion, not mere moments."

She idly rubbed her foot up and down his strong calf. "I tried, but my boast of restraint proved to be a false one."

"Ye had more than I."

"We can blame my uncle for this. 'Tis his fault we were kept apart so long that we were too starved for each other to endure long and sweet." She looked at him and tenderly caressed his cheek. "I can wait for long and sweet. We have a lifetime now."

"Aye." He sighed and watched her closely as he said, "There are a few things I need to tell you. I should have told ye them ere I asked ye to marry me, but I feared they would make ye so angry ye would say no."

Maldie tensed, fear briefly gripping her heart, then she forced herself to calm down. Balfour was a good man, too good to have many secrets or ones that would be too dark and horrifying to accept. She doubted he could even match the weight of the ones she had held tight to for so very long. Although she could not even begin to guess what he felt he had to confess to, she felt sure that she would find it easy to forgive and forget.

"Are these verra bad things ye are about to tell me?" she asked.

"Nay, but they willnae make ye think too kindly of me, I fear."

"Then spit them out, quickly, with no added words or explanations. This is not a night we should spend angry with each other, but 'tis also the perfect time for such truths." She took a deep breath and silently swore that she would be reasonable and would keep reminding herself of all he had forgiven her. "Tell me."

"Do ye recall the first time we shared this bed?"

"A foolish question. Aye, I do. Ye said ye couldnae play the game of seduction any longer, that ye wanted me too badly to keep taking a wee taste then having to step back."

"And I swear that was the truth. 'Twas just not the full truth, not the only reason I pushed ye into becoming my lover."

"Ye didnae have to push too hard," she murmured.

"I had seen Nigel's interest in you," he continued, ignoring her soft interruption. "I wanted to mark you that night, Maldie. I wanted to mark ye as mine and no one else's. I wanted Nigel to see as only a mon can that ye were mine. God's beard, I wanted ye to see it, too." He watched her cautiously, his eyes widening when he saw no sign of anger on her face. "I used the passion ye felt for me to push ye into bed ere ye were ready, because I wanted Nigel to ken that ye were taken."

"That is your big confession?" she asked. "Ye have been fretting o'er that for months, have ye?" She crossed her arms behind her head and fought the urge to laugh, afraid it might insult him.

"That and one or two other things," he said, not sure how to judge the odd mood she was in. He expected anger, but she looked almost amused.

"Tell me all."

"I didnae need to make ye come to Donncoill at all. Weel, at the time I didnae think so, for I kenned naught about Grizel. I looked at you, I wanted you, and then I thought of a way to keep ye near at hand. I had every intention of seducing you."

"Shameful."

Balfour narrowed his eyes and studied her closely. It looked as if she was trying very hard to control some strong emotion, but he could not begin to guess what feeling she was trying to hide. Although he was a little afraid to continue, he knew he had to. They could not begin their marriage with any secrets between them. She had confessed to all of her deceptions. It was only fair that he confess to all of his own.

"The last. . ."

"There is more?"

He just frowned and stubbornly continued, "I have already spoken of the time that I suspected you of betraying me, but I didnae tell ye all of the reasons why I did." He took a deep breath to steady himself, knowing he was going to appear a witless fool and that that brief time of idiocy could deeply offend her. "Aye, I think ye understand how I could suspect ye simply because ye became my lover." She nodded, her lips pressed tightly together. "Weel, 'twas a wee bit more than that which fed my suspicions. Not only had ye chosen me as your lover, but ye were a verra good one."

Her eyes grew very wide, she choked out the words *sweet Jesu,* turned onto her stomach, and buried her face in the pillow. Balfour was horrified. He had not anticipated that she would respond to his confession with tears. He awkwardly patted her on the back as he frantically tried to think of something to say to comfort her. A moment later he frowned, leaning down and futilely trying to see her face. He had never heard Maldie cry, but he began to be certain that she was not crying now. His eyes widened as he listened more closely to the muffled sounds she was making.

"Maldie, are ye laughing?" he demanded, his voice softened by shock and confusion.

She flopped onto her back, still chuckling as she wiped tears of laughter from her eyes. "Aye, and 'tis glad I am that ye finally guessed, for I was near to smothering myself in that cursed pillow. I am sorry, Balfour. I mean no insult." She reached out to touch his cheek. "Such dark sins ye confess."

"Now ye make jest of me," he murmured as he laid down in her arms, relaxing for the first time since he had decided to confess everything to her. "We are now mon and wife. I wanted us to begin our marriage with only the truth between us."

"A laudable plan. But, Balfour, ye worried yourself o'er naught. Aye, mayhap ye didnae act in the most honorable way, but compared to the lies I told and the deceptions I indulged in, I fear yours simply dinnae measure up." She grinned when he laughed.

"Then I declare ye the winner in the games we played with each other."

"Thank ye."

"Howbeit, it wasnae right for me to plot so hard to seduce you."

"Be at ease, my bonny brown mon. I was plotting as hard as ye at times." She readily returned his quick kiss. "I wanted you from the start as weel. Aye, mayhap I didnae plot and plan as ye did, but I grew verra skilled at telling myself lies, convincing myself that I could do as I pleased e'en though most of the world and its confessor would condemn me for it. And, aye, I was even able to unfairly set all blame upon your shoulders from time to time."

"Ye forgive a mon his faults verra easily."

"When his faults are that he wants me, desires me, and tries verra hard to get me, 'tis nay so hard. Nay e'en the last sin ye confessed to is verra easy to forgive. What woman can be hurt by the fact that the mon she loves thinks she is a good lover? In truth, I am just sorry that foolish women left ye feeling so unsure of your worth that ye could think it odd that *I* would want you."

"I love ye, Maldie Murray." He smiled faintly when she grimaced. "What have I said now?"

"Maldie Murray." She shook her head. "I didnae think this through verra weel at all. It has the taste of a lilt some minstrel would use when he cannae think of the words." She giggled as he laughed.

" 'Tis music to my ears. I can think of no sweeter sound than that of your name joined with mine."

She curled her arms around his neck. "Ye are getting much better with your flatteries, husband." Maldie covered his hand with hers when he began to caress her breasts, halting his gentle touch. "There is one more thing we must discuss ere we lose ourselves in the joys of our wedding night."

"No more confessions, please."

"Nay, I have no more. I saw ye speaking with Nigel ere we left the great hall. The solemn looks upon your faces told me he wasnae wishing ye weel, that ye spoke of much weightier matters." She decided not to tell him of how she had felt the deep sadness between him and Nigel, for Balfour sometimes found her ability to sense a person's feelings a little uncomfortable. "Is there some trouble lurking around the corner that ye havenae told me about?"

Balfour touched his forehead to hers. "Nay and aye. There is no enemy trying to kill me or mine or take my lands. This trouble lurks within our own family. Nigel willnae be at our morning feast."

"Why?" she asked in a soft voice, dreading his answer.

"He rides away at dawn to fight in France."

Maldie could hear the pain in his voice and she held him close. "I am so sorry, Balfour."

"This is not your doing."

"Of course it is my doing. 'Tis because of me he is leaving, isnae it?"

"Nay, 'tis because he loves you as any mon with good eyes and a heart must. I ken that ye did nothing to encourage him."

"I could have perhaps discouraged him more than I did."

"Nay." He idly brushed a few wisps of hair from her face. "Lass, we became lovers right before his verra eyes, and that didnae change how he felt. Ye telling him to look elsewhere certainly wouldnae have stopped him. Nothing could have stopped me."

"Or me," she said and sighed. "When we were apart and I thought ye didnae want me, I learned the pain of loving someone who doesnae love you. I would wish that upon no mon or woman. I at least had sweet memory to cling to."

"The fact that Nigel doesnae have that, that he has ne'er e'en kissed the one he longs for, may weel be his salvation. He believes he can cure himself."

"I pray he does, for his place is here with ye and Eric. He belongs at Donncoill, and I dinnae think he will be happy until he has come home again. Mayhap he will find what he seeks in France."

"As I found what I needed on the road to Dubhlinn," he said, and brushed a kiss over her mouth. "I would ne'er have guessed that my destiny would be standing there with tangled hair and a sharp tongue. I love ye, my green-eyed temptress."

"No more than I love ye."

"Do ye challenge me?" he asked, grinning down at her as he pinned her beneath his body.

"Aye, I do. Are ye mon enough to meet it?"

"It could take a long time to decide a winner."

"We have a lifetime," she murmured. "And I can think of no better way to spend our years together than in showing each other how much love we have."

"Neither can I, Maldie Murray. Neither can I."

THE MURRAY FAMILY LINEAGE

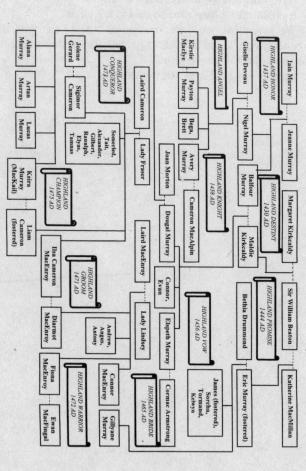

Please turn the page for an exciting sneak peek of

Hannah Howell's

HIGHLAND LOVER!

Scotland, Spring 1475

"Oof!"

Oof!? Dazed and struggling to catch her breath, Alana decided she must have made that noise herself. Hard dirt floors did not say *oof*. It was odd, however, how the rough stone walls of the oubliette made her voice sound so deep, almost manly. Just as she began to be able to breathe again, the hard dirt floor shifted beneath her.

It took Alana a moment to fully grasp the fact that she had not landed on the floor. She had landed on a person. That person had a deep, manly voice. It was not dirt or stone beneath her cheek, but cloth. There was also the steady throb of a heartbeat in the ear she had pressed against that cloth. Her fingers were hanging down a little and touching cool, slightly damp earth. She was sprawled on top of a man like a wanton.

Alana scrambled off the man, apologizing for some awkward placement of her knees and elbows as she did so. The man certainly knew how to curse. She stood and stared up at the three men looking down at her, the light from the lantern they held doing little more than illuminating their grinning, hairy faces.

"Ye cannae put me in here with a mon," she said.

"Got no place else to put ye," said the tallest of the three, a man called Clyde, whom she was fairly sure was the laird.

"I am a lady," she began.

"Ye are a wee, impudent child. Now, are ye going to tell us who ye are?"

"So ye can rob my people? Nay, I dinnae think so."

"Then ye stay where ye are."

She did not even have time to stutter out a protest. The grate was shut, and that faint source of light quickly disappeared as the Gowans walked away. Alana stared into the dark and wondered how everything had gone so wrong. All she had wanted to do was to help find her sister Keira, but none of her family had heeded her pleas or her insistence that she could truly help to find her twin. It had seemed such a clever idea to disguise herself as a young girl and follow her brothers, waiting for just the right moment to reveal herself. How she had enjoyed those little dreams of walking up to her poor, confused brothers and leading them straight to their sister. That had kept a smile upon her face and a jaunty spring in her step right up until the moment she had realized that not only had she lost her brothers' trail, but she also had absolutely no idea of where she was.

Feeling very sorry for herself and wondering why her gifts had so abruptly failed her just when she needed them the most, she had been cooking a rabbit and sulking when the Gowans had found her. Alana grimaced as she remembered how she had acted. Perhaps if she had been sweet and acted helpless, she would not be stuck in a hole in the ground with a man who was apparently relieving himself in a bucket. Maybe it would be wise to tell the Gowans who she was so that they could get some ransom for her and she could get out of here. Appalled by that moment of weakness, Alana proceeded to lecture herself in the hope of stiffening her resolve.

Gregor inwardly cursed as he finished relieving himself. It was not the best way to introduce himself to his fellow prisoner, but he really had had little choice. Having a body dropped on top of him and then being jabbed by elbows and knees had made ignoring his body's needs impossible. At least the dark provided a semblance of privacy.

He was just trying to figure out where she was when he realized she was muttering to herself. Clyde Gowan had called her an impudent child, but there was something in that low, husky voice that made him think of a woman. After she had landed on him and he had caught his breath, there had also been something about that soft, warm body that had also made him think of a woman despite the lack of fulsome curves. He shook his head as he cautiously stepped toward that voice.

Despite his caution, he took one step too many and came up hard against her back. She screeched softly and jumped, banging the top of her head against his chin. Gregor cursed softly as his teeth slammed together, sending a sharp, stinging pain through his head. He was a little surprised to hear her softly curse as well.

"Jesu, lass," he muttered, "ye have inflicted more bruises on me than those fools did when they grabbed me."

"Who are you?" Alana asked, wincing and rubbing at the painful spot on the top of her head, certain she could feel a lump rising.

"Gregor. And ye are?"

"Alana."

"Just Alana?"

"Just Gregor?"

"I will tell ye my full name if ye tell me yours."

"Nay, I dinnae think so. Someone could be listening, hoping we will do just that."

"And ye dinnae trust me as far as ye can spit, do ye?"

"Why should I? I dinnae ken who ye are. I cannae e'en see you." She looked around and then wondered why she bothered, since it was so dark she could not even see her own hand if she held it right in front of her face. "What did they put ye in here for?"

Alana suddenly feared she had been confined with a true criminal, perhaps even a rapist or murderer. She smothered that brief surge of panic by telling herself sharply not to be such an idiot. The Gowans wanted to ransom her. Even they were not stupid enough to risk losing that purse by setting her too close to a truly dangerous man.

"Ransom," he replied.

"Ah, me too. Are they roaming about the country plucking up people like daisies?"

Gregor chuckled and shook his head. "Only those who look as if they or their kinsmen might have a few coins weighting their purse. A mon was being ransomed e'en as they dragged me in. He was dressed fine, although his bonnie clothes were somewhat filthy from spending time in this hole. I was wearing my finest. I suspect your gown told them your kinsmen might have some coin. Did they kill your guards?"

Alana felt a blush heat her cheeks. "Nay, I was alone. I got a little lost."

She was lying, Gregor thought. Either she was a very poor liar, or the dark had made his senses keener, allowing him to hear the lie in her voice. "I hope your kinsmen punish the men weel for such carelessness."

Oh, someone would most certainly be punished, Alana thought. There was no doubt in her mind about that. This was one of those times when she wished her parents believed in beating a child. A few painful strokes of a rod would be far easier to endure than the lecture she would be given and, even worse, the confused disappointment her parents would reveal concerning her idiocy and disobedience.

"How long have ye been down here?" she asked, hoping to divert his attention from how and why she had been caught.

"Two days, I think. 'Tis difficult to know for certain. They gave me quite a few blankets; a privy bucket, which they pull up and empty each day; and food and water twice a day. What troubles me is who will win this game of ye stay there until ye tell me what I want to know. My clan isnae really poor, but they dinnae have coin to spare for a big ransom. Nay when they dinnae e'en ken what the money will be used for."

"Oh, didnae they tell ye?"

"I was unconscious for most of the time it took to get to this keep and be tossed in here. All I have heard since then is the thrice daily question about who I am. And I am assuming all these things happen daily, not just whene'er they feel inclined. There does seem to be a, weel, rhythm to it all. 'Tis how I decided I have been here for two days." He thought back over the past few days, too much of it spent in the dark with his own thoughts. "If I judge it aright, this may actually be the end of the third day, for I fell unconscious again when they threw me in here. I woke up to someone bellowing that it was time to sup, I got my food and water, and was told about the privy bucket and that blankets had been thrown down here."

"And 'tis night now. The moon was rising as we rode through the gates. So, three days in the dark. In a hole in the ground," she murmured, shivering at the thought of having to endure the same. "What did ye do?"

"Thought."

"Oh, dear. I think *that* would soon drive me quite mad."

"It wasnae a pleasant interlude."

"It certainly isnae. I am nay too fond of the dark," she

added softly and jumped slightly when a long arm was somewhat awkwardly wrapped around her shoulders.

"No one is, especially not the unrelenting dark of a place like this. So, ye were all alone when they caught ye. They didnae harm ye, did they?"

The soft, gentle tone of his question made Alana realize what he meant by *harm*. It struck her as odd that not once had she feared rape, yet her disguise as a child was certainly not enough to save her from that. "Nay, they just grabbed me, cursed me a lot for being impudent, and tossed me over a saddle."

Gregor smiled. "Impudent were ye?"

"That is as good a word for it as any other. There I was sitting quietly by a fire, cooking a rabbit I had been lucky enough to catch, and up ride five men who inform me that I am now their prisoner and that I had best tell them who I am so that they can send the ransom demand to my kinsmen. I told them that I had had a very upsetting day and the last thing I wished to deal with was smelly, hairy men telling me what to do, so they could just ride back to the rock they had crawled out from under. Or words to that effect," she added quietly.

In truth, she thought as she listened to Gregor chuckle, she had completely lost her temper. It was not something she often did, and she suspected some of her family would have been astonished. The Gowans had been. All five men had stared at her as if a dormouse had suddenly leapt at their throats. It had been rather invigorating until the Gowans had realized they were being held in place by insults from someone they could snap in half.

It was a little puzzling that she had not eluded capture. She was very fast, something often marveled at by her family; she could run for a very long way without tiring; and she could hide in the faintest of shadows. Yet mishap after mishap had plagued her as she had fled from the men, and they had barely raised a sweat in pursuing and capturing her. If she were a superstitious person, she would think some unseen hand of fate had been doing its best to make sure she was caught.

"Did they tell ye why they are grabbing so many for ransom?" Gregor asked.

"Oh, aye they did." Of course, one reason they had told her was because of all the things she had accused them of wanting the money for, such as useless debauchery and not something they badly needed like soap. "Defenses."

"What?"

"They have decided that this hovel requires stronger defenses. That requires coin or some fine goods to barter with, neither of which they possess. I gather they have heard of some troubles not so far away, and it has made them decide that they are too vulnerable. From what little I could see whilst hanging over Clyde's saddle, this is a very old tower house, one that was either neglected or damaged once, or both. It appears to have been repaired enough to be livable, but I did glimpse many things either missing or in need of repair. From what Clyde's wife said, this small holding was her dowry."

"Ye spoke to his wife?"

"Weel, nay. She was lecturing him from the moment he stepped inside all the way to the door leading down here. She doesnae approve of this. Told him that since he has begun this folly, he had best do a verra good job of it and gather a veritable fortune, for they will need some formidable defenses to protect them from all the enemies he is making."

Alana knew she ought to move away from him. When he had first draped his arm around her, she had welcomed what she saw as a gesture intended to comfort her, perhaps even an attempt to ease the fear of the dark she had confessed to. He still had his arm around her, and she had slowly edged closer to his warmth until she was now pressed hard up against his side.

He was a very tall man. Probably a bit taller than her overgrown brothers, she mused. Judging from where her cheek rested so nicely, she barely reached his breastbone. Since she was five feet tall, that made him several inches over six feet. Huddled up against him as she was, she could feel the strength in his body, despite what she felt like a lean build. Considering the fact that he had been held in this pit for almost three days, he smelled remarkably clean as well.

And the fact that she was noticing how good he smelled told her she really should move away from him, Alana thought. The problem was he felt good, very good. He felt warm, strong, and calming, all things she was sorely in need of at the moment. She started to console herself with the thought that she was not actually embracing him, only to realize that she had curled her arm around like a very trim waist.

She sighed inwardly, ruefully admitting that she liked where she was and that she had no inclination to leave his side. He thought she was a young girl, so she did not have to fear him thinking she was inviting him to take advantage of her. Alone with him in the dark, there was a comforting anonymity as well. Alana decided there was no harm in it all. In truth, she would not be surprised to discover that he found comfort in it, too, after days of being all alone in the dark.

"Where were ye headed, lass? Is there someone aside from the men ye were with who will start searching for ye?" Gregor asked, a little concerned about how good it felt to hold her, even though every instinct he had told him that Alana was not the child she pretended to be.

"Quite possibly." She doubted that the note she had left behind would do much to comfort her parents. "I was going to my sister."

"Ah, weel, then, I fear the Gowans may soon ken who ye are e'en if ye dinnae tell them."

"Oh, of course. What about you? Will anyone wonder where ye have gone?"

"Nay for a while yet."

They all thought he was still wooing his well-dowered bride. Gregor had had far too much time to think about that, about all of his reasons for searching for a well-dowered bride and about the one he had chosen. Mavis was a good woman, passably pretty, and she had both land and some coin to offer a husband. He had left her feeling almost victorious, the betrothal as good as settled, yet each hour he had sat here in the dark, alone with his thoughts, he had felt less and less pleased with himself. It did not feel *right*. He hated to think that his cousin Sigimor made sense about anything, yet it was that man's opinion that kept creeping through his mind. Mavis did not really feel *right*. She did not really *fit*.

He silently cursed. What did it matter? He was almost thirty years of age, and he had never found a woman who felt *right* or *fit*. Mavis gave him the chance to be his own man, to be laird of his own keep, and to have control over his own lands. Mavis was a sensible choice. He did not love her, but after so many years and so many women without feeling even a tickle of that, he doubted he was capable of loving any woman. Passion could be stirred with the right touch, and compatibility could be achieved with a little work. It would serve.

He was just about to ask Alana how extensive a search her kinsmen would mount for her when he heard the sound of someone approaching above them. "Stand o'er there, lass," he said as he nudged her to the left. "'Tis time for the bucket to be emptied and food and water lowered down to us. I dinnae want to be bumping into ye."

Alana immediately felt chilled as she left his side. She kept inching backward until she stumbled and fell onto a pile of blankets. She moved around until she was seated on them, her back against the cold stone wall. The grate was opened, and a rope with a hook at the end of it was lowered through the opening. The lantern this man carried produced enough light to at least allow them to see that rope. Gregor moved around as if he could see, and Alana suspected he had carefully mapped out his prison in his mind. She watched the bucket being raised up and another being lowered down. As Gregor reached for that bucket, she caught a faint glimpse of his form. He was indeed very tall and very lean. She cursed the darkness for hiding all else from her.

"We will need two buckets of water for washing in the morn," Gregor called up to the man, watching him as he carefully lowered the now empty privy bucket.

"Two?" the man snapped. "Why two?"

"One for me and one for the lass."

"Ye can both wash from the same one."

"A night down here leaves one verra dirty. A wee bucket of water is barely enough to get one person clean, ne'er mind two."

"I will see what the laird says."

Alana winced as the grate was slammed shut and that faint shaft of light disappeared. She tried to judge where Gregor was, listening carefully to his movements, but she was still a little startled when he sat down by her side. Then she caught the scent of cheese and still-warm bread, and her stomach growled a welcome.

Gregor laughed as he set the food out between them. "Careful how ye move, lass. The food rests between us. The Gowans do provide enough to eat, though 'tis plain fare."

"Better than none. Perhaps ye had better hand me things. I think I shall need a wee bit of time to become accustomed to moving about in this thick dark."

She tensed when she felt a hand pat her leg, but then something fell into her lap. Reaching down, she found a chunk of bread, which she immediately began to eat. Gregor was obviously just trying to be certain of where she sat as he shared out the food. She did wonder why a small part of her was disappointed by that.

"Best ye eat it all, lass. I havenae been troubled by vermin, but I have heard a few sounds that make me think they are near. Leaving food about will only bring them right to us."

Alana shivered. "I hate rats."

"As do I, which is why I fight the temptation to hoard food."

She nodded even though she knew he could not see her, and for a while, they silently ate. Once her stomach was full, Alana began to feel very tired, the rigors of the day catching up to her. Her eyes widened as she realized there was no place to make up her own bed; and she doubted there were enough blankets to do so anyway.

"Where do I sleep?" she asked, briefly glad of the dark, for it hid her blushes.

"Here with me," replied Gregor. "I will sleep next to the wall." He smiled, almost able to feel her tension. "Dinnae fret, lass. I willnae harm ye. I have ne'er harmed a child."

Of course, Alana thought and she relaxed. He thought she was a child. She had briefly forgotten her disguise. The thought of having to keep her binding on for days was not comforting, but it was for the best. Thinking her a child, Gregor treated her as he would a sister or his own child. If he knew she was a woman, he might well treat her as a convenient bedmate or try to make her one. She brutally silenced the part of her that whispered its disappointment, reminding it that she had no idea of what this man even looked like.

Once the food was gone, Gregor set the bucket aside. Alana heard him removing some clothing and then felt him crawl beneath the blankets. She quickly moved out of the way when she felt his feet nudge her hip. After a moment's thought, she loosened the laces on her gown and removed her boots before crawling under the blankets by his side. The chill of the place disappeared again, and she swallowed a sigh. Something about Gregor soothed her, made her able to face this imprisonment with some calm and courage, and she was simply too tired to try and figure out what that something was.

"On the morrow, we will begin to plan our escape," Gregor said.

"Ye have thought of a way out of here?"

"Only a small possibility. Sleep. Ye will need it."

That did not sound promising, Alana mused as she closed her eyes.

ABOUT THE AUTHOR

Hannah Howell is an award-winning author who lives with her family in Massachusetts. She is the author of over thirty Zebra historical romances and is currently working on a new historical romance featuring the Murrays, HIGHLAND AVENGER, coming in April 2012! Hannah loves hearing from readers, and you may visit her website: *www.hannahhowell.com.*